Odd Girl Out

Odd Girl Out

Elizabeth Jane Howard

PERENNIAL LIBRARY

Harper & Row, Publishers

New York, Cambridge, Philadelphia, San Francisco

London, Mexico City, São Paulo, Sydney

Odd Girl
Out

Part One

"**O**f *course* I don't mind, my darling. Of *course* I don't." She wore the top half of his pyjamas and was putting cherry jam on a piece of toast. She thought for a moment, and then added, "It will be lovely for me to have someone to talk to while you're in London."

Edmund Cornhill looked at his wife for some time without replying. At moments like these, he told himself, his customary feeling of devotion for her was shot with something positively *erotic*.

What he liked about her, he went on to himself—he was a man of incessant internal words, few of which reached the drum of human ear—was the way in which she always contrived to be rational about any sacrificing attitude he called upon her to make. She did not simply say that something would be all right, she said *why* it would be, and then, of course, it nearly always was. She was in bed, a place that he felt sure most wives did not occupy often enough: he never let her get up in the mornings until he had either set out for London, or otherwise begun his day.

"Stripes suit you," he said.

"Do they?"

"Or it may be the red and blue that is so becoming. You remind me of one of those delightful pre-war plays when the girl stays the night unexpectedly."

She said instantly, as he knew she would, "I love blue."

"She's been ill, or at least that's what it sounded like."

"I thought you said that Clara said she just needed a rest."

"She did say that. But she talked away about strain and needing a change, and the line kept fading out."

"Where did she telephone from?"

"Lucerne. But she wasn't staying there, she said, she was on her way to Paris."

"Goodness," said Anne politely.

Anne had been married to Edmund for nearly ten years, and the very faint spark of curiosity she had early evinced about Edmund's ex-stepmother's whereabouts had long since died. She was, Anne felt, bound to be somewhere, and, as very little experience had shown, almost certain to be on her way to somewhere else. One could not keep up with her unless one wanted to a great deal more than Anne had done. But Edmund *did* care—in an odd and rather touching way regarded his fleeting and attenuated relationship with her as some kind of heraldic feather in his cap. Whenever Clara came to England, he always had tea with her at Claridges'; he sent her a fiendishly expensive Christmas card every year and faithfully executed any of the dreary commissions which in her huge writing on beautiful postcards she exacted from him. He called her Clara and she called him darling.

"Do you remember that parrot we had of Clara's?"

He straightened up with the breakfast tray that he had been removing from the bed. "Of course I do. Why?"

"Nothing. I just remembered how bored it was—that's all."

) 4 (

"Parrots *are* bored: it was nothing to do with Clara."

She started to say that of course she hadn't meant that, when a scratching—as delicate as it was authoritative—interrupted them.

Edmund opened the door, and Ariadne made her customary graceful and noiseless entrance. She was black, and so seethingly pregnant that her body reminded one of a small muff into which somebody had crammed their hands in a vain effort to stop fidgeting. In spite of this, she leaped lightly onto the bed and fell upon her side within reach of Anne's hand. Anne stroked her neck, and she began to examine the end of one paw with critical care.

"When *are* you going to do it?" Anne asked her softly, but Ariadne merely shut her juicy eyes.

"As long as it's not on our bed," Edmund said as he went to run his bath. He said this every morning now, but neither Anne nor Ariadne took the slightest notice.

While Edmund was having his bath, Anne lay wishing he'd let her get up first: she hated wasting any of a beautiful morning in bed, and so she made lists, with her mind rambling lazily over the unrelated words as she wrote them on the back of Edmund's wine merchants' catalogue. *Muscari*, she wrote. They had not really liked being under the cedar; it was far too dry for them. If she wanted drifts of blue under the cedar, she would have to make do with bluebells. But then, bluebells were really their best in woods. If Edmund asked her what she wanted for her birthday, she would say a wood. But that would mean moving, and she never wanted to do that. To find a house, not too far from London, *on* a river, with a garden that contained, among other charms, a cedar, a mulberry, and a catalpa, was not something that could possibly happen twice to anyone, even if her husband was an estate agent. It had taken Edmund nearly a year to find it, and in spite of his professional sieving out of the impossibles, they must have looked at thirty or so houses. *Salmon trout*, she wrote, and thought how like the Walrus *and* the Carpenter her fishmongers were. When was this daughter of Clara's coming? And really, Edmund had better put her straight about who had been—or was—the girl's father. Clara had been married five times, not counting other prolonged relationships: the girl could as easily be a product of one of them as born in wedlock. But it would be as well to know—to be thoroughly briefed beforehand. . . . *Get bedside lamp mended,* she wrote. *Do roses,* she wrote. She meant, dead head, pick and arrange and spray and generally take care. Her old-fashioned shrubs were at their best towards the end of June, and this was a particularly good year for them.

It was Wednesday—the day that Edmund often looked at some country house for a client—occasionally even stayed the night in some distant market town or cathedral city; would ring her up in the evening to tell her what he had had for dinner and whether the house had been awful or charming, and would return the next day. On Wednesdays she would make some elaborate dish to be eaten on Thursday evening; would garden until it was nearly dark, and eat boiled eggs at the kitchen table with a novel propped against a loaf of bread. Afterwards, she would have a hot bath and wash her hair and write to Edmund's father, who lived in a Home in Cornwall. She tried to write these letters once a week; at least *made* herself write them on all the Wednesdays that Edmund was away. This compromise was not satisfactory to her: she was someone who continually felt that she was on the brink of order in her life, and that when she actually embarked upon it, her life would, so to speak, start afresh in a far more dynamic and significant manner. Order meant to her that duties of all kinds had both a time and a place for their performance. She was not sure whether pleasures were contained in either, but only insecure and unhappy people would try to plan for them.

Edmund was whistling a bit of the *Trout*—the bit that people always *do* whistle, if they whistle it at all. Soon he would be back in the bedroom wanting her to choose his shirt and tie and then changing her choice back to what she felt he could perfectly easily have chosen if she had not been there. One of the most noticeable things about Edmund was his predictability: to many this might equate with dullness; to Anne it was possibly his chief attraction. She had had enough of *un*predictable behaviour—

once—to last her for the rest of her life. She stretched, and got very slowly out of bed to consider Edmund's shirts. . . .

"How are *you?*"

"Pretty bloody." After a pause, she asked, "And you?"

"I'm all right, thanks." Both of their answers meant exactly the same thing, he thought: that they couldn't feel much worse but that the other one neither cared nor could do a thing about it if he or she had.

"And the kids?"

She answered at once with the kind of dreary triumph that had always irritated him. "They've got tonsilitis; or glandular fever; or mumps. They're both in bed, poor little sods."

"Have you got a doctor?"

"Of course I've *called* a doctor; I'm not absolutely mad. But doctors don't come the moment they're called these days, you know. She said she'd try to make it before lunch. Nobody's rung for you, if that's what you're calling about."

There ensued a frightful, minuscule, unknown amount of time, like watching somebody fall off a building, or the last grains of an egg timer, or somebody waiting to have their head chopped off; then he said, "It wasn't, actually. Actually, I'm on my way back."

She was silent for a moment; then, with an almost aggressive lack of curiosity, said, "Back where?"

He thought of counting three before he answered: "Home: back to you—and the kids."

She made a noise that sounded as though it was composed of a laugh, a cry, and a snort, and said, "Has she left you then? What a bloody silly question. She must have. You're not exactly the dutiful type, are you?"

Wanting to shout, Don't talk like a bad pre-war play, he said, "Yes: she *has* left me, you'll be glad to hear."

"Can't stand being alone."

"No. If I can't have what I want, at least I ought to do what I should."

) 7 (

"What makes you think I *want* you back?"

"It's not a matter of what you want, is it? That point always gets left out of these situations. It's what we can afford. I can't afford two establishments, and if you're to look after the kids properly, you can't work."

"She was keeping you, was she?"

"It doesn't matter what she was doing," he said, wanting to kill her for being so nasty about it. "She's gone. Left me: I could have lied to you about that, but at least I haven't. That's something, isn't it?"

"No—it bloody well *isn't*."

"*Why* isn't it?"

"You've just decided to come back because there's nothing better to do. That's marvellous, I must say." She was trying very hard not to burst into tears.

"It's not very marvellous for either of us. It never has been. I'll be home for lunch."

He put down the receiver, and lay back on the unmade bed. It was extraordinary how quickly this ritzy little Chelsea non-painter's studio had seemed to change the moment she had gone— what, four days and five nights ago now. When she had been there, it had had all the charms of a secret, romantic nest. It *was* very small—a two-roomed flat, in fact, with very mod cons—but it had seemed the perfect answer when they had first gone there. It belonged to one of her rich friends called Neville, who spent most of the summer in Ibiza and who, she had said casually, was always prepared to lend it to one when he wasn't in England— or, indeed, London: he apparently had a cottage in Hampshire as well, and a flat in Paris. But now—after these four days and five awful nights when he had simply drunk up all the remaining bottles of drink in the place, and even used up things like Worcester sauce and very old eggs on Prairie Oysters, and got sick of the few LP's, and smoked several hundred cigarettes, the place looked as though someone had had an unsuccessful party in it. The blackberry-coloured fitted carpets were covered with ash; he had burned marks on the edges of white-painted bookshelves; the bathroom and kitchen were a welter of squalor—of tide marks and dirty crockery, and things going bad in cups and basins and black-cracked soap and uninvitingly damp and dirty towels. He had only gone out for cigarettes, and he'd only stopped going out for them because his money had run out. He looked at the last packet that he had clenched in his hand while talking to Janet—there were only three left and he'd bent them. Damn. He was out of work, out of love, and had three people to keep. He wondered for the thousandth time where she was now. *She* should have been an actress, he thought viciously; *she* was the one: she would never have been out of work. She could make anyone believe anything for just as long as she chose. . . . He found he was crying again —not making much noise—just tears and the kind of snuffling he wouldn't have liked anybody else to have heard. He got off the bed and went to the bathroom: better try and shave with that ghastly blade that he knew he'd cut himself with but that was the only one left.

His face in the mirror looked so awful, and so different, that for a moment he was almost objectively impressed with his own grief. He would never be the same again, and, quite possibly, she *had* ruined his life. (But no; it was Janet who had done that: a blonde at drama school, wouldn't you know.) At moments like these, the rest of life can seem very long: visions of his ravaged and agonized middle and old age jerked tragically into his mind, like stills from some interminable film about suffering and the corrosion of a man: Dorian Gray, or Jekyll and Hyde, but the damage all done by plain heartbreak rather than plain evil. It was not *he* who had been wicked: he had not wanted to fall in love with her; he had not expected any more of life than to tool along with Janet and the kids, with the occasional girl on the side just to keep up his sexual morale. But *she* had picked *him* up, thrown herself at his head, dusted him off, and was now, no doubt, starting all over again. As he dabbed the blood off the first cut of his shave, he wondered again where the *hell* she had gone, gone so suddenly, and where in God's name she was now.

"Copper-bottomed; it does sound rude."

"It is this offal worm; it attacks the hulls of all sheeps—even yours, my darling."

"We never had any trouble in the Caribbean."

"It is a Mediterranean worm. If we do not have it done, we either do not cruise there or we one day seenk like stones."

"One thing after another. First Arabella—and then this. I'm not *made* of money."

She was wearing a silver-lamé leotard and grey tights, her head was encased in a black towelling turban, and she lay on her back with her legs over her head so that her toes touched the floor: he could only see her sideways. He started putting the marbles back into position on the solitaire board and answered, "Oh yes, you are, my darling. With a little flesh and blood thrown in, of course."

"Less flesh than there was. I've lost fifteen pounds in this boring place."

He had lost considerably more pounds of a different kind, and felt it better to change the subject.

"What has Arabella been up to?"

"Nothing unusual. In fact, I wish that girl would branch out into some form of originality."

"There was the affair with the lady sculptress," he pointed out. He was a fair man when indifferent, and he was certainly indifferent to his stepdaughter.

Clara sat up, crossed her legs, and began doing neck exercises. "That was sheer bravado. Well—call those people in Cowes and tell them to put on a copper bottom, but I want it done by the middle of July so that we can pick up the yacht at Nice after I've collected my things from Paris."

Her maid knocked and entered with a tray on which was a saucer of various pills and a jar of honey.

"Open the blinds, would you, Markham, and give me my dark glasses."

"They'll have to be the white ones, my lady; there was an

unfortunate accident with those that go with your exercising costume."

Markham was of indeterminate age, ugly, efficient, and spiteful: although she made a point of getting on with nobody, she had remained with Clara for over twenty years, so that now her indispensability safely counterbalanced her spite. She disliked all men, and had enormously enjoyed the various divorces and breakups that she had witnessed at such close hand. It was not clear what she felt about her mistress, but she looked after her clothes—kept in at least three different countries—with obsessive care. Only she knew that Clara possessed and occasionally wore nearly two hundred pairs of handmade shoes: she was a beautiful needlewoman and laundered all the superb underwear herself.

With the blinds up, sunlight the colour of melted butter filled the hotel room, making its pastel discretion seem drab. Prince Radamacz got up from his solitaire and wandered to the balcony. Outside, the postcard sky—mercilessly blue—made the lake hyacinth and the little sailing boats upon it seem like a brand-new set of toys as they scurried about in their aimless and miniature manner. The thought of being in one of them both bored and exasperated him. It was infuriating to have lost such a pleasure simply through being nearer death, and he had recently discovered that chronic comfort (or luxury) made him think a great deal about that.

"What happened to my *diamonté* glassess, then? Come on, Markham, out with it."

"It's not for me to say, my lady." In spite of Clara's currently being a princess, Markham unfailingly used this appellation; had, indeed, done so throughout Clara's various marriages: to Edmund's father—a professor of philosophy (English), to Arabella's father (Scottish), to a violinist (Hungarian), to an ornithologist count (French), and to a film star (American). But she had once, when Markham had first been engaged, been briefly allied in wedlock to an incredibly old Scottish baronet who had managed to die before even Clara could tire of him—he fell down half of a spiral staircase in his nasty Gothic castle on their honeymoon—and so, however much Clara might change her ways or her station, Markham could, or would, not.

"Markham!"

"Heythrop-Jones allowed the dog to eat them, my lady, if you must know."

"Not *eat*, Markham, surely."

"Crush them between his jaws, my lady. They will never be the same again."

"How foolish of him."

Markham looked sanctimonious. "Heythrop-Jones is given over to matters that do not appertain to your ladyship's affairs."

"I didn't mean Heythrop-Jones, Markham; I meant Major." She finished the last pill and yawned. "Vani! Let's leave this evening. This place is far too good and dull for us. Tell them we're leaving, Markham. Tell Heythrop-Jones to have the Rolls ready by three. Arrange a train for yourself to Paris. Don't bother with those wigs I had sent yesterday—have them sent back: I look like some sixties actress pretending to be some twenties actress in them. Cancel the masseur. Put in a call to Mr. Cornhill at his office in London. Draw me a bath. And the Prince would like his watch collected from Piguet. Or sent round—whichever is easiest. And you'll have to take Major in the train with you. Have the hotel pack him a decent meal. And one for yourself, of course." She thought for a moment, while Markham stood unblinking before her. "I'll wear the beige Chanel, the lizard boots—the beige ones, of course—and the Cartier topaz set. You choose my bag and gloves. I know I can rely on you for that."

"What about the Battenbergs?"

"Oh, them. Call them, Vani, and say we have to leave. Say anything. Say I'm having trouble with Arabella—say anything."

"She is not in Paris, is she?"

"I really haven't the slightest *idea* where she is. I am relying on good, dull Edmund to tell me."

"Christ—why don't they get *on* with it?"

She seemed to have been lying on a high, hard, humiliatingly uncomfortable table for hours. They had spread her legs apart, some hard-faced foreign bitch (probably a virgin, you bet) had swabbed her arm and casually and rather painfully stuck a needle into it. After that, they had seemed to retire to one corner of the room and simply confer—like extras in an opera, waiting for the leading characters to act. But nothing had *happened*.

"You may get up now."

"What do you mean?"

"It is finished."

"Famous last words," she said dreamily, very much disinclined to move; but the foreign bitch was approaching her with what she felt could only be described as brisk sadism.

"You will have to wear two sanitary towels. Here is the belt."

She found herself hoisted off the table. "If you would like to go in there, Miss Smith."

I'm not called Smith, you silly bitch, Arabella thought in the lavatory. She ached a bit and felt faint—with relief? The injection? And with some distant misery. She'd arranged things and it was horrible. When she didn't arrange things they got boring *and* horrible. What on earth was the alternative? She felt old and used up. Remarkably little could happen to one, it seemed, excepting squalid, day-to-day mishaps. She betted that smarmy little Romanian doctor didn't know what Christ had said on the Cross. But at least he'd been *on* the Cross—feeling, or perhaps knowing, that the whole death was worth a billion candles. This recent little death, if you could call it that, had been worth a hundred and fifty pounds. He had insisted on half the money beforehand, and would doubtless be waiting for the other half now. She had cashed the money this morning in fivers—she hated counting money and almost never did, but on this occasion she had needed more than this episode had cost her. Supposing he had cheated, and hadn't done it? But she was bleeding; he must have done *something*. And I don't much care what, she thought.

When she emerged from the lavatory, he was waiting for the

money, which she gave him by putting the fivers on the table. When she reached the end—seventy-five pounds—he patted her shoulder, put the money in his white overall pocket, and told her that she would be quite all right now but must go home and rest. He had a reddish moustache and very dark eyes; for a moment she wondered what the rest of his life was like. He must be stinking rich.

Outside, the sun seemed so strong that she fumbled about in her bag for her dark glasses. Home, she thought, ha ha. A strange house somewhere that she had never been in her life. But there was something familiar about *that*, as a prospect, when she came to think about it. She saw a cab and stopped and got into it just as her knees began to turn into melting wax.

Edmund sat in his handsome and dignified office, the comfort of which was temporarily, but lengthily, being destroyed by pile drivers and pneumatic drills. They were building an underground car park in the square outside, an operation that seemed to have been going on for months and that showed no signs whatever of completion, or even of progress. In consequence of this, the windows had to be shut and, even with the venetian blinds half drawn (making irritating bars of light and shade all over his papers), the place was far too hot.

". . . I am afraid that planning permission for rebuilding on a more convenient part of the site having been refused comma substantially detracts from the present value of the property full stop. We can comma of course comma appeal against the Council's decision comma but this would comma I am afraid comma take at least six months full stop. Perhaps you would care to consider what you would like done in this matter comma and if I can help you with any further advice will let me know comma otherwise I shall await your further instructions full stop. I am, etc."

Miss Hathaway looked up from her pad: her blond but visible moustache was beaded with sweat. "Shall I send this to Brown's Hotel or to the Malta address?"

Edmund consulted the spidery writing on dark-blue paper. "It's quite unclear where she is at present. The paper is from her old house, and she has simply put *Tuesday* at the head of the letter. Better ring Brown's and see whether she is still there, and if she isn't, air mail it, of course, to Malta."

The telephone rang. Miss Hathaway picked it up: her hands were nearly always moist—even in winter or when the windows were open—so that Edmund knew that the receiver would be clammy by the time it reached him.

After some delay, Miss Hathaway announced, "It is a personal call for you from Princess Radamacz."

"Thank you, that will be all, for the moment. I'll buzz if I want you."

He took the receiver, and when she had left the room, carefully wiped with the dark-blue silk handkerchief that Anne had not chosen for him that morning. A feeling of wordly excitement touched him: it was interesting to be somebody who calmly got calls of this nature.

"Clara?"

"Darling!"

"Where are you?"

"Darling, it's so silly, but still in Lucerne. But only for a moment. We're setting off for Paris, but I just wanted to know that my darling girl was safely ensconced with you before we go."

"What?"

"*Arabella*. I told her to go straight down to you. Isn't she there?"

"She hasn't got in touch with us; with me, anyway," he added, wondering, if she had been supposed to, why on earth not.

"Oh—I expect she'll just turn up then. *Do* tell me when she does. We'll be at the Ritz tonight. It is *so* maddening—the way she doesn't tell anyone what she is doing until after you've found that she's done it."

A Swiss operator broke in with a lot of unintelligible information. Over this, Clara said, "She's simply longing to stay with you. But *longing*. And you are an *angel* to have her. Only do be firm. Don't let her exploit you."

"How do you mean?"

"You know, darling—like *I* always do. She's only twenty-two. Far too young to be that sort of nuisance. Anyway, let me know. Must fly now. Bye now, darling. Call me in Paris."

The line went dead. He put back the receiver thoughtfully. A wave of responsibility engulfed him. What ought he to do? Logic, and a faint sense of grievance, came next: how *could* he do anything if he hadn't the slightest idea where the girl was? Loyalty, and what he considered to be his unique understanding of Clara, ended the brief procession of his thoughts: the girl was clearly yet another example of the younger generation, thoughtless, irresponsible, and selfish; Clara was simply being—as he felt she always really was—marvellous about her. There was nothing to be done, he decided with some satisfaction. This was his favourite conclusion about most things, and like most people's favourite anything, he was not able to indulge himself as often as he would have liked. Better get on with the booklet about Lea Manor. A large number of competent photographs had been taken, and it was now his business to choose which were most suitable for reproduction and to write—from his measured and statistical notes—an appealing text. There were seven hundred acres of reasonable dairy-farming land, and three farmhouses let with a fair return. But the house itself had dry rot, woodworm, no proper damp course, archaic plumbing, and what even an Eskimo would have regarded as laughable central heating. Although, probably, like so many of those primitive people, they were a damn sight better at essentials than was generally supposed. Sometimes he wished that he had travelled more, had a wider experience of life. Then he thought of his charming and comfortable house, so admirably run by the admirably satisfactory Anne, and knew that one could not have everything, and that on the whole he would rather be him. At least he could depend upon her, and his work, and what was going to happen from one week to the next. He smiled, because this sounded drab and only he knew that it wasn't, and pressed the buzzer for Miss Hathaway to bring in the pictures of Lea Manor.

When she had stopped crying, Janet yelled to the kids to shut up and climbed wearily up from the dark little room on the ground floor to what had been—and presumably was to start being again—her bedroom with Henry. In front of her dressing table, she looked at herself. She had not washed her hair since he had left and, by God, it looked like it. She looked at least thirty-five, she thought despairingly (in fact she was twenty-four, and had the kind of face—like most of us—that does not take kindly to chronic unhappiness). The trouble was that she did not any longer *love* Henry; he'd been too much of a bastard for too long for that: but the children and lack of money had eroded her appearance and her personality so that she could easily see why he did not love *her*. If he could be like he used to be; if he even pretended that I was all right for a bit, I'd get better. If I wasn't so bloody tired all the time, I'd like going to bed more: I'd have more initiative and we could go to the pub, because I'd damn well find a baby sitter. If we had a bit more bread, I'd feel better about shorts; and in the pub we always end up with shorts. If I go on drinking beer, which I've never liked anyway, he says I'm a kill-joy. That's what I am. I can't go back to the theatre—never was much good anyway, and I've lost my confidence. If he would just *start* the being nice, I might be able to follow it up.

There was practically nothing to eat in the house. She had to choose between getting some sausages and washing her hair. She hadn't had anything new to wear for—oh, well—before they'd had Luke. Luke was screaming now. The maisonette, in Belsize Park, had been cheap when they got it, and they could not now be turned out. But this, in turn, meant that the landlord did bugger-all about any maintenance. Water poured through the half-landing roof into the children's room, the house smelled of cats, and most of the rooms were dark from lack of sun. They were also too large to heat adequately, so that much of the year was always spent scorching (or not) before (or away from) some fiendishly expensive electric heater. The water was hardly ever hot: the place had been ostensibly furnished, which meant that nearly everything in it was gimcrack and ugly. The kitchen was a dank cave of inconvenience and discomfort. If only some television series would turn up for Henry, they might be able to get out of here: start a better, new life. Or at least get on with the old one against fewer odds. Janet was not by nature domesticated: she was not wonderful at inventing, running things up, decorating and making the best of a bad job. Nobody had taught her these things, and she had neither the initiative nor the intelligence to discover such tricks. So the flat stayed as awful as when they had first moved in, except that things like the roof and the hot water got worse.

She combed her greasy hair (blond hair, especially if it was very fine, always got greasy quickly anyhow), put on some lipstick, and changed into a black sweater: black was always better on the skin if you'd been crying a lot and not sleeping much. There were two eggs left, half a pint of milk, and a tin of corned beef. That would have to do, because, she now realized, she could neither go out to shop nor start washing her long hair in case the doctor came.

She climbed the next half flight to see why Luke was screaming.

After Edmund left for London, Anne realized that tomorrow —Thursday—was the tenth anniversary of their marriage. This meant that all her usual plans for the day must be changed. No gardening; no pottering about; no making those time-taking, minute alterations to the house that added up to all the difference in the end. She would have to go into Henley, and possibly Maidenhead, to buy interesting food and a present. It was going to be a very hot day; she hated shopping for food, but on the other hand, she loved buying presents. Edmund, unlike most husbands, was a most rewarding recipient. He liked clothes, antiques, wine, silver, glass, cuff links, snuff boxes, primitive paintings—there was really an enormous choice. Both Henley and Maidenhead were expensive for most of these things, but she certainly hadn't time to go to London. Anyway, she enjoyed spending most of her tiny legacy upon these occasions. Edmund was so generous to her, had so much changed her life from miserable and anxious poverty to comfort and stability, that, in a way, she felt she owed him anything that was privately hers. Last year, she had found a beautiful pair of ship's decanters with their original stoppers into which she had carefully decanted bottles of Cockburn '27 and Taylor '29. But perhaps for a decade of marriage one should get something more personal. Edmund took snuff: a good snuff box would be suitable. His favourite summer dinner of cold avocado soup, salmon trout, and raspberries would be easy: there would be time to have her hair cut. Anne wore hers cut as short as possible—had always done so from the moment Edmund had suggested it and then indulged them both in one of those nights of sensuality as satisfactory as it was startling to them both: a time that she could, and did, frequently recall, to conjure the first purely physical pleasure she had ever known. She had many times since had reason to be grateful to Edmund about her hair. But he was extremely fussy about its shape, and, as it was both thick and dark and fast-growing, she had to have it trimmed every three weeks. She picked up the wine merchants' catalogue and searched for another blank space on which to make a more urgent list. Perhaps she should get Edmund a gramophone record. He was particularly fond of opera and Strauss, but the only name of an opera by him that she knew was *Der Rosenkavalier*, which they already possessed. Still, the shop would know, and there would be catalogues. Anne was not particularly fond of music, but she did a great deal of *gros point* while Edmund listened to it, and she admired him for being interested in so many different things. *Brahms, Elgar, Tchycovsky*, she wrote. This last looked wrong, but she knew what she meant. When she got up, Ariadne raised her head and gazed, or rather stared, at her in a manner both meaningful and enigmatic. I might do it while you are out, and then I can do it where I please, was what it occurred to Anne that the stare might mean. When she had bathed and dressed in her blue linen trouser suit that became her rather straight and—as Edmund had remarked once—below the waist boyish figure, she lifted Ariadne off the bed and into the box in their bathroom that had been carefully prepared for the confinement. Ariadne got out of this immediately, shaking the fluff of a newly washed blanket delicately from each paw. They both raced for the bed. In the end, she had to be shut out while it was made; the communicating door between bedroom and bathroom closed, the bedroom door shut, and only the public way to this bathroom available. Ariadne thudded sulkily downstairs after her and waited for her breakfast to be served in order to refuse it until Anne had left.

It was going to be a *very* hot day. Anne loaded the MG with the bedside lamp, shopping baskets, and crates of empty lemonade bottles. Tonight, they would have Pimm's under the cedar; they might even have dinner out if she bought something to burn against the midges. Poor Edmund got dreadfully bitten, and she not at all: his skin was far more sensitive, or attractive, than hers.

Driving to Henley, she had a spasm of anxiety about this unknown girl coming to stay for an unknown amount of time. She herself had almost no separate friends from Edmund: half a dozen couples and a few other single people came and dined and stayed a night or for the week-end; she was an only child, both parents dead, and the only friend who had survived from her former (and to her now frightful) life was a woman—a literary agent—considerably older than Anne with whom Edmund got on extremely well. The few social occasions of her life were enjoyable, and probably necessary to preserve and sustain the delightful, domestic/married/erotic life that she and Edmund had somehow discovered or made or were subject to. She never felt lonely, even when Edmund was away, as there was always a great deal to do, and she was by nature a doer. She preferred to be doing something with—preferably—Edmund there, to simply being there—even with Edmund. Still, if one was so lucky and happy oneself, one ought to be able to have something to spare for any other person less fortunate. Anybody who had been brought up by Clara had probably been paralysed, made inarticulate with the constant frenzy of luxury travel and Clara's overwhelming personality. The thought of Clara with a daughter induced feelings in Anne that were as near maternal as she had ever become. She and Edmund had never had children, although they had never planned not to, but neither of them had felt any gap in their lives that people like Ariadne had not been able to fill. But to be Clara's daughter was a fate that Anne was perfectly able to recognize, although discretion would prevent her pointing it out to Edmund. The great thing about living seriously with one other person was to tell them very nearly, but not quite, everything. . . .

After the taxi had asked her several times, Arabella, feeling weak and awful, said crossly, "Oh, anywhere you like. The zoo, for all I care," she added, and much too soon later, the man announced that they had arrived.

"Where?" She didn't at all want to get out of the cab.

"Where you said—the zoo."

She had to take off her dark glasses to find her purse in her bag, and took so long over it that the man finally turned round to face her with his resentment, but by then she had found the money and handed it through to him. Then she *had* to move. Oh, God. Better to have gone to an hotel. But it was difficult in England just to go to an hotel for the inside of a day—wanting a bedroom, that is.

"Are you all *right?*"

"Never felt worse. Don't worry: you don't know me."

"Are you famous, then? Ought I to?

She put on her dark glasses again. "Wouldn't you like to know." The remark reminded her of one of the innumerable schools that she had experienced. She climbed stiffly out and found the driver, whose face, she now saw, was of a complexion onto which you could have dropped a fried egg without anyone's noticing, regarding her closely with very small, very brandy-coloured eyes. "Thanks," she said. "I'm feeling quite famous now."

"I only asked." He drove off, conscience relieved by resentment. He'd pop off to Warwick Avenue for his dinner: the cabman's Écu de France, he called it. He'd got his Dick Francis, and he'd get a Standard in Clifton Road. She'd given him a two-bob tip; she might be somebody.

Arabella found yet more money to get her into the zoo (Christ every time she *moved* it cost something) and sat down as soon as possible on a wooden bench. She ought to have gone to Candida's flat. She couldn't have, without going into everything. Candida was arriving—would probably by now have arrived—back from Sardinia. She simply didn't know anyone well enough to make use of them unless she was feeling well enough for it not to matter whether she made use of them or not. She wished it was not so hot; that she had a cool drink, and that she knew where the lavatories were. This last became an essential desire—so she got directed to them. After a long time there, she felt that she probably wasn't going to die and, unsure of what this meant to her, decided to practise getting through the day in an ordinary manner. She bought a bag of peanuts and went to see Guy, the gorilla. As it was a fine day, he was in his outside cage. He, alone, of all the apes, preserved a statuesque and regal gloom. He sat like someone trying to bear the indignities of the world with comprehending majesty. *His* life was awful, too: or at least he seemed to think it was, and that came to much the same thing. She tried to think of being a gorilla in the good old days: thousands of miles of territory upon which to prey—but herbivorously—and wondered whether Clara enjoyed being her age. He can't do anything because he's shut up, but what am I supposed to do? If you weren't shut up, you made contact—with someone, somehow. But *you* always seemed to last longer than *it*. I really do feel shut up, but I also feel that I have total, terrifying freedom. I can go anywhere, do anything that comes into my mind, and it doesn't matter in the least. Words like "committed," "viable," and "relevant" veered drunkenly through her mind. I can't do anything for people if I don't know anyone. And only one person has ever known me, or wanted to. She put that thought away into some grave that she had dug for it but never covered, left open for grief. She wished that she was four times as stupid, and twice as unattractive, and eight times nicer. What did nice mean? Caring about others. Working for World Peace; the poor; the diseased, the old, and the mad. The trouble was that she had never found time to care about others. She thought it was sweat, but found she was crying—or at least that there were tears on her face as well. I'll turn over a new leaf, she said inside herself to Guy. I'll be marvellous where I'm going. If I feel like this, everybody must feel it a bit; and as I feel so awful, I'll understand them like most people don't.

Guy hunched his immense shoulders and redirected his contemplation a fraction away from her. He knows it won't work, she thought. If she could have shared her peanuts with him, he might have been more co-operative. But DO NOT FEED GUY was on all the notices.

A keeper came along with a truck full of fruit and vegetables. Guy observed him without turning his head. As the keeper began selecting oranges, cabbage, carrots, and lettuce, she said, "Couldn't *I* give him something? Something you'd be giving him anyway, I mean?"

The keeper looked at her and then held out a banana. "You can try him with one of these. He won't take no notice, though. You'll have to come round this way."

When she held out the banana, Guy, without otherwise moving at all, put out one arm on the end of which was a gigantic and exhausted-looking work-worn hand, and took it.

"He doesn't mind you, then."

Guy examined the banana carefully, and then, with an absent-minded but dismissive gesture, put it down.

"He knows it's your banana, though. He knows it isn't a present."

"We've had to put a stop to all that. In the old days, people could feed nearly all the animals. But these days, you get some very funny jokers. . . ."

"How do you mean?"

"One gave an orange to a young African elephant. Stuffed

full of razor blades, it was. After that we had to tighten up the rules."

Arabella began to think of the elephant with the orange and, without the slightest warning, was sick. This made her cry.

"I'm awfully sorry," she gasped, leaning against Guy's cage and groping for a handkerchief.

The keeper gently moved her from Guy's possible reach, opened her bag for her, and took out the handkerchief.

"I'm so sorry," she said again.

"Don't you worry. We're used to cleaning up. Don't worry about that. Sorry I upset you." He led her back to the public fairway and put her on a bench.

"Look at the old boy," he said, as though to a child. "Look at Guy, now. He's eating your banana, see?"

Guy, who had turned to watch her when she had been sick, had now picked up the banana and was peeling it with careless virtuosity. In between each piece of peel, he watched to see whether she was watching, but as he stripped each piece he was intent upon the banana. This dual intensity was somehow comforting: he *made* her watch him, and not think. When he had eaten it, the keeper said, "Feeling better, are you?"

Realizing he meant her rather than Guy, she nodded.

"I should have a nice cup of tea and go home. You look a bit off colour to me."

"You've been very kind."

"That's all right, *madam*," he said, with an emphasis both kind and jaunty, and went back to Guy.

Feeling that she should move, so that at least she looked as though she was taking his advice, she got up and wandered past the ape house. People kept advising her to go home. Perhaps a cup of tea would make a difference of one kind or another. "How can you spend one hundred and fifty pounds and have nothing to show for it?" "That's just the point, you see, Mummy." But Clara wouldn't go as far as that. She gave Arabella a good deal of money, and when Arabella had spent it, and needed some more, she usually just provided it. Only sometimes she had a frenzy of going through Arabella's bank statements or travellers' cheques and complaining that she couldn't understand how Arabella got through it so fast with so few visible results, but this was usually only when she was tired of whoever she was living with —was venting some general discontentment about life upon her daughter.

Well, she needn't spend much in the country. She'd simply live on yoghurt and take health-giving walks and help about the house or be nice to the servants, whichever was applicable, and try to find out what the—what was their name?—Cornhills were interested in and talk about it. She would play with their children and get them all to love her. She had decided not to arrive until the evening to give herself more time to feel better, and although there seemed to be no signs of *that*, she always kept such promises made to herself. She'd taken all her luggage to Waterloo before going to that doctor, who even now was probably eating a hearty lunch in his rubber gloves to save time. It was only half past one. She decided to try and find something to eat, and then to sit somewhere dark and cool like the aquarium or reptile house or that place where all the nocturnal animals had had their time shifted round for them, to get through the next few hours. Self-pity was *absolutely* disgusting: it had no saving grace at all. Holding this firmly in mind (it was the only firm thing about her), she walked tremblingly to the cafeteria.

"It's the weather, you see; there's been a run on them. Everybody's been wanting salmon trout—can't get enough of them."

"Have you any salmon, then?"

The Carpenter turned to the back of the shop, where the Walrus was scaling sole under a running tap. "Any salmon left, John?"

The Walrus shook his shaggy head. "Might be a bit of frozen Canadian."

"Have some nice sole, madam. Lovely, they are." He picked one up and slapped it invitingly on the marble slab.

Anne picked out two soles and bought a pint of prawns to dress them. Edmund was very fond of sole. That would have to do.

"Tell him not to drive at such *breakneck* speed, Vani!"

After he had picked up the speaking tube and done so, the Prince said, with what was becoming his customary, faded, malice. "I have again and again said to you, my darling, that to choose chauffeurs for their appearance is a grave error."

"Don't be so silly. Heythrop-Jones is *utterly* gay. Just what one needs. Concentrate on the game."

The game was Scrabble, but as, from his point of view, he was playing it in yet another of his foreign languages, and Clara played her transistor rather loudly at the same time, the journey used up far too much of what remained of his energy. The Prince sighed and wondered whether Heythrop-Jones would kill them on one of these travellings.

Heythrop-Jones, who had slowed from eighty to seventy kilometres an hour, looked at the massive, waterproof watch given him by an ageing ski instructor (running to fat, poor Rudi was, and he dyed his hair) and wondered whether he'd make Paris in time to collect that charming young waiter who worked the afternoon shift before he had found something—not better but else—to do. He increased their speed again with imperceptible cunning. No good arriving much after seven. He might as well be driving a *hearse*.

Edmund lunched with his senior partner, an arrangement he had not the heart to get out of more than seventy per cent of the times he was asked. The old man was afflicted with a deafness particularly noticeable in restaurants, which meant that Edmund had to shout, which in turn made him sound banal and tedious while everybody else listened. Sir William was a very engaging old man, but he unwittingly touched continuously upon that chord of pathos that inhibited Edmund with an admixture of irritation and pity that does not make for a comfortable luncheon. His wife, to whom he had been absolutely devoted, had died some years ago, leaving him with two sons (Army and Foreign Office, and chronically abroad), and nothing else at all except his office. He was no longer really active there, but used it as a kind of club, where he read the *Times* and the *Daily Telegraph* from cover to cover; had a secretary who bought him razor blades and Floris toilet water and typed long letters to his sons and the editors of both newspapers that he read. He tried extremely hard to have lunch with Edmund—cheery little last-minute traps, like coming in at five to one rubbing his dry, mulberry-coloured hands and saying, "What about a spot of lunch? Miss Hathaway tells me you are free"—at least twice a week, apart from the formal engagements he made—"Lunch on the sixteenth, my boy. Few things we ought to discuss." "Ought to *discuss*," he would repeat more loudly, his once hawklike Lord Kitchener eyes now watery and pleading. He always repeated things more loudly because he thought that Edmund was deaf. If these ploys failed, he went stoically to Brooks's, where he had a drink with anyone who recognized him and did the crosswords. If he succeeded, he took Edmund to Wheeler's, or Wilton's, or Prunier's and lapsed into an almost agonizing nostalgic gaiety, ordering Krug and Yquem which he invariably said had been Irene's favourites, and eating dressed crab and raspberries, neither of which he'd really liked when she had been alive but which he ate now—in spite of indigestion from the first and terrible plate trouble from the second—because *they* had been her favourites, too.

"Funny thing," he would explain interminably to Edmund. "It's a kind of link, though. Trying to find out what she saw in the stuff." He would poke at his crab with heroic joviality: "Looks like dog's vomit, to me, I always used to say to her. Never put her off, though. She had a marvellous sense of humour. *Dog's vomit*," he would enunciate more clearly, and Edmund, touched, nauseated, and embarrassed, would cringingly change the subject.

Today, they were in Wheeler's, in St. James's. Edmund was eating his sole *Normande*—off the bone—and pretending to consult Sir William about Lea Manor. It was very hot, and he knew that the champagne would make him first sleepy and then give him a headache on the train. Sir William sometimes made a pertinent and shrewd remark or suggestion that turned out to be invaluable, but today his mind was not so oriented. He wanted to convince himself—and Edmund that life had been worth living, and this took him well back into the twenties. Yachts, actresses, wild week-ends all over the place; tailors' and wine merchants' bills; pawning his guns just before the Twelfth; private rooms; a girl he had thought he would have to marry—lasted them right up to what Sir William called pudding (black coffee and raspberries). "Then, of course, I met Irene. But you know about that," he ended, or, as Edmund could see, rather hoped that he had begun.

"Yes," Edmund said loudly.

"An Englishman's home is his castle, they say. Don't know who they are, or were, but *I* always say that the sexual equivalent to one's castle is one's wife. Marry the right girl, and you'll never look back. You're impregnable. I was incredibly lucky. *Lucky.* I often wonder," he continued, at top volume rumination, "whether sex hasn't got duller than it used to be—now that it's all over the place. You see three-quarters of a gal the moment you set eyes on her nowadays, and the whole lot, they tell me, at the drop of a miniskirt. We used to find ankles exciting. I'm not talking about the gals one picked up, d'you know—tarts and all that sort of thing—I mean the ones one *fell* for."

By now, the three remaining couples in the small top-floor room had dropped all pretence of attending to each other. Sir William took a hearty swig of Yquem and alarmingly changed his tactics from personal reminiscence to a loud, innocent, and to Edmund deeply embarrassing, cross-examination of Edmund's love/sex life. As Edmund had never been to bed with anyone except Anne, this should have been a simple conversation, but, he discovered as, indeed, any man might, that he was loath to tell Sir William and the entire company that he had only had one woman, and her legitimately. He parried, and Sir William, full of wine now, thrust, and the couples didn't pay their bills and listened.

"Terribly sorry, m'boy, to have embarrassed you," Sir William shouted, far too long after he had done so. "Had no idea. In my day we used to call a spade a spade, and a you-know-what a you-know-what. Men together, of course. Didn't talk to gals like that, and certainly not a lady."

Edmund, sweating, said that he really ought to be getting back to the office. Sir William insisted on paying, and outside the restaurant, said, "You've no idea how much I enjoyed that. Have the TV in the evenings, of course, but I do like a spot of conversation now and then. Anyway—take my advice, old boy. One rattling affair never did anyone any harm. Only enhances the real thing when you get it."

Edmund reminded him of Anne, who, it turned out, had completely slipped Sir William's memory. "Gad! And I went to your wedding. I'll tell you something—I'm getting old. Just as well poor Irene isn't here, I'd have started boring her to death." He then insisted on buying a large bunch of carnations for Edmund to take to Anne with his kindest regards, and so it came about that Edmund had to struggle in the rush hour with this wilting bundle to Waterloo.

"We don't *repair* lamps, madam, I'm afraid. Oh, no—we've never done that."

"Well, could you recommend someone to me who could?"

"It's hard to say, madam. We don't like recommending people, and I would question whether it was worth it. Nowadays people patch this sort of thing up themselves, or they buy a new one." He looked hopefully at rows of, to Anne, the awful little bedside lamps arrayed in his shop. His face, Anne thought, was unctuous with trying not to seem too unhelpful. All the lights on in the shop seemed to make it hotter than anywhere else.

"Well, thank you," she said. For nothing, she thought.

"Thank *you*, madam."

) 29 (

"Don't you want any?"

"Any what?"

"Corned beef."

"Have you got a cigarette?"

"Of course not!"

"What on earth do you mean by that?"

"I mean that I had to pay the electricity bill, I've got to buy food, and I didn't know how long the money had to last. Of *course* I couldn't buy fags."

"Oh, God!"

She stared at him, determined not to ask why oh, God, and feeling so awful she wanted to shriek.

"I wonder why you always manage to say the thing that will make me feel worst."

Silence.

"Well you see what I mean, don't you?"

"About what?"

"About the fact that money is always left out of this sort of mess. There are those two snivelling kids upstairs—that, incidentally, I never wanted in the least—and you've saddled me with having to ruin my life to continue a situation that neither of us gets a bloody thing out of. What about my art? What about my career? What the hell do you think is going to become of that if I have to take every job that radio or TV care to offer?"

Very different pictures of a succession of waiters, police constables, cab drivers, and the "Sir John, Mr. X will see you now" kind of bit part that was all he ever *did* get offered crossed both of their minds. The difference was that she couldn't see why on earth being married and a father made the slightest change in what parts he *was* offered, and he couldn't see why he need ever accept them if he was free of a family. He'd hold out for something really big.

"I don't know." It was defeat, or agreement, or acceptance of something worse and larger than anything she could deal with. In any case, she could not think of anything else to say.

Suddenly he put his head down upon his arms on the table. "Jan, I feel so awful about her. You wouldn't understand how awful I feel."

Losing one's love for someone was like an internal haemorrhage—nothing seen, just a slow dripping away, becoming weaker and weaker with pity and disrespect. "I'm very sorry," she said. She really was—for all of them.

Arabella spent more of the afternoon than she had intended in the cinema at Waterloo Station. She went because it was dark and cool and she could sit down, and then, later on, when she had seen the programme, catch a train without any more travelling. In fact, she fell asleep, and only woke up when, she realized, the documentary film about some South American and exceedingly primitive tribe was nearing its end for the second time. People whose gentle faces were daubed with fiercely unbecoming streaks of blue and yellow paint were slowly filing through tropical forest—the men carrying weapons, the women everything else. ". . . And so, we must reluctantly leave these primitive and fast-becoming-extinct Indians as they wend their simple way to make yet another temporary home farther into the interior where white man has yet to tread. . . ."

Someone was pinching her thigh. That was why she had woken up: someone was pinching it again. She glanced to her right, whence the pinch came, and the old brute was staring stolidly ahead at the screen, while his agile, creepy fingers worked their way steadily upwards. A left-handed karate chop would hurt her hand, and probably thigh, far more than it would damage him—she was too much out of practice. So she leaned towards him and said in a piercing whisper, "If you don't do up your flies and leave yourself alone, I'll call the attendant."

His hand shot back from her leg as though burned: plenty of people had heard her, and she decided to leave quickly to the left before he did. She stumbled out over people's legs and umbrellas and handbags to the rustle and murmur of people muttering to one another versions of what she had said. Outside, she wiped the silly expression of wounded disgust off her face, put on her dark glasses, and almost ran to the Station ladies'. There was a queue, and a beefy, drab woman was taking pennies, pulling plugs, and flicking lavatory seats with a much-used cloth. Arabella put paper all over hers as Nannie had taught her to do. It did not seem to be getting any better; in fact, it seemed to be worse. She walked out of the ladies' feeling distinctly weaker. She would have a strong drink before she caught the train; and, as she was jostled and pushed her way to the bar counter, she remembered how paltry drinks in England were. "Two double vodkas, please, with ice."

The barman pushed two glasses over to her. "Eleven shillings."

"And ice?"

"Ice in the bucket." He took her pound, slapped back the change, and turned to the next customer.

The ice proved to be three tiny, fast-melting cubes. She poured the vodkas into one glass and only succeeded in manoeuvring one piece of ice into it before the bucket was swept away from her. She drank the barely cold liquid fast: it was to do her good, and nothing to do with enjoyment. Then she went in to the front of the station in search of a porter to help her with all her luggage onto whatever would be the next train.

"The trouble is, you see, madam, that we could *wash* it, but we really couldn't undertake to *set* it. Not now. The girls will all be going home, you see. And also, madam needs a trim, if I am not much mistaken."

"Well, do you think you could just trim it, then?"

He gave a little prance of dismay.

"Ah, now, madam, don't be hard on me. You know my little ways. Wet, with a razor is how I've always worked on your head, and it *is* a weeny bit late to make a great change like that now."

"Well, could you *wet* it then, and trim it, and I'll set it when I get home?"

"You beat me, madam, you really do. I give in. I capitulate."

He snapped his fingers. "Marilyn! Would you rinse madam for a trim immediately."

A lethargic girl, in the heaviest eyelashes Anne had ever seen, drifted over. "Mr. Reginald, I have to take Mrs. Blueberry out in three minutes."

"Well, get Sharon, then. Be quick now: madam hasn't got all day."

Sharon, the newest, youngest apprentice, with greasy hair and frightened eyes, came running over with a mauve nylon overall, in which she inexpertly smothered Anne.

"Put madam in number three," called Mr. Reginald, as he went to collect his razor and a polo mint.

When she had been scalded, frozen, and half drowned by Sharon, he returned with razor in hand, mint in mouth, and settled down to his usual monologue upon sex crimes. He had just read a book about Rillington Place, and Anne heard far more than she cared to about exactly what Christie had done to various people and why Mr. Reginald thought he had done it. A miasma of sexual outrage, violence, and peppermint descended upon her and she gave up any pretence of reading *Country Life* or *Punch* as she weakly agreed with the random and rhetorical questions he periodically put to her. When he got to "You get some very funny people in this queer old world of ours," she knew he had more or less finished. Good thing too: she was going to be late home anyway.

Edmund caught his usual, but only just. This meant that he would have difficulty in finding a seat. He stumbled down the corridor of a coach that seemed entirely full of purple canvas luggage of varying shapes and sizes. It must all belong to one person, because it was all purple, but it seemed incredible that in this day and age anybody could travel with so much. It was a damned nuisance, anyway, he thought, as he stubbed his toe yet again on yet more of it.

When he got out at Twyford to change for Henley, he noticed that the purple luggage was being put out of the train too. Instantly, he thought of Clara's daughter. Of course! That was exactly the kind of luggage the girl would have. He looked up and down the platform for her. But the guard seemed to have got the only porter in sight to do the job and there was no sign of any owner. Eventually, when presumably all the luggage was out of the train, this fact seemed to strike the guard as well, and he disappeared, to return a moment later with a fair, tall, girl with spindly legs who looked half asleep. She wore a dark-brown suède miniskirt, white shirt, and dark glasses. She fumbled in some mysterious side pocket of her skirt and handed the guard what looked to Edmund like a pound. Then she turned to the porter.

"Apparently, I have to catch another train. Could you take me to it, with all this?" She absently kicked the nearest piece of luggage. The porter went to collect a barrow. Edmund advanced upon her.

"Are you by any chance Miss Dawick?"

"You must be Edmund Cornhill!"

"How did you know that?"

"Because you pronounced my name properly. Hardly anyone says 'Doik': they say 'Daywick,' or 'Darwick.' How do you do."

Edmund took her hand. It was dry but very hot. "I take it," he said, trying to sound very cosmopolitan about it, "that you are on your way to stay with us."

"That's right. Mummy—Clara, you know—told me to come down as soon as possible. Tonight was very nearly as soon as possible." Her white shirt, he noticed, was rather grubby, her thin legs were bare, and she wore old and rather dirty sandals that did up with a lot of leather thongs. The porter returned with the barrow and was now making a dog's dinner of getting all the cases and bags onto it.

"The train will come in here. It's hardly any distance," Edmund said clearly. "Did you ring Anne?"

"Anne?"

"My wife. To tell her that you were coming."

"Oh—your wife. No—I'm afraid I didn't." He could not tell

anything about her expression because of the dark glasses. "I'm sorry. I see I should have. I hate the telephone so much, you see." She fumbled in her bag, a battered-looking Greek one, slung over her shoulder, and produced another note, indubitably a pound this time, for the porter.

"That's far too much," Edmund muttered to her.

"I expect you're right. But I've got quite a lot of them, and I seem to have spent the whole day fumbling for change."

The train came in, and they and Arabella's luggage got and were put into it.

Once seated, Arabella took off her glasses and said, "It is extremely kind of you to have me." She had what really were violet shadows under her eyes and looked distinctly ill.

"Not at all," said Edmund heartily. "We've been looking forward to it."

"Will she be angry?"

"Who?"

"About me not ringing up."

"Anne? Good Lord, no!" Edmund backed up this statement with a reassuring laugh. As a matter of fact, he knew that she would rather have been told: she was a great preparer, and not, bless her heart, at her best with the impromptu.

"How many children have you got?"

"We haven't got any."

"Oh."

"Why did you think we had?"

"I don't know. Married people do, don't they? Especially if they live in the country. From what Mummy said about you, you sounded so settled that I thought you must have. Does she mind?"

"It was a mutual decision," said Edmund, a trifle stiffly.

"Oh," she said again, and then added, "a jolly patriotic one, if you ask me. Did you know that in . . . I think it is two hundred years' time, there will be only one square yard of earth for each person? And I can't think what they will do about gorillas. They really need square miles." She looked at him expectantly, to see whether he was interested in gorillas.

"Poor things," said Edmund. He clearly didn't mind a bit really.

"Although, I suppose if you *did* have children, it would be nice for *them.*"

"Oh? Why do you think so?"

"Well—being settled and all that. Children don't like being nomadic. I was one, so I know."

Edmund could think of no reply to this.

"I see you have an evening paper. Do read it, if you want to. I had some vodka at Waterloo and it's made me rather loquacious, but it will soon wear off."

Edmund, who had been thinking longingly of his *Standard*— he always read it on this last bit of the journey—picked it up from the seat beside him. This made him notice her feet, her ankles were elegantly crossed, but her toes did not look very clean. Clara's daughter, he thought: how extraordinary. He had not expected her to look like this, and was too tired and hot to start imagining what he had expected her to look like.

"Your mother rang me today," he said.

Arabella did not reply.

"She was on her way from Switzerland to Paris. She did not seem to know where you were."

"Well, she wouldn't have. I didn't tell her. I didn't know where *she* was, you see. But I don't suppose I would have if I had."

She shut her eyes. She really did not look at all well. Whooping it up at Annabels or something of the kind, he thought with indulgent envy. Girls like that probably spent their nights in night clubs, and their days getting ready for their nights.

"I hope you won't find it too quiet in the country."

"Why should I? Is it especially quiet?"

"Well, it is not at all like London."

"If it was, you wouldn't come all this way, would you? It is funny, how small journeys in England always seem so long and complicated. In Africa or America you go hundreds—or thousands—of miles and hardly notice it."

"Have you travelled a great deal?"

) 36 (

"Far too much. I think I'd better go to sleep for a bit so that I make sense when we arrive."

The bit, however, was only about ten minutes: Edmund had to touch her to make her wake. When she woke up, she looked frightened. She sat up and put on her dark glasses.

"Why do you wear them?"

"Oh—just so that I can see people first. Before they see me, I mean."

There ensued a long and, to Edmund, awful time during which they heaved and lumped her eleven pieces of luggage to the car park. By the time they reached that, he had no doubt at all about the number, and each one seemed to be filled with stones. The Rover was not a small car, but by the time everything had been stowed, including the wretched carnations, Arabella was sitting in front with two bags on her knees and at her feet and Edmund had difficulty in changing gear. He was sweating, and wondering whether he should have rung Anne from the station to warn her. Too late now. They set off.

"I think Oscar Wilde was quite wrong about nature, don't you? Green is the only colour you can't have too much of. Think of red: butchers' shops and the insides of people and Communism. Or black: all the old Greek women in the world gathered together and execution blocks and a good many people's hair. Green is much more accommodating."

"I suppose it is."

"I'm sorry I bore you. I probably won't tomorrow. It's quite difficult at first finding out what the other person is interested in. That's why dinner parties are such a boon."

He nearly looked at her—took his eyes off the road and looked at her. "How do you mean?"

"Well—I mean, if one is turning out to be no good at it, one gets a kind of commercial break between courses. Then you try the other person. Do you have television?"

"We hardly ever watch it, though."

"I do: all the time, when it's available. It's the most marvellous way of taking your mind off something and putting it on to something else."

Edmund, turning off into the lane that led to his house, thought longingly of the candlelit evenings when either he told Anne what had happened that day or they listened to records chosen by him. Perhaps *she* would watch TV by herself. She's like a sort of old child, he thought irritably.

"I'm most dreadfully sorry, but I'm going to be sick. Could you stop the car please, for a moment?"

Edmund speeded up round the bend to where there was a comparatively straight piece of road: not the ideal place to park by any means, but road caution fought with his loathing of anyone's being sick, and lost.

"Open the door, please," she said in a muffled voice.

Edmund leaned over her gingerly and opened the door. Arabella shot out and disappeared towards the back of the car. He turned on the car radio in order not to hear her.

She came back, looking paler, if possible, than before. After a moment, when she had settled herself into the front seat again, Edmund asked as heartily as he could, "Everything all right now?"

"Better, anyway. Oh, don't turn off the Haydn. I like these variations."

"Do you like music, then?"

"That's like saying, 'Do you like people, or children, or animals.' I like some. I think Haydn's keyboard music is his best thing. The opposite of Mozart, really."

Edmund said nothing to this. It was very tiring, getting real answers back to formal or rhetorical questions. Then, a few minutes later, he was able to say, "Here we are."

The narrow, curving drive was empty. Anne must have put her car away. He drove to the front door, because of all the luggage, and when he switched off the engine, there was the sound of bees and the delicious smell of lemons and honey coming from the Kiftsgate that covered the porch. Arabella got stiffly out and looked at the house and then round it. It was very pretty, she decided, and her spirits, which seemed to have sunk to well below zero, rose a point.

Edmund, anxious to lose no time about it, began calling for Anne while Arabella stood on one leg and watched him. After a moment, a towel-turbaned head looked out of a top window, saw Arabella, nearly withdrew, and then changed its mind.

"Hullo, *darling*. This is Miss Dawick. By an extraordinary chance she was on the same train."

"One second." The head disappeared. Edmund laughed uncomfortably. "She's obviously setting her hair," he explained, but did not add that she loathed anyone to see her doing it. He began to heave the luggage out of the car, with Arabella ineffectually helping.

Just as he had finished. Anne appeared, in a housecoat and without the turban.

"This is Clara's daughter—Annabel, isn't it? This is Anne."

"How do you do," Anne said.

"My name is actually Arabella—but sometimes I am called Arbell. How do you do. It is very kind of you to have me."

"Is this all your luggage?"

"If you mean is this *all* my luggage, yes, it is. If you mean what a lot, I'm afraid I had to bring everything, because there was nowhere to put it, really."

"I'm sorry nothing is ready for you: Edmund didn't tell me you were coming, you see, or of course I would have got everything ready."

"I did tell you she was coming, darling."

"Yes, but not when."

"I didn't know when. I just met her on the train."

"It's my fault," said Arabella quickly. "I'm awfully sorry. I didn't know until yesterday that I could come today, and I'm terribly bad at ringing up people I don't know."

"Well, it's lovely that you've got here."

Edmund glanced at his wife approvingly.

"Edmund, you take the two big ones, and we'll follow you with what we can manage."

They trooped, or filed, into the house; Edmund led the way with the women after him. At the head of the stairs, he paused, and asked, "Which room, darling?"

"I think the big spare, then she'll have plenty of room."

The spare room had three windows, white-painted panelling, and a yellow carpet. Anne put down the bag she had been carrying and began opening the sashes. "Goodness, it is hot in here," she was saying. There were a number of dead bluebottles on the sills. "I don't think Mrs. Gregory can even have *done* this room today. I'll get you some sheets and things." She bustled away, and Edmund plodded after her to get more of the purple luggage.

Arabella stood in the middle of the room alone. A pang of sharp, familiar sadness overcame her. Here she was again: staying somewhere where other people spent their lives. It had obviously been a very bad thing not to ring up. I've started all wrong, she thought miserably: I've got to make it all right somehow.

When Anne came back with the linen, she said, "What a beautiful room this is. Oh, please don't bother to make my bed: I can perfectly well do it myself." She waited a moment, and then said, "I really *am* sorry that I didn't ring up. I see how thoughtless it was."

"That's perfectly all right. Let's do the bed together: we can make it in two ticks."

Arabella was very bad, if not hopeless, at making beds. She always seemed to be the wrong end, and obviously knew nothing of hospital corners. Eventually, Anne did most of it for her. "You've got two blankets on the bed and there's one in the cupboard, in case you need it. Now I'll leave you to unpack a bit, and whenever you feel like it, come down and have a drink. Down the stairs, and the second door on your right.'

There was a basin in the room. Arabella found her sponge bag, laid out its contents on the glass shelf, and washed her face with very hot water, a practice she always found comforting. She looked out of the windows. They were at different angles of the room: two looked out onto the drive and the other one onto a lawn with a beautiful and drooping old tree and wide, neat flower beds crammed with flowers. A blackbird was creaking about in the wisteria, making fussy, clucking sounds, as though someone had come to stay the night with *him* or her whom they did not expect. She groped in her Greek bag for her comb and dragged it through her hair. She had sweated so much, what with the heat and sickness, that it was dank and streaky. Her shirt was dirty and so were her feet. She decided to find a loo, and if there was a bathroom, perhaps she might have a quick shower.

Outside her room, everything was very quiet, as though she was the only person in the house. A clock downstairs chimed a tinny, silken sound. The passage had flower prints mounted in olive-green canvas and framed in gold. She turned left outside her room because there was more passage there away from the staircase, and a number of white-painted doors. The first one was the linen cupboard, and she shut it again quickly, afraid that someone would see her and think she was prying. The next was a very small single room with a single white bed in it. Opposite, then. Here were three doors, and the first she found was the loo. Next to it was a bathroom, but it had no shower, and she felt it was too much to have a bath without asking. She trailed back to her room and washed her feet in the basin: very uncomfortable, but she stood on her own shirt—the dirty one—not to spoil the carpet. Then she began hunting in her bags for a clean shirt. She could not find one and, as she felt cold and queasy, decided on a sleeveless cashmere. I don't want a drink, *or* dinner, she thought; I just want to go to bed.

Downstairs, Edmund was opening a bottle of wine, while Anne added to the salad.

"But if Clara rang you today, and seemed to think she was with us, why didn't you *tell* me?"

"It never occurred to me that she wouldn't ring up. And anyway, if you've been in Maidenhead or Henley all day, it wouldn't have been any use would it?"

"No."

"Well, don't *worry* about it." He put a hand lightly on her shoulder, and when it was there, pressed down a little. "Have a sherry. It's far too hot to argue about a silly schoolgirl."

"Is that what she is?"

"*I* don't know. She behaved rather like one. She was sick in the car coming from the station."

"*In* the car?"

"No—out of it, luckily. I got her out in time." He handed her a glass. "Oh—Sir William insisted on sending you these." He indicated the wilting bunch on the draining board.

"Oh! Oh!" she repeated after seeing them. "How kind of him. Did you have lunch with him, then?"

"Yes. Worse than usual. I've had *the* most awful day. London is like a steam oven."

"So have I. Nothing has gone right." They started to tell each other about the day, until one of them heard Arabella descending the stairs. Anne put the carnations in water, and Edmund fetched another glass for their guest.

They dined off *salade Niçoise* and cold lamb. Arabella ate very little. They found themselves telling her about their days, and she listened and tried very hard to understand them. After the meal, Edmund went to make coffee.

"He always makes it," Anne told Arabella. "We go into the sitting room."

Arabella followed her obediently into the long, low-ceilinged room, nearly dark now, in spite of the french windows looking onto the lawn and several other windows as well. Anne lit a standard lamp by the open fireplace and instantly it was assailed by tiny moths veering and tapping upon the shade.

"We'll have to shut the big window, anyway, or else sit in the dark."

Arabella stood irresolutely by the lamp, wondering whether they were having the kind of evening they would anyway have without her.

Anne, coming back from shutting the french window, suddenly saw her, as it were, for the first time: her head bent down to look at a foot scuffing a dead moth from the carpet; with the miniskirt and her small breasts in the scanty sweater, she looked leggy and forlorn, like someone who had just lost her identity as a child and had not yet found anything to put in its place. Before she had thought about it, she said, "Poor thing, you look very tired. You aren't feeling homesick, by any chance, are you?"

But Arabella answered in a colourless voice. "Oh, no. I couldn't be *that*. I've nowhere to be it for." But she did sit down —on the floor—and at the same moment, Edmund came in with the coffee tray and Anne sneezed.

"I told you, you should have finished your hair off. Arabella wouldn't have minded a bit, would you?"

"Oh, no."

"Now coffee, and what. Arabella? There's brandy, Marc, and Mirabelle."

"I'd like some brandy, please."

Edmund gave her what Arabella privately described as "mingy English."

"Darling? Your usual?"

"Yes, please."

Edmund poured her a much more generous Mirabelle, while Anne dispensed coffee.

A not very peaceful silence reigned. Edmund cast himself upon the sofa with a slightly exaggerated air of comfort; Anne perched upon the arm—nearest his feet and also the lamp—of this piece of furniture, and Arabella continued to be on the floor with cup and glass ranged round her. Edmund sipped his Marc and took a swig of coffee. Any two of them might have been able to converse, but three—or this particular combination of it— seemed to make this impossible. Anne was by now thoroughly curious about Arabella, but this simply meant that only direct and unduly personal questions occurred to her. Edmund could only think of the minutiae he was in the habit of exchanging with Anne at this time of the evening, and felt inhibited by the realization that this would exclude Arabella. Arabella, who was feeling not too good, felt that she could hardly say, "I've had an abortion this morning, and so I feel pretty ropey. Would you mind if I went to bed?" but nothing else occurred to her. In the end, they settled for a record of Scarlatti, and either listened or thought their own thoughts.

When the record was over, Arabella got to her feet and said, "Would you mind if I went to bed now? I've had rather a long day. And would it be all right for me to have a bath?"

Both Cornhills seemed instantly animated at the idea of her going to bed. She noticed this, and with a final effort to be the right kind of guest said that she had found her way to the bathroom, thank you, and she was sure she would find the passage lights. This made Anne recall this morning's failure with the bedside lamp.

"Edmund, darling, could she have the one out of your study, just for this evening?"

Edmund said of course, and went to get it. This left Arabella stranded: she felt she could hardly stump up to bed and expect Edmund (or Anne, come to that) to install the new lamp for her. So she said, "That was lovely Scarlatti. Was it by any chance played by Nina Milkina?"

Anne went to the gramophone to look. "Yes, it was. However did you know?"

"I didn't exactly know: I sort of guessed. You see, I knew a good many people it couldn't be—like George Malcolm or Horowitz—but it sounded too good to be anybody else."

"I didn't know you were musical."

"One of my stepfathers was, and he conducted a sort of blitz on my musical education. It was awful while it lasted, but in retrospect it's turned out to be good thing. It's provided me with a resource, and I'm a bit short of them."

Edmund reappeared with an anglepoise lamp half folded in his arms—like some old vulture, Arabella thought. "No, no, I'll take it up for you. Then I'll be sure it works."

At the door, Arabella paused, turned to Anne, and said, "What happens in the mornings?"

"Well, we usually have breakfast in bed.'

"Oh, that would be lovely. Could I sleep a bit, though, and not be too early? Just this once?"

"Of course."

"Good night, then, and thank you again for having me."

"Good night, Arabella. I do hope you sleep well."

When Edmund came downstairs again, he found Anne collecting Arabella's coffee cup and glass off the floor.

"That was a bit cool. Expecting breakfast in bed. Who is supposed to supply it?"

Anne said, "Oh, I can easily do her a tray while you are having your bath."

"I don't like to think of you having your mornings upset by a total stranger."

"Well, she won't go on being one, and I'm sure we shall find a compromise."

Edmund kissed her lightly on her now almost-dry hair. Compromises suited him, nearly as well as not having to come to a decision.

"What do you think of her?"

Anne thought many things before replying neutrally, "She seems not at all well: not herself, as they say. So I don't think I know. I'll have to wait and see."

"Leave the tray for Mrs. Gregory, and come to bed."

"What do *you* think of her?" Anne asked.

"My dear, I have no thoughts of her at all. She simply isn't the kind of person who comes into my orbit. If she becomes obtrusive, we'll get rid of her. I'll tell Clara to fetch her away. I don't want our island disturbed."

"Island" was what he called their continuous and very private life together. Anne had once thought this a trifle precious, but now she simply accepted it as apt. Their joint lives *were* an island, with occasional trips to some mainland or other for domestic or social supplies. Edmund got into bed beside her, and felt her small but luxuriant naked body. She arched her back slightly at his touch, and the beginnings of their great mutual pleasure began.

Arabella managed quite well all the time she was having her bath, unpacking her night things, cleaning her teeth, and doing her hair into one thick plait. She also took her mind off things while she struggled to get the anglepoise into a sensible position, but when it either glared at her or collapsed, she gave up, turned it off, lay rigidly on her back in the dark, and cried without making any sound at all.

Part Two

---∞---

Neither Edmund nor Anne mentioned their anniversary the next morning: Edmund because he had forgotten, and Anne because she thought Edmund liked to keep any celebration of it until the evening. This formula had persisted ever since their first year, when Anne had put a packet on the breakfast tray and wept when Edmund had not seemed— as indeed he had not—to notice it. He had then, with great presence of mind, said no, no, it was not that he had forgotten —how could he?—it was simply that he wanted the festivities to be when he came home from the office and could really enjoy them. In London, he had rushed to Harvey and Gore and bought an eighteenth-century paste necklace of peacock blue, and then, in Fortnum's a bottle of Mitsouko and a jar of caviare. He had then told his secretary that she must always remind him of

Anne's birthday and this particular anniversary on the mornings of these dates. All subsequent secretaries had been faithful in this respect, and Edmund preferred to buy presents under the pressure of time: it made him more generous and inspired. On her birthday, he took Anne out to dinner; on their anniversary she cooked him a feast. This morning, however, both were in any case preoccupied: Edmund wondering what on earth he could say to Clara if Anne and Arabella didn't get *on*; Anne because she realized that she would have to dash into Maidenhead for a third sole, because, of course, Arabella was going to be there, stopping its being the kind of evening it usually was. . . .

". . . let Mrs. Gregory get her breakfast for her," Edmund was saying.

"Oh, I don't mind doing it."

"You're a saint: you don't mind anything."

"Anyway, Mrs. Gregory doesn't get here until ten."

"Well, she can wait till ten, then, can't she?"

"Don't worry about it, honestly."

"*I'm* not worrying; I just don't want you to."

"Well, then, I just won't. Have a good day, darling. Thank Sir William for those loathsome flowers."

"You know, I rather like your hair when it hasn't been set. You look like some Victorian waif—a Pip or an Oliver." He picked up a lock of it and let it fall back against her forehead. "I'll tell him they are your favourite flowers."

"Don't! He's so kind, he'll keep giving them to me."

"My dear, he doesn't remember anything. He forgot about *you* yesterday. Kept on about me having a jolly good affair with somebody."

"Horrible old man!"

"No no no. Dear old deaf creature. He simply thinks he's the only person in the world who's had a perfect marriage." He bent to kiss her. "Little does he know."

He was gone: she was alone—except for Ariadne, who lay like a creature stuffed so full that her eyes were glassy—at the end of the bed. And, of course, except for Arabella.

Arabella woke to find herself alone in a strange bed. It did not take her long to remember where she was, only about a second's fear; no bed was strange after the first night. She lay, perfectly still, trying partly to remember, partly not to remember what it had been like yesterday. Pretty awful: she thought of some other awful days in her life to see where it stood, and discovered that she was really only thinking of particular awful *bits* of days; sometimes just moments that had pounced on her, revelations, things she had half not been meant to know but had found out, people who suddenly turned into somebody else, being stranded in places where she knew no one, starting to feel ill and having to disguise it, trying to find out what people, or any one person, expected of her, thunderstorms when she was alone, being sent for to be talked to by Clara and so on. One didn't remember whole days for long, only the landslides in them—the peak, or falling-off-the-peak, moments, as it were. As days she could remember, yesterday stood pretty high for awfulness. In her experience, awful times were usually followed by a dull calm: nothing very much happened, or if it did, one was simply blinded by some preceding dazzle of catastrophe and didn't notice it. It was amazing, how one stretched and shrank to and from occasions, and how you seemed always to be handed just the right amount more than you could stand, in fact, that hating it, you *could* stand. She decided that she must spend the day being the perfect guest, and also finding out whether she wanted to be a guest of any kind. The less she wanted that, the easier it would be to be perfect. Instant perfect worked with a surprising number of people, and nearly everybody could be it: chronic perfect was being a saint, and saints, like dragons or angels, were simply mythological kicks for the imagination. She was just deciding to get up and go to the loo, when there was a knock on her door. She pretended to be asleep, and after two more knocks, the door was opened and somebody came in with a tray: Anne, she saw, through nearly closed eyes. While Anne deposited the tray and drew the curtains, she went through the motions of waking up.

"Here's your breakfast. I hope you slept well."

"Marvellously." She sat up. "It's awfully kind of you. When you said breakfast in bed, I never thought—"

"Of course you didn't. But it's quite all right. We have to start early because of Edmund's getting to London." She had moved Arabella's bedside table so that it swivelled over the bed. Sunlight filled the room, and also showed that it was covered with slightly unpacked luggage.

Arabella saw Anne seeing this and said quickly. "I was so tired last night, I couldn't even remember where my night things were. That's why it's such chaos." She swung her legs over the side of the bed and then said, "Actually—that's barely true. I'm *always* chaotic, and so I've got awfully good at thinking of reasons why I'm like that. I must go along the passage. Please don't go —won't be a minute."

So Anne waited while Arabella put on the sort of dressing-gown that fearfully fat opera singers wear for evening love scenes —a huge, apparently shapeless but trailing garment of sea-green wool—and disappeared for a long time. At least it seemed long to Anne, who felt a mixture of curiosity and discomfort at the girl's being here at all. When she returned, Anne saw that the dressing-gown—or whatever it called itself—was, in fact, mysteriously attractive, or at least Arabella had got the secret of wearing it: with her single plait of hair and colourless face, she looked like some majestic, and at the same time touching, invalid. She threw the wrap aside and climbed carefully back into bed.

"Edmund said you'd been ill."

"I don't know why he said that. I haven't been exactly *ill*. What a lovely great breakfast."

"Perhaps it was just that Clara—your mother—said you needed a rest."

"She always says something like that. I need rests, and she needs new men." She drank some orange juice and began pouring out coffee. "And an egg!" she exclaimed, with what seemed to Anne simulated gaiety. "Goodness! You are kind to me."

"You look as though you need feeding up a bit."

"Oh—I always look like that. Even after huge meals in French restaurants, I look like an advertisement for Oxfam. So don't worry. I'm the kind of person who doing good to doesn't make the slightest difference, and doing bad to—' her voice trailed off. They looked at each other. "Makes the slightest difference," Arabella finished. There was short, charged silence.

"Eat your egg before it gets cold," Anne said gently. She felt as though she was dealing with some foreign child, and for someone who had never cared about or wanted children, this was strange.

Arabella ate her egg and indeed everything else that was edible upon the tray while Anne smoked and talked to her. Their conversation actually consisted of their asking each other questions; neither felt able to comment upon many of the replies; each felt a certain constraint, or shyness, with the other. Each had a genuine desire to know about the other's life, but Arabella felt that hers had been too improper for Anne, and Anne felt that hers had been too dull for Arabella for either to enlighten the other very much. Their day was therefore fraught with half truths embedded in much goodwill.

"Goodness, what a lot of marvellous clothes you have!" Anne had exclaimed during the hour that it took her to help with the tremendous unpacking. "Did Clara—your mother—give them all to you?"

"Well—some. She's always buying new clothes because she's always changing her size and she hates waste, so she makes Markham alter them for me. Markham's her creepy maid. Whenever she has a new honeymoon, I come in for a lot of junk. Don't wear it, though. But due to my Scottish blood, I suppose, I don't throw it away, either. Except that dressing-gown. I do wear that. It's Dior, and it wasn't actually made for her—she just bought it off the top floor."

"The top floor?"

"Where they sell off the actual models. Frightfully cheap, in a way."

"Don't you have *any* clothes that were yours to start with?"

"Some: not many—but some. Jeans and things. I usually buy a lot of one thing while I'm at it. Like that suitcase. It's full of shirts that I bought in Rome. Haven't worn most of them."

There must have been dozens of them, Anne thought, as the case was carelessly opened to display the neat plastic envelopes, each containing a different coloured shirt—all made by Pucci, she noticed.

"How beautiful!" Anne was particularly fond of shirts: Edmund liked her in them, especially with men's trousers that suited that part of her figure so well.

"Have some!"

"Oh, no!"

"Please do. Please choose whatever you like. I haven't worn them, honestly."

"It's not that. I wouldn't mind *that* in the least. They wouldn't fit me. I'm—I'm much larger than you."

"Try one on. They're quite loose on me."

"Well, I will, some time. That's very sweet of you."

"No, *now*. Otherwise, we might forget. What's your favourite colour?" She was sitting on her heels in front of the open case, rummaging among the collection of packets. "Blue! I bet it's blue." She held up a turquoise silk shirt, and before Anne could stop her, she had pulled it out and was undoing the buttons.

Anne was wearing a trouser suit, navy, with a sleeveless top and a white shirt. She had taken off the sleeveless top and received the shirt that Arabella held out to her before she realized that undressing further in front of the girl was going to embarrass her—so much that she could not possibly do it. This shocked her, and for a minute, she could not think what to do to get out of the silly, entirely surprising, but impossible situation. Finally, she gabbled something about wanting to see what it looked like in her own glass and escaped to her bedroom

What's the *matter* with me? she thought, but really, she knew. Her breasts had always been too large for the rest of her: she had suffered agonies as a schoolgirl, and all her life she had worn heavily built brassières that were a little too tight. Since she had married Edmund, she had been able to afford to have them especially made for her, but nobody *but* Edmund—or the lady who made the bras—ever saw her in or out of them.

She had shut the door, taken off the white shirt, and thrust her arms into the delectable turquoise silk, but of course, the two edges did not begin to meet in front. She took it off quickly: she could not have borne to do that in front of Arabella.

When she went back to return the shirt, Arabella was standing by the window. She was wearing a pair of white jeans and nothing else at all. She turned to face Anne with total unself-consciousness.

"No good?"

"I'm afraid not. Thank you, all the same." Oh, God, she thought, she's like I've always wanted to be: small, and firm, and perfect.

"Chuck it over, then. I might as well wear it."

"How old are you, Arabella?"

"Twenty-two."

Anne was thirty-nine, but she had never looked like that— not at any age.

Arabella was buttoning on the turquoise shirt. Then she pulled off the elastic band holding her plait and ran her fingers through her hair. In the sunlight, it was the colour of tobacco.

"Did we unpack my brush?"

"Yes. I put it on the dressing table. What about the rest of your cases?"

"Let's leave them. Do one or two a day." Her head was tilted to one side as she vigorously brushed hair down onto one shoulder. "What would *you* be doing if I wasn't here?"

"Why do you ask that?"

"Well—I hoped I could help you to do it—whatever it was. I went to a finishing-off place where they even taught you to do housework. And wait at table. I'm a marvellous parlour-maid. I was awfully bad at the housework, though. Another girl used to do it for me. You don't have any servants, do you?"

"We have a very nice daily woman who cleans everything. But otherwise, no, we don't."

"Oh, goody. It's much more peaceful—and free. What *would* you be doing?"

Anne explained about the anniversary—ten years of marriage —to be celebrated that evening.

"Golly! Ten years! How marvellous! Wouldn't you like me to go out, or something? I mean, I could go to the cinema and have a Wimpy or whatever they're called. Honestly, I wouldn't mind a bit." She was rubbing cream from a tiny pot onto her face. "Or I could dress up and pretend to be the parlourmaid. No. That would be silly and ghastly. Forget it. I often have ideas with no discrimination about them. But I've never *met* anyone who's been married for ten years and pleased about it. You should see Clara after eighteen months with anybody. Like a rogue elephant in velvet."

"She's not *fat*, is she?"

"No: but elephants aren't *fat*. Just overpowering. Mammalian juggernauts. That's like Clara."

"Do you . . . find her . . . difficult?"

"Difficult? Yeah—that's about what I find her."

She was stuffing the clothes she had worn yesterday into the wastepaper basket.

"That's not a dirty-clothes basket!" Anne said, wondering how on earth Arabella could think that it was.

"It's a trash basket, isn't it? I don't want these clothes, you see, ever again."

"Oh."

They went downstairs to the kitchen, Anne carrying the breakfast tray in spite of Arabella's protests. The kitchen was a large country one: slate-floored, with an Aga and pine dresser that occupied one whole wall. It looked out onto the kitchen part of the garden. There were geraniums on the window sill, in front of which was a round, pine table, where Ariadne sat watching the flies that skittered and zoomed above her head.

"Is that cat yours?"

"Yes. Ariadne. She's half Greek, and about to produce a huge family."

Arabella sat on the edge of the table and stroked the cat's head. Ariadne rose to her feet, arching her neck in acknowledgment, but her attention was still upon the flies: she knew that sooner or later one of them would make a mistake and fly too low; nothing could distract her from this eventuality.

"What will you do with them all?"

"Find homes for them," Anne answered more lightly than she felt. Ariadne's procreative life was as regular as it was prolific, and all obvious outlets for her progeny were long used up. "Why? Do you know anybody who would like one?"

"I hardly know anyone in England. I mean—*know*. *I* would love one all to myself." A picture of her living in a tiny, thatched cottage on the edge of some moor with a cat came to mind.

"But you travel so much, you couldn't really have an animal, could you?"

"It might pin me down. There!"

A fly had come down, Ariadne had caught it with one neat movement, and crunched it up almost before she had resumed sitting on the table.

"Isn't it bad for her?"

"It doesn't matter what it is for her. She just does as she likes."

"All the time?"

"I think all the time."

"Goodness! I wish I was a cat. Even if it meant being demoted, from the reincarnation point of view, I think I should prefer it."

Anne was clearing up everybody's breakfast. "Don't you like—"

"Being me? No. Hardly ever. I simply haven't got the hang of it at all. I just don't know what—" She stopped and stared at the bare foot she was swinging against the table leg.

"What? What don't you know?"

"What to do with myself, I suppose." Her hair hung down so that Anne could not see her face.

"What are *you* going to do?" she added almost at once. (To stop me asking anything more, Anne thought.)

"Pick raspberries for dinner. Like to come?"

"Oh, *yes!* I haven't done that since I was in Scotland when I was four."

What an extraordinary thing to be able to say and remember, Anne thought.

They took a colander and a chip basket and went out of the back door to the kitchen garden. The fruit cage was at the end of it. It was already hot, and the air smelled of lavender and warm box from the miniature hedges each side of the cinder paths. Arabella was barefoot.

"Don't you mind no shoes?"

"Not really. Anyway, we didn't get to the case with the shoes in it. No—honestly, I like the feeling."

When they reached the cage, there was the usual adventurous and panic-stricken bird inside, making short spluttering flights up to the chicken wire and down again, then bustling and clucking about the bushes and canes of fruit.

"We'll leave the door open for him, and he may have the sense to find it."

"Supposing he doesn't, he'd still be all right, wouldn't he, with so much to eat?"

"He'd start fussing about his family."

"Do *all* birds have families?"

"I think so; most of them. At this time of year, anyway."

"Lucky them."

"To have a family? Or just to have a family for part of the year?"

"Oh—both, I should think. Where shall I start?"

"Let's do a row each. There won't be an awful lot yet, as it's rather early for them."

"You mean, 'Don't eat any or there won't be enough'?"

Anne, feeling rather caught out, laughed, and said, "Something like that."

They picked in silence until Arabella said, "Do you have brothers and sisters?"

"No. I'm an only child."

"I'm one of them too. I hate it, don't you?"

"I've never really thought about it. My mother died when I was born, so I was brought up with an aunt and her child."

"What became of it, the other child? Do you see him or whoever it is?"

"She was a girl, and the moment she was old enough, she emigrated to New Zealand. She's married there, now."

"Still—you had someone to be a child *with*. That must have been fun."

"Well—in a way." Anne thought, as she had not done for some time, of the bleak and run-down rectory in Leicestershire where nothing had been fun, really, but one had always known, with dismal certainty, where one was. "It was the kind of house where one was always eating the stale bread to use it up and never having new. And the garden. You could see everything in it from everywhere—it wasn't at all exciting: just safe. I don't know whether that constitutes a happy childhood, do you?"

Arabella sat back on her heels and thought. "I simply don't know."

"What about yours? Your childhood, I mean."

There was a long pause. "I moved about so much, you see. I never had time to have any friends, or *haunts*—you know, like apple trees or favourite chairs for reading in—because we were always going to some other place."

"That must have been exciting."

Arabella said flatly, "Yes, I suppose it was." She thought about some of it, trying to choose something about it that Anne would be shocked by but in an understanding way. "All those stepfathers. Sometimes they made passes, and sometimes they didn't, but they never really *liked* me.'

Anne rose to this, "But that must have been when you were older."

"You'd be surprised. I was ten when *that* began. Well, anyway, I hadn't even started the curse. The kind of men Clara goes in for are pretty decadent, if you ask me. Horrible, *casual* old Humberts: they weren't in the least obsessed, just experimenting."

There was another pause, and then Anne said softly, "Poor Arabella. How awful for you."

Somehow, that had been too easy: she wanted Anne to be too sorry for her to be able to say so. "It didn't matter at all, in fact. I soon got the hang of things. I used to steal back money that Clara had given them off them. Even if they found out, they couldn't say."

"I suppose you went to school?"

"I went to—let me think (she didn't need to, in the least: this was routine)—fourteen schools in different places. Not always different *countries*: sometimes I ran away, or got expelled. I speak three languages and I can't spell in any of them."

Whether this was meant to be a boast or a derogation, there was something dull, or stock, about it; it sounded as though Arabella had often made it before. But then, Anne considered, if one kept moving about and meeting new people, one would be likely to go through the same hoops with them. She licked the juice off her fingers and got to her feet. "I've finished, and I should think we have enough."

"Let me see yours. *Far* more than I've got."

"I've just had more practice. I don't suppose you were an expert when you were four."

"I ate most of them. Has the bird got out?"

"Can't hear him, so I think he must have. Remind me to find out how he got *in*."

"Do you do all the gardening?" Arabella asked, as they walked back up the path.

"A very old man called Leaf comes once a week. Otherwise, I do."

"Is he really called that: Mr. Leaf?"

"Well, people who've known him for more than forty years call him Ken, but I'm not in that privileged position. He's very good at fruit and vegetables, but otherwise he only likes dahlias and chrysanthemums the size of soup plates. Size is what he goes in for."

They had reached the kitchen. It was completely tidy and there was the sound of a Hoover from upstairs. Ariadne had gone.

Anne explained that she had to go to collect some fish (tact forbade her saying *a* fish); she would not be long, she said, implying that she did not wish Arabella to go with her, and Arabella, whose manners for all occasions of this kind were excellent, said she would love to go and look at the books and records in the sitting-room, if that was all right. Mrs. Gregory, upstairs, was apprised of Arabella, and Anne set off for Henley with feelings of some relief. It was oddly tiring, being all the time with somebody whom you did not know at all. In a way, you were forced to find out too much about them too fast. But then, I am used to and happy about being alone, except for Edmund, she reflected.

Mrs. Gregory left quite soon, and the moment that she had done so, Arabella rushed to explore the house properly. She started upstairs, on the basis that Anne would not get back for at least another twenty minutes, and she could presumably be anywhere on the ground floor with impunity. But not in their bedroom. This was the place that she most wanted to see, and she found it easily—it being the opposite end of the small house to hers. The walls were covered with a Morris wallpaper of tiger lilies: the curtains were pale-green raw silk, the carpet looking like *gros point* of fleurs-de-lis. They had an enormous bed covered with a patchwork quilt, and very pretty, if sparse, furniture. There was a photograph of Anne, in trousers, on some sort of yacht, on what was clearly Edmund's chest of drawers, and a picture of Edmund, looking incredibly inexperienced, sitting in a deck chair with a drink in his hand, on Anne's dressing table. The bathroom led off the bedroom, and this was a little den of luxury, Arabella quickly observed. Thick white carpet, sunken bath, shower, mahogany and gilt fittings, and a shelf of books by the loo. She looked: *Diary of a Nobody*, *The Specialist*, Giles' car-

) 59 (

toons, and a Penguin book of crosswords—the stock shelf for lavatories, she knew. There was a venetian blind over the window, and a huge, old print of Oxfordshire hung on the wall over the bath. There were also some dull, cautiously green plants on a shelf near the window. There was Guerlain soap and Weil oil and an electric toothbrush. On the back of the door hung white and blue peignoirs of rich towelling. There was a basket rocking chair covered with the same Morris pattern of lilies that was the paper in the bedroom. What did she *expect* to find? Because all of this was neither surprising nor *un*surprising, it didn't tell her anything, and she had told herself that her curiosity was not idle: she needed to *know* what they were like, these people she was going to live with. Back in the bedroom, she opened a few cupboards and drawers. Everything lay or hung in perfect order. Anne seemed to go in for conservative, rather mannish clothes, and Edmund just for Englishmen's suits: dull and expensive and well cared for. No powder was spilt, no dirty clothes tucked away, each shoe was shining, the drawers were all lined with flowered paper of felt; everything was comfortable and all *right*. She thought about Anne. Small, boyish, except for her breasts, very short hair, little make-up, pleasant, not a *sexy* character at all. She thought about Edmund. He had the slightly haggard, unfinished appearance of somebody who ought to be twenty years younger than he was. Did they have a smashing time in bed together? Perhaps they had neither of them ever considered that there were lots of different kinds of people, and so, once committed, they had simply settled down with each other. Perhaps that was the way to make the best of anything. A kind of desert-island outlook—only first you choose the island: living in that sort of geographical emergency, you would have to make the best of it. She tried to imagine being on a desert island with Edmund. . . . Then she heard the car, and ran quickly downstairs to the sitting-room.

While Anne drove to fetch the fish, she found herself thinking exclusively of Arabella. Poor child! The idea of her being molested by a series of spiderish old stepfathers filled Anne with protective revulsion. It was a wonder the child wasn't a neurotic wreck: stuck in the amber of some interminable analysis. Clara must—apart from anything else that she was—be a really wicked woman, or at least a wicked mother, which, if you *had* a daughter, came to much the same thing. Arabella's offer to go out on this particular evening was especially endearing: after all, she had hardly arrived, and had clearly spent most of her life feeling that she was not wanted. "Casual old Humberts," she had said. Anne read a good many novels, and this allusion to *Lolita* had not escaped her. Obviously, Arabella must read novels too. It was something they had in common. She shall have a lovely time with *us*, anyway, Anne decided, almost reaching the flesh-on-her-bones, colour-in-her-cheeks attitude. People *could* be helped, or changed.

She remembered what a tense, panic-stricken wreck she had been when she had first met Edmund. She had only been on her own for about three months, sharing a dark, beetle-infested flat in Earls Court with two other single working girls. The relief at getting away from Waldo, of his really not knowing where she was and therefore unable to manifest at any old hour, drunk, aggressive, maudlin, and often just plain frightening, had been so great at first, that the very dullness/simplicity of life with two bachelor girls had seemed wonderful. But they were all short of money: the other two vied with each other for getting taken out in the evenings, and there seemed to be an unspoken rule that if this was happening (to them, not Anne at that time), whoever it was could borrow anything from the others, could have the only hot bath the flat grudgingly afforded its occupants every twenty-four hours, had the run—later on in the evening—of the only sitting-room (the others would have gone to bed or pretend to be out), and could expect breakfast made for her in the morning because she would have been so late the night before. After a few weeks of Diana and Mary taking turns with these privileges (and clearly despising her for not seeming able to compete), Anne had grown to dread coming back from her dull job of being an assistant's assistant on a magazine devoted to warning people of the dangers of chemicals in all fields of life either to eat a chop with whichever envious flatmate had *not* got "something on" or boil an egg entirely alone and listen to the indifferent radio. Sometimes, she wrote letters to the aunt in Leicestershire, saying how all right, or much better, she was without Waldo. The flat had really been a kind of unplaced persons' camp: that is to say that nobody intended staying there a moment longer than she could help, and meanwhile it had all the air of temporary marking-time squalor. Furniture that managed to be uncomfortable, rickety, and hideous: people's smalls always hanging in the dank bathroom or steaming readily in front of the only efficient gas fire—in the sitting-room. She used to live on novels from the public library, on the vicarious excitements of the evenings spent by the other two, and, occasionally, on going to the local Odeon by herself.

She met Edmund because he had been brought back to the flat by somebody who had obviously not dared face it alone with Mary. Edmund had been very shy, had sat on the edge of a chair that all three girls knew was on the last of one of its precarious legs, twisting a glass of lukewarm beer in his hands and smiling when anybody looked at him. He had been at school with Mary's dinner partner, but once this fact or explanation had been exposed, nobody had very much to say. It was clear to Anne that Mary had not wanted him to come back at all, had meant to have her Noel all to herself. This made her embark upon a highly coloured and completely untrue account of what mad times the three girls had in the flat together—the never-a-dull-moment, who-knew-what-would-happen-next stuff—with Diana loyally supporting her, Noel feeding the right questions, and Anne neutrally silent. She had not known either of these girls before: her joining them had been the result of an advertisement. Eventually, exhaustion, boredom, and embarrassment had made her decide to smoke one of tomorrow's cigarettes (the ration was ten a day). Instantly, Edmund began to get up to light it for her, and as he did so, the leg of the chair broke and he and it subsided ungracefully on the floor. This caused a disproportionate fuss of several kinds. Edmund apologized without stopping while Noel plied him with the kind of badinage only tolerated by people who have been forced to live together in an institution, Mary giggled uncontrollably, and Diana exclaimed incessantly how furious the landlord would be. Anne began telling Edmund that it wasn't in the least his fault, discovered that her voice was trembling with the strain of disliking her flatmates, and finally fled to the bathroom just before she burst into tears. That had been the beginning of several things. The start of her realizing how awful she felt about the breakup with Waldo—how hopeless, how guilty, how despairing. Plenty of people had had far more to bear than she and for far longer: she was weak, ungenerous, and incompatible. No wonder she had failed: had left someone badly in need of help because she was too selfish to care enough to help him. But it had also been the beginning of a relationship with Edmund. He had arrived two days later with another chair—far better than the one that had collapsed under him; had caught Anne in one of her blackest and uncontrollable moods of depression; had been kind enough to her to make her cry and had then spent weeks of evenings trying to make her feel better. In the face of her unhappiness, his shyness left him: able to comfort, he became unafraid in her company. Discovering that he always seemed to know what was best for her was the best thing that could happen to either of them: she admired and depended upon him; he relied upon her admiration until he was sure that he could only marry a girl of such discernment. The romance grew to this point and Edmund proposed in Boulestin's restaurant after a performance at Covent Garden of *Der Rosenkavalier*. Anne's divorce was on its way—Waldo having obligingly provided her with straightforward means to this end—but it was not through, nor would it be for several more months. Anne, who by then longed for Edmund with a violence that both delighted and frightened her, began to propose in her turn that they should, sexually speaking, at least, anticipate her freedom, but Edmund would not hear of it. Passionate embraces in cabs, outside front doors, even in cinemas was as far as he would go, and it was some difficult weeks later before Anne began to understand why. He was actually afraid. He had told her repeatedly that he had never loved anyone else, and she realized that if this was indeed so, then he had almost certainly never been to bed with anyone. This touched her in a completely new way; the dimension of a protective tenderness was added to her desire. It was then that she really fell in love with him, and by the time they married understood how to seduce him without his knowing it. They had lived together now for ten years in a state of comfort and harmony that —judging largely from what she read about them—few people seemed to enjoy. If she could change from what she had been ten and a half years ago (and, after all, she had been through some pretty shocking experiences during her Waldo period), surely if she was loved and understood, if she really felt that they were concerned about her, Arabella could also be helped. She was much younger now than Anne had been when she met Edmund. They must unite in helping her. She drove back from the fishmonger's with that slightly priggish feeling of euphoria that very general benevolent decisions are inclined to produce.

". . . The one thing you can't expect with nomadic peoples is a sense of responsibility about land. Land is simply something you rove over and, when you feel like it, depradate—sorry, a little bit sensitive there, are you?"

Edmund, stifled by rolls of cotton wool, a tube in his mouth that was loudly dehydrating him, and terrified that if he made any sound the high speed drill would zip through his tongue, at least, rolled his eyes in a confirming manner.

"Let's have a look and see how we are getting on."

(For heaven's sake, thought Edmund with hatred and terror, if you don't know *that*, you don't know anything.)

"Quite a bit more to do, I'm afraid. You've let this cavity get rather out of hand, you know. I really think a little prick would be the thing," he added—for the third time that morning. When Edmund was able to speak, he had explained that novocain

) 64 (

ruined his taste buds and made his face feel like a huge, painfully mobile boulder. He did not wish to spend his anniversary with Anne in this manner. Now, however, worn down by time and fear and pain, he sullenly agreed. Mr. Berkshire swabbed his gum with ether—witheringly cold—filled his syringe, and stabbed Edmund with all the finesse and consideration of a professional torturer. Edmund felt as though the skin on his gum was being inflated beyond endurance, but this was quickly followed by a swelling silence, as though size was simply taking the place of pain.

". . . It's just something that people who don't know the Arabs cannot understand. The wandering-Jew stuff is all nonsense. Jews only wandered when they were forced to. But you try and keep a Berber or a Kurd pinned down to one spot, and you get trouble at once. How are we getting on?" He massaged Edmund's gum with a white, muscular finger. "I think we're just about ready." He unhooked his drill, and Edmund watched his foot ready to press on the lever to set it going. "You know what my solution to the whole Middle East problem would be?" Just as Edmund decided that it would be unwise to shake his head, Mr. Berkshire began high-speed drilling again. "I'd give the Israelis the whole of North Africa, and let them get on with it. It would be the end of the desert in half a dozen generations. The Arabs wouldn't like it, but they never know when they are well off. That's what I'd do: rinse would you, please."

Edmund sluiced water round what felt like the inside of a football and spat feebly into the bowl with its miniature whirlpool—spat, or rather let the water come out: his muscles for spitting had vanished.

"I don't know what you think, but, to me, it's a perfectly sound and logical solution." He stood poised with the drill again, while Edmund feverishly agreed. He always found himself in this situation with Mr. Berkshire, whose interests were wide and whose opinions were many. Mr. Berkshire had fixed his life, he thought, with vicious weakness, so that nobody could disagree with him—about anything.

"Just a little more. I think this will be the end of it. Not feeling anything, are you?"

Edmund indicated, God knew how, that he wasn't.

"I once crossed the Sahara in an old Ford that belonged to my wife's mother. That's a wide-open space for you. It made a very nice change. Bit of an eye-opener, too. The wife didn't care for it—just a little wider, please—but there's nothing like getting first-hand information. The world's made up these days of vicarious experience—and we all know what that leads to. Rinse, please."

"Don't we?" he continued, stuffing new rolls of cotton wool into Edmund's football mouth. Edmund's eyes, on these occasions, became, he felt, about as hammily expressive as a star in an early silent film. Mr. Berkshire began mixing something tiny on a glass plate. "Everybody thinks they know what life is like for everyone else these days, and if you ask me, they have less idea than they ever had. Public communications are nothing but a snare and deception." He blew some hot, or cold, air into Edmund's empty cave. "It's all a question of scale," he continued; he really enjoyed talking, and at home his wife interrupted him. "One gets into a *rut*"; he was ramming cement home into the wide-open space he had created for the purpose. "Whenever I feel like that, I go off and do something I've never done before: it makes a diversion, stops one asking what on earth one is doing with one's life. Just stay as you are." He was using the miniature battering ram to drive the cement home: this felt to Edmund like dwarf, distant thunderbolts. In front of him was a picture of two poodles wearing pink and blue ribbons and unbearably anthropomorphic expressions. "Boy Meets Girl," the picture was titled. He wondered whether Mr. Berkshire's house was full of such things. Mr. Berkshire was washing his white, clever hands and drying them on a lilac towel. "That's fixed you up for a bit, I think" he said.

"Wha you doagh this ear?" Edmund heard himself trying to say.

Mr. Berkshire laughed genially. "Just popping over to Corsica for a couple of weeks. It's the wife's turn, you see. We take turns. Next year, I'm taking her to the Cape Verde Islands. If you don't like it, you can lump it, I've said—because, between you and me, there would be a lot to be said for married couples' having separate holidays. We all need a real change from time to time." He began removing the cotton wool and dehydrating tube from Edmund's mouth. "We've had fifteen years of an exceptionally happy marriage, but you've only got one life, haven't you. Rinse now, if you would. It isn't, of course, that one *wants* another woman, but one doesn't like to feel that one can't have one. If the occasion arose, that is. Well," he finished sincerely and kindly, "I hope I shan't have to see you for many a long day."

Edmund tried to smile with the rubber earthquake that was presumably his face.

"Thang you," he said.

Later, in Bond Street, wandering, waiting for inspiration about Anne's present to strike him, Edmund wondered fleetingly what it would be like to be buying a present for a woman he hardly knew. Much more difficult in some ways: he probably wouldn't know her taste or even her size (he was here seized by a spasm of what he refused to admit was excitement), but then again, much easier in others: if she hardly knew him she would probably like any present, or at least couldn't say that she didn't. Eventually, after looking at several pieces of jewellery which he either didn't like or couldn't afford, he settled for a shop that sold expensive and pretty sportswear. Here again, he seemed unlucky: the suède waistcoat was two sizes too small, the sweaters much too thick for the time of year, and a royal-blue silk shirt again too small. In the end, he found something that would fit Anne and thought would do, but he didn't feel the usual glow of triumphant kindness that he associated with these occasions.

Anne and Arabella lunched off salami and salad in the garden. They sat, or rather lay, upon the lawn close to the herbaceous border that Anne worked so hard to make. Bees and butterflies were busy or happy according to their natures, the sky was that heavy, pale blue that goes with hot and humid days in England, and there were the merest breaths of wind. Arabella had tied back her hair; her white jeans were stained with raspberry juice. When they had finished the meal, she produced two Mars bars from nowhere in particular and offered one to Anne.

"I can't. I have to think of my shape."

"Poor you." In the end, Arabella ate them both, and then lay on her front and said, "Would you mind if I took off my shirt?"

"Of course not," Anne said immediately and dishonestly. (But why should she mind? What difference did it make?)

As Arabella lay there, Anne, looking, realized how extraordinarily beautiful a young, bony back could be. The colour, the texture, and the curves, the delineation of bone and muscle suddenly made her wish that she was able to sculpt or in some way fashion this position, age, and quantity of shape that was alive, and changing, and there.

"I know this is an awkward question."

"What?"

"Do you, by any chance, have some of those good, damn-awful sanitary towels?"

"I don't, I'm afraid. I've got Tampax."

"I don't think I can cope with them yet. I had an abortion yesterday. I'm still bleeding like a pig."

"Arabella! Oh! Poor girl! Why didn't you tell me earlier?' She had made an instinctive move towards the prone figure, and when she touched her, Arabella sat up.

"Sorry—I didn't think. Also, honestly, I didn't know you well enough to ask you when you went out this morning. Also, I didn't think I'd need them. Perhaps that bloody man was a charlatan. Could I borrow your car and get some?"

She was sitting three-quarters facing Anne. Her nipples really were like the raspberries.

"I'll get them for you. You have a rest, and I'll get them."

And that was how they both spent their afternoons. Arabella slept on the lawn, while Anne, having cleared up the lunch, went back to the chemist in Henley to buy what was needed. She was full of anonymous indignation and the warm and faintly exciting sensation of being needed by someone other than Edmund.

When Anne got back, there was no sign of Arabella on the lawn. She hurried into the house and called, but there was no answer. Unaccountable anxiety (she might simply be asleep on her bed, after all) made her run upstairs to Arabella's room. The door was open and there were a whole lot of new clothes all over the floor, but still no sign of Arabella. She called again, and then, from the window at the end of the passage, saw her in the vegetable garden. She was walking slowly about, examining things and occasionally picking them. She was wearing her shirt again, which was just as well, in case old Leaf took it into his head to come and water something—a useful whim that seized him on hot evenings. She opened the sash window and called, and Arabella turned at once to the window.

"I've done a surprise for you."

"What?"

"I'll come in and show you. Don't go into the drawing-room until I come. I do hope you'll like it—them, actually. You see, I'm not much good at cooking, so I thought at least I could do these for you."

She opened the drawing-room door and preceded Anne into the room, turning so that she could watch her face. "*Do* you like them?"

"They" were two flower—or rather vegetable and plant—arrangements. One was almost entirely of runner-bean flowers, the scarlet and white set off by pieces of ilex. This had been arranged in Anne's only piece of Dresden, a china basket embossed with clover carnations. The other arrangement had been made in Edmund's much prized and extremely valuable Sung jar. This consisted of artichokes and sprays of Albertine roses and some white phlox that Anne had been meaning to keep for seed. The jar, which Anne knew leaked slightly, was on Edmund's inlaid chess table. Then she noticed Arabella watching to see whether she was, not just pleased, but amazed and delighted.

"They're lovely. Tremendously unusual," she added, feeling inadequate.

"I thought you'd like them. After all, you oughtn't to do flowers for your own anniversary." She looked so anxious to have pleased, and so pleased at having tried, that Anne felt awful to have to start worrying about a mat for the jar and the risk of Mrs. Gregory next morning. Mrs. Gregory, as Edmund had remarked, broke only the best.

"They're marvellous, and it was kind and sweet of you to take the trouble. Now. Supposing you have a rest and a bath while I get dinner under way, and then we'll both be ready for drinks when Edmund gets back?"

"All right. You do *like* them, don't you? You don't regard the whole thing as a presumption? I so love doing it, and usually they're just awful shop flowers that you can't."

"Yes, I do." More reassurances, and Arabella went upstairs. Anne fetched a deep soup plate for the Sung jar and dried the table that fortunately had only begun to be damp. My artichokes, she thought: six of them! Goodness knows how many runner beans had been left. But why should it matter? Poor Arabella, not feeling well at all, had tried to be surprising and helpful. Nobody could resent that. She was not much more than a child. I'm nearly old enough to have been her mother, she thought, rubbing away at the chequered satin-and-ebony woods. But not quite. Heavens —that *would* make her feel old.

Edmund had had a really fearful day. The heat in London had been the worst sticky, breathless kind, where any gust of air reeked of diesel fumes or hot people. His face had gone on seeming to be a large, different, alien part of himself: he had not wanted lunch; Sir William had sent for him with some crackpot suggestion of going to Greece—to *Greece* of all places—to look at villas for rich, nomadic clients, a proposition that Edmund had said he would consider, meaning that he would allow time to elapse before turning it down. He had also found himself obliged to look at a huge and horrible house near Ladbroke Square (Mr. Hacking, who usually did this kind of thing, being on holiday) which was inhabited by an old, mad, midget-sized widow who was so demented by loneliness that it took him the best part of two hours to see the property while she pattered and chattered after him. All the windows in the seven-story house were tightly closed so that everything smelled of dust and sweat and old clothes. The widow insisted on making him a cup of tea, which he had neither the heart nor the spirit to refuse, but with which, due to the partial paralysis of his mouth, he scalded his tongue. There were also some rock cakes—most rightly named: they reminded him of tiny, fly-blown crags; these he managed to reject. By the time he escaped, he had just decided to take a taxi to Waterloo and blow the expense, when he remembered that he had left Anne's present in the office, and if he wasn't very careful, it would get locked up there. This meant abandoning the taxi and queuing for a call box and getting Miss Hathaway to wait for him. He finally caught his train and had one, irritable, wish that that girl was not going to be there, interrupting his quiet, soothing anniversary, before he settled down to his paper. At least he wasn't going to have to struggle with hundreds of pieces of purple luggage.

While Anne cooked the dinner, Arabella did some more unpacking. She felt that both Edmund and Anne should have presents, and this meant a pretty thorough search through everything that hadn't been unpacked in order to find suitable objects. Then she decided that she ought to appear in a festive manner, and this, too, took time. She was feeling distinctly better, and the challenge of being a success with people whom she hardly knew always made her try—about her appearance and her behaviour. By the time she had dressed and gone down to the drawing-room, Edmund and Anne were already there. Anne was wearing a blue silk dress and Edmund was opening some champagne. Arabella wore a trouser suit made of brown pleated chiffon, her hair hung silkily about her shoulders and in a thin, wandering fringe on her forehead, and she had put on some heavy, dark-brown eyelashes that matched her brown velvet slippers. She carried two very badly packed boxes and reeked of a peppery scent. She did not exactly make an entrance; rather threw open the door as though she had not expected anyone to be there, and then, finding that they were, became shy, almost coltish.

"I didn't mean to interrupt" is what she said.

"You're just in time for some champagne," Edmund said.

Anne said, "What a marvellous dress, or outfit, or whatever you call it."

"Mummy gave it to me for my birthday: I haven't worn it before."

Edmund had got the cork out of the bottle and poured the first fizzy bit into the glass that Anne held out to him. All three glasses were filled, and then, holding hers near her mouth, Arabella said, "Well—jolly good luck, or whatever." She drank and then added, "Not that you seem to need it."

"Why don't we?"

She turned to Anne. "Well—everything seems so marvellous, and usually people drink toasts when they expect everything to be awful."

"These are for you," she added, and presented them each with a box. Everybody became, in different ways, embarrassed. Edmund did not want her to give him a present at all; Anne was terrified that she wouldn't like whatever it was and find herself unable to lie about it; and Arabella was seriously concerned that she might have chosen the wrong things.

And so she had, in a way. Edmund's present was a snuff box, enamelled in green and set with crystal and rubies. Anne's was a caftan of peacock silk heavily embroidered in silver.

"My God—this looks like Fabergé!"

"It is, actually. One of my stepfathers came by it, and then I came by him and subsequently it. So it isn't at all kind of me." She watched Anne now, who had opened her box and was pulling back the tissue paper.

"This is beautiful."

"You ought to put it on now," Edmund said, thereby destroying Anne's picture of herself, and also making it impossible for her not to change.

"I will." Anne disappeared with the caftan obediently.

Edmund offered Arabella a Gauloise, which she accepted as he said, 'You've rather taken the wind out of *my* sails, at least. I haven't given Anne her present yet, but it certainly doesn't match up to yours.'

"Oh, dear. Oh, well. I'm not nicer, or anything, I just *have* more. You know how it is. Damn: it's gone out, I'm hopeless with Gauloises. Could you light it, please?"

Because she smelled so delicious, he tried to ignore that: this made him notice that she had a long, curving mouth and Italian forehead and those very simple arched eyebrows that made him think of some painting he knew well. He could not remember what colour the eyes had been or were, but he could not, come to that, determine the colour of Arabella's.

"Thank you for my box. It really is a beauty: you shouldn't have given it to me."

"You can't say that to people! You can say that you don't like something, but you can't say that people shouldn't give you— *anything!*"

There was a silence while she gulped the rest of her champagne before saying, "Giving people things is nothing. It's usually some kind of indirect bribe. Have this, and don't be a nuisance for a bit."

"Is that why you gave me this box?"

"No." She was blushing, he noticed, and wouldn't look at him. "I just felt like it. But, of course, I hoped you'd like me more if I gave it to you than if I didn't. Or are you chock full of moral rectitude?"

"Of course not." Like most people, Edmund liked to feel that his moral rectitude was a decently chronic, but unflamboyant, affair.

"Oh, good. I haven't got any. I should think I'm probably the most *un*moral person you've ever met."

"I very much doubt it." Gallantry and slight resentment at his supposed inexperience combined here, but before he was able to enlarge upon either, Anne could be heard coming uncertainly down the stairs. I suppose she talks so much, poor girl, because she hasn't had enough people to talk *to*, Edmund thought, his mind still confusedly upon Arabella.

"It's a little too long for me," Anne said, and indeed it was. She could not walk without holding it up, and this did not suit the dress. It was also too shapeless for so small a woman, making her look as though underneath it all she was probably pregnant. But Edmund admired her in it, and poured them all more champagne: Arabella glowed with successful generosity, and both Anne and Edmund worried and wondered about their private presents to each other. These were, as they had always been, duly presented before dinner. Anne had a pair of eighteenth-century cuff links of purple foiled paste for Edmund. Edmund's present was a very thin, chiffon shirt embroidered with cornflowers and tying round the waist. Arabella exaggerated her admiration for both presents, which embarrassed Anne, who realized this, and charmed Edmund, who did not. When the champagne was finished, they went in to dinner.

The dining-room was small and rich and dark, and Anne had lit candles, round which tiny moths were hopelessly riveted. On the round, rosewood table lay three plates of *hors d'oeuvre:* tomato, anchovy, some kind of egg, and two or three huge prawns. A bowl of creamy roses lay in the centre: these were Anne's—she had explained about Arabella's touching extravaganzas and begged Edmund not to mind about his Sung jar.

As they sat down, Arabella looked expectantly from one to the other. They saw this, and Edmund said, "Well? Do you want me to pass you the salt, or are you wondering what you are going to drink with this?"

"I was wondering what you were—what we were—going to talk about. I mean, it's not like a restaurant, where either someone is trying to seduce you or get you to buy something silly, and isn't like dinner with Mummy and whoever it might be, because she often plays Scrabble through meals, and I get heavy looks from the current stepfather and I sulk. So I just wondered."

Anne, who, by now, thought she understood that Arabella must be used to so many and such varied parties where people talked all the time, said kindly, "What would you like to talk about?"

"Well—the state of the world?"

"Very bad for the digestion," Edmund said promptly.

"The arts; religion; social progress. What happened to you today. Then," she added.

Anne said, "I can't talk about the arts. I love reading, but I don't know enough about all the arts to talk about them. I don't believe in God. You know what happened to me today. That pretty well rules me out."

Edmund said, "I went to the dentist. But, not unnaturally, he did all the talking. I was cowed and gagged into agreeing with every single thing he said." Then he turned to Anne and said, "Are you sure you don't believe in God? I don't mean any particular established church, but just God?"

"I'm not sure, I suppose. I don't think I like thinking about it for long enough to come to an opinion."

Arabella seized on this. "That's the trouble, isn't it? God has got pre-empted by so many awful people who make a society out of Him that you haven't a hope of finding anything out for yourself. But I bet there's a God, all right. And I think he's pretty malevolent, if you ask me. Nobody agreed with Him enough, and that always makes organizers angry. They'd rather you didn't know and cared than didn't care and knew. What about politics? Are they a topic?"

Edmund said, "Anne and I agree about that. We're both Tory to the bone."

"But doesn't that mean that you talk about it more, rather than less? I mean, if you disagreed, I can see you'd have one whacking argument, but if you agree, don't you keep on worrying about details? Details in politics are enormous."

She picked her prawns to pieces with delicate, sharp fingers and sucked the heads and tails with animal enjoyment.

Anne said again, "What would *you* like to talk about, Arabella?"

"Well, if I'm not very careful about it—and I hardly ever am —I end up talking about myself. Often simply *to* myself, but that doesn't make it any more interesting."

Anne said to Edmund, "But you often *do* talk about the state of the world. When you're very tired and have had an awful day."

Before Edmund could reply, Arabella remarked cheerfully, "But then, there's other things: like malnutrition and sex and what people smell like and whether it matters whether you're brave or not."

Edmund fetched a bottle from the sideboard and began pouring wine. "I talked about the train strike rather a lot, because it was such a damn nuisance to me. Perhaps that comes under the heading of talking about myself?"

"Well, darling, it was natural: it *was* awful for you."

"You probably talked about it a good deal *to* yourself as well, I expect. Golly—what super wine. Sancerre. One of my best wines."

"You mean Edmund thought about it to himself."

"No—talked. That's what people do nearly all the time. They call it thinking. In my opinion, hardly anyone thinks at all. I expect financiers and novelists and scientists and that crowd think a bit in their baths, but, ten to one, when they do get any idea about anything, they haven't the slightest notion where it came from."

"You think most of the inventions and ideas in the world have been accidents?"

Anne was collecting plates. Everything else, being cold, was in the room.

"Not *accidents*, exactly. More like dandelions. There's such a terrific amount of seed that some of it's got to get rooted. Like sperm and children."

This last observation unhinged both Anne and Edmund: Anne because of Arabella's earlier confidence that day, and Edmund because he spasmodically, and uncomfortably, wondered whether Anne didn't have any children because she knew he didn't want them.

Anne laid a silver-lustre dish of cold sole covered with a sauce that she had almost invented, of sour cream, chopped walnuts, and horse-radish. There was a large salad in an olive-wood bowl that Edmund began dressing. Arabella finished the wine in her glass and said, "What I really meant was please do talk about whatever you *would* talk about if only I wasn't here. I just meant that I don't want to change or spoil anything."

Anne put another dish of beautifully made new-potato salad beside the fish. Edmund passed the bottle to Arabella. "Help yourself."

As Edmund watched Anne helping the fish, he said, almost belligerently, "Of *course* you can talk about the arts, Anne, darling: you love pictures and music and far more poetry than I do."

"Loving or liking isn't knowing."

"But God's strewth, hardly anyone *knows* what they are talking about, do they?"

Anne passed a plate to Arabella and said, almost maternally, "I suppose knowing is a relative business. I live on such an island that I don't feel I know anything outside it any more. Not that I *mind*," she added, seeing Edmund's face, and at the same time choosing the best piece of fish for him. "I couldn't wish for anything more: you *know* that."

"What a marvellous dinner." Arabella had helped herself to the salads and begun upon her fish. She had decided to coast a bit, and also discovered that she was ravenously hungry.

Edmund met Anne's eyes and raised his glass. They drank to each other silently while Arabella's silky hair was bent over her plate.

"The thing is that of course you're not spoiling anything, but you can't expect not to change it."

Arabella looked at her. "I suppose not. But this is family life, isn't it? I'm totally inexperienced about that. I had a kind of nursery life until I went to schools, but after that—"

"After that?"

She gave Edmund a look that was not really describable—or that, anyway, he would not have attempted to describe. "Oh—after that. Nothing. You know. Moving around. Night clubs. Restaurants. Hotels. Rented villas. Millions of schools, of course. Nowhere you could take for granted. All places where people had to take *you* for granted, if you know what I mean. Or not, as the case might be. Often not, in fact. I should think I've been a howling failure most of the time, but, you bet, I made sure of its being howling while I was about it. "Could not do worse if she tried," is what I aimed at in school reports, but nobody had the wit for *that* kind of nutshell."

Edmund, who found his curiosity about her proliferating, said, "What would you *like* to do?"

"Have some more fish." She passed her plate. "Oh—find some cause, I suppose. It is so awful finding that nearly everything that people say are the best things in life aren't. I don't care a damn what they cost, I mind, what they turn out to *be.*"

"What sort of things?" Anne handed back her plate.

"Oh—drink, and freedom, and things being beautiful, and sex. A total frost, if you ask me. But I suspect that that is because I've been so damnably brought up. I'm frigid, I think, and they tell me. And I don't know what to *try* for. It's like any serious experience: hardly anyone can describe it: they simply bore you by going on about whatever it is being unique. I wouldn't mind if all my best things were everybody else's, as long as they really were mine too. The opposite of Mummy, in fact. She can't bear having a dress that anyone else has got. Well, I wouldn't care a damn if a million people were wearing it, so long as *I* liked wearing it. But somehow nothing works out that way. *I* don't like whatever it is, and people keep saying that its an exception to some bloody rule. What would you do about that?"

Edmund, rather dazed, said, "I don't know."

"Could I have some more of that delicious potato salad, do you think?"

A moment later, her mouth full, but without, mysteriously, seeming to be so, she said, "Of course, food's a very good thing in life, but I suppose when one gets to be thirty—or old, anyway—you can't eat what you like because of fatness or middle-age spread. My mother fights the battles of her bulges from morning till night. You quite quickly reach a conflict between vanity and greed, don't you? Which would *you* go for?" She had turned to Anne.

"Greed, I think. I don't think I have enough to be vain about."

Edmund looked prim, which meant, Anne knew, that he was displeased.

"You have me. *I* don't want you to get greedy and shapeless. I like a little vanity in women."

Arabella turned to Anne. "You see? It *is* a man's world. He really thinks he ought to be able to choose your pleasures or vices or whatever they are."

Anne answered with a hint of tranquil disapproval. "I don't mind a man's world, you see. I seem to have a very good life in it."

She was getting, with difficulty, to her feet, in order to change the plates. Her dress was so long that all movement was tricky if one had to use hands to carry things. Edmund sprang to his feet to help her. Arabella put her elbows on the table and said vehemently, "Well, I *hate* a man's world. There's absolutely no valid reason for it any more. Men hide behind our menstruating and having children—which, incidentally, neither you nor I are doing—to try and make us do all the dull things, calling it protection. It's the biggest confidence trick of all time. They've done their level best to stop us doing anything interesting, and now they say we couldn't do these things. It's as bad as people being against Jews in the eighteenth century for being money lenders, when that was all they were allowed to be."

Edmund said mildly and therefore, to Arabella, maddeningly, "Women don't seem to have written much poetry or music. You don't get women sculpting much or conducting orchestras or being architects."

"You get awful houses because of men being architects. And you *do* get women being poets and musicians and prime ministers or presidents. And look at Elisabet Ney."

"Never heard of her."

"There you are! A woman sculptor. Granddaughter of Maréchal Ney."

"But surely it's a point in my favour, that I *haven't* heard of her."

Anne said, as though to two children, "Have some raspberries. And stop quarrelling."

"We're not quarrelling, but I do hate being wrong about things. No. I do so like being *right* about them. And if I didn't think there was some cosmic social reason for my being such a frost, I couldn't bear it."

Here, the telephone rang. Edmund went to answer it, and Arabella said, "It's my mother: I know it is."

Anne gave her the cream bowl and said, "You aren't a frost, of course you aren't. You simply haven't had time to find out what you really want. Of course it's not your mother," she added soothingly.

But it was. After what seemed a very long time to Anne, and no time at all to Arabella, he came back into the dining-room saying, "Clara. She'd like to speak to you."

Arabella left the room without a word.

"Does she know where it is?"

"If she doesn't, she'll come back and ask. Edmund!"

"Yes?"

"She's been having an awful time. She had an abortion yesterday."

"Good God! Is she all right?"

"Seems to be. What I mean is she hasn't talked about the man or anything, but I think she's feeling pretty bad, and we ought to be kind to her."

"*I'm* not being *un*kind to her, am I?"

"No. I just thought you ought to know."

He walked round the table and put a hand on her shoulder. "Good, kind Anne. You always think about other people. You are being so nice about her."

"I think she's fascinating—very interesting—I mean, one doesn't often meet people of her age, and they're quite different."

"I don't think that they're all that different from us—" But at that moment Arabella returned. Her face looked as though some-one had taken a handful of soft snow and rubbed it. She was still pale, but glowing with—fright?—indignation?—resentment? Something certainly unknown to both Edmund and Anne.

She said, "Look here. She wants me to go to Paris and to *Nice*. She wants me to go on her horrible yacht, and hang about in Paris until I can go on her horrible yacht with her ghastly friends and one particularly ghastly one who she'll try and get me married to."

Anne and Edmund gazed at her, separately unable to deal with this situation.

"It's not that she *wants* me in Paris. She just wants me to go to bloody old Cartier and collect her emeralds they've been reset-ting so that she can wear them at least once in Paris. Can you imagine that?"

Anne said, "What did you tell her?"

"I didn't *tell* her anything. I can't, you see."

Edmund said, "Well, really, I should have thought that Cartier could arrange to send her necklace or whatever it is to her them-selves."

"Yes," Anne said, "and then you could join her much later if she wants you to go on the yacht."

Arabella, who had been standing in the doorway, now turned to its lintel and, without the slightest warning, burst into racking sobs. "Can't! You don't understand! Hates me—just wants to spoil anything that looks like being all right!"

Anne said gently, "But I'm sure you needn't go tomorrow, just because she says that. Why not agree to go in a week or so, when you feel better? A yachting holiday would probably do you good."

Arabella turned towards them: tears were streaming down her face like rain on the window of a car with no windscreen wiper. "I don't— Oh! Well, I promise I won't stay here more than a week—or ten days at the most? Would that be all right?"

Edmund, who had got to his feet when she re-entered the room, now went towards her. "You shall stay here exactly as long as you like. Of course we don't want to turn you out! Do we Anne?"

"Oh no! I never meant that. We shall both love having you."

"You tell her that you are perfectly happy where you are, and that we don't want you to go," Edmund said firmly.

"Oh, *please! You* tell her. Tell her that you want me to stay. She might believe you. She never believes me. Unless you don't?" She looked frantically at each of them.

"Is she still on the telephone, then?"

"Yes, yes. She's waiting to be told. Something—by someone. I just don't want it to be me. She'll stop my allowance—well, that's what she'd start with—you don't know what she's like.'

Anne said, "You tell her, darling."

"What?" He was clearly uncomfortable at having to take both such a firm and distant line.

"Tell her that Arabella wants to stay with us, and that we want to have her."

Edmund squared his shoulders. "Right."

When he had gone, Arabella flew to Anne, knelt by her chair, and said, "You're so kind—you don't *know* how kind you are." It was extraordinary how she could stream with tears and go on looking beautiful and not have to blow her nose, Anne thought. She wanted to feel "poor little thing," but there was something about Arabella's appearance and state that went well beyond that. She put out her hand to stroke Arabella's hair and, touching it, felt vaguely frightened.

In their bedroom, Edmund said, "You shouldn't have tried to make her go on the yacht. She clearly didn't like the idea, and it made her feel unwanted."

"I didn't try to do that. I honestly thought that it might be good for her."

"She obviously finds Clara impossible as a mother, so how

could it do her good? Do you mean that you would really rather that she went?"

Anne had been struggling out of the huge caftan, which now fell in Tiepolo-like folds to her feet. "Of course not. No: I *was* trying to think for her."

"Of course you were. You don't know Clara as I do. That robe is too big for you."

"Don't I know it!"

"Don't sound so ungrateful: it was a very sweet gesture."

Anne said—crossly, for her, "After all, it was *I* who told you what to say to Clara."

Edmund came behind her and undid her brassière. "Don't let's talk about Arabella," he said as he pulled the straps off her shoulders and marvelled and enjoyed how he could not encompass her breasts with his hands. Her faint but, to him, erotic shame that he could always sense from his touch at these moments made it easy and unnecessary to give the girl another thought.

"Oh, darling. I'll get into bed."

He turned off all the lights, excepting the usual one, and stripped back the bedclothes. She lay on her side, half turned away from him, waiting: her short, dark hair ruffled; none of her skin white excepting her breasts and the arches of her feet; she lay with one knee raised and tucked under the other so that the curves and the straight parts of her body were as clear as a good drawing.

"I have always wanted to say, 'Have you met Mrs. Cornhill? She is at her best without any clothes.'"

"Do you really find me . . . all right?"

He lay pressed to her back. "You've never asked me that since the first time."

She was so easy, and he wanted her so much that both of them could torment and delight themselves with time. It was strange that, after everything that he had said and done, the thought of Arabella, alone in her bed, came to Anne, intercepting the sated, familiar contentment.

) 83 (

"I do hope she is not too unhappy," she murmured, but Edmund did not reply: he was asleep.

In Paris, the Prince said peevishly, "I am *not* responsible for this daughter of yours. But if she is to recur in whatever conversations we may have, naturally I am made provident about trying to settle the situation."

Clara was in a bath, surrounded by marble and expensive-smelling steam. "Well—*why* did you make me call about her? Why ask her on the yacht? Why ask—*beg* for trouble?"

The Prince, who hated being in bathrooms when fully dressed, and was far too old and experienced to appear in any other way before Clara excepting at carefully pre-arranged moments, answered, "To have her on the yacht was not for pleasure, but to get her married. That is what any parent must have in mind. She will soon become too old, too rich, too self-assured—an impossible combination for any man of taste and discretion. Ludwig would be a match, at least."

"He hasn't got a penny!"

"There is no need for him to have a little of what she will have so much. We were at school together. His castle is virtually uninhabitable: it would give her something to do."

Clara did not reply. The fact that Baron Potsdam was a contemporary of Vani's, and therefore several years older than she herself admitted to being, was not something to bring up. It was true that she would prefer Arabella to be married, and therefore morally, if not financially, off her plate, but the Prince's notion of parental discipline was fearfully outmoded like so much of the rest of him, and nothing but the sternest and most old-fashioned methods would ever get Arabella to the altar with Ludwig, who had absolutely nothing to recommend him except his mouldering estate and a title that was hardly recognized outside his own country and deeply resented within it. The trouble was that anybody whom Arabella might want to marry and whom Clara would regard as being suitable would almost certainly turn out to be somebody she wanted herself, and would therefore probably take. Fortune hunters were out, unless they had such striking compensations that she would prefer Arabella not to be struck first, so so speak. She yawned.

"Give me my towel and tell Markham to tell them to bring the drinks next door. We'll revise the guest list. Dear, dull Edmund seemed charmed to have her under his roof."

She stood up and wound the pale-pink towel round her like a sarong. She was wearing a turban to match, and held out a tiny, freckled hand with silver-tipped nails. The Prince received it gallantly enough, but he, too, yawned and wished for the third time since arriving in Paris that he was dining alone or with some congenial member of his own sex at The Travellers'.

"Have who?"

"What do you mean, Vani?"

"What I have been meaning is who would Edmund be charmed to have under his roof?"

"Oh, Vani! Please do not bore me like that! Arabella, of course."

"Sometimes I have noticed that it is as a pig that you treat me." He was at the bathroom door, gazing at her with the elaborate reproach that reminded her of a large and stupid dog.

"Not a *pig*, darling—never a pig. And I am sure," she added with her spasmodic candour, "that sometimes I must bore you also. That is what is so dreadful in life: this continual choice between being lonely and being bored."

The Prince again lifted her hand—this time to his thin, dry lips. "Of course, you are incapable of boring me, my darling." He did not believe in candour—never had.

They lay in the same bed together in the dark, each one rightly sure that the other was awake, each pretending that he, or the other one, was asleep. Earlier, he had tried to make love to her —even just to have her—to try and wash some of the guilty, miserable defeat out of their systems. But it hadn't worked. He couldn't even get started; her hair smelled of cooking oil; her body felt both undernourished and flabby, poor and unresponsive to his hands. But it made her cry all right: anything, *anything* could do that, he thought viciously, if *I* come into it. It seemed insulting to him that she should cry, when he was so much—so far more—unhappy than she could have any idea of. *And*, when, feeling like that, he should pluck up any courage at all. He gave up fairly soon, said he was sorry, told her not to cry, wiped a bit of her face with the—not very clean—sheets (Christ—you'd think she'd think of that, when he'd said he was coming home) and then abandoned himself to his private, dull, endlessly repetitive despair.

Janet lay rigidly apart from him: she was cold, her head ached, and what emotion she felt was anaemic outrage. Surely he could have had the sense and feeling not to try that—straight from one bed to another; surely he must see that it would take time and affection (the words sounded like pieces of period costume as she thought them) for anything ever to be all right again. So he was simply trying to prove to her that it wasn't—never could be. If he loved her, if he cared about her, if he felt anything for the children, surely he would not attempt anything so important as their lives together with such mechanical unzest? I don't understand him, she thought. But that thought had no effect upon her at all. I wish I was dead. That, at least, had the element of gesture about it. She lay under the stiff, felty blankets, hugging this endful possibility and wringing comfort thereby. People would be sorry then: they would have some inkling of what she must have been through. *He* would be sorry. I hate that young, rich, selfish bitch. Hatred was like brandy, or adrenalin: it did not make her sleep but almost glad when Luke started crying and she had to get up to him. She was careful about not waking her anyway wakeful husband.

Arabella lay in bed, with the black cat, Ariadne, beside her. She, the cat, had been in the bedroom, and on the bed at that, when Arabella went upstairs. Arabella had removed as much of the bedspread as it was possible to do, and Ariadne's umbrage at being moved at all had quickly died down. She now lay with her body under the clothes and her head leaning heavily against Arabella's neck. She was purring with the professional smoothness that denoted both years of practice and incessant vibration. Arabella was smiling in the dark that suited them both. Saved, she thought; and, this time yesterday—or the day before that . . . If Ariadne was thinking, it could only be any minute now, as Arabella could feel the minuscule thumping and writhing within her tightly stretched fur. "You have them with me: I don't mind; I would like it," Arabella whispered, and Ariadne washed a paw briskly and then Arabella's neck. No offence meant, but nobody likes being told what to do when they will be doing it anyway. "They're awfully kind, nice, different people. I hope they will love me."

An owl was near them outside in the garden. The windows were open, and the scent of stocks and tobacco and jasmine and roses could be smelled. The end of daytime allowed the night noises. Moonlight fell in one delicate shaft across the littered carpet. Arabella lay, with the warm fur next to her, absorbing the extraordinary pleasure of being at home in a strange place.

Part Three

 week later, Ariadne had
five kittens just below Arabella's pillows on her bed. This
news was broken to Anne and Edmund by Arabella knocking
on their bedroom door while they were having their usual
private breakfast. Anne, wearing his black-and-white striped
pyjama jacket was eating toast and mulberry jelly, and Edmund, wearing the other half of the pyjamas, was shaving
with the bathroom door open.

"She's had them!"

At the same time that Edmund said, "What?" Anne cried,
"How many?"

"Five. Three quite black, one striped, and one black-and-
white. I thought she was starting last night, so I slept on the
floor."

"You *what*?" Edmund appeared with half his face still soapy: he used a cutthroat.

"Slept on the floor. I was perfectly comfortable. It was just that I didn't know how much room she wanted. It was all very neat, though: hardly any blood."

Anne started to get out of bed, and then changed her mind. She had nothing on beneath the bedclothes. Edmund, who regretted having appeared in such a farcical manner, retreated to the bathroom again. "It's perfectly absurd to let a mere cat throw you out of your own bed."

"No cats are mere," Arabella answered. "Anyway, it's not my own bed: I'm just staying, Ariadne *lives* here." She sat on the end of the bed on Edmund's side. "Do you think I could take her some breakfast? Something festive, like sardines?"

Anne smiled at her. She really looked, and was, childishly excited; and Anne felt on her side about it. Birth was no mean affair. "Of course," she said, "on the third shelf towards the left-hand end of the larder."

"The thing is that I'll find them all right, but I simply cannot open tins. I break that key thing, and the tin gets all jagged, and then I can't get whatever it is out and cut myself."

"You get them, and a saucer, and bring them up to me."

"And some milk," she called: Ariadne hated milk that had been heated.

"All right." Arabella went, leaving the door open.

The moment that she had left, Anne leapt out of bed and put on her dressing-gown. Edmund, who had cut himself, reappeared with a bit of Kleenex stuck to the wound, and said, "Really! You shouldn't have let her do that."

"Let who do what?"

"Let that blasted spoiled cat have her kittens all over the poor girl's bed."

"The poor girl has been encouraging her. I don't think it matters at all. All *you've* ever said is 'as long as it's not on *our* bed.'"

"She's been ill and needs proper sleep. Besides, she's coming to London with me today."

"Is she?" It was the first time that Anne had heard of this plan.

Edmund started rummaging in his shirt drawer. After a moment of this, he said, without looking up, "She said she wanted to do some shopping, and so I thought we might as well go on the same train. It saves trouble."

Before Anne had time to ask—or to decide not to ask, "What trouble?"—Arabella returned with the sardines and a bottle of milk.

"She won't need a whole tin." Anne opened it with instant skill, put two fish on her coffee saucer, and mashed them up with her knife. Then she took Edmund's saucer and said, "I'll come with you. You'll have to hurry if you're going on the same train as Edmund."

"Oh, golly! I thought you said car, so there wasn't such a hurry."

"I did, but still we'll have to be off in twenty minutes."

While Anne followed Arabella to her bedroom, she wondered why Edmund had said train when he obviously meant car. He only went to London by car when he had to view some house outside London, and this, she knew, usually meant that he was away for the night. But he never went away for the night without saying something about it—usually, several things about it—the previous evening.

Ariadne lay on her side in the shape of a half moon. She was purring, and flexing and reflexing her paws as the five tadpole heads butted and felt for milk. Whe she saw Anne and Arabella, she raised her head slightly, the volume of purring increased, and she opened and shut her eyes very slowly as though she was broad-mindedly acknowledging outrageous compliments. Her thick black tail beat gently against the pillows: she was in a state of voluptuous triumph. Anne held out the saucer of sardines; she observed but did not attend to them. But when Arabella dipped her finger in the saucer of milk and held it out, Ariadne cleaned it with her raspberry tongue, and then, getting slowly to her feet, arched her back in a luxurious stretch, yawned, and, walking carefully over her children, jumped lightly to the floor and settled down to the milk that Arabella had placed for her.

"You'd better get dressed quickly if you're going with Edmund."

"I'll have a lightning bath."

While she was gone, Anne looked with mingled irritation and amusement at the state of the room. Arabella had slept under an eider down and with what looked like her winter coat as a pillow. Clothes, as usual, were everywhere, powder spilled, scent prevalent. On the dressing-table chair lay a buttercup-yellow linen suit with navy-blue stockings and yellow shoes beside it. Her London outfit, thought Anne. Some feeling of . . . not precisely anxiety, nor resentment touched her; she imagined a day in London with Arabella: shopping for things that she, Anne, could not possibly afford. Anne would sit in a spidery gilt chair, while Arabella paraded and asked her advice. They would lunch off a little, very expensive food, like oysters at the bar at Bentleys. Perhaps they would look at some pictures in the afternoon, and then Anne would do the one dull thing she had to do in London: take that wretched lamp to be mended at a place in the King's Road. But she had not been asked. Edmund and Arabella had made this plan without reference to her at all. But, then, Edmund had to go to his office, and heaven only knew what Arabella had to do. She probably had friends in London, people of her own age whom she wished to see. She would have a good chance to get on with some serious gardening—something that had proved impossible with Arabella about. There was plenty to do; she hated London, really; it was foolish to worry.

Arabella came back in her bathrobe and with wet hair. She dressed with a speed that was remarkable, but her hair dripped on down her back, making small dark circles on the yellow linen.

"You can't go to London with your hair like that!"

"It'll dry in half an hour if Edmund'll put the hood down. It was filthy: practically lice-ridden." She began cramming all kinds of things into a yellow leather bag. She hung a heavy gold pendant round her neck. It had a complicated safety clasp. "Could you do it for me? It's an awful nuisance, but Greg gave it to me, and swore it was pre-Columbian, so Clara *forced* me to have this done."

"Who was Greg?"

"Greg? Well—he was a kind of a film star Mummy married for a bit. The only good thing about him was his place in Mexico. Otherwise he was just a muscle-bound bore. A sort of out-of-work Tarzan, not able to make up his mind whether it was Mummy or I who was Jane. Mummy won, of course, but *I* didn't want him, so there was no problem: except it would be lovely to beat her at her own game."

Edmund called, without much hope, as Anne could hear, "Are you ready?"

"Two ticks." She brushed her wet hair vigorously, and drops of water spurted from the brush and her head. Ariadne had finished her milk and returned to her young.

"I'll get her off here before you come back."

"No need. No need at all."

"You *are* coming back?"

Arabella swung round from the dressing table. "Of course I am! I love it here! It's just that I've got to do some things in London. I rather left things in a mess. You know."

Anne didn't know, but thought she understood. Arabella had never referred to the situation that had led to her abortion, and Anne now imagined that there must be things she had to settle, somehow, with someone. For all Anne knew, the poor girl had been suffering about whoever it was but not feeling strong enough to face it.

"You'd better take a mac," she said, far more confidently. "They said it was going to thunder and rain."

"Haven't got one. They're either too cold or else you sweat in them. I really prefer getting wet."

Edmund now appeared at the door. There was hardly any Kleenex stuck to his face now.

"Look!" said Anne.

"Very nice," he answered absently, and then looked across the room at Arabella. "How much longer are you going to be?"

Anne said, "If you're taking the car, it doesn't matter so much."

Edmund said, almost sharply, "I have to take the car when I'm going out of town to view. But don't worry, we'll be back for dinner."

Which they were not.

It took some time to get the top down.

"In America, you simply push a button and it all folds up of itself."

"I dare say it does," Edmund replied. He hated getting his hands dirty with the top, and he did not like driving with it down, as the wind always messed up his hair. He could not think why he had bought the MG in the first place, and determined upon changing it as soon as possible.

"What a heavenly car." Arabella said this in what he privately described as her affected voice. "And my hair will soon dry in the sun."

"There isn't much sun." There wasn't; it was hazy and still, with the feeling of a storm lying in wait.

"In a minute, I shall say, 'Are you cross with me?' and you'll say, 'Of course not,' but you will have been and you'll be glad I noticed and minded."

Edmund found himself smiling. He glanced at her: the tobacco hair was streaming out behind her so that one ear could be seen —not quite so pale as her face and charmingly elaborate in contrast to the long, simple curve from her cheekbone to her chin.

"All right; and then what will you say?"

"I don't know whether you like having conversations when you are driving. Only very good and very bad drivers do, I find."

"And which am I?"

"Well—you might be somewhere in between."

Edmund decided to use the M4, after all.

"Let's assume I'm very bad," he said, "and see what that leads to."

There was a short silence, and he glanced at her again. Her long pale hands were folded together in her lap. She bit her nails, he noticed, as he had noticed before.

"Do you ever have parties?" she asked eventually.

"Not really what you would call parties. Sometimes a friend of Anne's comes to stay the night, and once a year my father comes to visit us—"

"The one who married Clara?" she interrupted.

"Of course. I've only got one father."

"Lucky old you. So—in a way, we are related?"

"Only by marriage. Not really related."

"Oh,"

She sounded so forlorn that he added, "But in a way, of course, we are quite as much related as some cousins are."

"It's clever of you not to have parties."

"Why?"

"I suppose it's because you simply don't need them. Parties are for hunting aren't they?"

"You could say that," he answered, although the idea had never actually struck him.

"And for being hunted, of course."

"Do you like parties, Arabella?"

"You mean, do I like being hunted? That's a hopeless question. To begin with, hunters and hunted aren't divided between the sexes. To go on with, *people* aren't."

Edmund, unable, or unwilling, to take in the implication of this last remark, accelerated: they were approaching the round-about for the M4. People aren't *what*? he thought: hunters or hunted, or divided into the sexes? He had an uneasy feeling that she meant the latter; he also felt in the uncomfortable position of being knocked off his avuncular pedestal—which would never do. He began to drive fast to take their minds off anything that they might have been on.

Arabella threw back her head, saying, "I love speed. I don't mean drugs," she added quickly (and to Edmund incomprehensibly), "I mean going fast. I had a dear little car once—hotted up and all—but I fell into a ravine with it. Had to have twenty-three stitches, but no amount of cobbling would do the poor car any good."

"You *do* drive well," she said some miles later, as she took out a brush from her yellow bag and began brushing her hair. "What are you going to do all day?"

"The usual things. Go to the office. Dictate letters. Answer the telephone. Go and see a probably frightful house somewhere in Hertfordshire. What are you going to do?"

"Nothing much. Mooch around. I've got one or two things to get and do, but not much."

He wondered, not for the first time, why she had been so anxious to come to London at all. "Does that mean that you would like me to give you lunch?"

"Yes. That's what I was hoping you would say."

"Where would you like it?"

"A surprise. I would like to come to your office and see you doing your stuff, and then you take me somewhere I don't know."

"I don't know what you don't know."

"Well, then, you'll simply have to guess, won't you? Things shouldn't be easy. Simple, but not easy."

"All right." Edmund suddenly felt his best: in command of what he felt was a worldly situation that he understood. He could easily take the girl somewhere really good that she wouldn't know. It would be fun. It would save him from Sir William. That was the thing. That, of course, was the main thing.

"Where do you want me to drop you?" he asked as they approached Chiswick.

"Oh—anywhere: King's Road would be super."

So he dropped her, as she asked, near Oakley Street. She had brushed her hair and covered it with a dark-blue silk scarf. It was only after he had dropped her that he began to wonder and worry about whether she knew the name of his office or where it was.

His mind alternated between delightful places to lunch and the likelihood of her not finding him.

Anne went shopping in Henley. She decided that she would do a great deal of this; stock up for at least a week, and then have a picnic lunch in the garden with the newest Elizabeth Taylor novel, and *then* get down to a good afternoon's gardening. When she went back to Arabella's room, Ariadne had eaten the sardines, but made it plain that she did not wish to be moved. Anne, who loved her, and also had a fear of what primitive persons might do to their young if too much pressed, left her to her own devices, which was really the best, if not the only, thing to do with a cat. She thought of Arabella having a turgid lunch with ex-lover (he *must* be that, surely?)—awful silences, and nobody eating anything, but working themselves up to saying the unsayable.

"I'm sorry about it all."

"Oh, well—there it is. People don't plan to ruin one another. They just do it." (In the past week, she had picked up a good deal of Arabella's idiom.)

Entirely by herself, and much influenced by the past week, she certainly didn't indulge, but nerved herself to remember what life with Waldo had been like. Full of drink, casual unfaithfulness, never knowing when and—worse still—how he would return. Total insecurity: emotional, financial, and, if, indeed, that came into it, spiritual. Waldo had not noticed, or ever cared a damn, what she felt like, or whether she ate or drank or was lonely, or frightened, or unfulfilled. His answer to all this had been—quite rightly—that he wasn't cut out to be a husband at all. They had only married because Anne had honestly thought she was pregnant, and because she had felt that abortion was wrong, and going back to what wasn't really her family would be insupportable. So she had married Waldo and *that* had turned out to be both wrong *and* insupportable. Edmund had saved her. If it wasn't for Edmund, she could imagine having turned on the gas in that awful flat one night, or throwing herself into the river, or something of the kind. She had been so lucky that she could only hope that—in the end—something of the same sort would happen to Arabella.

The reasons that Arabella had wanted to be dropped off in the King's Road were that she thought she might like to buy something stunning to have lunch in, and also that she had the uncomfortable feeling that Neville's flat might have been left in a state that would preclude his ever offering it to her again. She decided to get this over first.

"Well, dear, it *was* rather a complete and utter shambles, and a weeny bit naughty of you. I had the impression"—his brilliantly blue eyes were fixed upon her face—"that either a good time had been had by everybody, or that nobody had enjoyed themselves the teeniest bit."

"They hadn't much, I'm afraid. *I* didn't, anyway."

He brushed his thick silver hair with a sensitive hand. "Did you simply hop it and leave Mr. X in charge?"

Arabella nodded.

"I guessed it. Well, he was certainly no home-maker, if you'll forgive the expression."

"Look—I really want to pay for the damage and all that. That's really what I came about."

"That's simply sweet of you, darling, but Rodney and I both felt the whole thing was getting a trifle *vieux jeu*: we wanted to do it over, and this gave us a lovely excuse."

For the first time, Arabella actually looked at the small sitting-room in which she had spent what now seemed so much time, and where Neville was kindly giving her coffee out of a wobbly Spanish cup and saucer. It did not seem very different—simply a slightly more cramped open space in her life than she had imagined. Neville's pretty prints and china were back on the shelves: the books looked the same; there were some beautifully arranged flowers, but the gramophone and curtains were absent, she saw. Oh, God! He'd probably burned holes in them and broken the machine.

"Don't worry, dear. I'll send you a tiny bill for Mrs. Hotchkiss's spring cleaning, but, otherwise, as I say, we're quite excited at our new plans. Rodney has done some fabulous drawings, and he's happy as a lark out matching things all day. Have some more coffee?"

"No, thanks, I really ought to be going: I've got to shop." She put a dutiful, household expression on her face, but he was not deceived.

"Darling, you're just like your mother: you know you adore it. Like most of us."

"Well, you like it, too."

"Oh, no, dear. I like *collecting* things—that's entirely and utterly different. I'd far rather come by them, you know, like dear Queen Mary, than have to go about writing cheques or carrying wads of dreadful dirty paper money that you don't know who's touched it. What are you going to buy?"

"A clothe. Do you know anywhere good?"

"Just one clothe? Oh, well, you won't mind what it costs. Shall I come with you, dear?"

"It's awfully kind of you," Arabella said hastily, "but I'm meeting someone jolly soon, so I'll have to do it far too quickly. I'd love you to come when it's a serious buy: you've got such marvellous taste, Mummy says."

"Say no more. By the way, your dear mother called from Paris yesterday to know if the flat was all right."

"What did you say?"

"I said *perfect*, dear—not a hair out of place."

"You *are* kind." Arabella said this with sincere gratitude: he was.

"I know, darling. It's my reputation: I like to keep it up. It takes such years to acquire that one mustn't let one's behaviour slip for a second—or bingo! goes the lot. And then what have you? Like black people, and women, and ugly people, I have to try harder, as they say in America."

"But you are all right—aren't you, Neville? I mean—Rodney —"

"I worship him, and he's really very fond of me. But the simple fact is that Rodney is fifteen years younger than me. One day, he'll be off, and I'll have nobody's shoulder to cry on but my own. It's not like marriage, you see, dear: it's far more precarious. None of the kiddywinks lark, or any moral brakes on that straight people have."

"People *can* be married without children and be all right." As she said this, she was conscious of feelings composed of, or perhaps confused by, envy, and a sense of challenge.

"Ah, but if people do that, they have to live on some kind of island. Rodney would hate that. He adores meeting new people all the time." For a moment, his chubby, rubicund, gentle features became something quite different: had momentarily the sternness of dignified anxiety—something always to be faced and eventually to be encountered, grappled with, and accepted. Arabella got up and kissed him.

"I've got a shoulder or two," she said.

"Dear girl, I *know* you have," he answered with the utmost emphasis and, behind it, lack of conviction.

She managed to get him to let her write a cheque for Mrs. Hotchkiss, and they parted with mutual affection and relief.

Edmund spent a morning entirely on edge. Everything seemed to be going wrong. Advertisements in two reputable papers were proving to have contained misprints that inaugurated a spate of angry telephone calls. He had a row with a rival firm with whom they had hitherto amiably collaborated. Miss Hathaway had a summer cold of the most noticeable nature. The drilling in the square seemed incessant, and to bely any jokes people made about British workmen: either one hundred and two workmen were drilling for forty seconds each in quick succession, or they had got hold of some black-leg obsessed maniac who was prepared to drill himself to Australia. The heat and now certainty of thunder made everybody irritable. The office boy had an appalling sty that made his cheeky ineptitude verge upon the pathetic. Edmund hated having any of his feelings about people confused in this way. Sir William could talk—or shout—about nothing but Greece and the villa possibility and how important it was that Edmund should go there and see what might be done. "*Islands*— even!" he thundered. "We can't let the matter drop." Edmund went through the old rigmarole about nobody who wasn't Greek being allowed a house (he refused to call it a villa) with any coast line at all. "There are ways of getting round *that*," Sir William had replied, knowing that Edmund knew that there were, but that they were not ways that had ever been a practice in the firm. Geoffrey the junior partner's wife was having a baby, and he seemed to consider that this amounted to a qualification for sick leave. Edmund told Miss Hathaway to book a table for two at three—carefully considered—restaurants for one-fifteen, and her lack of both initiative and demur about this maddened him. He might easily end up having a miserable lunch at one of them alone. He told Sir William that he was lunching with a client and then going to Hertfordshire to look at the house near Barnet. Sir William had tried—quite unforgivably, in Edmund's view—to share the lunch. So when Arabella turned up at one-fourteen in a white crepe trouser suit, he really didn't know whether to scream with self-pity or shout for joy. The whole office would realize that he was having lunch with her: it would have been unspeakably awful if she hadn't turned up.

Arabella's late arrival meant that she had no opportunity to see Edmund at work, which, in fact, *he* found unexpectedly disappointed him: it also cut down the choice of restaurants to the only one they could get to without being unreasonably late. And so— and perhaps it was the best of the three—they found themselves at Prunier's.

"Of course, you must have been here before."

"No. Only in Paris. They have two there—both awfully delicious, I must say. I do love sea food, don't you?"

Edmund agreed. He also liked the excellent waiters and not

being jammed against everybody else. It was not an original, but still perfectly sensible, choice. Arabella drank some Chambéry, and he had—uncharacteristically—a Gibson. Menus were brought. Remembering that it is more difficult to talk to someone if you sit side by side, he had opted for the chair opposite her banquette. The restaurant was only half full, and they were well separated from the other people lunching. They both looked at the menus for some moments and then at each other. There was a certain, to Edmund, delightful constraint.

"Not the time of year for oysters," he said.

"I don't like them. Savarin put me off. You know, the people not being able to open them fast enough for him."

"*Foie gras?*"

"Oh, no! All those wretched geese with their feet pinned to the ground and awful collars round their necks so that they can't be sick or regurgitate or whatever. You should *never* eat that."

"What else shouldn't you eat?"

"Veal—certainly. They make them have such awful lives nowadays."

"But you're not a vegetarian?"

"No. I just don't think anyone has the right to make animals have a dreadful life and *then* kill them for food. I think they ought to think about that. It's quite all right to eat meat, but people ought to mind about how it has lived and how it's killed."

"Bernard Shaw said that, for all we knew, vegetables had just as much sensitivity."

"He wouldn't have cared, though, would he? Anyhow, he ended his life on whisky and liver injections, which seems a bit out of place if you are keen on no alcohol and being a vegetarian."

"What extraordinary things you know!"

"It's not that. It's just that there is so much to know that anything might turn out to be relevant and sound extraordinary."

"The *pâté Traktir* is delicious."

"Yes, I know: I'd love that."

"Would you like some salmon afterwards?"

"No, thank you. I once went in a boat when I was staying in Scotland with my Nan, and they caught salmon trout and whacked them on their heads and they certainly didn't die and everybody said that fish couldn't feel. I was sick. I did it in the boat to show them."

"That might apply to any fish. I thought you said you liked sea food."

"I do: I haven't got any serious principles, only amateur ones. I'd like a sole—just plain grilled. I expect *it* had an awful end, but, you see, I wouldn't know about it."

Edmund ordered the *pâté* and sole for both of them, and was then presented with a wine list. "I know you like Sancerre."

She nodded. "Fine. If I drink too much wine in the middle of the day I become torpid or—"

"Or?"

"Hopeless," she answered. He hadn't the slightest idea what that meant.

After they had ordered the food and drink, there was another silence. It was all rather like a thunderstorm, Edmund felt: either the air would be cleared by some cosmic row or they would both go on feeling on some kind of brink.

"You've changed your clothes, I see."

"Yes. Have you got a Gauloise?"

He hadn't but they could be easily got, and he acquired some. When Arabella had had one lit for her, she inhaled it, carefully, and blew the smoke out of his direction.

"Are you in love with someone?" Edmund asked suddenly.

"No. I don't have to pretend, you see, so—no. In a minute, you're going to say it's a pity that I have so much money. You may be right, but at least it means that I don't have to pretend to love someone because I need him practically."

"What makes you think that you are in such a minority position there?"

Their *pâtés* were brought and put before them. Arabella at once put out her cigarette. "I don't know if I am. But a lot of people want to make up to you because you've got money, and *because* you've got money, you needn't let them." She picked up her fork and ate a sorrel square of her *pâté*. Then she said, "You seem to be encouraging me to talk about myself."

"I am."

"Well, to put it as briefly as possible, I don't know what the *hell* I'm supposed to be doing. I just drift on—any asset is supposed to be a responsibility and a pleasure. I don't seem to recognize the first, and I don't at all manage the pleasure bit. I don't belong anywhere, to anyone, you see: that seems to be where most people start their lives—I don't mean artists or monks or dictators. Just supposing you haven't got any vocation, how *do* you start? I'd like a safe place to experiment from."

Without thinking, Edmund said, "You're safe with us."

"I know! I can't tell you how much I realize that."

While she finished her *pâté*, he looked at her more carefully than he had ever done before. The white trouser suit, attractive though it was, did not really become her—what was it?—almost Florentine appearance: in fact, her face alone distinctly reminded him of some painting, or of someone *in* a painting; he imagined her in sprigged muslin with her feet bare, dancing with a wreath of leaves or flowers on hair cut and flowing much as it did now: perhaps it was not sprigged or embroidered muslin at all, but something more diaphanous. . . . For no reason that he was prepared to consider, other than that it was for no reason at all, he felt fleetingly faint. The sensation had passed before his attention, and, above all, hers, needed to be drawn to it.

"You haven't finished your *pâté*."

He drank some wine. "Do you want it?"

"If you don't, yes, please."

Comfortable feelings of kindly command, of comforting, eldercounsinly superiority took possession. "Will you have room for your sole?"

"Easily."

She was so slender that he marvelled at how much she habitually ate. Slender, indeed! If he were her older brother, he would probably call her scraggy. Just then, she picked up her wine glass and held it out to his so that they touched. They drank and she smiled—her long, curving smile that stopped the rest of her face looking too long and oval.

Edmund thought of the drive to Hadley Common and the house whose keys were in his pocket. He smiled, and she laughed, just as he thought she was going to ask him what he was smiling at.

They ate their fish, and, like most people attracted by any mystery, he began to ask her questions. He was amazed and fascinated by how little he knew of her. The week at Mulberry Lodge, with its simple and leisurely routine peppered by her presence, had nonetheless revealed nothing about her beyond small, commonplace discoveries. She liked to sleep a great deal; she washed her hair continually; she did not like her mother; she had moments of childish, almost operatic affectation; she did not wear shoes very much; she was extremely untidy; her knowledge was so startlingly general, erratic, and in every sense unspecific that she was unexpectedly good company or none at all. She was very young, and privileged in ways that she did not seem—as supposedly most of the young would not—to recognize. Now he found himself cross-examining her, and she would answer each question with apparent artlessness, but also, he felt, with enigmatic reservations that were beyond his experience in sophistication.

"*Have* you ever been in love?"

"Oh, of course, I have thought so."

"Once?"

"Often. Little and often."

"But has it made you unhappy? Or happy? Or changed you?"

"I can't know that," she had answered, making it very clear that it was the last part of the question she referred to.

Before he had thought very clearly, he had persisted. "But apart from men—I suppose—*have* you ever needed anyone, or cared about them?"

Her face changed. They were eating chocolate mousse—again, chosen by her. She did not stop eating it, but said, "Yes. I did care about one person, in the sense that you mean. I mean, I *needed* them. My Scottish nurse. That sounds awfully corny, but I can't remember when I didn't know her, and she was always *there*, you see, being the same, saying the same things, someone I could always go to and stay with. I didn't have to consider whether *she* loved *me*—it wasn't part of it at all. She was old, and rather fierce and often funny, because she said things so well, but I don't think it would have mattered what she was like about being funny; it was her always being *there*, never letting you down in that simple way, until—" She stopped, and without any warning, tears began to slip down her face. She took no notice of them—went on eating her mousse, swallowed, and said rapidly, "My mother suddenly sent me to a boarding school, and when I heard she was going to do it, I rushed to Nan and said I didn't want to go and it was an awful idea, and Nan could stop it, because my mother took notice of her because it made me less trouble, you see, and Nan said . . . she said—it was the worst surprising thing in my life—that it would be the best idea, and I should go at once. I had an awful row with her about it, and she was just as rocklike or obstinate about it as she'd always been about anything. They made me go, and I did everything bad I could think of to get expelled so that I could go back to her, but it was no good: they put up with anything for that one term." She stopped eating the mousse and put her hands onto her face to move the tears off it. "She had cancer, you see. She knew. She never told me. She didn't think it would be good for me to be about while she died of it. It was her idea—the boarding school. But she never *told* me, and when I came home for the holidays, she was dead. So I didn't come home, I had to go to my mother in America. I never said good-bye to her: she didn't understand that I'd rather have been able to do that. She thought she was protecting me: what she'd always done, only then I didn't understand the protection. I thought she'd let me down, and by the time I found out that she hadn't, she was gone, dead, burned up. I couldn't tell her that I was sorry. That was the person I cared about."

After a long silence, during which she stopped brushing the

tears off her face and drank some wine, Edmund said, "How old were you then?"

"Seven. It was ages ago. They weren't much good at cancer then. The pain, I mean."

He handed her a cigarette and lit it. He felt the only thing to do was to go on asking questions. She was blowing her nose when he asked the next one, and said, "Sorry. What?"

"Had you always been in Scotland until then?"

"Most of the time. She knew my father, you see, she lived on his estate. If I was sent for to godawful places like Geneva or London or New York, she always came with me. But the best times were in Scotland."

"And since then?"

"I've knocked about all over the place. You know what my mother's life is like. Well, perhaps you don't, but I do."

"Have you ever been back there?"

"No. There was nothing to go back for. There's nothing to go anywhere for, come to that, but at least most places are neutral."

Coffee was brought them. "Would you like a liqueur?"

"I'd like a brandy. I've never talked about that before. To myself, endlessly, but not to another person."

"Does it make it better?"

"Nothing will make it better. *You know*, that's all."

She drank the brandy as though she'd been ship-wrecked, and then the scalding coffee. Then she said, "I'm going to find a ladies' and wash my face."

He drank his coffee (he had refrained from brandy) and paid the bill.

Outside, a dense and almost colourless sky seemed to be pressing down upon them. She said, "What are we going to do now?"

So of course he said fetch his car from the garage and drive to see the house near Barnet. He wanted to put the top up, as he was sure it was going to rain, but she said, "Oh, do let's wait until it does. It would be lovely to have rain when we are driving fast."

She settled in the car, lit another Gauloise from the packet he had given her, and said, in a studiedly off-hand voice, "Thanks for a super lunch. It was very kind of you, and I *did* enjoy bits of it, actually."

After some driving and no conversation, she said, "What do you think your father and my mother must have been like? Together, I mean?"

"I can't honestly remember. I was at a prep school most of the time."

"There wasn't much of that, was there? Time, I mean."

"I can't remember that, either. She was always very nice to me —Clara, she made me call her. She used to come to Sports Day and the Winter Play. At least," he added honestly, "she did for that year. All the other boys were impressed by her. The first time, I wondered whether she mightn't be a bit too much—you know—"

"Flamboyant?"

"Exactly. Well, she never was. She always managed to wear the right hats and look wonderful and not silly in them. And she always gave me the presents I most wanted, which my father would never have afforded me. I was very disappointed when she left."

"Disappointed! What an extraordinary word to use!"

"It's what I was."

"It's what you think now you were. I bet it's not how you put it to yourself at the time."

Indeed, he had not, he now was forced to recall. His father had written him a—what seemed at the time—pompous letter; well, probably it had been: "Your stepmother and I have most unfortunately agreed that we must part. So I am afraid you will have to make do with your dull old father. Clara and I shall always, I hope, remain the best of friends" (how mysterious *that* had seemed to Edmund then, as his best friend, Hastings minor, *was* his best friend precisely because they *did* want to spend as much time as possible together: if Clara and his father were going to remain the best of friends, why didn't the silly nits stay in the same house, then?) "but," his father had continued, "our lives are not really compatible."

"I felt awful about it. It was frightfully dull after she had gone. No flat in London, no treats, just a dreary little oast house in Sussex, with my father stuck in his study all day and a series of housekeepers who hated me having friends to stay."

"Of course, I hadn't been born or thought of then."

Egocentric, she is, he thought, and said, "Good God, no. You're much younger than I am."

"How old are you?"

"Thirty-eight."

"Mm. That's fine for a man."

He could think of nothing to say in reply and so didn't. They were now out on Hendon Way: there was very little traffic and he felt the urge to arrive at this house. Get the work out of the way as soon as possible. Why?

"Will this house be full of horrible people?"

"No. They've gone abroad."

"Their horrible furniture, then?"

"No. They've taken or stored that. It will be empty, dusty, and probably full of shutters that we'll pinch our hands having to open."

"Still—the best way to see a house."

As they reached Barnet, huge, reluctant drops of rain began to fall. By the time Edmund had consulted his map and been misdirected, there were surgical forks of lightning of fluorescent brilliance, followed by the pause before distant thunder.

The house was mostly Georgian—a bit mucked about, but in a splendid position. They drove through battered and half-rotten gates. A miscellany of outbuildings confronted them, with one black-painted door into the house itself.

"The house first," said Edmund. "And whether you like it or not, I'm going to put the top up now. I don't want to drive home on sodden seats."

"Even *talking* about the top makes you cross."

She went away through some garden door while he struggled with it. It was pointless having a drophead in England; but even the thought of choosing and buying a new car gave him a sense

) 109 (

of power and luxury: it was changing something in his situation, a thing he hardly ever did.

He walked through the garden door, now left open, through which Arabella had gone. She was standing beneath a huge cedar, looking up into the sky. She looked like a contemporary immortal —if there could be such a creature—her hair streaming further down her back with her upturned head, the white crape clinging and flowing when she moved. She had kicked off her shoes and they lay tossed upon the lawn. The lawn had not been cut for some time; it was covered with daisies and clover and the odd buttercup, excepting where she stood under the great, dark tree. Beyond her stretched more lawns, studded with trees at graceful intervals. He thought she had not seen him, but before he could stop watching her, she said, "There's a broken-down old greenhouse with a lot of grapes. Mildewed, though. Shall we explore?"

"I must do the house first, I'm afraid."

She started towards him, and he said, "You really had better wear shoes in the house. With the carpets up, the floors will have horrible headless nails."

"O.K."

When he opened the black back door, they found themselves standing in a square, dark hall from which there seemed to be two staircases and a number of doors. It was much cooler in the house than outside it. Edmund had a bunch of keys and began opening the doors, but little more light emerged, until Arabella undid some shutters in one of the rooms. There were three sets of these, and they undid them all. A large and beautiful room, looking out upon the garden where he had just found her was to be seen. The room was not exactly dirty, but the pile of soot in the fireplace, the floorboards—waxed at their surround and dry and bare in the centre—gave the place an unkempt and vulnerable air. The paint was an ugly grey-green and also dusty. In one corner of the room was a dirty white telephone resting upon dog-eared old directories. There were the usual bleached gaps on the walls where pictures had hung, and a huge spider's web had been woven from a pelmet board to its pulleys. Dead flies lay on the window sills in their dozens, and the windows themselves were dirty. Edmund got out a steel rule and began measuring the dimensions of the room.

"Have you got to do that to all the rooms?"

"I ought to. Usually, I have a junior with me for that kind of thing, but his wife is having a baby."

"What a bore for you." She stood at the window looking out on the garden.

What a bore for *her*, he thought, is what she really means. He wondered if he could go through with the whole laborious business, measuring each room and listing it in his book for reference when it came to advertising the house for auction. Better not, he decided suddenly: get a general impression of the place, count the bedrooms and so forth, note salient features, and send young Geoffrey up to do the donkey work next week. There was plenty of time—in one way—for that, anyhow.

So, in the end, they tore through the house in an almost cursory manner. Arabella was fascinated by what few things had been left. A bottle of Dettol in one bathroom: "How can *anyone* have wanted black baths and salmon-pink tiles?" A straw hat and some tennis shoes in an upstairs passage. In one or two of the minor bedrooms, curtains still hung, bleached and dirty with the sun and neglect. One lavatory smelled of seaweed, and Edmund said he thought there was wet rot. In the kitchen was a plastic bowl full of sprouting potatoes and a calendar about the beauties of Scotland. It had not been turned since February, where there was a dramatic and sinister picture of Loch Ness. There were a number of good rooms, but one end of the house had been recently and horribly built. Bits of underfelt lay obscenely on some bits of floor, like horizontal fungus. There were yellowing piles of newspapers, a croquet mallet—split—a photograph album, very small and old, with Victorian ladies sitting on basket chairs out of doors, parasols poised. Under one was written *Miss Fawcett?* in pale ink.

"You'd think they haven't been here for *years*! Oh, do let's explore the garden."

Edmund agreed to this. He knew that it was large, and that he ought to walk the boundaries with the map he had with him, but he also knew by now that he would do no such thing. He and Arabella would simply go about looking at it as though they were prospective buyers at their first viewing. By now, he did not mind this at all.

The garden was in a jungle state of desuetude: weeds were everywhere. The top lawn descended to a second, where was a tangled rose garden and sundial: thence further descent, past more noble trees, to a third lawn in the middle of which was a pond or miniature lake. It had an off-centre well-scaped island, containing one weeping willow and some iris out of flower. Pigeons flew heavily out of bushes like people leaving a theatre of which they disapprove. Rabbits cavorted and then escaped their attention just in time. A huge, old, buddleia was spattered with either tortoise-shell or painted-lady butterflies. Arabella seemed delighted by the whole thing. "But the lake's the best," she said. It had stone coping round it, warmed from the recent sun, and she lay down to look through the water-lily leaves for fish. "There must be fish," she said. Edmund sat beside her reclining body.

"There *are* fish! It's marvellous, isn't it?"

"It is a remarkable property to find so near London."

"Oh, God! Do stop being a surveyor."

There was a particularly violent streak of lightning, followed at once by a tremendous crashing of thunder just overhead.

"Do you mind thunder?"

"Not if I'm with someone. It's exciting, so there must be some fear in it."

She was very close to him: he noted her heavy, curved eyelids, her pale well-boned face; her hair that he wanted to touch, because its appearance made one want to feel it; her half-serious, half he-didn't-know-what expression. She had kicked off her shoes again, and her feet, also pale, but the colour of parchment with white insteps, made a deep and, to him, extraordinary impression. She leaned towards him and said, "Light me a cigarette.

There's going to be the most awful storm—you'll see."

There was. The lightning and thunder followed at louder and more frequent intervals. Single, large drops of rain fell upon them freakishly, but each thought the other had not noticed. Arabella had turned onto her back; had undone the top of her trouser suit for Edmund to discover that there was nothing beneath it but her flesh—her breasts and the surrounding skin. A sense of unreality and longing for that overcame him. He would have her if it was the last and only thing that he did.

She was not unwilling. Precarious sensuality, incredible promise, and opportunity fought with his desire—to be the best she had ever had, without knowing what that could possibly be. By the time she was naked, the rain had begun to fall but seemed only an erotic chorus—necessary but unimportant. Once he had begun to make love to her, to discover and tell her how beautiful she was, she was utterly silent: still, almost relaxed, open to him, but leading nothing: almost waiting—for anything. Her cigarette lay upon the grass, unsmoked and quickly put out by the rain.

When he could wait no longer, Edmund flooded her as though all the years of his life had been saved for this moment. Then she put her arms slowly round his neck and kissed him. Afterwards, he propped himself up to look down at her face, to read and remember it: her eyes, the colour of the deepest, dark, still water, as unfathomable, looked back: he felt that he would never forget her and that he knew nothing. He started to ask her something, and she put her cool, rain-soaked hand over his mouth—for a moment—long enough to stop him. Rain was now pouring, beating down upon them, her hair was stranded and dark with it, and sometimes drops fell upon her eyes and she shut them so that the drops rolled down like tears.

The storm was passing, over them towards the east; meanwhile, they were both, he realized, without dry clothes of any kind, excepting for a macintosh he kept in the boot of his car. As he thought of this, Arabella sat up, clasped her hands round her knees, and said, "It will stop in a minute."

She was right. A ragged streak the color of old lemon peel

appeared in the sky. The rain became slower; the air was refreshed.

"We should have put our clothes under the cedar; then, at least, they would have been dry."

She seized the tail of her hair and wrung it out and the water ran down each side of her spine. The sun came out of the passing cloud and shone suddenly in a shaft upon the weeping willow on the island. Each side of the shaft seemed a curtain of mist and dusty shadow. Sunlight broadened across the small lake and, after a moment or two, the steam began to rise and there was a steely peacock-coloured dragonfly. Arabella saw him first. Edmund had put most of the clothes he had taken off on again, and very uncomfortable they felt. She had made no move to dress, and he wished, as many people have done at such moments, that he could draw, or have a drawing of her as she was now. As he was thinking this, she said, "I suppose the poor old Gauloises are wet through?"

"They were in your bag."

"They were—in the car. I just put them in my pocket when I got out. Oh, yes—they're done for."

"What about your suit?"

I expect it's shrunk like mad."

He watched, as though he was parting from her, while she pulled the trousers up her, stood, and struggled with the zip. "Can't do it up: it's stuck, somehow."

"Let me try."

"No. It doesn't matter. The top half will cover the worst of it." She thrust her arms into the crumpled, clinging stuff. "It feels lovely and cool." The sun was now everywhere, the birds no longer silent. She put a bare foot upon the stone coping and said, "Stone cold: that didn't take long."

The grass was steaming now, the daisies opening to the sun, but the buddleia, bowed down with its weight of rain, had lost its butterflies. The house, with its shutters closed, looked both blind and anonymously dull. He wanted to take her in his arms, to make all kinds of promises, declarations, reassurances: to hold her and ask her all the things that he did not know about her, to set some seal upon this, to him, unprecedented experience. But she gave one more look at the lake and turned towards the house, saying, "Do you think I could pick some of the roses? Nobody wants them, do they?"

He followed her, carrying her shoes. The rose garden was overgrown with bindweed and thistles, and in the end she picked only three roses, carefully choosing different coloured buds. "They will come out if I put them into hot water when we get home."

This simple remark staggered and confused him so much that he found himself literally unable to consider its implications. Instead, he made sure that he had locked the black back door properly, got his macintosh out of the boot; decided that, although he could have done with it himself, she needed covering more than he, and so offered it to her.

"By the way, what became of your other clothes? I mean the ones you came to London in?"

"I left them at the shop where I bought this. They'll send them home. It was easier than carting them about all day."

There it was again. "Home." Mulberry Lodge: Anne—his wife.

"I tell you a good thing we could do. You stop at a Marks and Spencer and buy me a dry outfit. I know my size: it'll be quite easy. And we could get some more cigarettes."

He looked once more at her before starting the car. Her head was thrown back against the seat: she had a very long, and round, white neck, and he remembered that all her limbs were so formed; that her slenderness was made of lengths and never interrupted any curve. He wanted to kiss her once more, before they left this place, after which he felt that everything he had always known might become *un*known, and that everything he had found in her might recede or vanish into a myth of his life. But looking at her calm face, whose expression was still—and indeed had never stopped being—mysterious to him, he did not dare. He sighed, started the car, and backed it out of the rotting gates.

He drove down the hill through Barnet and turned right into

Barnet and Totteridge Lanes. The sun was now steady; there were lakes beside the lane with swans on them. When he reached the main road, he said, "Are you always called Arabella? Do you have no other names?"

"*She* used to call me Arbell: you know, like Arbell Stuart."

He didn't know. But then she said, "My middle name is Flora. After my father's mother. Awful name—I never use it."

Flora. That was it. The Botticelli picture "Allegory of Spring." She was girl, nymph, goddess, bare-footed, beflowered, casting them random upon the dark ground, where they grew as they fell. He had never in his life seen anyone who sprang, as it were, from a picture. He wondered whether to tell her this, and decided that it should be his secret about her. He needed one: there might be no other.

"What about Marks and Sparks?"

"We'll have to go to one in London. We'd have to go that way more or less, so we might as well find a good one."

"The best ones are Oxford Street and Edgware Road."

"Look, I may not be able to park. Wouldn't *you* rather choose the things and I'll drive round the block?"

"I don't mind in the least about choosing things, and honestly, I don't think I'm decent enough for a respectable chain store."

Her nipples showed through the damp and shrunken white crepe, and he saw what she meant.

"We'll try Edgware Road first, as it's nearest."

"You are nice not to ask too many same questions."

He thought about that all the way to finding a parking metre, which turned out to be miraculously easy.

"What do you want me to get?"

"I'm a fourteen. Either trousers and a shirt, or a trouser suit, or a dress or a skirt. Not black: I look awful in it—like a scarecrow. I wouldn't mind a long woollen jacket—haven't got one." She was fumbling in her yellow bag and produced a wad of five-pound notes. "Here."

"It's ungallant to take them, but I'll have to because I didn't cash a cheque this morning."

"Even if you had, it wouldn't be ungallant. Go on: choose something pretty and a surprise."

Marks and Spencer was not Edmund's milieu; that is to say, he had never been in one of their shops in his life; he had never casually, as it were, outfitted a girl, and was anyway in a condition that was variously composed of euphoria, anxiety, and, above all, a feeling that everything that was happening was either unreal or extremely frightening. The brilliantly lit shop, with its multitude of goods, its scores of customers all looking as though they knew exactly what to do and how to do it almost paralysed him, and for some moments he stood just inside the doors gazing at the enormous scene. He pulled himself together, through years of practice and therefore mechanical effort, and set about finding the section or sections that had women's clothes. After some searching, the feeling—God knew where—intervened, that he must get back to her or she would not be there, would have vanished or simply walked out of the car, and he hastily bought some orange velvet jeans, a pink shirt made of some mysterious modern material but, he thought, a good colour, and a long white cardigan. She had not said anything about underclothes, but he bought her a pair of pants in case she had taken that for granted. He was astonished at how cheap and how simple it all seemed to be, and, by the time he had finished, he was almost enjoying it. "My girl got soaked to the skin, so I had to pop in to Marks and Sparks and fit her out," he heard himself thinking of saying—but, then, there was nobody to say that sort of thing to. He didn't know anyone who would receive the information with the slightest interest or admiration. Or at least nobody like that whom he would *want* to say it to.

When he returned to the car, Arabella was asleep. He remembered then that she had also wanted cigarettes, and so went off to find a tobacconist. But there was a near-by pub, and, as it was nearly six, he decided to blow the Gauloises, and buy any old fags and half a bottle of brandy. They might both need it before the day ended.

She was still asleep. Asleep, she looked like eighteenth-century sculpture. He wondered then about the differences depicting women in art. Paint them in clothes, draw them naked, and sculpt them in repose seemed a satisfactory formula—at least for Arabella. He got into the car and touched her right-hand cheekbone with his hand. As he did this, and she awoke, he trembled, with a renewed and agonizing longing.

He said with tentative daring, "Here are your clothes, my darling Arbell." He thrust the paper carriers into her lap. "But how are you to get into them?"

"Oh—that won't be difficult: I can change in the car, without anyone noticing."

Can you indeed! he thought, but he said, patiently, "Do you mean while I'm driving, or while we're parked here?"

They were in a back street, but it was only a little past six, and the sun had not set. "Oh—here. I'd better see what you've brought me, and then I'll think of the cleverest way to put them on."

"Although, really," she added, as she undid all three carriers, "as I'm getting from indecent to decent, people ought to be grateful: policemen and so on."

She was pleased with the trousers and delighted by the colour of the shirt to go with them. The white cardigan she liked, she said, but it would not last on her for five minutes. "The moment I wear white something happens to it." She wrapped it round her shoulders, and began undoing and wriggling her arms out of the white crepe top.

"Would you undo the buttons on the shirt for me? You see? I'm awfully good at this. Do you know why?"

When he didn't answer, she said cheerfully, "Because my Nan used to dress all inside her dressing-gown with her back turned to me in the mornings. Then, I thought it was just a Nannie's thing. She was being decent, of course." She had fastened the shirt now, and put the cardigan over her knees. "This is going to be worse, because they've shrunk so frightfully, and I can't stand up. Oh—new pants as well! That was thoughtful of you."

Edmund, to give himself something to do, and to take his mind off the relentless feeling that he was parting from her body exactly when he couldn't bear to, lit one of the cigarettes and took a swig of brandy.

"Oh! Light me one! Surely you didn't get brandy and them at Marks?"

"No. I went to a pub. You said cigarettes, and I felt like the brandy. Do us both good. Stop us catching cold."

"Do us good, all right. But you needn't worry about colds: we shan't catch them. Not in those circumstances. You see—if the top was *down*, I could have stood up to get the jeans on. As it is, I'll have to get out of the car. Still, thanks to the pants, it'll only be decent exposure." She opened the door, thrust her feet into the jeans and drew them up her. He handed her the cigarette he had lit for her as she got back into her seat, and then thought that if he took his jacket off, at least his shirt would dry.

"Do you know what I would like now?"

He handed her the brandy bottle. She drank some and said, "Well, that, certainly, but what I feel like now is a ham sandwich. Shall we go to a pub, do you think, on the way home?"

"All right." He wanted, or felt that it was essential, to talk to her, to define in some way their state, and difficult though this might be in any circumstance, it would clearly be worse while he was trying to drive through the rush-hour traffic. "Here's your money: I owe you for the brandy, I'm afraid."

"No, you don't. Think of all the booze I've consumed during the last week."

He took her to a pub on Campden Hill that he knew had a back garden where one could drink in summer. It was early enough for them easily to find a bench and table, but full enough for him to be conscious of the way in which other people looked at Arabella. This filled him with pride and at the same time caused him embarrassment: he simply was not accustomed either to be envied or speculated upon. It would make talking to her even more difficult, he thought.

"What would you like to drink?"

"Just a ham sandwich. Oh, yes, and a Bloody Mary. Or can't pubs make them?"

"I should think they could. I'm awfully sorry to ask you again, but could I borrow another of your fivers?"

"Course. I'm dying for a loo. Where do you think it would be?"

"I'll ask for you while I'm ordering. You stay here and keep our bench. Don't let anyone else take it."

Edmund ordered, went to the gents', where he also combed his hair. This made him look at himself—trying to imagine how a stranger would see him, and also to see whether he seemed to have changed at all on the outside. His clear-cut, rather sombre face looked back at him: the morning's razor cut was now scarcely visible. He wondered whether his entire life had been changed or whether he had simply impersonated someone—to himself or, worse, to her. Simple, she had said things should be —not easy, but simple. As he went back to the bar, he thought rather grimly that perhaps they had had the simplicity and were now to embark upon the unease.

Arabella had collected a young basset hound, who stood on his or her hind legs, with its head upon her lap and its ample ears draped upon her knees. She was talking to it, and Edmund could immediately spot the owner from his smug and indulgent expression.

"The ladies' is inside on the right," he said, taking no notice of the hound, who gave him a mournful, bloodshot glance and ambled off to its owner.

Arabella took her bag and left him. Edmund had decided to drink beer as he had the drive (and God knows what else) before him, but he, too, had found that he wanted to eat. The garden had that curious smell of wet soot that so often occurs in London after heavy rain. Occasionally, drops fell from the trees in next-door gardens. He drank some of his bitter and had a momentary feeling of pure and carefree happiness. Here he was, in a pub on a summer evening with a beautiful girl whom he hardly knew, but with whom he had had the most extraordinary and exciting experience of his life: without warning, too; suddenly, he, who had spent ten or more years of pleasant but naturally familiar routine, had been violently and completely moved from it. Moved, he supposed, rather than removed. For what did she expect? Arabella? She had not so far behaved as though she expected anything, but this might simply be because she was so sure of what she expected. For her to think that what had happened by the lake was a mere, isolated, incident was intolerable for him, but anything else she might think could well prove to be that too.

When she returned, nearly all the dozen or so people in the garden either stopped talking to each other or continued with their heads turned in her direction. She sat down and immediately attacked the plate of sandwiches. "Some are for me," Edmund said in the kind of way that he hoped would publicly establish that they were simply very old friends.

"All right. Eat away. They are good, aren't they?"

When the sandwiches were gone, they had cigarettes and drank their drinks in a silence that Edmund broke, rather desperately, by saying, "I'm sorry if this seems to you idiotic and naïve and all that, but how do you feel—about me, I mean?"

She turned to look at him and said, "How do *you* feel about *me?*"

"I can't tell you here. At least, I'm not even sure if I know: what I mean is what did you *want* out of the situation?"

"I just wanted you to love me more." And when he didn't reply, she said, "Has it made you do that?"

There was a pause; he shut his eyes, because again, for a moment he felt dizzy, aching for the need of her, but light-headed with some nameless relief. Then he answered, "Yes. Yes, it has made me feel that."

"Oh, good!" she said warmly, like someone admiring some public, athletic, or artistic achievement. "That's the thing. We mustn't be late for dinner, because Anne will have made a super one, I bet, so shouldn't we go?"

Jettisoning his view of guilt, alternatives, relative values, and responsibility, Edmund decided to take what seemed to him an extraordinary (and probably false) attitude at its face value, and said with what sounded to him like totally false sophistication, "Yes, we'd better."

So they went: down Church Street and Wright's Lane onto the Cromwell Road in order to reach the M4. The weather was changing again. The sun, surrounded by livid colour, was sinking, but clouds were crowding it, and it was clear that there was going to be another storm. Driving was slow: they were scarcely out of London before the rain began again, this time with a fierce, professional insistence. They had hardly gone ten miles before the puncture occurred. Edmund, who had been in the right-hand of the three lanes, had, with difficulty to manoeuvre himself into the left and to hobble to the shoulder. The tire was absolutely and completely flat. For a moment, Edmund simply sat cursing. Punctures were sufficiently rare to seem an outrage. The rain drummed down on the canvas roof; the huge road was glistening and roaring with traffic; he knew that the jack was a brute to use and that the wheel, originally put on by a garage, would be horribly stiff to get off. So, "Damn the bloody thing," he said again.

"I'll help you."

"Oh, no, you won't. There's only one mac, and not a single Marks and Spencer between here and Henley." He got the macintosh from the back of the car, found the torch that he kept for map reading, and got out. The boot opened, but he had then to lever up what felt like an asbestos sheet with nothing to get hold of under which would be the spare and tools. Lorries, who were sticking more faithfully than usual to the nearside lane, drove past in an irregular stream, but regularly spraying him with water. He got out the tools and began struggling with the jack. Unfortunately for him, it was a nearside back tire, so that he did not even have the intermittent advantage of the headlights of the deluging lorries. The skies were so dark with the storm that the kind of evening summer light that in any other circumstance there would have been was not there. The jack slipped twice after he had begun to wind it. He began to realize that he would probably have to ask Arabella to help in the end, as he would not be able to undo the incredibly tight wing bolts unless he had someone holding the torch. He got the jack properly into position and wound it laboriously to the required height. By now, the lorries were unnerving him: they made so much noise and seemed to come so near that it was hard to believe that he was really out of their way. Arabella opened her window, stuck her head out, and said, "Are you O.K.? Sure you don't want any help?"

"Not yet, anyway. Thank you," he said.

But the real troubles were to come. He got the hub cap off the wheel, but then found that he was utterly unable to move a single one of the nuts. He heaved, and turned, and half strained his wrist, but nothing moved at all. The lorries went rolling by: Trust them not to stop, he thought, and then thought that if he saw a man changing a tire on a pouring night, the chances were that he wouldn't, either. He had one more go, and gave up. He'd have to get help of some kind, although God knew how far he would have to walk down this murderous road to find it. He went back to Arabella.

"It sounds feeble, I know, but I can't shift the nuts on the wheel at all. I'll have to get help."

"There was a sign saying TELEPHONE HALF A MILE a little way back."

"Well—you stay here: you're quite safe, and I'll go and telephone. I'll leave you the cigarettes and the brandy."

"Poor you," she said, "what a ghastly bore," She smiled at him, and it lasted him for at least fifty yards. After fifty yards, the shoulder ceased, and he had the choice of walking down or upon a steep slope or being run over by a lorry. Quite an easy choice to make, he thought, lurching down the slope, and as he thought this, stumbled, turned his ankle, and fell full length onto what seemed like oily grass. When he got up, he could only limp, with pain. There were lights of a housing estate below him, and he decided to make for them rather than endure the possible near half mile of slope before encountering the motorway telephone.

Just as he thought this, he saw another shoulder looming and the telephone box. That was something. He limped towards it.

It was curious, Anne found, how her mind ran on Waldo, about whom she tried, and usually successfully, never to think. It was all right while she was shopping. She bought a duck for the evening meal, cod's roe, various cold meats and salamis from the shop that had such things; cheeses in different stages of ripeness, an ox tongue to cook; some ox liver for Ariadne, who adored it, and certainly would need good food for the next few weeks; some crabs from the Walrus, who was alone, the Carpenter being on holiday: "He can't stand them: it's the wife who makes him do it. Comes back a wreck. He's never known what to do with himself without his TV and the fish. There you are, madam. Three lovely young crabs. I've removed the parts we can't fancy. Going away this year, are you? Oh, well, there's nothing like home. Brian says the one thing he can't stand is a new experience." Anne also went to buy selective tins: pimento, anchovy, sardine, tomato purée. Then she got herself a new comb and some sandals and returned to silent, sunlit Mulberry Lodge.

For lunch she had a picnic under the cedar and read *The Wedding Group*. At half past two, she reluctantly abandoned this pleasure, got into her jeans, and started weeding the main herbaceous border. She had not mulched it enough: weeds were rampant; phlox needed staking; dead heads of roses had to be cut; the spin trim to be used for the grass borders. But once she had stopped shopping and reading, her thoughts ran alternately upon Arabella's day in London and her own brief and horrible life with Waldo. She had met him in a pub; she remembered how he had been surrounded by a circle of acquaintances, who were being entertained by him. He had never been a good or successful actor, but, remembering that night, she realized why he had wanted to be one at all. He was at his best with people he hardly knew, met casually with drinks available. Then he could make a remarkable impression—as, indeed, he had upon her. He had had, no doubt still had, a beautiful voice; he was a good if repetitive story-teller (oh, how she had got to know those set pieces, which seemed to occur so casually, by heart), and he treated all women he met, irrespective of their ages or appearance, with a courtly admiration. If, as she was, they were clearly unattached, he treated them to even more of the same, and on this evening, Anne had felt dazzled by seeming to have attracted more of his attention than at least three other girls more obviously attractive than she. It was long afterwards she found that he had slept with two of them and that the third was a Lesbian. When they had married, she had thought of their lives in terms of her looking after a potentially great artist, hitherto incapacitated by lack of the right care and feminine background. He had encouraged her in this, and the first bad moment had come when he said, waving a huge, unpaid telephone bill, "But you have four thousand a year. This little thing will be nothing to you." Of course, she had had nothing of the kind. She had come into a small legacy of fifteen hundred pounds, and being young, and covertly under-privileged as she had always been in the rectory in Leicestershire, she had launched out into a new wardrobe, a holiday in Italy, and a few objects that made her look as though she was financially comfortable. When she told him, he pretended that it made no difference, but from that moment, that was exactly what it did. It must, she felt, be pretty awful to feel that you have been married for your money if you've got it, but somehow it was worse feeling this when you hadn't. You had no choice, she discovered. If she had had money, she could perhaps have paid for his good humour; as things were, she could do nothing of the kind. When she had thought herself pregnant, she had thought he would be pleased: he took it so operatically in his stride that she did have fleeting anxieties. But as soon as she found herself married and, as it turned out, *not* pregnant, his attitude had quickly reverted to what, she then understood, it must always have been. His attitude was that she had trapped him—in more ways than one. They had a very small, but mercifully rent-controlled, flat in Fulham; he took to using it simply as somewhere to sleep things off, change his shirts, and, occasionally, if he felt like it, eat a meal she had prepared. She soon found that if ends were to meet at all, she must get some sort of job, and so took manuscripts home from an agency and did a good deal of exceedingly hard, underpaid work. Waldo's behaviour to her, she realized afterwards, had, from the moment he had discovered that she was as poor as he, been designed to get rid of her at almost any cost. Eventually, having spiritlessly endured his indifference and sneering (her class, her appearance, her total lack of artistic talent all came in here), she was galvanized by his unexpectedly knocking her across the room when he came back one night angry drunk and she had not made him a meal. The shock, the cut on her forehead, the feeling of sick fright that she could ever have tried to spend her life with someone so alien and hostile, forced her to escape. She remembered now rinsing the wettex pad under the kitchen tap and holding it to her forehead for what seemed ages until the bleeding stopped, and then, early the next morning, while he was still asleep, packing one case and leaving. She had had breakfast at an ABC near South Kensington, and then, feeling that she was still far too near his territory, walked all the way up Exhibition Road to the Park and sat on a seat by the Serpentine. He might have killed me, she had kept thinking. Indeed, had she stayed, there was a very good chance that he might do just that, by mistake, of course, as he seemed to do most things.

She sat back on her heels and looked up at the sky. It was going to rain quite soon, but meanwhile there was a hot, windless silence: the birds had stopped singing—a sure sign of impending storm. She must finish staking, or delphiniums, phlox, peonies, would all suffer. She got up from her weeding, took the trug to the compost heap, and fetched bamboo and twine from the greenhouse. It was silly to think about Waldo any more. He had gone to Canada, she had heard in some remote way, and she remembered that his going had seemed the absolute and final release from him.

It was only, she supposed, because Arabella was so young that she felt anxious for her, and that was what had made her remember her own youth. She was nearly forty: she hoped that Edmund did not mind; but then she smiled at the mere thought of him and knew that he didn't. He rather liked being a year younger than she was; he liked, although it was not openly admitted, a degree of what amounted to almost maternal care—in everything, that is, excepting sex. Only somebody whose sex life was as satisfactory as hers could objectively appreciate the beauty of a young girl such as Arabella. For she found, during this last week, that Arabella's appearance had become increasingly fascinating to her: as she came to recognize her looks in general, so particular aspects of them had continued to reveal themselves. She was marvellously of a piece: it was difficult to imagine, say, somebody with her high, oval forehead, *not* having a long neck to go with it; that somebody with rounded, but elongated limbs would not also have long slender feet with high arches and most articulate toes, hands whose fingers were long without being bony; whose skin seemed all of one colour—not white, not cream, but something like the peony she was now tying. She was dreadfully untidy, of course, but she was always wanting to help, adored Ariadne, who was still majestically ensconced upon her bed, and she seemed profoundly grateful and happy to stay with them. Edmund seemed to like her quite as well: indeed, the whole experiment was turning out far better than Anne felt any experiment that had anything whatever to do with Clara had any right to do. The first, heavy drops of rain had begun; she was nowhere near finished. She decided to plough on; even if she got wet through, a hot bath would put her right.

By the time Edmund got back to his car, accompanied by two very pleasant policemen in their patrol car, who told him that they were getting a lot of punctures on this section of the M4, he found that Arabella, soaked to the skin again, was squatting by the wheel holding the torch while a man in an oilskin was putting the final touches to the wing nuts on the spare.

"This tremendously kind man stopped, and he said you always have to kick the thing to move the nuts."

"That's right," the man agreed, straightening up. "Beats me why the garages have to screw them up so infernally tight. Course you wouldn't want your wheels flying off in all directions, but there's such a thing as compromise. Nasty little jacks, these, too. Course if you'd had one of those flash lamps, your poor daughter wouldn't have had to get soaked to the skin."

There was a brief silence: Edmund fought with resentment, rage, being made to feel a fool in more ways than one, but at once, so to speak: the police walked round the car as though they expected that there was something more seriously wrong with it, and one of them asked to see the flat tire.

Finally, Edmund managed to say, "It was very kind of you to stop and help."

"Don't mention it," the man said cheerfully. He had a small, bright-red clipped moustache. "Always glad to help a lady in trouble."

"Would you like a nip of brandy?"

Edmund cast a furious glance at her. He had been idiotically concerned that his breath smelled of drink, and that one of the policemen would notice and start those ghastly tests, and here was the wretched girl implying that they always went about loaded with alcohol.

"No, thanks, all the same. I must be getting. It's a nasty flat, isn't it? Looks like a big nail to me."

The policeman examining it shook his head, but in agreement. "Had too much of this lately. As though someone was doing it on purpose. Well, there it is, sir. *You* seem all right, thanks to this gentleman here."

"I'm sorry to have bothered you," Edmund said, wondering how much longer they were all five of them going to go on standing in the pouring rain.

"Thank you so very much for all your help." This was Arabella to red moustache.

"Pleasure. Good night, all." And he went off to his own car.

Just as Edmund was beginning to worry that his licence was out of date, or that there was some other unknown and unlawful aspect to his car that the policemen were about to pounce upon him for, *they* said good night and went off to their car, from which distant radio squawks could now be heard. He and Arabella were left alone. He put the flat back in the boot, together with the tools he had been so useless with, and slammed it shut. "For God's sake! Why don't you get into the car? You'll be soaked again."

"I'm that already."

They both got into the car in silence, until she said, "Why are you limping?"

"I fell on a damn slope."

She laughed with genuine, and therefore maddening, amusement. "On top of everything else, you sprained your ankle? Oh, poor Edmund!"

"You don't sound very sorry for me."

"*You* didn't sound very grateful to that awfully nice man who did all the changing of the tire."

"I thanked him."

"Only just. And you sounded sulky about it."

"I expect your gratitude more than made up for that."

She laughed again. "It was funny, his thinking I was your daughter."

"Was it?"

"Oh—have some brandy, and stop being cross."

He took the bottle, and when he had drunk some, said, "And that's another thing. Why on earth did you shout about brandy in front of the police? You might have got us into trouble."

"There's no law against having drink in cars in England, is there? You talk as though this was a police state. You sound like a silly student."

Edmund, who had been about to start the car, without in the least meaning to, suddenly lost his temper. "I suppose you've never heard of the breathalyser? I suppose it didn't occur to you that after walking miles and getting the police, I felt a bit of a damn fool to come back and find that, instead of staying in the car as we arranged, you'd picked someone up and made him do the job? You simply thought how clever you were and how stupid I was not to *know* that you have to *kick* the bloody wheel?"

Arabella, her teeth chattering, said, "I was simply trying to help. After all, it's I who have got wet through, not you."

His anger dissolved as suddenly as it seemed to have manifested. "Darling!" He touched her shoulder; she was, indeed, absolutely wet through and obviously very cold. He felt not only a fool but a brute, the kind of farcically horrific combination he had only ever attributed to other men.

"It's all right," she said, but stiffly. "And I'm not your darling: that's all too clear."

"Look, have a swig; go on, you need it. And what about your white cardigan thing. You could at least take off that shirt and put it on instead.

She accepted the brandy—now nearly finished—without answering. Then he saw that she was crying—not a great deal, but any tears at all coming from her were more than he could bear. He started gently undoing her shirt, and she was quite passive. He pulled it off her shoulders, and then took the cuffs and drew the sleeves from her arms. She felt icy, and her small breasts were starting with cold. He remembered a chamois-leather kept for wiping the windscreen, reached for it and rubbed her back for some minutes with firm, circular movements. She leaned forward a little to allow this. When he felt that she was a little warmer and that part of her, at least, was dry, he pushed her back against the seat. The long white cardigan was behind them: he took it and put it round her shoulders. She remained still: he put her arms into the jacket—it was like dressing a doll. When the garment was on her, he pulled the edges of it together over her breasts—he wanted to kiss them; not to do that was his penance, but as he began to do up the top button, his face was so near to hers that he stopped to smooth the tears from it with his fingers. "I do love you, darling Arbell. I am very sorry indeed to have behaved so badly to you. I know you were trying to help. It was entirely my fault. Please forgive me. May I kiss you?"

She shut her eyes without moving, and he kissed her mouth,

tasting the brandy on it, put his hands round her small, rounded waist, feeling her cool, tender skin, smelling—past the brandy—her own particular scent that he had noticed by the lake, forgotten, and would now never forget: he did not dare to stop kissing her mouth, because, out of his love, all his senses were alerted to knowing that this was not like the lake—for her, anyway. She needed affection, reassurance, anything but his needing her body. It took him an unknown amount of time to reach the kind of calm and control where he could take his mouth from hers, stroke back the wet strands of her hair, smile—for she had opened her eyes when he stopped kissing her, and they looked at him with such appalling uncertainty and practiced fear, of he didn't know what, that he could only go on doing up her jacket and say, "This is really the kind of thing that only cousins could do for each other."

She smiled then, and it brought tears to his eyes. Without knowing why, he said briskly, "I'm going to take you to a pub to dry out, and give you more ham sandwiches and altogether stop you getting pneumonia."

He started the car, turned on the heater, and, waiting for a gap between lorries, drove back onto the road.

"Yes," she said, to any or all of that.

By the time Anne had finished her staking, she was soaked through. She had not realized how long this had taken her, but when she went back into the house, meaning to have a hot bath and change, some instinct made her go and see how Ariadne was getting on. It was a good thing she did so; one of the kittens had died, and Ariadne was in a state of great distress. She had removed all her live children onto the eiderdown on the floor; but she kept going back and forth to the dead one—cleaning it, picking it up by its poor little inert scruff of the neck and putting it down again. Had it died earlier, she would have demolished it. Anne got her some milk and some of the ox liver, which she chopped raw, and while Ariadne was examining these offerings, removed the dead kitten. She then got half a cardboard dress box, which she lined with newspaper and Ariadne's own blanket, and put her and the kittens into it. Ariadne, who had drunk some of the milk, instantly began lifting each protesting kitten out of the box and back onto the eiderdown. Anne decided that they were in no state to argue with each other, and so she waited until all four kittens had been moved, and then tried to feed Ariadne with some of the liver by hand. Ariadne took one piece out of courtesy, but dropped it on the carpet and returned to her young, carefully washing the taint of Anne's hands upon them from their meagre fur. Anne then considered Arabella's now vacated bed: it was true that it had been an extremely tidy birthing, but there was still some blood on pillow cases and the top sheet. The bed would have to be changed. For no reason that she could afterwards understand, Anne felt that she must change and make the bed before she did anything else. The result of this was that, by the time she had finished, she was shivering and cold to the bone. It was nearly six o'clock. Should she have a bath, and *then* light the drawing-room fire and start on cooking dinner, or should she get the chores over and then have a bath? She decided on one whisky to keep her going, and at least start the fire and the duck in the oven, as she liked to cook the latter very slowly. She bent down to kiss Ariadne's forehead. This was endured, rather than enjoyed: she thought that perhaps she had better grill the liver slightly, as this was usually more popular. She took the saucer down to the kitchen. By now she was shivering. She poured herself a generous whisky and drank a little of it neat, before putting any water into it. At this point she began to wonder whether Edmund and Arabella would return together, or whether she would get a call from the station and have to fetch the girl. She lit the drawing-room fire, grilled the liver, and put the duck in the oven. If Arabella *did* ring up she would have to go quickly and so she had better get dry and changed as fast as possible. So she compromised with a hot shower and put on a jersey trouser suit. The drawing-room fire had gone out, and this annoyingly meant going out doors to fetch more coal, and a hunt for the fire lighters that Edmund disapproved of because he said they made the room smell of paraffin. By now it was nearly seven. The fast train from London would have arrived by now, so it looked as though Arabella might be returning with Edmund. And Edmund, since he had not been going away for the night might be home at any minute. She fetched material for relighting the fire, stayed with it until it was going, and turned the duck over onto its other breast. It was still raining hard. She drew all the curtains, and even considered putting on the heating, as it felt so dank—or she did. Then she had another drink, curled up on the sofa, and went on with her novel. But it did not, or could not, absorb her as it had before. She kept thinking that she heard a car, listening, and either she had heard one but it was going on up the lane or she was mistaken. She decided to play the gramophone so that she would not hear the cars, if there were any, and so that she could do the rest of the cooking with something to take her mind off being alone. She had a soup in her deep-freeze; chestnut, but, she felt, suitable for this weather. She had an orange-and-watercress salad, and there was a ripe piece of Brie. By a quarter to eight, the duck was nearly ready, she had had a third drink, and was both irritated and anxious.

The pub that Edmund chose, or found, was one of those awful ones where the brewers had done everything, with power and no imagination whatsoever, to entice the young. This meant Muzak: horrible sub-fluorescent lighting; a kind of hygienic olde-worldeiness that was neither comfortable nor intimate. It had, in fact, a small proportion of the regulars it had always enjoyed, plus a few people—like Edmund—who didn't know what they were in for. The landlord had Second World War moustaches, and his wife looked as though nothing good had happened to her since the late forties. It was difficult to get food: "We don't do snacks in the evenings. There is the Tudor Lounge." This meant ploughing through a three-course meal of the kind that has rightly made Britain infamous on the Continent. The menu was written in Continentalese: everything upon it turned out to be canned, frozen, and overcooked. But Arabella managed to dry out most of her jeans in front of the Magicoal in the huge neo-Tudor fireplace, and they had a cherry Heering each to warm them up. Arabella stood in front of the Magicoal, lifting her white cardigan to get her jeans warm, and Edmund sat very near her, simply enjoying her presence. At this point, neither of them had discovered that snacks at night were unavailable and, for different reasons, neither cared. Edmund had veered from not wanting Arabella to take him seriously to not wanting to spoil what seemed to him the most serious day in his life. He had drunk enough throughout the day to feel able to cope with this unfamiliar kind of euphoria. It was not that all feelings of responsibility had left him, so much as he realized that, as he had so many, he was due for a change. It would be madness to throw away the chance of dinner alone with Arabella when the—as far as he knew—only opportunity for it occurred. He also felt, rather defiantly, that his recent behavior in the car warranted some return. He felt that now there were a thousand things he wanted to ask her, to know about her, nearly all of them neither the kind of questions that could be asked unless they were alone nor, if asked, not answered. Her abortion: the man concerned had begun to concern *him*. He must be a rotten creature or else the kind of competition—i.e., with a licence to be rotten and get away with it—that Edmund did not at all care for. She must be protected from such ventures. She stood now four feet away from him, her legs apart, her hands lifting the jersey, her little glowing drink upon the phony oak table. A spotted, rather nasty, timid, and pathetic waiter (the very combination of person that Edmund could not bear) had now arrived with the menu.

"Darling," he began and read aloud: "*Scampi à la provençale. Escargots.* Smoked salmon. *Vichyssoise.*"

She made a friendly, deliciously intimate face. "Oh, dear. Smoked salmon sounds the safest."

"Two smoked salmon."

"Right. Now, listen. *Coq au vin; rognons sauté avec le vin rouge;* duck *à l'orange*, and turbot *hollandaise*."

"Duck, please."

"Two duck, then."

"And vegetables, *m'sieur?*"

"Mushrooms and a green salad," she said before he could read anything.

The waiter bowed: "Here is the wine list."

The wine list was not very long and, as far as Edmund could see, filled with uninteresting and overpriced wines. He decided to decide without asking her upon a St. Émilion, which would probably turn out to be dull, but which, he felt, they would not notice.

"Have another drink," he said; he wanted one himself.

She drained the small glass and held it out to him.

"Yes, please. It's delicious."

At the bar, the landlord's wife served him enviously. Whatever her idea of fun might be, she clearly wasn't having it, and did not much enjoy seeing other people full of any kind of cheer. When Edmund remarked upon the filthy weather (he had to say something), she said give her Majorca any day, and this was England for you. He decided against offering her a drink; she simply wasn't nice enough.

"I've stopped actually steaming, so I might as well sit down. How long do you think dinner will be, because I'd better make this drink last, and they are a bit like chocolates, you drink them without noticing enough?"

"Long enough for them to unfreeze the smoked salmon."

She giggled and said, "And warm up bits of tepid duck. I don't mind how awful it is, I'm famished."

For some reason, this made Edmund look at the time. It was just after eight. He knew that Anne would be wondering what on earth had happened to him; he was never late without telling her—she would be worrying, she might even be thinking . . .

"Back in a minute," he said to Arabella, putting the cigarettes and his lighter on the table.

He had seen where the telephone was as they had come in. It was in a box and conveniently situated just outside the gents'. He went into the box and stood waiting to see what he felt he ought to do and what he felt he could bear to do. It was the kind of decision that he was utterly unused to and found that he very much disliked. He would far rather have done nothing at all about it, but he recognized that even doing nothing at all would, in fact, be doing something. It would be leaving Anne in the dark as to his whereabouts. He'd have to telephone her. So he did.

"But where *are* you?" she said, at least twice. She sounded either cross or a bit drunk, or both.

"At a pub. We had this awful puncture, you see, and I simply couldn't get the wheel off and had to walk miles to get help, and Arabella got soaked to the skin, so I really had to take her somewhere to dry off."

"Well, when *will* you be back? The duck's ready now."

"We can't just yet, I'm afraid. She—she wanted a bath, and somehow we couldn't do that without agreeing to have a meal here."

"I can't see what on earth having a bath has got to do with a meal."

"Well, I can't explain now. It's the *place*. They aren't exactly co-operative. But I thought she'd get pneumonia if she didn't have a bath and get her clothes dry, and you can't just march in anywhere and ask for that."

"But where *are* you?" she asked for the third time.

"It sounds extraordinary," he said, making it sound just like that, "but I really don't know. I just took the first pub that came along."

"But—"

"We'll be back as soon as she's bathed and we've eaten something. Don't worry, darling."

"But where did you *get* the puncture?"

Edmund waited one second and then cut them off by putting his finger firmly on the receiver rest. Then he replaced the telephone, stood for a moment, and went to wash and think what lies he would have to ask Arabella to tell. The fact that they were a bare seven miles from Mulberry Lodge was bad; that could not be told: therefore, they must not have had the puncture where they had in fact had it. God, he thought, and this is only the beginning, or possibly the *end*, of something. He was in a state (his and most people's usual one) of not in the least wishing to have to decide something that would radically alter his life. He would have liked to feel that he had simply acquired another dimension, as it were; not a matter of conflict or alternatives, just an enrichment.

When he returned to Arabella, she said, "They've been to say our dinner is ready."

They finished their drinks and went into the dining-room. This was a mixture of what is laughingly known as roughcast, imitation beams and hideously expensive flock-and-gold wallpaper. They sat at a small, round oak table with uncomfortable oak chairs. There was a plastic rose and sprig of lily of the valley in an earthenware juglet. There were paper napkins and cutlery of the kind that you could take anywhere and do anything to without impairing its original and barely functional appearance: forks with two prongs, blunt knives, and spoons with so small a declivity that you would rather have drunk your soup from a bowl.

The smoked salmon arrived with a tiny wedge of lemon and curling pieces of brown bread and butter.

"Could we have the wine now?" Arabella asked. "I simply love wine with smoked salmon."

Throughout the—expectedly terrible—meal, she was very gay and entertaining, telling him stories about holidays spent with Clara in various emotional and geographical circumstances. It all started with her saying how funny it was that the only, what she described as serious, men in her mother's life whom she had not known had been Edmund's father and her own. "Mine died in a matter of weeks, leaving her pregnant with me—I bet that made her furious. . . ."

"Why do you bet that?"

"Well—she's never had any others, has she? And it can't be for want of opportunity. Well, so my poor father passed on, as Nan put it, and yours, I suppose, was far too dignified ever to come trying to have reconciliation scenes and borrow money.

"No, he would never have done either of those things."

"Well—the ghastly violinist did; he never stopped: cables, flowers, awful scenes like silent films, with him on his knees with his arms round her crying and screaming in Hungarian—saying she'd ruined his art. It's funny how often people say that to each other. It's about the most difficult thing to ruin, I should have thought, if one had any in the first place. Anyhow, I always seemed to be about, and my mother learned to say 'Not in front of the child' in about six different languages, but as the situations were practically identical, of course I always knew what she meant."

"Weren't any of them nice to you?"

"Oh—*nice*. They thought they were: they all tried to kind of bribe me or show how good they were with me until they realized that my mother didn't care a damn what they were like with me, and then, of course, no holds were barred. For them, that is."

"Didn't your mother mind? Or find out?"

"Only once: with Greg. But I think she sort of knew, because I kept suddenly being sent off to summer schools and courses and awful group holidays, and it was usually after someone or other had made a pass. This duck is awful, isn't it? I don't care though: I wasn't being rude, just saying what it is."

Edmund, who had long ceased feeling at all hungry, had finished the wine, and was wondering whether to get at least a half bottle more, began to feel that time was running out, nothing that he wanted to say had been said, and, worse, nothing that he *had* to say was getting said either.

"Then there was this awful old thing called Jean-Pierre Louis. Le Comte de Rossignol. He looked like a dirty old lithograph of someone: kind of grey and dry and full of dull good manners and no feeling at all. He had a vast château somewhere in the middle of France that he'd inherited because nearly all of his family were mad. Actually, he could easily have murdered them. He had frightfully thin lips with lines going vertically down onto them, and his eyes were so close together that I honestly thought they might run into each other one day. His nose was very long and pointed and he could wriggle it like a rabbit: he was always doing it when things weren't in good taste, which they hardly ever were. He was foul to servants and animals, and he collected seventeenth-century pewter—very pretty—and all his cousins were spotty and speechless and they loathed me and I loathed them. Clara did up the house and gave parties, and to begin with he liked it, but then he got fussy about who she asked. He had very bad breath—I should think it was constipation: it often goes with meanness, have you noticed? He was incredibly mean. He crept about turning off the heating and the lights. It was a jolly good thing he mostly kissed people's hands or they would have fainted. Could I have a cigarette now? I've just about got to the end of this athletic duck."

Edmund gave her one, asked for coffee, and, while it was coming, took a deep breath and said, "Arabella! Arbell! What are we going to do?"

"How do you mean?"

"Well— Oh, you must know what I mean."

"I won't be sure till you say it."

"After today—this afternoon—it's not the kind of thing I usually do. I can't—"

She put a hand out over the table and touched his. "Don't. You'll simply foul everything up with plans and promises and lies. Just leave it."

"But it isn't as simple as that. You might like it to be, and it may well *be* for you, but I'm married."

"Well, that makes things simpler for you than for me, doesn't it? I mean, you love Anne, and there she is. By the way, did you ring her up?"

"Yes. And immediately I found I was lying to her. That's what I mean. You're not a child. You must understand some of what I'm talking about."

"I'm certainly not a child. Well, what lies did you tell her?"

The coffee arrived at this moment, and they waited in silence while it was poured out.

"I told her—I implied—that the puncture had taken place

miles away, and that you got so wet you had to go somewhere to dry your clothes and have a bath. And we couldn't do that without having dinner in the place."

"Why couldn't you just say that we had a puncture and I got wet and then we got hungry?"

"Because we're about fifteen minutes'—no less—drive from home, and there was no reason why we shouldn't have gone there."

"I didn't know that. Well, why didn't we?"

"Because," he said, feeling both angry and enslaved, "I *wanted* to have dinner alone with you. I thought you wanted that too."

"Oh," she said wearily. "Want. In my experience, men want things to happen, make them happen, and then tell lies. I just *let* things happen. I don't tell lies."

"For God's sake, I didn't take you to that house in Barnet to — I'm not *trying* to put any onus on you: I'm just trying to explain that, for one reason or another, you *are* going to have to tell lies."

"Anne isn't going to say, 'Have you had a fuck with Edmund?' She'd never do that."

Edmund, shocked by this expression, said, "You don't understand."

"I understand very well. Isn't this situation all the wrong way round? Oughtn't you to feel jolly glad I'm not picking the whole situation over—today, and the future—and making some sort of horrible mincemeat of it? I'm not, you see. I don't expect anything of people. I don't live with a kind of emotional security, like cash in the bank. We probably shan't ever do that again. There it is. You can't have it both ways, and most of the time most people don't have it any way at all. I *do* know that, I can tell you."

They both drank some boiled, bitter coffee, and Edmund tried to assemble his thoughts. Before he could do so, she said calmly, "I'm not 'becoming your mistress,' in case that's what you are afraid of. I told you why I did it. I wouldn't dream of getting in your or Anne's way, whatever that may be. You're behaving like men say women do. Don't. I won't, and you needn't. You may be short of excitement, but that's a luxury shortage. Try being me."

"I can't, can I?"

"No. So just you leave it alone."

He looked at her: because he had no idea how she felt now, he thought that perhaps he had never known what she had felt. This made it more difficult to know what to do—about anything. Then she said, as though she knew what he was trying to think, "Look. If you want me to connive at the lies you've already told, I will, because I can see that it might make things bad for you if I don't. But *don't tell* any more. O.K.?"

"All right," Feeling humiliated at a position she seemed to have put him into, he reiterated, "We had the puncture miles away. You got wet through, and we thought you'd better dry your clothes and have a bath. That meant dinner. The reason I didn't ring before was that I was staggering about in the dark trying to get help."

She nodded and then looked away from him. Then she said, very sadly, "It is extraordinary how everybody seems to have a little conspiracy in the cupboard—like a skeleton. Perhaps we'd better go now."

So they did. Edmund paid the bill. Outside, the rain had stopped, everything was dripping and the air smelled of moss. In the car, she said, "Perhaps you'd rather I went away? Perhaps that would make things easier for you?"

He stared at her. She was not looking at him but straight ahead, with her hands folded—no fingers to be seen. The thought of losing her, of her disappearing from his life, was intolerable. He had not considered it; but now, as she suggested it, he knew that it was, or would be.

"Of course not! Please don't think of it; don't say it. We are both exceedingly fond of you. Anne told me. I think she feels about you rather as she might about a daughter."

She smiled faintly, and then said, "Nobody has ever thought of me like that."

"Well—a younger sister, then: you know what I mean. She wants to look after you—to protect you."

She gave a deep sigh, of contentment, and, although he could not name it, of hope.

Getting back and facing Anne turned out to be far easier than Edmund had expected. To begin with, she was—unusually for her—a little drunk, or possibly feverish. She looked flushed: the kitchen was in an uncharacteristic mess, and she was in the middle of brewing some hot and also alcoholic drink. Halves of squeezed lemons lay all over the draining board, brown sugar had been spilled from its jar, and the whisky bottle was on the shelf by the stove. She was wearing her winter dressing-gown.

"Hullo, darling," said Edmund, kissing her forehead and altogether approaching the situation in a manner tempered with apology plus its not really being his fault.

"Hullo," said Arabella. "How's Ariadne?"

"One of the kittens died, but I spirited it away. I've tried to get her off your bed, but she simply carried them all back. It's all right, otherwise. They're supposed not to be able to count up to more than two or something."

"I bet they know. I mean, it wouldn't just be a matter of counting, would it? They aren't all the *same*. What are you making?"

"I got so wet gardening," she sneezed, "afraid I've caught a cold. You'd better have some too, if you got so wet."

"Good idea," said Edmund. "We've all got pretty wet, one way and another."

"I got deluged twice!" Arabella said cheerfully. "Once when Edmund took me to see this house with a fabulous garden, and then when we had the puncture."

Oh, God! thought Edmund, as he fetched glasses and spoons to put in them. What on earth will she say next?

"Oh, you went viewing with Edmund, did you?" said Anne. "And did you see poor old Sir William?"

"No: missed him. I was nearly late for lunch, you see, because I had to see someone in the morning and then I got bogged down shopping."

"I thought your clothes were different."

"They got different again later. I bought a lovely white unsensible trouser suit and got soaked. So then Edmund had to get me these from Marks and Sparks. Then I got wet in *them*. You see why I have to have so many clothes. I'm no good with them."

"But what about the ones you went to London in?"

"Oh, those. I left them in the shop, not wanting to cart them about and not thinking about the rain."

"I told you it would rain," Anne said, the maternal note—missing during the last few exchanges—back in her voice.

"Well, *you* got wet too."

"It was entirely my own fault. I simply had to finish my bit of gardening. Here we are." She started to pour—rather sloppily—the delicious-smelling hot toddy into the glasses that Edmund held out.

"I must just go and see Ariadne. Back in a second."

When Arabella had gone, Anne looked more carefully at Edmund and said, "Why didn't you tell me you were taking her out to lunch? I mean, I don't *mind* in the least; it just seems so odd your not saying anything about it."

"I didn't know I was taking her. You know what a mysterious girl she is. I thought she had a day packed with secret missions in London, and I was just the chauffeur, so to speak, and then it turned out that she just had one person to see and didn't know what to do with herself all day. You don't mind, do you?"

"I said I didn't mind," she said almost crossly, and added on a different note, "I expect she had to see you-know-who and it all turned out worse than she had thought it would. Good thing you took her out to cheer her up."

" 'You-know-who'?"

"You *know*. The *man*." Anne almost hissed, as they could hear Arabella coming back.

) 143 (

After she had returned, full of loving enthusiasm for Ariadne's family, and Edmund had given her her glass of toddy, he suddenly thought, so *that* was what she was doing. Seeing the last man who— A wave of what he thought was disgust, but was really jealousy, struck him. Perhaps she had been to bed with hundreds of men. Perhaps it meant nothing to her at all. Perhaps she had been acting the whole time. He leaned against the dresser and shut his eyes, as the vision of her naked and streaming below him recurred.

"Darling—are you ill or something? Do you think you've got a cold as well?"

"As well as what?"

"As me." She sneezed again.

Arabella said, "Perhaps we've all got colds and it will be like a siege, with Ariadne going out and bringing us back mice and birds for sustenance." She giggled and then added, "We'd soon find out if she could count then."

"I've put a camp bed in your room. Or you could have the other room. Only it's rather cold because we haven't put the heating on there for weeks."

"I'd much rather be with her."

Edmund drained his glass. "I'm going to have a hot shower."

"You should as well, Arabella. Don't worry—I'm not going to bother to wash up tonight."

For a moment, Edmund visualized himself standing under a hot shower beside, or rather facing, Arabella: he would kiss her, and there would be no room for the water to fall between their bodies. . . .

"Good night," he said.

As soon as Edmund had gone, Arabella put her arms around Anne and said, "Honestly, I'm awfully sorry about us not getting back for dinner. I bet you made a lovely one, as usual, and we should have rung you earlier, only Edmund had to use a police box for the puncture trouble."

Anne said, "That's all right." Then she added, "At least you notice that I must have cooked it."

"Men aren't so good at that. What did you make? Can we have it tomorrow?"

"I did a duck, with morello cherries."

"That's extraordinary. We had the most awful duck you can imagine in the ghastly place we went to. All tough and stringy and greasy—the kind that makes you feel you ought to be jolly glad it's duck, if you know what I mean."

"Where did you have dinner?"

"Honestly, I don't know. It was raining so hard, and when we saw a pub sign that said it had a restaurant, we just ran like drowned rats. You're not cross, are you?"

"Was your . . . morning all right?"

Instantly, she became remote. "I suppose so. Rather what I expected, really."

Anne looked at her: she was sitting on the kitchen table, one bare foot swinging just off the floor. "Dear Arabella. I didn't mean to pry. Only I couldn't bear—" she stopped and finished her drink rather shakily.

"What?"

"Well, if you want to know, I couldn't bear to think of you unhappily in love with someone who was horrible to you. I know what it's like, and I couldn't bear it for you."

Arabella smiled faintly. 'You are *so kind:* nobody's ever been so kind since I was a child. But don't worry: I'm not in love with anyone. I'd know if I was, and I'm not."

After that, they went upstairs together, and everybody went to bed.

In bed, Anne said to Edmund: "Everything's all right."

"How do you mean?"

"She's *not* in love with anyone. So whoever it was this morning didn't hurt her too much."

Anne, full of whisky, lemon, and Codis, fell asleep at once, while Edmund lay, trying to sort out whether Arabella had meant it when she said she didn't tell lies, and whether he would mind more if this were true or untrue. He wished that he was

) 145 (

able to put into words—or thoughts—what he wanted, but found this impossible. He felt, at the same time, very tired and very much awake.

Arabella slept with Ariadne and her brood. This turned out to be practical, and from Arabella's point of view, a good thing. They managed to share the bed, with Ariadne's back turned to Arabella and the kittens on the far side. Ariadne was full of vibrating warmth, but, with her back turned, her whiskers were not in evidence, and, in fact, everybody fell asleep as soon as their various heads settled on the pillow. Everybody, thought Arabella sleepily, felt at home.

Part Four

The next morning was hot and bright and fresh, but Edmund woke feeling only the first of these things; and this, he realized, was because Anne, breathing heavily beside him, seemed to have some kind of fever. She was certainly much too hot, and there were far too many bedclothes on their bed—more than their usual number in summer. He twitched a couple of blankets off his side of the bed and lay on his back for a few minutes remembering a number of disparate occurrences and states of mind. His mouth felt dry and dirty; he had a slight headache and a considerable thirst; in fact, he had a hangover. Anne seemed deeply asleep; he settled for a long, hot bath, some Alka-Seltzer, and a good deal of coffee before he woke her. To this end, he took his equipment out of their adjoining bathroom and went along the passage to the one used by Arabella. Then he realized that he had left the Alka-Seltzer behind, and, swearing softly, went down to the kitchen, where some was usually kept. He drank two in hot water—the taste was like white wool in his mouth and he nearly retched, but he knew it would make him feel better, and so it did. The bath, in which he lay for longer than usual, made him sweat, but that, too, he felt was a good thing. After all, he had a day's work in front of him whatever he felt like. He decided to make the coffee in his bathrobe to give the sweat time to die down. The breakfast tray that Anne invariably laid at night in the kitchen ready for the morning was not laid, and he was both irritated and surprised to find how long it took him to lay it and how difficult it was not to forget things and then to find them. As he padded upstairs with the laden tray, he thought of Arabella in her room and an overwhelming desire simply to see her, asleep in bed, overtook him. He put the tray carefully down on a passage table, poured out a mug of black coffee with some sugar, which was how he knew by now that she liked it, and knocked softly on her door. He was only bringing her some coffee, after all. There was no answer from within. He opened the door gently. Arabella lay in the half light of the half-drawn curtains, one arm thrown over Ariadne's back. Ariadne raised her head and stared steadily at him in an outfacing manner. What was he doing here? her look implied. Arabella did not stir.

"I've brought you some coffee."

She turned her face towards the door, but did not seem to see him.

"Too early: too sleepy yet," she murmured, turned so that he could see only the silky tangle of her hair and the fact that she seemed naked except for the sheet half covering her shoulder. He moved nearer the bed. Ariadne sat up, yawned, and then, curling one protective arm round her kittens, lay down again. He was interrupting.

"Arbell! Darling! Wouldn't you like some coffee? I've got to go to London in half an hour and I shan't see you all day."

Arabella raised herself onto one elbow and looked at him.

"No. Thank you. I just want to sleep some more. Thank you," she said again, retreating into warm unconsciousness.

It was no good. He went out of the room, shutting the door behind him. He did not like coffee with sugar in it. He poured it down the basin and rinsed it out. Then he picked up the tray again and returned to his bedroom. Anne was half awake and clearly feverish. She looked flushed, which did not become her, and said that she did not want coffee, only fruit juice. He gave her his as well as her own; felt vaguely annoyed that she did not seem to notice or thank him, and drank three mugs of coffee, the third while he was shaving.

"I think I've got a temperature."

"Better take it and find out."

"The thermometer's in the cupboard."

He put down his cutthroat, reached in the cupboard, expecting it to be in its case, but it was not and rolled into the basin below, where it broke.

"Damn!"

"What?"

"I've broken the damn thing. It wasn't in its case. Oh, blast, there's glass all over the basin." He began picking out the larger pieces, but the scum from his shaving made this a precarious business, and in no time he cut himself.

"Oh, *damn!*"

"Now what is it?"

"Cut myself, that's all."

"You're always cutting yourself with that razor. Much better if you used the electric one I bought you."

"It wasn't the razor. It was the thermometer."

"You don't mean to say you've broken it!"

"Of course I've broken it. How could I have cut myself on it if I hadn't?"

He ran his right hand under the tap, while with his left he tried to undo the elastoplast tin.

"What *are* you doing now?"

"Oh, don't be maddening, Anne. I'm trying to stop the blood and get a plaster on; then I'll get you another thermometer."

"There isn't another. You broke the last one last Christmas, don't you remember?"

He did. "Do you mean to say that in all these months you haven't got another one?"

"I didn't see the point. What's the use of having two of everything? It only makes one break things more. Anyway," she added a moment later, "I know I've got a temperature: my eyes hurt when I move them."

"Better get the doctor, then."

"You don't sound very sympathetic, I must say."

"I've got a train to catch, as you perfectly well know. And there's a telephone by your bed. Ring him now. Catch him before he goes out."

She wanted to say, "You didn't have a train to catch yesterday," but desisted: she really did feel rotten, and those, as she knew, were the only times when they nearly quarrelled—not quite, but nearly.

"All right, darling."

"Be sure to call me at the office if you're feeling really bad."

"I'll be all right. I'm sure Arabella will look after me."

He was getting late, and his hangover had by no means subsided. He seized a shirt and tie out of the drawer without asking her opinion on them and dressed as quickly as possible.

"Mrs. Gregory will look after you anyway. I'm sorry you feel ill. I expect it's just a summer cold. You stay in bed until she comes."

He bent down and gave her a cautious peck on the top of her head. He did not want to catch whatever it was. The bed smelled of boiled eggs, which faintly nauseated him. "See you this evening."

"At least dinner is done."

A parting shot, he thought viciously, as he started the car and clashed his gears. Arabella's white suit lay in a crumpled heap on the front seat. He took it out: it smelled faintly of her scent; on second thoughts, he put it back in the car; and then, on third ones, took it out again and put it on the steps that leaned against one wall of the garage. Then he drove out of the drive as fast as possible and went to the station.

By the time he reached Waterloo, all freshness and brightness of the day had gone, and he was submerged in a sticky, sunless heat. He was late at the office and, for once, Sir William wasn't and had been asking for him. After an hour of shouting on both sides, not acrimonious but argumentative and conducted on the familiar basis of each thinking the other deaf, it became clear to him that Sir William had set his heart upon Edmund's going to Greece: nobody else would do. "Take someone with you. Take your wife," he shouted, suddenly remembering Edmund's state. "You could do the whole thing in a week, but I shan't complain if you take more. These Greek chaps take their time about things —you'll probably need more than a week."

"When do you want me to go?"

"Got your secretary to book you on a plane on Friday night."

"Tomorrow?"

"*Friday* night."

"That *is* tomorrow."

"I said Friday."

"It doesn't give me much time."

"What for?"

The alarming simplicity of this question floored Edmund.

"I don't speak Greek, you know."

"Speak what you like. It's all the same to them. It's what you *see* I'm interested in, not what you say to the foreign chaps. But if we're not quick off the mark, the market will be lost. Lost," he repeated loudly, and Edmund's head ached more than ever.

"Right. Well, I'll go and consider my plan of action," he said. This was what he nearly always said to Sir William when presented with an awful/impossible/absurd mission, and what he usually meant was that he was going to spend a long time thinking how to do nothing at all about whatever it was, or, if the worst came to the worst, how to effect some compromise (Edmund's not having to do anything, but finding somebody who would or could).

He really found decisions of any kind intolerable; he liked things simply to *happen*, or go on in the same way. He sent Miss Hathaway off to do some routine brochure-sending-out to clients, and sat at his large desk in a state of very unquiet peace. Arabella liked things simply to happen: if he could take *her* to Athens! He thought of it: an evening flight, with dinner on the plane—champagne to celebrate their holiday. Emerging into the hot night, lit with yellow lights, pointing out the sights to her from a racketing taxi, taking her to a small *taverna* that he happened to know about —tourists didn't go there, it was the real thing—sharing a bed with her in one of those new, air-conditioned hotels; the night, the morning with bread and honey and coffee; the joys of bathing with her both in the sea and the hotel: of going about with her in a place where nobody could know or mind that they were together. Perhaps, even, she had never been there; it would be his chance to show her the most beautiful country in Europe, to sit for hours drinking the delicious wine and being kindly, courte-ously attended by people who would simply admire him for having such a beautiful girl. . . .

Anne would want to go. Anne had never been to Greece and enjoyed travelling far more than he. She would jump at this chance, want it to be their holiday, to stay far longer than a week. Anne had always wanted to go to Greece, and he had never taken her.

They could not leave Arabella behind, alone.

Perhaps they might all three go?

Oh, God, what a dreadful thought. He could, he hoped, just about manage the situation at Mulberry Lodge, but, on unfamil-iar ground, he did not know what he would do. He had some fair idea of what he would feel like, and this made him terrified of his possible behaviour. Anne would find out: with none of the domestic routine, the props of so many things that were not only taken for granted but required time and attention, all of her would be centred on Edmund and their common, foreign ground. No, it was out of the question for all three of them to go. But if Anne was ill, would that make it reasonable for him to take Arabella? Or, if he did not openly do so, supposing she left Mulberry Lodge—Clara wanted her, or something of the kind— and then went secretly to Greece with him? But she had said, with some vehemence, that she would not tell lies. He thought about lying for a bit and came to the depressing conclusion that telling them depended nearly always on how much the person concerned wanted to. He knew now that *he* would: a situation that twenty-four hours ago he would have regarded as wrong, out of—*his*—character, and not something that any decent, honourable married man would or should dream of. But *she*, Arabella, seemed not to have reached that state, or perhaps, he thought adoringly, she was immune to it. She was simply too young, too innocent, too pure to allow of such a thing. She had said that she loved Anne, and indeed she seemed to. If Anne was ill, and therefore conveniently unable to accompany him to Greece, he had a gloomy feeling that Arabella would *want* to stay and look after her. Perhaps if they all went, it *would* be better. It would be best if they need not go at all, but when he had suggested that young Geoffrey should go instead of him, Sir William had, with some reason, replied that he must be mad. Young Geoffrey was just about up to doing the donkey work about the house in Barnet, but to send him on this kind of thing—new baby and all— was out of the question. He'd *go*, of course, if he was sent, but he'd make a mess of it. Edmund was going to have to go: he decided to postpone whether this should be alone or in whatever company until he got home in the evening and could test the atmosphere. He sent for Geoffrey and briefed him on the Barnet house. At this point, Sir William got him on the intercom and made the really terrible suggestion that he and Edmund should go to Greece together. By the time Edmund got himself out of that one, he knew that he was in for the journey, either ficti- tiously accompanied or no.

"I've brought you this." It was a huge glass jug of what looked like orange juice.

"Oh, thank you. The only thing I feel like. But what a lot!"

"I squeezed twenty oranges. It's so awful not having enough. And if you've got a temperature, it's jolly good for you."

"I think I must have. My eyes don't fit."

"If you think you have, you certainly have, and the kinds one has when one doesn't notice don't often matter. I think thermometers are silly, really. Suppose it broke in your mouth and you swallowed the mercury. Ariadne's starving. Could I cook her the rabbit I saw in the larder?"

"It would be very kind of you."

"The only thing is, how do I do it? I've been looking up rabbit in some of your marvellous cookery books and they go on and on about prunes and cream and cider and bits of streaky bacon, and I shouldn't think Ariadne would care for any of those."

"You just put it in a saucepan with cold water and a little salt and stew it gently until it is cooked."

"Nothing about your Aga seems very gentle to me: kettles boil while you sneeze, and toast blackens in that grill thing in a second."

"You use asbestos mats. Mrs. Gregory will show you."

"Is there anything else that you would like?"

"I'd love some paper handkerchiefs from the bathroom." She watched Arabella, looking very businesslike in faded jeans and what looked like a man's shirt. She had tied her hair back with a piece of blue wool, and she was barefoot, as usual.

"What else shall I do?" she asked eagerly. "Just tell me, and I'll do it. I'll pretend to be you for the day and run the house and all."

"I did all the shopping yesterday, and there'll be the duck for you and Edmund tonight. Mrs. Gregory will change the sheets —oh—I don't think there's anything special. Your lunch. Can you manage that?"

"I'll come and ask you what I'd better have when I've had a bit of a choose out of what's around. I had scrambled eggs with Ariadne for breakfast. I mean I scrambled rather a lot, and she seems to favour them, so we shared. Although you wouldn't think so to see her now. I could pick the fruit and take off dead heads and other ladylike things. Or I could just play the gramophone, or would you rather I mowed the lawn?"

Anne smiled weakly. "You do whatever you like."

"All right."

She went away, but came back shortly with a rather ugly little brass gong that Edmund's father had once given them for Christmas. "If you want me, bang on this: I'll be bound to hear."

When she had gone again, Anne took some Codis with some of the orange juice and fell into a feverish trance. Her throat was sore, her glands round her neck hurt if she touched them, and her head ached: she began to wonder whether she had flu.

The morning passed with the single interruption of Mrs. Gregory's enquiring in a stage whisper whether she would like her bed made or the room done. Unable to face the conversation that this would entail, Anne said no, thank you, and Mrs. Gregory padded forlornly away: she loved illness; Mrs. Cornhill looked very poorly to her, and she began to consider from her personal experience of medical predicaments what they might all be facing now. Glandular fever, she thought, remembering Auntie going right through from Michaelmas to the New Year with it. Or mumps, she speculated, thinking of Lizzie and the twins and that dreadful holiday they had in Ilfracombe. Jaundice, struck her as an inspiration just as she entered the kitchen, to find Miss Dawick messing up the kitchen table (just scrubbed) with ever so many roses. This last notion seemed to her such a good one and so terrible that she had to voice it. "It could be jaundice," she said, in what Arabella by now described as her church voice. "Too soon to say, but it's quite on the cards. It's About. Mrs. Mixmaster from the school said there was ever such a lot of it About."

"But Mrs. Cornhill doesn't go to school."

"If it's About—people who catch it, catch it. In my opinion, miss, the doctor should be informed."

"But don't people go all yellow with jaundice?"

"By the time they do that, it's been known to be too late."

"Oh, Mrs. Gregory!"

"Mark you, Dr. Travers is no good at all: his patients never seem to have anything. But any professional opinion is better than nothing, which, with the best will in the world, is all that you or I can be. We don't *know* all the diseases, you see. It's no good barking up the wrong tree when the horse is out of the stable. That's what did for Gregory. He would *not* have a doctor until his legs were so bad that nothing could be done with them." By now, she had made two huge mugs of Nescafé, and drank hers standing to show that it was not an actual break. But conversation—particularly of a disastrous nature—was something she was perennially short of, and Miss Dawick, a nice young girl, although she looked a touch tubercular to her—small chance there of making old bones—was very nice to *talk* to. She was doing the roses for Mrs. Cornhill, she said. Mrs. Gregory instantly forgave her the mess on the table. All sick rooms should have flowers, and real ladies nearly always made a mess whatever they did. "Only don't forget to remove them at night. Flowers do terrible things at night to sick people. That's why you'll find the corridors of hospitals lined with the vases."

"Have you got the doctor's number?"

"It's in the address book in the hall, miss, but it won't do any good now. He'll be out on his rounds—diagonizing flu and colds. It's all he seems to think of. That and rheumatism—and the Lord knows there's nothing he can do about that."

"Well—when I take the flowers up, I'll ask her whether she would like me to call him."

"You could do that," Mrs. Gregory conceded, but grudgingly: it was clear that she was going to be off the premises before there could be any emergency for her to rise to. But she had Miss Blenkinsopp down the lane, and she was getting on the late side. If she arrived in time, Miss Blenkinsopp gave her a hot dinner; it not, not. She took off her overall, hung it on its peg by the kitchen door, and took her coat and matching bottle-green hat off the hanger and shelf above it. Her hair was the colour of bleached wood. "If only her troubles were little ones," she remarked as she buttoned up her coat. "A house without children isn't the same at all. But there it is. Nature is mysterious—you have to grant that."

"Thank you for all your help," Arabella said, wondering what on earth Mrs. Gregory had just been driving at.

"Anyways—I'll see you tomorrow: you can count on that, whatever. And if that Leaf comes round this afternoon, he's to get one sandwich to his tea and no cake. That's what he gets, but he'll try anything." She left then, and Arabella realized that she wanted Anne to be pregnant, and that she had been talking about the gardener.

Arabella threw her mug of Nescafé down the sink, lit a cigarette, and tried to sort out whether Mrs. Gregory's views on the seriousness of Anne's illness could be founded on anything more than macabre hope. No, she decided: Anne was about as ill as poor Jane Bennet had been after her silly mother had made her ride miles in the rain to catch young Bingley. She went carefully upstairs with the roses for Anne.

Anne was crying. This shook Arabella so much that she put the roses on the floor and knelt by Anne's bed: Anne went on not saying anything, with tears falling, and Arabella, after a moment, took her in her arms and, with one hand, stroked the short, damp strands of hair from Anne's forehead.

"What is it, darling? Do you feel awful?"

"I don't know."

"Do you think it would be a good idea if I rang the doctor?"

Anne seemed to assent to this, but stayed in Arabella's arms. Then she said, "I don't know why. I just have an awful feeling of fear and foreboding."

"You mustn't. It's just because you feel ill. Have a little more orange juice—you've hardly drunk any, and it's supposed to do you good."

She relinquished her hold on Anne gently, poured out a glass of the juice, and then propped her up in her arms again to drink it. When Anne had drunk a little, she said, almost pettishly, "*I* don't want to see a doctor in the least, but it'll be the first thing Edmund asks when he comes home, and, if I haven't, he'll pretend I'm pretending."

"Well—I'll call him. Would you like me to change your sheets and get you some water to wash in?"

"I'd love some clean sheets. I just couldn't face Mrs. Gregory. I could wash, if you could bear to do the sheets."

"Of course. Where are they?"

"The linen cupboard's the door after yours down the passage, just before you go downstairs. Our sheets are on the second shelf on the left-hand side."

"All right. But I'll ring the doctor first."

When she had gone on these missions, Anne sat up and swung her legs over the side of the bed. She felt faint, and the effort made her sweat again. She must get a dressing-gown or something before Arabella came back. What she really wanted was a tepid bath: she felt so squalid and somehow it seemed a waste of clean sheets not to have one. She got herself to the bathroom, put a towel round her, and started both taps of the bath. Then she weakly cleaned her teeth: the inside of her mouth had that slippery, viscous feeling that she associated with fever. Better get on with the bath before Dr. Travers turned up and told her that she'd better not have one.

By the time Arabella returned with the linen, she had run the bath and was sitting on the bathroom stool waiting to explain this so that Arabella would not come in when she was naked. Arabella said O.K., and that Dr. Travers was out but that his wife was getting a message to him and was sure he'd be along some time in the afternoon. "But don't lock the bathroom door, in case you faint or anything," she added.

This made Anne try to hurry with her bath, and when she got out of it, everything dissolved and went dark and she found herself on the floor with Arabella bending over her.

"It's all right. You did faint. I shouldn't have let you bath alone. Don't cry," she added, and Anne realized that tears of weakness and of shame had begun again. Arabella picked up the bath towel, lifted Anne from under her arms, and put her on the stool. Then she wrapped the towel round her and began gently to dry her.

"I feel so—"

"Never mind."

"So squalid—and hopeless." Then she looked up at Arabella, who was leaning over her carefully drying the back of her neck. "I'm no good without clothes: I look awful; can't help it, it simply makes me feel—"

"You look lovely. *Far* better without clothes. That's jolly unusual, I must say. If I was Edmund, I would say, 'Do meet Mrs. Cornhill: she looks much better out of her clothes.'"

Anne looked up at her: the clear, heavy-lidded eyes looked into her own with nothing but the sweet sincerity of truth. Then she bent down and kissed Anne's mouth—a cool, still kiss that seemed to go on for a long time. She did not say anything at all, but when she stopped, she wrapped the towel round Anne and led her back into the bedroom. The room had been aired: the bed was made. "The only thing is," Arabella said in a perfectly normal voice, "that I didn't know where your night-gowns were, and doctors usually seem to expect night-gowns."

Anne sat on the edge of the bed. She felt now entirely at ease, even light-hearted: almost as though she was enjoying being ill and Arabella looking after her.

"In the second drawer down. You choose. They're pretty dull, I'm afraid, because I hardly ever wear them."

Arabella had a careful search. "They are, aren't they? Well, try this." She threw an old white nylon edged with coffee-coloured lace into Anne's lap.

Anne stood up to pull it over her head. Arabella was not looking at her, but the feeling of intimacy and ease permeated the room. She was putting the bowl of roses on the dressing table, where Anne could see them.

"Is there any champagne in the house?"

"I'm almost sure there is. Why?"

"Because, before the doctor comes, I thought we might have a little orange juice and champagne together, if you see what I mean. It doesn't do you anything but good, but doctors aren't trained to think like that."

"Let's have some then." Anne got gratefully into bed, and Arabella pulled the sheets and (now, only two) blankets over her. "Right," she said gaily. "If there *is* any in the house, you can trust me to find it. Don't get cold. Would you like some kind of bed wrap?"

"No. It's hot, really: I'll just lie down till you come back."

While Arabella was away, Anne lay and thought about her; about being ill, and the fact that up till now, nobody had ever been kind about it. In the rectory in Leicestershire, the medical minimum was done for you, but you were made to feel that you were letting the side down. When she had married Waldo, any indisposition was a personal cut at him. When she married Edmund, he invariably fussed, something which he did not at all like to do. That seemed to sum up her experience of being ill and people's responses to it. Arabella contrived to make her feel unfortunate, all right, and even attractive: she made a party out of what had previously turned out to be various kinds of bloody nuisance. The roses were beautifully arranged. One window was open, and warm sunlight streamed across a band of carpet and the bed. It would be lovely to drink the drink that Arabella had suggested. She got out of bed and found her scent spray with Bandit in it. A little of that and she felt better than ever, although too weak to brush or comb out her hair. Arabella will do it for me, she thought, subsiding among the pillows (Arabella had thoughtfully provided her with two extra ones).

Arabella duly returned with a bottle of champagne. "Couldn't find any halves, but so much the better," she said. She seemed to have no difficulty in opening it: clearly champagne had come her way far more often than sardines. She had also brought some ice. When she had made two glasses, she handed one to Anne and said, "What a lovely smell. Bandit, isn't it?"

"Yes. Do you know *all* the scents?"

"Well, most of them. Clara is always trying out new ones—or she *was*, but now she has one made for her. I used to get the rejects. You know, when she changed men, she nearly always changed scents. What shall we drink to? You getting well?"

"And you not catching whatever it is."

"All right then, to both of us."

When they had both drunk a glass each and Arabella had recharged them, she said, 'Would you like me to do your hair? I mean, I know it's awfully tiring when one's feeling awful."

"Yes, please. I was going to ask you, actually."

"It's extraordinary, isn't it, how ill one has to be before one *doesn't* sort of tidy up for doctors." She had sought and found Anne's brush and comb and now sat herself beside Anne so that she could get to work on it. "Mrs. Gregory seems rather keen on illness. She quite seemed to hope that you had jaundice."

"I've had it years ago. What Mrs. Gregory is always hoping is that I'm pregnant."

"Oh." Arabella brushed away for a moment, before she asked casually, "And do you wish you were?"

"God, no. Edmund would hate it. It isn't his line at all. He likes to be the first person to be looked after in this house, and if I had a baby he mightn't be."

"Oh. What lovely, thick hair you have. Shall I backcomb it a little? It will make it even prettier."

"Do you know *how* to?"

"Easy. Easier on someone else, of course."

"Would you like children, Arabella?"

"I'd like six. A huge family, and I'd live in one place, except they'd all go for their holidays to another same place every year. With me, of course."

"And your husband?"

"Haven't thought about him. Whenever I try, all the men I've ever met sort of go misty and merge: I feel I wouldn't know which was which, or who they were. "Still," she added cheerfully, "I could always just have the children and to hell with whoever begot them. Like Ariadne," she ended, after further thought.

"I wouldn't like that for you. I'd like you to be tremendously happily married: have the children, of course, if that's what you want, but have a really reliable, good man."

"Like Edmund?"

"Mm. Something like that."

Arabella did not reply, but when she had finished Anne's hair, she fetched a hand mirror, and as she gave it to her said, "Of course, I could always adopt them. Then there would be no fuss about a man at all. There. Do you like it?"

She had somehow managed to make Anne look as though she had been to the most expensive hairdresser and/or at the same time done absolutely nothing about her hair.

"It's marvellous. I *am* impressed."

"It's easy, really. I've watched fiendish old Markham doing Clara's for years. You can't help learning—even without meaning to. Look—we'd better sink this before the good doctor comes."

By the time Dr. Travers did arrive, Anne had had another sleep and, although when he took her temperature it was over a hundred, she seemed in good spirits to him. "Another of these summer colds," he said. "They always seem to be worse than the winter ones, because one doesn't expect them. Let's look at your throat now."

"My glands hurt," Anne said, beginning to feel an impostor.

He felt them with cool, dry, experienced fingers. "Yes: a bit swollen. Had a headache, have you?"

Anne nodded. He looked approvingly at the glass of orange juice by her bed. "Plenty of fluids—that's the thing. I think we won't put you on any antibiotic straightaway. Probably no need. But if your temperature is up tonight, better let me know tomorrow morning early."

"I'm afraid my husband broke the thermometer."

"Well, couldn't that remarkably attractive Botticelli-like creature who let me in nip into Henley and get one?"

"I don't know whether she can drive." As Anne said this, she thought, Of course, she *is* like Botticelli. Her opinion of Dr. Travers—never very low—went up.

He said, "Well, I'll ask her as I go down, and if she can't, you'll just have to have this one. Don't worry: it's always happening to me. People these days seem to regard a thermometer much as they regard a leech—an outmoded manner of dealing with ailments. But if you have a temperature tonight, or tomorrow morning, you'll have to stay put. All right?"

"Can I eat things?"

"Anything you feel like. You're a sensible young woman, aren't you; well, stick to your instincts. They're thoroughly reliable if kept in a sensible working condition."

He stood up, and something prompted Anne to say, "Have you had your holiday, yet?"

"No: we're going in September—to Greece. Before the flu starts, and after the children are back at school. I'm damn well having a holiday without them. Never see my wife nowadays. Death to the National Health."

And off he went.

A bit later, Arabella came up to say that although she *could* drive a car, she hadn't for ages in England, so Dr. Travers had left a thermometer. Also, Mr. Leaf had turned up, and she was making him one sandwich, but what of? Anne told her. Arabella reported that Ariadne had eaten enough rabbit for five, which was just about fair, considering her family, but left her supper rather in question. Anne said there were bound to be pieces of duck, so that was all right. Anne felt sleepy, and slightly drunk from the champagne. When Arabella suggested some more Codis and a sleep, she thankfully agreed. She was still fast asleep when Edmund got home.

He arrived by the usual train and his car, and put it straight into the garage. He noticed at once that Arabella had not moved her white trouser suit and felt unnaturally aggrieved. Surely she would have had the sense? When he went into the house, it was to the sound of Scarlatti played by Nina Milkina, that unbeatable and instantly recognizable player of the composer. Arabella met him at the sitting-room door: she was dressed in a long, crushed-velvet skirt the colour of apricots and a black chiffon shirt that left everything to be desired. Before he could make any move of the slightest kind, she said, "Anne's in bed. She's either got flu, or some kind of summer cold. But she's all right: you needn't worry. I got the doctor, who was fearfully sensible and nice, and I've done all the proper things about our dinner and fed Mr. Leaf and Ariadne, so everything's fine, really."

"Has Anne got a temperature?"

"Yes—actually. It's nearly a hundred and one. But she's asleep now, and I thought the thing would be for us to have dinner and then see if she felt like anything."

"Marvellous idea. What I need is a drink."

"Oh—I've made you one. With cucumber and vodka. It's tremendously reviving." She went into the kitchen and returned to the sitting-room with a misty jug. The Scarlatti was still going on. "I adore Scarlatti," she said. "Partly because only musicians can play him. I bet that Spanish princess was hard put to it, as indeed she should have been. And that's my last highbrow remark for the night. Here you are."

Edmund drank the drink she offered him, sank into one of the two comfortable arm-chairs, and stopped thinking about anything. This was the way life should be, he thought unthinkingly, no problems, no decisions; simply a charming situation that he hadn't arranged but that was—never so gently—sprung upon him.

The Scarlatti came to its close. All of life, accepted, understood, sad, gay, heroic, and inevitable and absurd had come to their ears in the space of a few sonatas. Then Arabella said, "I've put our dinner on the trolley. Thought we might eat in here, as it's cosier."

"Do you think I should go up and see if Anne's all right?" He very much hoped that she would say no, which she did.

"I've been up at half-hour intervals all the afternoon. She's fine. If you could just open a tin of *consommé* for me, I think that's what she will want when she wakes up."

When they had eaten the duck and cherries, and some salad and cheese, Edmund told her about the Greece situation. Her response was immediate and depressing.

"How lucky that just when you have to go, I am here to look after Anne."

"That's one way of looking at it."

She lit a cigarette, curled herself more comfortably in the arm-chair with her legs tucked under her, and said, "You mean, she'll be frightfully disappointed not to be well enough to go with you?"

"No. Well—yes, she might be that, but that's not what I meant."

She leaned forward to pick up her wine glass, and he noticed the difference of her lips: the top one narrow, indented, very much curved and turning up at the corners; the bottom lip a simple, and rather full crescent, its texture reminding him of some piece of a fruit.

"I think you know perfectly well what I meant: you're just pretending not to."

"Not pretending: I just wanted to be sure. You seriously think that I could zip off to Greece with you, leaving Anne ill and alone in bed. What would we say to her? 'So sorry you can't come, Anne, but you do understand, don't you? Edmund hates to go alone, and I'm so used to travelling that I'm practically Miss Cook.'"

When he didn't reply, she went on, "Or had you thought of pretending to go alone; lying to her; pretending to get me sent off to Clara in Paris, and then really joining you at the airport?"

So much had he thought about both these possibilities that he could think of nothing to say. She put down her wine glass, now empty, and said, "Or perhaps you were thinking of all three of us going together? But Anne's being ill has foiled that? Well? Which was it?"

He said miserably, "I've thought of all of them. All day. I've thought of every possible combination—including my not going. But that's no good. I've got to go. My boss insists. He even suggested coming with me."

"But why are you making something so complicated out of such a simple situation?"

"It doesn't feel simple to me. You don't seem to understand me in the least. I love you. I don't think I've ever felt like this in my life."

She said, more gently, "But you love Anne. You've loved her for years, and she feels the same."

"I don't know what I feel about Anne any more. I don't know what I feel about anything—even you—excepting that I can't bear the thought of going away from you. But whatever it is that I do feel about you has stopped me knowing what I feel about anything else. Can't you understand *that?*"

He got up to get them some brandy.

When he returned, and handed her a glass, she said, "Look. I may *not* understand what you are saying *or* feeling because every time anyone says anything like that they usually mean something different by it. But I do know one thing. If you aren't jolly careful, you'll ruin everything."

"What do you mean?"

"Can't say any more. The awful thing is that if one has to try and give anyone advice about *themselves*—not what they ought to do for a living, or whether they should believe in God, but advice about the sort of thing you're trying to make me give you advice about—one disrespects the person. If they take the advice, you simply feel they're a weaky, and if they don't, they're a baddy. It gets like Western films. So it's no good from either of our points of view for me to try to tell you what you ought to feel and then what you ought to do about it. You stick to what you know about the situation, and I'll stick to what I know. If you decide to tell lies, that's up to you, but I've told you I won't."

"But I have to ask you something."

She turned her pale, carved face to him and said impassively, "Yes?"

"Do you—do you love *me* at all?"

"Oh—that. I love you, I love Anne, I love Ariadne, I love this house and yours and my life in it: I love the summer here, and the garden and the river. I love Scarlatti and being in one place and not being with Clara and having money and my good health. But in the sense you mean, no: I don't love you—I don't love anyone. I never have. Except the one, dead person I told you about. And as I don't love anyone, I'm a private menace. That will be the next thing you tell me when you are angry. That, and that it would have been so much better for me if I hadn't had so much money. Although why money should make me—in your sense—heartless I really don't know. But those are the two things people say. Could I have some more brandy, please? These conversations always seem to use up a hell of a lot of alcohol."

He gave her some more brandy in silence. Then, he said, "You don't know what it's like to yearn for someone? To feel that every moment that you aren't with them is dead time: that you are either half asleep or too much alive waiting to be with them again? That if other people say their name, or if you see or touch anything that belongs to them, you get a kind of second-hand shock of joy and longing? You don't know any of that?"

She shook her head.

He wanted then to take her firmly in his arms and impose any of his heart or body upon her without any more words, since they seemed to do nothing but make fragments of his pride, but before he could begin to do this, she said something that made it impossible.

"Of *course* I know about yearning for someone. And all the other things you say about it happen to me too, but you see I don't know *who for*. I've never met the person. I can't imagine what they are like. I have to make them up. I have to invent their names or what belongs to them. It's all pretending— quite useless." She looked down at the glass she was holding in her lap and then said, so that he could hardly hear her, "It isn't that I don't try. I've tried all the ways I can think of."

Because he *did* care for her, he had then a sudden, uncertain but fearful glimpse of her life and knew that he would have neither the courage nor resolution to live it. This appalled him: he had always thought of himself as the protector, the manly man who arranged for the comfort and security of others. But what she had just said seemed almost to reverse their positions: it was she who seemed able to pioneer, to settle for no half truth or mere comfort; it was he who, like a woman, wanted now to pick over their personal situation with no reference to the generalities of their lives. He wanted to talk about his love for her—to be domestically reassured, even to be emotionally pressed into a difficult scene in which the only agonizing comfort was that they each felt the same. That was it. He wanted them to feel the same about each other; it would then follow that they would be in the same cleft stick—every cliché about the *ménage à trois* that every *ménage à trois* has been through would be pursued: the caring about the third person, the anxiety for them, the private, unspoken determination to do what they wanted to do while of course wishing very much not to hurt them; the mounting amazement that the third person did not see what was so patently and violently felt, the conclusion that they were of different clay; the snatched moments of lust that simply could not be forgone, the guilt that they had occurred, the resentment that they had had to be snatched, the paralysis of being driven into a situation where there was no going back and no way out except through action —violence and guilt, and decisions of one awful kind or another: the very things that went most against his emotional grain. Yes, but if only they could *talk* about them, surely everything would seem easier—easier and better? He looked at her so gracefully disposed in her chair, head a little bent, so that the high, oval forehead and the marked curve of her eyelids were best seen: as he watched her, she put up one hand to move the shorter strands of hair to one side of her face. There was something weary about the gesture, as though a piece of her had been worn and used passed bearing: for the first time it occurred to him that perhaps she suffered, although in a way that he could not conceive of. He said heavily, but with intended kindness, "Perhaps it is a good thing that I am going to Greece alone: it will give me a chance to think."

But she answered at once, "There is nothing whatever to think about." She unexpectedly put out a hand to touch his, and repeated almost as though she was pleading with him. "Nothing. Don't do that: I beg you."

It was a plea, but one that he could not in the least understand. He took her hand and kissed it: she smiled, her faint and ageless smile of sheer and mere acceptance.

Upstairs, after she had had some hot *consommé*, Anne said, "Darling, I really don't think you should sleep in here tonight: I must be awfully infectious."

So he went to the other spare room alone, without even having to try, for the sake of appearances, not to want *her* the whole night.

The next morning, Anne's temperature was down to ninety-nine, but she felt, if anything, worse, she said. Edmund explained about Greece while he was shaving: he felt so exhausted by his wakeful night that he hardly cared about her response, and was therefore uncharacteristically uncircuitous. He had to go that evening, he said: Sir William insisted upon it. He might be away a couple of weeks: he was not sure until he got to Athens how many islands he was supposed to visit. It was a pity that she was ill and could not go, but he was sure that Arabella would look after her. He would send a cable or telephone as soon as he knew when he would be able to return. He did not at *all* want to go alone, he said more than once, and Anne knew better than to pity herself aloud for being too ill to accompany him. "About Arabella, though," she began, and his heart leapt. Was she, as a miracle, going to suggest herself that Arabella went with him? For company? He was tying his tie when she said this and his fingers froze, but he managed not to turn from the glass.

"What about her?"

"Supposing Clara rings up with one of her imperative telephone calls? You know, saying Arabella must go to Paris or Nice or somewhere immediately. What shall I do?"

"Tell her you're ill and that Arabella is nursing you. Tell her Arabella is ill. For goodness sake, tell her anything you like. Only don't let Arabella go. She—she doesn't want to. She told me."

"She told me too. All right—I'll be brave, if I have to, and cope with her."

As Edmund bent hurriedly to kiss the top of her head as a farewell, she said, "So funny. Dr. Travers called her 'that Botticelli-like creature' when he saw her yesterday. He only saw her for a moment, and it had never occurred to me, but he's quite right, isn't he? She's like that girl, or goddess or nymph or something out of 'Primavera.' "

Edmund was cramming spare shirts, etc. into his case. He did not answer at once, but eventually said coldly, "What an extraordinary thing for a doctor to say."

Anne laughed in the indulgent way that she had done for years but that now maddened him for the first time. "You are so narrow-minded, darling. Why you should think a doctor neither knows nor cares about pictures, I cannot imagine."

Finally, before he actually left, she said, "Please. If you find somewhere very beautiful, do consider it for us. Dr. Travers is going to Greece in September. People do go there, you know, and I should love it so much."

"You sound as though you are in love with Dr. Travers."

"Of course I am. Madly. Arabella did my hair specially for him. Have a good time, my darling. Take care of yourself. I shall miss you."

He did not answer this, but turned towards her with a fleeting, harassed smile and lifted his hand as a kind of indoor wave of good-bye. Poor Edmund, Anne thought, as she lay back again in bed (her throat still hurt), he so much *hated* going abroad, and going abroad alone must be anathema to him.

He had not expected to see Arabella again, but she was in the kitchen squeezing oranges. She was wearing an extraordinary sea-green garment that trailed upon the floor and had such wide sleeves that she had to keep tossing them back up to her shoulders to keep them out of the way of her hands and the juice.

"I'm off now," he said as casually as possible.

"I hope you have a lovely and interesting time," she answered politely—but really politely, as though she meant that she did hope just that.

He paused; everything, the time of day, what lay ahead of him, and her attitude precluded any serious leave-taking. Perhaps it was just as well.

"I'll do my best to look after everything until you come back," she said, and then she turned and saw his face, and immediately went to him and flung her arms round his neck. "Dear Edmund: I meant have a lovely time. I know you don't think you will, but I *hope* you will." She kissed him on each side of his face and hugged him. "Don't look so terribly sad. You are only going to Greece for a fortnight! Think! It might be Siberia for a year. Take your Siberia-for-a-year face off, please: I can't bear to think of you tooling off to Waterloo and Cavendish Square and Heathrow and all those outlandish places so full of doom." She gave him a final hug; he managed a wan smile: shamefully, he was very near tears.

"Good-bye, Arbell. Look after yourself as well."

He hurried out to the garage on that.

Arabella finished squeezing the immense number of oranges she thought necessary for Anne, and then trailed slowly and carefully upstairs with the jug. Ariadne, who heard her, came out of their—by now—joint bedroom to see what arrangements had been made for her. Seeing Arabella, she trotted along the passage after her into Anne's bedroom.

"Ariadne has come to see you about the housekeeping. I think, in spite of what I told Dr. Travers yesterday, I think I had better risk your car and buy some more suitable food for her. She did not really enjoy the duck much, because of the cherries and orange that was inside it. It was delicious, though; I meant to tell you. Supposing I get you some breakfast, and then we do a list of Ariadne food and I go out and get it?"

Anne, who had been trying hard to read and finding that it

only made her headache worse, put down the book and said, "I'm just a frightful bore. I'm so sorry." She had reached the stage where self-pity for being ill and the boredom of not feeling well enough to do anything that she wanted were beginning to weigh upon her, so that these apologies sounded almost like an accusation. "Is the doctor coming?" she asked.

"Have you got a temperature?"

"Ninety-nine, but I feel worse than yesterday. Can't think why —it's most unfair."

"Well, then, I must ring him up: he told me to if you weren't normal. I'll find out when he's coming so that I can time the shopping visit."

Ariadne jumped up onto the bed with Anne, who put out a hand to stroke her, but after a single glance of distaste, Ariadne jumped down again and looked questingly at Arabella.

"We'll have to open another tin. She's frantic. Those kittens have about fifty snacks a day."

"Bring up a tin: I'll open it."

"I promise I'll try and learn how this time."

"Will you ring the doctor, or shall I?"

"Oh—sorry. I will, of course."

The doctor would come after lunch, Arabella announced, so perhaps she had better do the shopping as soon as Mrs. Gregory arrived. Anne drank some orange juice, and then said that she didn't feel like it today. Then she added fretfully, "It is so like life that Edmund has to go somewhere that I madly want to go to as well, and then I should be ill. I am hardly ever ill; Edmund can hardly ever be persuaded abroad: it does seem unfair.'

"Well, if it's any comfort to you, I really don't think he wanted to go in the least."

"Don't you? Don't you think he's secretly excited? He seemed most odd this morning—not at all himself."

"Perhaps that is just because he *didn't* want to go."

Anne looked doubtful. "Perhaps it was. But I simply can't *imagine* not wanting to go, can you? Oh yes, I suppose you can, because you've travelled so much."

"Oh, *I'd* much rather stay here—with you. I hated Greece the only time I went."

"Tell me about it."

"When I've done the shopping. Could I have the keys of your MG?"

"They're in my purse: on there."

"If you feel up to it, I should have a bath while Mrs. Gregory does your bed: then you needn't get let in for too much doom."

"All right: good idea. Remember to drive on the *left*," she called.

Arabella went off after putting on some jeans and a shirt, collecting some sandals and shopping baskets. She hadn't the slightest idea how to get to Henley or Maidenhead, but felt no qualms about this. Someone would tell her, or she would simply find one of them.

Left-hand side of the road, she told herself as she got into the car. I wish I had a friendly small dog with me. *My* dog, was what she thought next. It was another lovely day: wild roses were out in the hedgerows, and poppies and cow parsley. There were many other pretty decorations to the banks and hedges of the lane that led to and from Mulberry Lodge, but soon she was on a wider, duller, road. The sky was unusually blue for England, and the road like steel. She drove with great caution, letting everyone pass her, because then she could notice things and think about them. She was also making a mental list of what she wanted to buy. It was true what Neville—of the Chelsea flat—had said: she did love shopping; if that was all she had inherited from Clara, she would be lucky, she thought. She had planned to buy Anne a present—or even several presents—as well as unheard of delicacies for Ariadne. She landed up in Maidenhead, which was probably just as well, since the larger the place, the better the choice. She put the car in a car park, locked it, and started to explore. She bought a huge boiling fowl for Ariadne, and then two rabbits, and then, passing a fishmonger who looked quite good, she asked him what fish would be suitable for a cat. Whiting or coley, he said, pointing to rather dry, curled-up silvery fish, and slabs of awful stuff that wasn't even white. She bought some plaice for Ariadne, and a lump of cod that was much whiter than the other stuff, and saw scarlet contorted crabs on display. Surrounded by crushed ice and parsley, they looked most inviting, and Arabella bought two. All this food shopping first was a mistake, she realized, as it had used up the shopping basket and was heavy and hot to carry. So she asked the fishmonger if she could leave the basket with him while she got some other things. She then bought a hundred Disque Bleu and some toothpaste, and set about the present. She had wanted to find a night-gown for Anne that was neither dull nor vulgar, but this proved extremely difficult. Then she passed a jeweller who had a mixture of antique and everyday stuff. In the window, among almost everything else one could think of, was an eighteenth-century ring: crystal and enamel and gold. She went in. It was thirty-five pounds, the man said. Arabella tried it on. It slipped onto her second finger easily, therefore it must fit a finger of Anne's. She bought it at once. The jeweller put it into a dull little box with the cheapest kind of cotton wool. "Haven't you anything nicer than that?" He hadn't, nor did he care. She put the box in her bag, and went to Boots for better cotton wool. Then she bought some toilet water of reliable make, was astounded that they did not sell Guerlain soap, and wondered whether she would find her way back to the fishmonger. On her way back to him, she found one of the innumerable boutiques that spring like mushrooms on any reasonably well-heeled ground. They had a night-gown—made of chiffon and lace—that she decided would be perfectly suitable for Anne. It was the colour of the inside of an avocado pear with charcoal-coloured lace, and was, she was told, indelibly pleated. It was expensive, but Arabella did not notice the cost of things much, so she bought it with nothing but a feeling of triumph. Then she bought a bottle of Delamain, since she did not really enjoy the Cornhills' brandy, and finally staggered with the shopping basket from the fishmonger plus everything else to the small, boiling-hot car. It took her some time to find her way home, but she did not mind.

She was wondering what she should tell Anne about Greece. Was she meant to tell her about its beauties, so that she, Anne, would feel happy about Edmund's going there, or should she say what a frightful time, she, Arabella, had had there, thus making Anne less envious? It did not matter from her own point of view in the least: it *was* a most beautiful country and she *had* had a perfectly awful time there. It had been during the Comte de Rossignol's era; Clara had rented a yacht, and the Comte had (practically simultaneously) tried to rape her and to marry her off to one of his hideous, half-mad—or at any rate moronic—relatives. The yacht had been of the size to make bedroom intrigue all too easy: the crew were well trained and practised in ignoring all relationships between their employers: Clara had been tiring of the Comte (and about time, too, Arabella had thought), but her worst moment had been when she had realized, or thought that she had realized, that Clara's intention had been to give the Comte his *congé* on account of his behaviour with her daughter. What Arabella might have to go through to achieve this denouement seemed not to have mattered to Clara in the least. I think I started actually hating her then, Arabella thought.

By now, she was nearly home and pretended that she was returning to a large family, one of whom was having a birthday. The dog, she thought—if only there was a dog, sitting on the front seat beside her now, pretending it could see out of the window.

By the time she got back, Mrs. Gregory had left. As she put the car into the garage, she thought, Supposing this was *my* house, *my* home, and all the children were sitting in the kitchen having lunch with Nan. But everything was silent, and nothing of the kind was taking place.

Once Edmund had announced his intention of going alone to Greece, Sir William treated him with grandiose compunction, as though he was about to embark upon a very expensive and dangerous operation from which there was but a small chance of his recovery. "Got the right stuff to take with you? I don't mean clothes and all that, I mean really good stuff for the stomach: you can't keep your bowels sound over there for twenty-four hours. Either you're so bound up you're swilling down Andrews every other minute and can't eat a thing, or else—and Irene always used to find this—you've got the trots. And Greek lavatories are no joke. Mind you, I haven't been there since Irene and I went together before the war, and they have tarted them up a bit since my day, but in my day they took a lot of beating. It's not simply the *stench*, it's finding them at all, and then keeping them to yourself. I used to have to stand guard for Irene. *Lavatories*," he roared, mistaking Edmund's expression for one of non-comprehension. "I'd advise you to take these," and he thrust an old, round, discoloured pill box into Edmund's unwilling hands. *The Pills*, was written in faded spidery ink: *Take three every two hours.* "Mind you, if you can get that floor polish they call wine down, you'll stand a much better chance. I used to drink a tumbler before breakfast. Very binding, and all that pine what's-it they put in acts as some kind of disinfectant." Mercifully, at this point, his telephone rang, and he stumped back into his own office to take the call.

Young Geoffrey knocked and entered with a sheaf of papers. Edmund was about to say that he would deal with them on his return, when he noticed that some of the papers were photographs, and his eye was attracted by a huge cedar tree with a house showing framed within its gigantic branches.

"The owners of the Barnet property have sent these."

"Oh, good: let me have them. When are you going up there to measure?"

"I thought this afternoon, sir, if that's all right with you. The pictures aren't very good, sir; I wondered whether you'd like me to take some more."

"I'll look through them and let you know."

Alone, Edmund lit a cigarette and, putting all but the photographs aside, started to look at the one that had first attracted him. It was the tree under which she had been standing with her head turned to the sky—he would never forget seeing her thus.

There were a number of dull pictures taken from different aspects, but showing the house to be what it was: Georgian—late —with a good deal of mucking about. Then there were three pictures of the garden. One taken from the house and showing the descending lawns and beautiful trees; one rather blurred of the rose garden and its sundial; and one of the lake, taken, he thought, much from where he and Arabella had lain together during the storm. He put the first one of the tree, and this last one of the lake into his wallet: they were a little too large and he had to cut one side with his pocket knife. Then he returned the rest of the pictures to the sheaf. He called Geoffrey and told him yes, take as many pictures as he could, and particularly of the garden. "The lake," he said, wondering whether his voice could be heard to be shaking: "take the lake from several aspects. The garden is the best part of the property—that, and its proximity to London, of course."

"I hope you have a good trip, sir."

"Thanks."

He looked at his watch. It was only twelve, and his aeroplane did not take off until nine. He decided to get the hell out before Sir William asked him to lunch or gave him any more frightening and useless advice. He had the memoranda of whom he was to see and when neatly typed by Miss Hathaway in his brief case. He checked once more that he had his passport, air ticket, and travellers' cheques. Oh, yes—he had all of them. He wanted badly to ring Mulberry Lodge, but even if *she* answered, there was a fair chance that Anne would pick up the extension in the bedroom. There were hours to be got through: he did not feel at all like lunch; he had a few things to get, like film for his camera, dark glasses, and some paperbacks to read on the plane, but however much he spun out these missions there were going to be hours in which to dread the journey, the flight, leaving Arabella, his feelings about her, and, worse, his feelings about Anne. He would do his shopping, take his bags to the air terminal, and then find some quiet, cool, cinema with a meaningless film where he could make a definite attempt to think things out. And he would have his hair cut. It always looked better a couple of weeks after it had been cut, and he did not intend to be away for more than two weeks.

In Paris, Clara put down the telephone and said, "I no longer care whether the damn bottom of the boat falls out or not. I will *not* spend any more time in this heat in this city. Already it is difficult to sleep at night, and nothing amusing is happening."

"Where would the amusing things be being?"

"Oh—*Vani*! Where one makes them, of course. But my clothes are done, and Paris is filling up with tourists. Everybody is going away to their country houses or somewhere or other. This hotel is becoming like a railway station. One is continually having to send flowers to arrivals and departures. And there is nobody worth playing bridge with. And *you* aren't enjoying it, Vani. You said this morning that you had no plans for the day."

"I am immensely accustomed to boredom," the Prince reminded her gently. He had never seen the point of life at all, and therefore had few relative values when it came to entertainment. Comfort was a necessity, and it had taken him all of what little energy he possessed to make sure of that.

"Well, I'm not. Or, if you like, I refuse to be."

"A woman of spirit," he said languidly: "that is the only thing to be."

"I suggest that we go to Cannes, and harry them about the yacht, and if they can't be harried, we just take off."

"There would be a spice of danger about that," he agreed. He was not uncourageous: the Titanic would have suited him down to the floor of the Atlantic.

"Right. Markham!"

She appeared at once.

"We'll go to Cannes tomorrow. Pack. Get my furs stored. Tell Heythrop-Jones. Send a telegram to the hotel and another to the captain of the yacht. Give Cartier the things you know I won't want to take. Fetch me the guest list for the yacht."

Markham, who always mysteriously knew the order in which

to carry out batches of directions, reappeared with the guest list at once. Clara and Vani were sitting in their suite. She was drinking vodka with ice, and he was drinking Ricard *en tomate*. Neither of them wanted lunch, but there was really nothing else to do with the two hours in the middle of the day. A menu lay on a marble table.

Clara ran her eye over the list. It had, of course, been made by her, but she was not happy with it. It was too—*familiar*. It contained the usual collection of a dull banker and his harmless wife; a young American starlet with the French director who believed in certain aspects of her to the point of idolatry; the middle-aged adventurer who had really done one-fifth of the things he claimed to have done—one of which was totally to lose his Australian accent except when he totally lost his temper; a woman, older than Clara and considerably poorer, who could be counted on to be a good sport in any sense of that word in return for a little free luxury; and Vani's dull friend, Ludwig Potsdam—who, Clara supposed, might just be suitable for Arabella, since she must marry the girl to someone sooner rather than later. Then there were the possibles: either not yet asked or not yet sure. There was an Italian painter whom Clara felt would probably make the largest contribution to the party, but he had a wife and children, and Italian law interfered with anything but his casual pleasure. There was an unmarried British Cabinet minister, but Clara suspected his celibacy as either being a choice (impossible) or the kind of cleverness that she had become rather frightened of. There was the youngish daughter of an English duke, but she could only be considered in relation to the rest. She was highly intelligent, totally unself-conscious, and extremely rich. She therefore constituted the kind of competition that Clara could no longer contemplate. Oh, dear, the balance between being bored and being humiliated! Vani was not a possible life mate. But she was unused to being alone and regarded it as out of the question. Surely the point of the cruise must be to get Arabella married. That would be one load off her mind.

"Markham! Put in a call to the Cornhills tonight. About eight o'clock."

The Prince looked gloomily at the menu. It had everything he would expect upon it, and this was exactly what he would have expected. He sighed. They might as well go as stay: the only thing that he actually enjoyed in life was gambling, and he had used up the allowance Clara gave him for that nearly two days ago. He had considered cutting his wrists in one of the two handsome marble baths the hotel provided them with, but he had discarded the idea as it might turn out to be uncomfortable, and Clara was notoriously unable to leave him alone in the evenings. Perhaps the yacht would sink, and he could either save someone's life, or lose his own. But even there, one would have to use discretion. Clara was as shut as a clam about the contents of her will, and so, to be on the safe side, he would probably have to save the life of the English banker, the only results of which could easily amount to no more than a case of champagne or a gold watch. The *uncertainty* of life! If only it amused him. He decided upon *oeufs Bénédictine* and cold roast beef. He did not wish to die: he wished to be young with illusions—something he had never managed. He wondered whether he would, in fact, prefer the company of handsome young men. The trouble about money was that it seemed to prolong all kinds of things one had not thought of, and then give one far too much time in which to think about them.

Anne had followed Arabella's advice about Mrs. Gregory, who practically spring-cleaned her bedroom and won, because Anne could not think of anything more to do in the bathroom, and longed weakly to be back in bed. Mrs. Gregory hoped she was feeling better, but clearly did not think so. Anne said she *was* better, but Mrs. Gregory looked at her with such dark solicitude that when she had left, Anne felt obliged to take her temperature again. It was over a hundred: and, forgetting the likely effects of a hot bath, Anne, with nothing to do but fret about her condition, accepted the hot drink offered her by Mrs. Gregory, took two more Codis and fell asleep. Mrs. Gregory, who had realized that Mr. Cornhill was going Abroad, and also from a note left for her in Arabella's large, clear writing that she had gone shopping but would be back in plenty of time for lunch, tidied Arabella's room ferociously, putting away every single object that was lying about the room. This was to register her approval of Arabella, whom she regarded as a very nice young lady indeed, but her system for the storage of Arabella's numerous and assorted possessions underwent several changes of policy while she was doing it, which meant that Arabella was unable to find anything she wanted for days. Long-playing records went into the under-clothes drawer, mainly because Arabella had so few of the latter, but many other strange combinations were effected before Mrs. Gregory was satisfied that nothing—excepting Ariadne, of course—was lying about. Then she tiptoed to Anne's bedroom, found her asleep, took the empty cup away, and left to catch a bus to Henley to do her shopping.

Janet stood patiently in the queue in the post office with her book in her hands. Henry had been offered two days' filming as the man who drove the getaway truck in a robbery for a TV series. Naturally, he was not paid in advance, but it made Janet feel slightly better about drawing out three more of her private, precious pounds. She gazed at the posters of places in the country or by the sea that told you how to address an envelope properly. The handwriting had that anonymous clarity that she associated with letters in films. She looked at the thatched cottages and seaside bungalows with longing. If only she could take the kids away for a week or two; Luke might get over his tonsilitis. The doctor had said that he would have to have them out, really, but not until he had thoroughly recovered from his present bout. Samantha was better: she had reached the whining stage where she could not think of anything to do, and indeed there was precious little, poor little sod. But Luke still sat about listlessly, cried a good deal at night, and was off his food. The woman in front of her was buying fifteen postal orders of different denominations: she always got behind someone like that, Janet thought. When it was her turn and she pushed the post-office savings book through the grid and asked for her three pounds, the woman counted them out in a second, stamped her book, and returned it. Janet looked at the page. Now she had precisely twenty-three pounds left. She went to one of the form-filling booths to look once more at her shopping list. Bread, two Penguin biscuits for the children, half a pound of Stork, two pounds of granulated, one packet of corn flakes, a packet of Tide, a quarter of tea, one Nescafé (save enough to pay milkman), a pound of sausages, a half of streaky bacon, two lambs' breasts, bones for stock, five pounds of potatoes, one of carrots (old), three of onions, one pound of tomatoes (Luke would sometimes eat a tomato sandwich), three oranges, and one lettuce. Cheese! She must somehow have enough for cheese. One pound of Cheddar, she wrote, and crossed Tampax and lavatory paper off the list. Substitutes could be found for them. Perhaps a tin of peaches—for the children. But really she needed a pound of Stork, they ate so much bread. One pot of Hartley's jam. Two tins of corned beef and two of sardines. She felt a surge of panic. She was going to have to write down the price of every bloody thing she collected in the supermarket, in case she outran her budget. This had happened to her once, and the embarrassment and humiliation had been so awful, with the woman at the adding machine furious at having to do it again, and the people behind her irritable and impatient, and she trying to think what to do without—she would not on any account go through that again. Sometimes there were bargains to be picked up at the supermarket, and the butcher was always nice to her. She decided to start with him, since what she spent there depended so much on his mood/generosity. Her luck was out. Ernie was on holiday, a sour-faced man said: he had gone to Eastbourne for two weeks. What could he do for her? Janet looked anxiously about: not much was on display because of the heat. Breasts of lamb? she asked. He'd have to cut her them, he said grudgingly; how about some nice lamb chops? At six and six a pound, they were out of the question. Well, stewing lamb, she

said, but that was three and eight, as opposed to the breasts at two
and four. It would have to be breasts. When he returned from the
deep freeze with a side of lamb, the telephone rang, and he went
to answer it. His demeanour changed on the telephone. Yes, they
had some lovely fillet. A whole one. Yes: yes, he would bring it
round himself between one and two. While he was on the telephone, Janet tried to see whether there were any bones in sight.
There weren't. She hadn't the courage to ask, since the moment
he was off the telephone, the man reverted to his sourness. Damn
it, she thought, it is for the kids: I ought to have more guts. "Have
you any marrow or veal bones?"

"Got a dog, have you?"

"No I want them for soup."

He went away again, and returned with a few miserable bones
that he chopped viciously on his board and charged her one and
six for. So much for the butcher. Why the hell didn't Henry get
his National Assistance? But she didn't want to go into that,
because she was fairly sure that he did, and the money went on
booze and fags when he was out. She tried the baker for any of
yesterday's bread—far cheaper when they had it, but today there
was none. She was sweating with the heat, and at the same time
feeling cold. The supermarket was cool, but very full. This meant
that people were always jostling you when you stopped to write
down the price of anything, and she had never been very good
at adding up. The bargains were some Polish jam of unnamed
variety—she bought a jar instead of Hartley's—and some very
battered-looking tins of sardines—she bought them as well. She
did the cheese last, when she could work out how much she dared
buy. The woman weighed the Cheddar and said, "Four and eight,
is that too much?" It was, but Janet didn't dare say so—it simply
meant that she would have to cut down on the milk for a day. It
was better than having a scene about the cheese: she really had
to cut down on them these days.

She walked the quarter of a mile home, weighed down with
two string bags. Henry would be waiting for her. I am going back
to my family, she thought: two children I can't afford to look after

properly and a husband who thinks they are entirely my fault. She wondered fleetingly how much longer she was going to be able to stand any of it. She felt weak from lack of affection and food and any kind of hope. If she tried to divorce him, perhaps then, one way or another, she *would* get some money: the lawyers or whoever would force him to send her enough for the children, or she would be able to claim National Assistance for herself. But she hadn't the faintest idea how to set about any of it, and the thought of trying to find people who might tell her irrationally terrified her. She didn't want people to *know*. Lawyers cost money; she didn't know any: it was almost impossible to get out without the children, and with Henry going to be out on location for—she didn't know how many days it would turn out to be— she was stuck. She had never been a very practical creature: had shown a small talent for acting at the school who had given her a scholarship (where she had met Henry), and her family had emigrated to Australia just after she had married him. They had no idea—and not much interest—about her circumstances, and she retained a kind of pride (Scots) that had narrowed down now to her only form of self-respect. She must just grit her teeth and get on with it. As she walked down the hill, she stopped for a rest from the shopping bags and found she was crying. If I could go back now and he would say, "What marvels you have done with three pounds," she thought, instead of "Why the hell have you been so long?" She picked up the bags again, having wiped her face with her hot, dirty fingers. Only fifty yards to go.

He opened the door when she rang and looked at her as though she was someone he—quite objectively—simply did not want to see. "Why the hell have you been so long?" he said.

"You've been so long, I thought you were never coming back." Anne sat up in bed and looked at Arabella with expectant trust and affection. "It is awful," she went on: "you've hardly been here a fortnight, and already I can't think what I'd do without you."

Arabella looked at her with unaffected delight. "Oh, *good*," she said. "Listen: I've bought a lot of sensible things for Ariadne, but possibly some rather silly things for us. How are you feeling?"

"*Much* better. I felt worse after my bath, but that was partly Mrs. Gregory feeling that I must be. What have you bought?"

Arabella told her about the things for Ariadne, and Anne, though she privately thought plaice too good even for such a cat, made no criticism. Arabella's description of the coley "like half-frozen slabs of awfully dirty underclothes" and the whiting as some sort of decoration that somebody had made of a cheap and unusual material made her laugh and ask for champagne. "Why not?" she said quickly, more to herself than to Arabella: "Edmund wouldn't mind in the least. He'd be glad that we were enjoying ourselves."

"Let me just tell you about one of the silly things."

"Just one, then."

"Two huge crabs."

"That doesn't sound particularly silly to me."

"But when I got them home, they aren't at all like you have them in restaurants. They're—well, *whole*, and I don't at all know what to do with them."

"Well, you could bring them up here and I could show you. After lunch—or after champagne, anyway. Have you brought any cigarettes?"

"Yes, but won't they make your throat sore?"

"Yes, but I want one."

"O.K."

Downstairs, Arabella realized that she had not thought about lunch at all. She would have to make an omelet—the only dish that she knew how to make. She got some champagne and glasses and decided to give the presents as she felt like it. She put a rabbit on for Ariadne, as she had been taught to do, and went back to Anne with cigarettes, the drink, and the presents in a carrier bag. She felt full of excitement, as she loved giving presents even more than shopping.

After the first glass, Anne said, "Can people tell when you have been drinking champagne? On your breath, I mean?"

"You mean Dr. Travers? I bet not, on the whole. The Gauloise won't fox him though. Not unless you clean your teeth like mad and we open the windows and I let him in with one dripping out of my mouth. Would an omelet be all right for lunch?"

"It would be lovely, but there is a cold chicken, or a cooling chicken, in the larder. I asked Mrs. Gregory to do it for us, and she's a brilliant roaster."

"Oh, well—let's have that. We can always fall back on my omelets, and, as we might have to fall quite often, the later the better. I can't make anything else," she explained. "Perhaps, when you are better, you'd teach me to cook. I really ought to learn, and all they taught at the awful place I went to was things like *chou* pastry, which I hate, so I didn't learn properly on purpose. Or do you think it is socially wrong for very rich people to be able to cook?"

"Why?"

"Oh, you know. Creating unemployment—that sort of thing. That would be bad, wouldn't it?"

"Are you very rich?"

"I think I must be, because Clara is usually pretty mean about doling out money, but I've noticed that since I was twenty-one she jolly well doles it out, if you see what I mean. Which would argue that whether she likes it or not, some of the dough *is* actually mine. Although I have to ask for it so far. I think when I'm twenty-five—years away—then I may get control. That's why she's so hell-bent on getting me married before then. She knows I'd never be manageable once I got my paws on the loot."

"But she can't *make* you marry anyone you don't want to marry."

Arabella took a defiant swig. "No, she can't, can she?"

"What will you do when you do get it?"

"Ah. That's the thousand-dollar question. If you want to know, I've kept a loose-leaf book for years. With plans in it."

"Why loose-leaf?"

"So that I can tear out the looniest plans when I outgrow them.

It stays quite a thin book," she added sadly, "although I bought six lots of refills."

"Will you show it to me some time?"

"If you swear not to laugh, I might. I've never shown it to anyone, you see, on account of that danger. It's laid out on a double-spread system. One side says *Good for Arabella* and the other side says *Nice for Arabella*, and so far they don't seem to fit much. Here's a present for you." She threw the bottle of toilet water onto the bed and Anne's lap. Anne was delighted, and Arabella watched her and got the maximum pleasure from her delight.

"Lovely: I'd run out, and this is one of my favourites. I do love being given presents, don't you?"

"I don't know: I don't get them much. It's a bit like being known to be a super cook. People wouldn't ask you out to dinner, because they would always think you could do it better than they could. People always seem to feel that I could buy a better whatever-it-might-be for myself."

"Oh—*poor* you."

"*I* don't mind. Poor rich me. I do love giving presents, though. Here's another for you."

"Arabella—really! You shouldn't."

"Anne—really! I can do what I damn well like."

This time it was the night-dress. "I thought you might as well give Dr. Travers some fun for his money. It's not actually a night-gown," she explained, as Anne speechlessly unfolded it. "It's supposed to be what some extraordinary sort of person does nothing in in the evenings. You do like it, don't you?"

"Yes, Oh, yes. But it seems so—*much*."

"Well, you admitted your night-dresses weren't up to much, and you haven't *got* to wear it in bed."

Anne said, "If I wasn't infectious, I'd kiss you."

Arabella said, "I never catch things. Do kiss me." She went to the bed and bent down so that Anne could do this. Anne kissed her face and, inevitably remembering the earlier kiss that had been quite different, wondered immediately about hurting Arabella's feelings. The precedent for mouths had been set: the last thing she could bear to do would be to hurt this generous, affectionate creature. She moved Arabella's face so that she could kiss her mouth. When she did this, Arabella kissed her back, with a strength and sweetness of affection, and also, it seemed to Anne, a hunger for being loved that moved her in more ways than one. She's never had a man she has loved, Anne knew then: she feels safe with me. It's as though nobody has loved her, poor darling. She put her hands each side of Arabella's neck and stroked the silky hair and soft skin kept warm by the hair. "*I* love you, anyway," she said, and then wished very much that she had not put it so badly. But—'I love *you*, also," Arabella said, and her voice was both warm and light. Everything was all right. Everything, in fact, was surprisingly good. They both had some more champagne, and then Arabella fetched the chicken and two little salads that Mrs. Gregory had laid out with a bottle of Heinz mayonnaise.

"Oh, good!" Arabella had said about the latter. "I do so prefer things out of bottles that people have made for everyone. I really adore this stuff, and it is surprisingly difficult to get in restaurants. I suppose they save money making their beastly own."

When they had nearly finished, she said, "When you're feeling better, can we take a boat and go for a picnic on the river?"

"Of course we can. It would be lovely. We really waste the river: Edmund gets back too late—you know, it is all dusk and midges biting away at one. But we could go in the morning."

"Now. I'm going to give Ariadne a substantial snack. You could get into your gown, or whatever it is. Dr. T. is due any time now."

Dr. Travers turned up while Arabella was boning the rabbit. She went to the door, which she opened with a tea towel wrapped round her hand.

"What have you done to yourself?"

"I'm sticky with rabbit. Nothing. Anne is upstairs," she added unnecessarily.

"How is she today?"

"Better, I think, but it seems to come and go. She doesn't seem to be having an actual cold."

When Dr. Travers came down, he said, "Well, I think you're right about the cold. I think she's got glandular fever."

"Oh. What does one do about that?"

"Nothing, I'm afraid. One goes to bed when one feels ill and gets up when one feels all right."

"How long does it go on for?"

"Seldom longer than three months. Sometimes much less than that. She doesn't seem a very bad case. Her temperature's normal at the moment."

"Three *months*!"

"Well, don't let's look on the black side of things. She may get over it in a few weeks. By the way, from your point of view, Miss—"

"Dawick."

"Dawick, if you are the kind of person who's going to catch it, you'll catch it, and if you're not, you won't."

"I'm not," said Arabella firmly. She had gone back to the laborious boning of rabbit. Dr. Travers smiled at her clumsiness and determination.

"Well, let her do what she feels like doing. Fairer to other people if she didn't go to cinemas and things like that, but otherwise . . . Oh, and see she takes her temperature twice a day. If it goes up a great deal, give me a call. Otherwise I'll come and see her next week. Her husband's away, I gather?"

"Yes—but only for about two weeks."

"I have no doubt that you will hold the fort admirably. Who is all that rabbit for? Are you making a pie?"

"Good God, no. I'm a one-off cook: omelets. This is for the cat. She has had four kittens, so if you hear of a good home, we'd be most obliged to you."

"Right. I won't forget. But nearly all the homes I visit don't have any vacancies."

"Do you want some tea?" Arabella asked; he seemed to be

hanging about rather, and she thought that possibly English doctors got tea wherever they went.

"Thank you, no, I must be going. Don't hesitate to call me if you are worried about Mrs. Cornhill."

And he went.

When Arabella had fed Ariadne a huge meal of rabbit and separate bowl of top of milk, she looked in on Anne, who was reading.

"Sorry about your whatever-it-is fever."

"It is a bore, isn't it? Just as well Edmund is away, really. He hates me to be ill."

"Shall I go and pick things in the garden while you have a rest? Then, if you're feeling all right, I could bring the crabs up to you and you could show me how to unhinge them."

"That would be lovely. I keep feeling sleepy. Pick some raspberries—there should be a lot more by now. And peas, if you like."

"Could I pick some roses as well? Or a mixed bunch of things?"

Ordinarily, Anne would not have liked other people picking her flowers, but she liked the idea of Arabella doing it.

"I'll be awfully careful," Arabella said.

"Pick anything you like."

"If you want me, use the gong. I'll hear it easily."

"I shan't want you. I'm perfectly all right, just sleepy."

"How long have you . . . cared—for me, Clint?"

"I fell in love with you, baby, right from the very first moment I saw you coming out of that movie."

It's time *I* got out of *this* movie, Edmund thought with a start. He had been not exactly asleep, but in a kind of trance where his eyes remained open, he had no thoughts of any kind, and he had not the slightest idea who Clint was or the girl he was now vociferously kissing. He looked at his watch: he had been in the cinema for well over two hours. It was nearly seven; he could reasonably make for the air terminal. It wasn't that he wasn't perfectly all right: he simply felt dazed and hot and rather thirsty. These feelings soon gave way to sheer fright at what lay ahead. At the terminal, he managed to get a double whisky and ginger ale before catching a bus to Heathrow. The bus, after Cromwell Road and Hammersmith, ascended the M4. The M4. It would be that: the last time he had travelled it had been with Arbell, nearly forty-eight hours ago. He leaned back in his seat and gave himself entirely over to anxiety and self-pity. If only she was with him now! The bliss—the gorgeous feeling of excitement and irresponsibility! As it was, he was faced with a probably exhausting and unrewarding mission with all the rigors of being in a country where he could not speak the language. Perhaps, when he reached the airport, he *would* ring Mulberry Lodge. There was a chance that she would answer; that he would at least hear her voice. The bus was full, and next to him sat a man with dark glasses, a soft hat, and a cigar the chronic smoke of which blew steadily in Edmund's direction. The bus also contained a child who was whining without pause, and what looked like a honeymoon couple—since they radiated a self-conscious sexual awareness of each other that no amount of staring into space, hands creeping together as though they led a life of their own, could erase. I'll get drunk, Edmund thought. That's what aeroplanes are for. Then I shan't care *what* happens. The trouble with this idea was that he already didn't care what happened, and that was the trouble. He *wanted* to care. It suddenly seemed urgent that the wretched bus should arrive in time for him to telephone.

It didn't. By the time his luggage had been weighed—a long queue—they were calling for his flight number. The telephone boxes also had queues attached to them, so that he could comfort himself that he hadn't missed ringing by a hair's breadth. Through customs and passport control, they were put into a bus, where they waited interminably—presumably for those persons brave enough to make telephone calls, risk losing their plane, and keep everyone else waiting, Edmund thought. They drove for what seemed like miles to the plane. Everybody managed to get out of the bus before Edmund, which simply meant that he had a seat between two other people near the front. Where, if you crashed, you had least chance, he thought. He had not had lunch and was now longing for some more drink, but this was clearly going to take time. He wondered whether he had married Anne out of cowardice, or some mysterious sense of inferiority. Then he felt a complex of disloyalties. All men of his age underwent some emotional upheaval, he imagined. He couldn't actually think of anyone who had, but then he didn't know any man well enough to know that about him. He wanted to look at himself in a glass, but there wasn't one. The lights of the airport—vari-coloured and in dramatic patterns for the take-off paths—were reflected in the windows. Stewardesses in their tight, well-cut skirts were mincing or hobbling up and down the gangways, putting up—with infinite patience—with the clash between first, or rare, experiences and day-to-day routine. "No smoking now, sir. Fasten your seat belts. Shall I put that on the rack for you? Dinner will be served approximately half an hour after take-off. Drinks will be served as soon as we are airborne. Would you like a paper? No smoking, I'm afraid, until after take-off."

When this finally occurred, Edmund—as a lone man—was easily able to procure a double whisky and ginger ale. The small plastic table that was pulled out for him by the stewardess as she served his drink made him feel safe and cared for in an alien world. Perhaps he would not even want dinner. His stewardess was small and dark, with pancake make-up and false eyelashes. She had large breasts, and he thought of Anne again; and then of *her*, with those small, childish protuberances that made him feel so agonizingly protective. There was a delicacy about her that he had never dreamed of. That, and her surprising, and patchy, sophistication. It would have been unbearable if she had seemed all of a piece. Perhaps she *was* exactly that, but it was unknown to him. She was beautiful, and brave and honest, and who, meeting that, could not love it? He took the pictures of the house in Barnet out of his wallet to look again at the cedar tree and the lake.

Sir William sat in the huge, dank room that Irene had called his study. Its large windows faced north and looked out onto the back wall of a mews, and Sir William was so used to being too cold in it that even on this midsummer night he had, out of habit, the old astrakhan car rug from the even older Bentley (now sold) on his knees. He was, as usual, watching television and eating a bowl of corn flakes. He enjoyed almost all television immensely, even when facts—as he saw them—or people—as he saw them—seemed erroneous or out of place. "Silly young monkeys," he muttered, as a pop group came to the end of its gesticulations that had been emphasized by a steady, monotonous thud and applause filled the empty room. His favourite programmes were "Miss World," ballroom-dancing contests, party political broadcasts, and American gangster films. How Irene would have laughed at this lot! Their clothes and all that hair all over the place and their voices that ranged from America to Liverpool. . . . Dammit! His right eye was watering again. As the commercial began, he put down the empty bowl on a table and fetched himself his nightly Scotch. He always had a Scotch after his corn flakes. As he was a poor sleeper these days, he watched until there was nothing left to watch, right through the pop groups, the news, serials, or arm-chair theatre, to intellectual discussions about pretty well anything to God. The ways in which they managed to go on about God impressed him deeply: with apparently no trouble at all they could bring Him into damn nearly anything. One minute a feller was talking about trees or the East End or sports, and the next moment he'd applied it all to God. He stood when they played the Queen (next to Irene, she was the finest woman he knew) and then switched everything off and stumped up two flights of stairs to bed. He slept now in his dressing-room: Irene's room was just as she had left it, and sometimes he went in to see that everything was all right—but not often, and not for long. It was funny, he told himself, what a long time it seemed to take to get over it. So many people had told him that he would that he had come to believe them, but it still didn't happen. Going back to his (her) house was still a nightly ordeal, but he resisted any casual efforts of his sons or friends to move him to a flat. This house had been theirs, so he was going to go on being in it.

As he drank the last of his Scotch now, the news began with its headlines of disaster and deadlock, and he wondered suddenly how young Edmund was getting on with his journey to Greece. Must be in the air by now. He was a bit of a stuffy egg, as well as being deaf, which was extraordinary for a young feller who hadn't been under heavy fire: he didn't seem to have the gusto for life that Sir William would have liked in his successor. But, then, he hadn't got Irene: it was women like Irene who made a man tick. By God, he'd been lucky. His left eye was watering now, as he found it often did in the evenings. Better go and see some eye feller about them. If only, he thought, letting himself have one thought for once about her, if only she hadn't died, *be* would have taken her to Greece and she would have enjoyed every minute of it. The other thing he found he often had to do in the evenings was to pull himself together. He did so now—clearing his throat and blowing his nose very loudly, so that he missed how many Russian technicians were now operating in Egypt.

"I can't wear it for cracking up crabs: you said it was for doing nothing in."

"I know, but you looked so smashing in it."

"You're not hurt! It's not because I don't like it. It's because I like it so much."

They were sitting side by side at the large kitchen table, with hammers and picks and a dish, getting the crabs done.

"Once," said Arabella dreamily—they had both had drinks made by her that were so cold that their strength had been momentarily concealed—"Once, I got a black wool beard that hooked behind the ears. I wore it for about three weeks. *All the time.* I loved it so, you see. And it annoyed Clara awfully in hotels."

"Edmund will be in his aeroplane by now."

"You aren't missing him too much, are you?"

"I would be, if you weren't here. Now look: this is the poison bit." Anne had a sharp knife and showed Arabella how to cut this out.

"Would it really kill you if you ate it?"

"I've never tested it to see. But, yes, I think it easily might. The fishmonger should have taken them out for you."

"Those sort of people always know I don't know."

"Let's just have crab and lettuce and masses of raspberries and cream," Anne said, as the crab dismemberment was drawing to a close.

"Yes, let's. There's a little of that drink I made left. Shall we have that first?"

"Of course." Anne felt surprisingly well and slightly drunk. "And you tell me more about your book."

"I'll tell you bits about the principle of it. You see, what I feel is," she went on, having gone to the fridge, collected the jug of drink, and poured out the rest of it for both of them, "*is*, that if I really *am* rich, I ought to be good and useful to somebody or some people. But I can't properly think how. I mean, you know, Dr. Schweitzer and Josephine Baker and all the people who find a way of being needed. They don't even need money to start with. But all I seem to have is money. On the other hand, I wouldn't begin to know how to start a leper colony or how to run a huge crowd of adopted children. I could just give all the money away, but so far that has always just come under the heading of *Good for Arabella* and never *Nice* for her. I suppose I want my pound of flesh in gratitude or having a purpose in return. I want to know what I'm *for*, and I can't simply be for a million dollars, or whatever I turn out to have."

"I think you should start by being married to somebody you really respect and care for."

"Like you, you mean?"

"Well—I don't know about that. I love Edmund: I haven't got any special gifts or advantages, so I suppose I haven't thought beyond the fact that I love him."

"And respect him?"

Anne thought before answering. "Yes: I do, I suppose. For a man."

"Ah! Then men aren't necessarily the answer. But children might be."

"I've honestly never wanted them. Edmund has filled the bill for me."

Arabella drained her glass and said, "Do you believe in lies?"

"How on earth do you mean 'believe in' them?"

"I mean, do you think it is quite all right for people to tell them?"

"Of course not. Except when it doesn't matter."

"When doesn't it matter?"

"Well—when you would hurt somebody very much if you told them something they don't need or want to know."

"Surely needing and wanting could be different?"

Anne said slowly, because she was having to think about it, "Yes, I suppose they could. But," she finished more lightly, "One can trust one's instinct there. To get that sort of thing right. Do you still want Heinz with your crab?" she asked a few minutes later, when the shells has been consigned to the rubbish and the table was being laid.

"If you don't mind. If you don't feel it's an insult to your home brew."

"Of course not. Let's both have what we like."

"It's funny, isn't it, how some kinds of being drunk simply make you feel hungry and happy? And other kinds don't at all?"

"Is that what you are?"

"Oh, yes: I'm quite drunk, but in a very good way."

Anne noticed how her chin was charmingly and neatly square, which, by itself, would not seem to go with the rest of her face at all, but, in fact, was exactly the right finish.

When Anne had lit the lamp on the kitchen table, they ate their meal there, with a bowl of cooling water to dip their fingers in and damp tea cloths to wipe them. Ariadne soon smelled the crab and walked, or picked her way, round the table making her wishes plain. Occasionally, a neat, hooked paw collected a piece of fish, and in the end, as they had far too much, they gave her the smaller claws. These she took singly to the floor and crunched up with professional skill and satisfaction.

"Glad to get away from those boring, demanding kittens," Anne remarked.

"Well—wanting a change, anyway. Everybody except me seems to want that."

"But you only don't want one because you're always having them. I mean, you'd soon get bored with here if you found you *had* to stay."

"Gosh—I wouldn't."

The telephone rang, and Arabella, with what seemed to Anne to be a sixth sense, said, "I know who that is: my mother. Don't let's answer it."

It went on ringing. Anne said, "It might be Edmund. He might have missed his plane."

"Well, then, *you* answer it."

"But if it *is* your mother, it would be much better if you did, because then you could say that Edmund was away and I'm frightfully ill and you have to stay to look after me."

Arabella gave her a look composed of fear and resentment in equal proportions.

The telephone still rang: by now it had got on both their nerves, and they knew it must be answered. Arabella got slowly up from the table, wiping her hands on the tea cloth, and walked slowly and rather unsteadily out of the kitchen into the hall, where the telephone was.

Anne listened. The conversation began in French, with Arabella accepting the call from presumably a Paris operator. It then became clear that she was talking to her mother in English and French that seemed interchangeable. What struck Anne with a surge of love and protection was the way in which Arabella's voice—in either language—seemed to change when talking to her mother. She sounded defiant, childish, inadequate, obstinate, and generally bad at expressing herself. She couldn't come to Paris or Nice, she said; she was nursing Mrs. Cornhill: Edmund was abroad—no, she didn't know how long for, but there was nobody else in the house, and she couldn't leave. *Pas de domestiques.* Ludwig *who? Merde!* She wasn't going to get off with some grasping old toad old enough to be her father. She hated yachts. She loathed St. Tropez. She was perfectly all right where she was. She was twenty-two. Tell that to Vani. No. No. *Non.* All right. Call next week, but she wouldn't change her mind. She needed some more money. Her dentist had charged her nearly two hundred pounds for crowning. Please. It was her money anyway, wasn't it? Without it, she would never come: if it was sent or accorded her, she might change her mind. No, she did not want to speak to . . . *Bon soir,* Vani. *Je suis infirmière pour une femme qui est souffrante. Avec une maladie très dangereuse. Oui. Maman ne comprend pas.* Please leave me alone, Mummy—I'm perfectly all right where I am. No I told you—they *want* me to stay. I daresay you don't, but it's true. They like having me—they said so. He only went this evening. *N'oubliez pas les livres, s'il vous plaît, maman, parce que je suis trop pauvre.* I *can't.* I've told you—I simply can't leave a very ill person alone in a house. *Ludwig est horrible—je le déteste. Je ne veux pas de château. Je suis très contente ici. Maman!* . . .

When she came back, Anne started to give her a cigarette; she crumpled it up in her fingers and said, "I tell *her* lies, anyway," and burst into tears.

A moment later, she said, "She doesn't believe them, of course, but she never tries to find out what I really mean. Oh! Why does she have to be *so awful?* Why couldn't she just be a nothing mother, bored with me and leaving me alone?" She was wiping her face with the crab-ridden cloth. Anne got some brandy and gave her a glass without saying anything. Arabella's relationship with her mother was something so entirely outside her own experience that she felt afraid to give advice or pronounce any sort of judgment upon it. Arabella drank some brandy. Anne wanted to say, "You are twenty-two. If you hate her so much, why don't you just get free of her?" But she realized that if, indeed, the situation was as simple as that, she would not need to say it.

Arabella sat down again at her place and put her elbows on the table.

"I hate her so much that if only I could think of the kind of lies that would make her never want to see me again, I'd tell them like a shot. But I'm not clever enough. The things you'd think she'd mind, she doesn't seem to, and the other way round."

"Who's Ludwig? I couldn't help hearing what you were saying."

"Ludwig is some little German punk with a broken-down castle who's looking for some rich, dumb fool to marry. I expect he's related to Vani—nearly all really awful people are. It would settle me down. Get me out of the way. He's a Catholic, you see, and I'm a lapsed one, so I'd *never* get away from him. His breath is like the ghastly old dungeons in his castle. His family are haemophilic, so most of the time he stays indoors collecting stamps. I hate him," she added unnecessarily.

Anne gave her another cigarette and lit it for her. "Now listen. This is the twentieth century. You can't be made to marry someone you really hate. You must calm down a bit, darling, about all of it."

"Yes: yes, I must. But the difference is that Clara does seem to be my only living relative, and I think I must secretly be somebody who's meant to have a lot of them, and if I just get out as far as she's concerned—where *to?* I just seem to know a lot of people in the *wrong* way, if you see what I mean. I mean people you go to parties with, or skiing or swimming or anyway are generally meant to be well and having a jolly good old expensive time with, but nobody who I could ring and say I just feel awful and I haven't a penny and don't know what to do. Clara has always held money over my head ever since I can remember, and it must have worked a bit, because honestly I don't know now what I'd do without it."

Anne said, "When Edmund comes back, perhaps he would be

able to find out whether you *have* got any money that is really your own. Then you could claim it, and then you would feel freer."

"And if he found out that I *haven't* got any money of my own?"

"Then, at least you would know. You could choose. A lot of people don't have money, you know. And it doesn't force them into being unhappy."

"Well, I know I've got a little. I could probably buy a very small branch-line disused railway station and live in it with some animals."

"Have some raspberries."

"That reminds me. Hang on a minute." She went to the fridge and brought out the bowl of raspberries. Then she fetched a smaller bowl of whipped cream. Encircling its apex was the crystal-and-enamel ring.

"That's your third, and last, present: for the time being. I thought it looked better on cream than cotton wool—even Boots' best. You take it, and lick the cream off, and put it on," she added.

Anne, looking once at the eager, tear-stained face, did simply as she was told. The ring fitted her third finger. It was very beautiful. She said so.

"It's nothing. It's just what money can buy," Arabella said in her hard, childish voice.

"Darling Arabella—you don't feel that you have to bribe *me?*"

"No. No, of course I don't. I just thought that you might like it."

At this point, Ariadne leapt neatly up onto the table beside Arabella and began systematically cleaning the crab from the cloth off her face. Anne looked down at the extremely pretty ring: it was exactly the kind of ring that she most liked; it only seemed passingly strange that it should have been given to her by Arabella rather than by Edmund. But then, over the years, she had become used to being given presents only by Edmund. She looked across the table at Arabella, whose tears had not stopped, although Ariadne was making pretty good headway with them.

Arabella said, "Bribed by crab. It's because I dried my face with that crabby cloth."

Anne said, "But she also loves you."

"Does she? Does she really?"

"Of course she does. Otherwise she would never have had her children in your bed."

Arabella put out a hand and stroked Ariadne's back long and lovingly. Ariadne arched her back, rubbed her cheek against Arabella, and then got on with the job.

"I love my ring. It isn't at all just what money can buy. Think of all the awful things that that can do. Horse brasses, and milk chocolate, and dahlias, and cocktail cabinets—"

"You really *do* like it?"

"I told you: I love it. Thank you, darling."

Arabella looked at her so intently when she asked the last question, and also while it was being answered, that Anne felt suddenly shy—not exactly ill at ease nor embarrassed, but plain shy. The silence that followed promoted a feeling of tension, which had something oddly exciting about it.

We are sitting at the kitchen table having dinner, and the cat is here, so why do I wonder or care about what will happen next? "Let's have some raspberries," she said.

"You have some. I don't think I want any."

"I don't much, either. Shall we have coffee, then?"

"Yes. And I bought a special brandy. We'll have that." Ariadne left her, jumped off the table, and walked silently out of the room.

Anne made the coffee, while Arabella cleared away the crab and raspberries and cream. Clearing things up made everything homely again, and they agreed to take the coffee and brandy into the sitting-room. This was filled with a kind of plush twilight, as though the heat of the sun had actually imprinted a warmth to the colours of the room. It was at the same time romantic and snug. Arabella, as though she had lived in the house for years, sought and found a record—a concerto of C. P. E. Bach. She played it very quietly. "Men always hate you to play the gramophone like this," she said, "but we aren't men."

Anne, pouring out the coffee, said, "Do you think we are much nicer than men?"

"I think we are kinder—and more gentle with people. I don't think we would make wars or have the kinds of fights that men seem unable to do without."

"Perhaps we are *kinder*, anyway."

"Men would say it was because we are less intelligent, and therefore have a smaller horizon. It's easier to operate in a smaller sphere."

"Why should it be? I should have thought that that might make it more difficult."

"For men, it would be. But I think more things please us, and fewer things make us ask questions. That's probably our bodies —far more time-taking."

"How's your body?" Anne took the brandy as she asked this. "I mean, after what happened in London."

"Oh. As good as new. Or bad, as the case might be. What fascinates me," she continued, curling herself up on the sofa, "is how men harp on the inferior intellect of women. I mean— honestly—take the average man! When you get down to average, it's common sense you're after—and I should have thought that women have far more of that."

"I don't know. I think the intellect idea comes from women's being far worse educated than men for so many years. That's nearly always been the arrangement—unless you were a Tudor princess or something rare like they were."

Arabella looked at her with real pleasure. "I do like talking to you," she said. "None of the over- or undertones one gets so drearily accustomed to."

"Like?"

"Like: 'Most women seem to me wholly unintelligent, but you aren't like most women.'"

"Oh—that old stuff! Only men who don't really like women say that sort of thing."

"But what I mean is that we've been accustomed for hundreds

of years to *not* having our brains or minds sharpened, that we are at a general disadvantage. I mean there jolly well *is* a sex structure everywhere, whereas class structures are becoming more and more parochial. You have to be a manly kind of woman to get on, professionally speaking, but you can be any sort of man and be O.K."

"Well—you used not to be. Think of Oscar Wilde."

They both thought of Oscar Wilde. Anne thought of John Gielgud's performance as Jack Worthing, and Arabella thought of staying in the hotel in Sloane Street and having a drink before lunch and someone telling her that this was where Wilde had sat drinking hock and Seltzer and waiting to be picked up by the police.

"He would have said that he had the bad luck or bad management to live in the wrong country at the wrong time. Anyway, he went through it all for them: it doesn't count any more, and quite a lot of that is due to him. But all the women who have worked away at equal opportunities for us—from voting onwards—have always been laughed at by men."

When she said this, Anne looked seriously at the beautiful and very young girl before her and said, "You've probably got enough money to do something good for yourself that would turn out to be good for other people."

Arabella sighed. "Oh, yes. A great many people would say it was the least I could do, and that is such a mothy goal, isn't it? I suppose you mean, get myself educated—"

"Or qualified to do something?"

"It would have to start with education. You know, like you can't be a doctor without Latin and mathematics. I feel too old. Too well, too lucky, too lonely, and too *far gone* to do any of that. I expect my mind's already gone to seed. Some people's do, you know, at a terrifying rate. I bet that's the kind I've got."

Anne said, almost timidly, "You seem very intelligent to me."

"Do I, now? Yes, but supposing as *well* as being intelligent I am also rather silly—that's a perfectly disreputable and usual combination, particularly with women; it would mean that I'm too silly to understand how to use my intelligence."

Without asking each other, they both had some more coffee, and brandy to go with it.

"I think," Anne said peacefully, "that I'm just another of those people with a large amount of common sense. I don't think I'm intelligent at all—and certainly not gifted in any way. I'm probably what men mean when they talk approvingly about a feminine woman."

"Yes, I think you are. Lucky you."

"Why?"

"Well, it's much better to be approved of than not. Unless you've got a jolly good reason for being disapproved of, of course. Like Florence Nightingale. Or Joan of Arc."

"But then there are those maddening in-between women, like Jane Austen and Elizabeth Fry, who had jolly good reasons for what they did and managed not to get disapproved of too much while they were doing them."

Arabella, who did not know who Elizabeth Fry was, thought of asking, but decided not to. There seemed to be so very much to talk about that there would be plenty of time to find out about her. What she wanted to do was to find out about Anne. As this curiosity seemed to be mutual, they exchanged confidences, tales of the past, opinions about ideas, God, politics, and back to the differences between men and women.

"The trouble is, *I* think," Arabella said—on her third brandy by now, "is that there are quite simply too many bloody people on this earth for them to be free. I mean, they're bound to be exploited, just because there are so many of them. The trouble about exploitation is that it used to be quite a family or national affair, and now it's become a ghastly great international ideological split. It's much more like the Protestant/Catholic rub that there used to be. I mean, when people honestly thought that the other side would go to hell—which was a real place to them—if they didn't recant. I'm sure the Communists really do feel (I mean the ones who've been educated to that way of thinking) that the rest of us are bound for some kind of material hell. And we think they are. And this means that brave and intelligent people go on being martyred, and everybody puts up with wars because they feel the other side does represent hell in the old-fashioned sense."

"Well, I think Communism *would* be hell," Anne said.

"You may be right. What I mean is that most people aren't given the chance of knowing what anything would be like. There is no sort of free referendum, which in turn means that millions of people can spend their lives starving or undernourished and certainly not *told* anything at all about any other possibility for them. These people are all over the place. If you asked them what they wanted, they'd say, 'Enough to eat.' "

"What about the people who have got enough to eat and still unhold situations that pretty well ensure that the others won't have?"

"That's the rub. Each side would say that it was the other side who aided and abetted that."

"*You* seem to have some ideas about what should happen. Why don't you do something about it?"

"Because I don't want to have any truck with any idea unless I thought it had a chance of working. And I can't think of any idea that would. I keep trying, but I don't have that peculiar gift for being actively contained within my capacities. Drink," she added, a moment later, "always makes me use longer words in a rather hit-or-miss manner."

"But it would be arrogant, surely, to think you could change the whole world? Surely the most anyone can do is to make the best and most of whatever their piece of it seems to be?"

"There, my darling Anne, is our difference. You have the common sense to see that, and act upon it, and I have simply the arrogance—as you say—and consequent laziness to think like somebody who I am not."

The record had long since finished. Arabella got slowly up from the sofa and took it off the gramophone and turned the machine off.

"Let's go to bed," she said.

Upstairs, Anne said, "I must see Ariadne's brood."

They went to Arabella's room together, to find that the kittens and their mother had entirely taken over the bed.

"Oh, really," Anne said. "You can't put up with that."

"What can I do about it? I know: I could come and sleep in your room. You've got a huge bed, and I'm a very quiet sleeper. And if you felt ill in the night, there I'd be."

Anne simply nodded. She felt, as it was suggested, that it would be far nicer to spend the night with Arabella than by herself. They got on so well that it could only be comforting and friendly as an arrangement. "You get your night-gown and come along," was all she said.

When Arabella joined her some ten minutes later, Anne had arrayed herself in the new present: she was also wearing the ring. Arabella appeared in her green trailing garment and, on being asked, opened the windows so that the smell of jasmine and night-scented stocks came into the dusky room. She drew the curtains apart and turned off the light by her side of the bed. Then she pulled off the green robe, under which she wore nothing, and slipped into bed.

"Good night, darling Anne," she said. "You have made such a difference to my life."

She put her arms round Anne and again they kissed. This, which now had the charm of being both new and at the same time on the way to being customary, gave each far more pleasure than the times before. Anne felt a kind of loving admiration for beautiful Arabella, and Arabella was overcome by the warm certainty of being loved. When they had stopped kissing, Anne said, "You do smell nice."

"It's me: it isn't anything out of a bottle. It's supposed to run in the family." Then, she added, "You smell nice, too."

They lay for a few minutes of entire and peaceful amity: neither, then, would rather have been in any other circumstances. Then Arabella withdrew her arms from round Anne's shoulders and said, "I feel a bit drunk and rather sleepy. And I love being in bed with you." She kissed Anne's face—turned towards her—

and her neck, and then her left breast. Then she turned over onto her other side and went to sleep.

Anne, whose breast responded to the kiss—a faint shock of excitement that resounded throughout her body—waited until it was over to think about it, and then decided that there was nothing to think about. Women *are* nicer than men, was the only ripple of an idea that spent itself as she, too, drifted in to sleep.

Edmund, having survived his journey, climbed out of his aeroplane into the hot, spiced air; went through the formalities at the airport, got into a taxi, and was driven riotously into the centre of Athens. He was staying at the Olympic Palace, one of the newer hotels that was admirably run by dispossessed Greeks from Cairo. His room was cold with the air conditioning; furnished as though for an immensely privileged prisoner—nothing unnecessary, everything that could be needed for one night. He waited until the charming boy who had brought his bags to the room had gone, and then went to the window. By peering to his right, he could see the floodlit Parthenon. By not peering at all, very yellow lights, palm trees, traffic, and immense buildings in a state of decomposition or erection were before him. The shock of change, inevitably experienced by any but the constant traveller or the person oblivious to any environment whatsoever, hit him. He tried to think about Mulberry Lodge and its inhabitants, and a confused picture of Anne, feverish and somehow unattractively vulnerable because of her illness, occurred and was uneasily dismissed.

He tried to think about Arabella, in her room, surrounded by Ariadne and her kittens, and at once his mind broke out into a kind of rash of loneliness and longing and distance from her. He tried to think about her calmly—with an indulgent tenderness, to recognize that this separation, by its sudden and temporary nature, would probably be better in the end. But all rational thought dissolved into simply wanting to see, touch, hear and be with her. He had also an aching curiosity about whether *she* was now feeling as he felt, or at all like it, or even a little of some part of it. He decided to drink some of the bottle he had bought on the plane, and to write to her. And so, with water from the tap, and whisky from his briefcase, he set about covering a piece of the hotel air-mail paper.

"My darling Arbell," he began, "I miss you quite unbearably." He crossed out "quite," wrote "Why are you not here? With me?" and then realized that he would have to use a new sheet of paper. Love letters could not have words crossed out in them. He began again. "Darling Arbell, I miss you. Why *etc.*" "I think about you all the time," he proceeded. But this brought him to a halt. There had not been very much time, and it was not true. Love letters must surely be both extreme and truthful to find their mark. He had had no practice at all at such measures. "I don't think I have ever loved anyone in the way that I love you." *Think?* He crossed that out, recognizing that this would have to be a draft: the real letter would have to be written out at the end—when he had managed to express his feelings with all due emotion and sincerity. For he *did* love her, and wanted to tell her so: no question about that. "I keep remembering the lake and the rain—your streaming beauty as the sun came out. . . ." He was away; amazed at himself—his pen rushed back and forth. He finished and poured himself another (neat) whisky without noticing as he covered the page with all the things he might have said to whoever it should have been when he was twenty-one. It was not until he reached the end of the page and the second whisky that he was brought to a sudden and complete standstill. He could not possibly send a letter of this kind—or, really, of any significant kind—to Arabella. Arabella, living with Anne, would be put in an impossible position. The Greek stamp, his handwriting, everything, would give it away. But if he could not write what he felt to Arabella, what was the point of writing at all? He was too tired and had drunk too much to be able to think. It was Anne whom he should be writing to, but he would think about that tomorrow: he had no news for her and could not imagine writing her a letter that contained anything else. The great thing to do about these situations was, he thought, as he got ready for bed, that if one was in any doubt, do nothing. He must retain his sang-froid. He did not consider the problem of retaining what he had never, so far, turned out either to need or employ.

Janet lay alone in bed. She was hungry, and anxious and depressed and sorry for everything that was, or was not, happening to her. When she had got back with the shopping to Henry's expected greeting (if you could call it that), he had gone on to say that he had to leave that afternoon for his two or three days' work filming in Oswestry. She didn't believe him, and then she did, and then she didn't care much which was right. She asked him for money; knowing that he probably hadn't got any, and that, if he had, *she* wouldn't get it, and then washed and ironed his supposedly drip-dry shirt, as he required her to do. His going meant that the food she had brought could be made to last far longer; it also meant that she was in the same state of anxious and monotonous suspension that seemed to be all her life now. She had fed the children, and Henry had had a bath—which meant that nobody else could for God knew how long. She thought how marvellous it would be to be somewhere like the Arts Theatre Club with—well, practically anyone—telling her what a good actress she was going to be and giving her delicious food and drink. Henry went at about four; then she tried ringing a few friends, but they all knew what her life and situation was like, and they were all too near it to want any experience—even second-hand. She couldn't say, "Come and have a drink and tell me the gossip," because there wasn't any drink. She couldn't even make anyone a decent meal. In the end, she found a middle-aged mid-European actress—good at her work, but unbeautiful and unwanted except for neurotic character parts. This woman turned up, and they ate corned-beef hash while the woman told her what sods men were, and Henry in particular. She was glad when Lisa went. The woman combined a hatred of men with a maddening, Freudian-all-knowing comprehension of Janet's life. She had brought a quarter bottle of gin with her, and, after what might be described as more than her fair share of this, her Lesbian tendencies became distressingly apparent. Janet found this at once horrifying and absurd. She didn't want to go to bed with any bloody woman, thank you very much. And men were not all as Lisa described them, although she was disastrously right about Henry. Whenever Janet tried to be practical about her situation, Lisa accused her of being cold, and British, and practical. She disposed or, or ignored, the children as one might bedbugs or influenza. Nothing chronically serious, simply the products of ill management. When she left, she said how marvellous it had been to have a serious talk with anyone in this country, and Janet tried to imagine what an unserious talk could have been like. She had wanted to be cheered, not sneered at. So now she was back—not exactly where she had started—hardly anyone, she reflected, could ever be that, but back to the stalemate of her life that she reckoned a hell of a lot of people had to contend with. No career, because of the children; no money, because of Henry. The children because of Henry; and no alternative to Henry because of the children. Luke began his nightly howling. She got, shivering, out of bed to try and deal with that.

Part Five

Arabella woke early in the morning. Because the curtains were not drawn, the first sunlight woke her, and she lay in the pretty room in the comfortable bed and thought how good everything was. Anne, asleep, looked far younger, more vulnerable, and even more feminine than Anne awake. She lay on her side, turned towards Arabella, with one corner of the pillow bent under itself to raise her head. Her short and dark hair was in curly disarray, her eyes fast shut, and the look of resolution that is often apparent in people fast and seriously asleep made Arabella feel older, protective, and full of affection. She watched Anne quietly for some time: there seemed to be no dividing line at all between the kinds of feeling one could have for somebody. Women *are far* nicer than men, occurred to her as a thought (it was one that she had had before in her life):

they seemed to set more store by continuous affection; they did not regard sex as a kind of foray from which one emerged at square one; they liked talking when given the chance—about sex when given the chance—and they were not, or hardly ever, so concerned with their pride, their *amour propre*, their conceit or whatever. They were humbler, more grateful creatures, taking human relations seriously and acute about any reciprocation. She is a nice, good, dear, even darling girl, Arabella thought, and I'd give anything in the world to have breasts like that. How wonderful it would be if *she*, Arabella, could have a child—in the family, so to speak—and they could all live happily (in the same place) ever after. I conceive at the drop of a hat, she thought; Anne doesn't want children, but if I looked after them, she'd simply find out how good it was having them. Edmund could supply the children, and Anne and I could have a lovely time bringing them up. What seemed absolutely extraordinary to her was the way most people told you beforehand that anything but the most tried principles of social relations couldn't work out. How did they know, if they'd never tried them? But they wouldn't try them, because they were so afraid that if they *didn't* work out, everybody else would be able to tell them why not. I mustn't spoil things, she thought: Anne—like most people, would think something was wrong with her if I could make her as happy as Edmund clearly can. She hoped that Edmund would find he had to stay in Greece much longer than he had expected to do.

After four days (it was now Tuesday), Edmund realized that Sir William had been right about the potentialities in Greece; he also realized that he was not going to manage to do what had been expected of him in two weeks. He therefore sent two cables: one to Sir William explaining that it would all take longer than he had thought, and one to Anne explaining that it would all take longer than he had thought. By now, he had been on trips to Hydra and Spetsai, and then, branching out a bit, to Naxos, Ios, and Paros. All this took a great deal of time. The first part, the

Hydra-Spetsai part, was relatively easy, but the other islands bore little or no relation to one another, which meant that in between each excursion he had to return to Piraeus (or Athens) and start again. He drank innumerable cups of coffee and ouzo with various people. He took to sleeping after lunch—when possible—sometime after four in the afternoon, and not expecting to dine until ten or eleven at night. He journeyed with Greeks whose command of English was more than adequate, who provided him with ravishingly pretty girls in the evening who spoke not a word of his language. After four days, the superiority of men over women in Greece caught hold, and he went to bed with a very young, dark-haired girl, who was entirely acquiescent to his deepest wish. He began to enjoy himself. The incredible and continuous beauty of the country had reached his senses; the excellent food and wine—so much decried by those who have had no experience of it—made him feel both exceedingly well and partially happy. Arabella receded in his mind, and Anne was hardly there at all. He congratulated himself on how adaptable he was, and enjoyed his total lack of emotional responsibility.

"Think how *awful* it would have been, having this cheating disease with Edmund going off every morning, and no you."

"Well, you don't have to, because here Edmund isn't, and here I am."

They were making raspberry jam together. Anne's illness came and went, much as Dr. Travers had predicted, but when she felt ill, they both repaired to her bedroom, where Arabella had moved the television set, and sat or lay in bed together watching it in a desultory way.

"It really tells you too little about too much of the world," Arabella had said, quite soon after this regime had established itself: "so one can really afford to be pretty frivolous about it. It's a kind of 'gather ye causes while ye may' policy which it's easy not to take too seriously."

By now, they ate rather expensive food procured by Arabella and either not needing to be prepared at all or done by Anne. The

) 213 (

raspberry jam was simply a daytime pursuit, because Anne happened to feel up to it. By now, Arabella had abandoned her room to Ariadne, and Anne enjoyed their evenings together in her bedroom. They drank rather a lot, because Arabella seemed to arrange that, and Anne felt—after the stories of lecherous stepfathers—that Arabella was owed almost anything. There was no more news of Clara, but if there had been, Anne felt able to deal with her, whatever her temperature turned out to be at such a time.

After Edmund's cable had arrived, Arabella said, "Well, he must be enjoying himself, or he wouldn't want to stay longer. Isn't that marvellous?"

"He's never been away so long."

"But you're all right, aren't you? So when he comes back, you won't make him feel guilty."

"Of course not."

The jam was setting: Anne had put little bits of it on saucers, and now it was behaving as it should. Anne put it into the warmed jars, and Arabella wrote out what it was in her best writing.

"What are we having for dinner?"

"I thought quite a lot of champagne, and then some smoked trout."

"I'm a bit tired."

"We'll have it in bed."

By now, Arabella had taken to having her baths at night in Anne's bathroom. Embarrassment about their naked selves had ceased between them. Each had reason for envying—or admiring —the other. As Arabella got into bed with Anne (it was Thursday by now), she said, "Are you missing Edmund? I mean, your sex life and all that?"

"The funny thing is that I don't think I am." Anne laughed rather nervously after this remark, and then said, "It's extraordinary. Sometimes I wish *you* were a man."

"Why?"

"I don't know exactly. I suppose because I enjoy our life together so much that I don't want— I mean, I wish there wasn't a stopping point."

"There isn't one, really."

Arabella turned out the single light remaining in the room. "I can make you feel wonderful: I can't give you a child, but you don't want that."

"No—I don't want—" Anne began, and then Arabella started to kiss her, and her whole body responded to her mouth being kissed. Arabella kissed her mouth, and then her breasts—in between, she said how lovely they were—and as her hands moved down over Anne's body, there was nothing but the most sensitive excitement.

"You taste like moss down here," Arabella said, and Anne reached, overcame, and was ready for the next peak of pleasure. "I love you," Arabella said, at exactly the right moment. Anne was lost, in love, in feeling, in the perfect balance of equality. Arabella would not be doing any of this unless she wanted to: Anne could abandon herself to Arabella's desires without question. She did not know what Arabella expected of her in return; in one sense, she had the uncertain passivity of a virgin, but when Arabella made her cry out from her extreme joy, she flung her arms round her lover and heard Arabella utter a sound of both triumph and gratitude, followed by a long, shuddering sigh of contentment.

They lay then in complete silence until the last tremor of each body was spent, and then Arabella whispered, "Do you love me, Anne? *Do* you?" And Anne, with arms still round—and not to break whatever this spell was—whispered back, "I *do* love you— with all my—" But here Arabella covered her mouth with a hand, and then they kissed once more: to Anne, it was the most gentle, the most loving kiss that she had ever given or received in her life. Then they slept.

Edmund was away, in fact, for just over five weeks. This was partly because he twice got stuck on islands owing to bad weather conditions, and got once, but once and for all, most thoroughly stuck with his opposite number in Athens. Mr. Andros was a jolly, even frenetically friendly man, but the consequence of this was that his life was spent on several levels at once. Business was his pleasure, and women were his relaxation, and he seemed to have more than his fair share of both. Whenever Edmund went to meet him, his telephone rang without stopping; whenever they met outside Mr. Andros's office, a wealth of social and emotional intercourse intervened. Mr. Andros combined the inability to say no to absolutely everyone, with an immense interest in plans, possibilities, alternatives and conspiracies: if arrangements fell through, which they frequently did, he hardly noticed it, so bent was he on what they would or might be doing whatever happened to anything. Once, in desperation, Edmund visited his house, where he met a melancholy wife and two children: she had no idea where her husband was, and seemed surprised that this should in the least surprise Edmund. Mr. Andros was perpetually concerned that Edmund should be enjoying himself and went to considerable and various lengths to secure this state, or, at least, to give it the maximum chance. But Mr. Andros's life was so enriched by the complexities of friends and/or business acquaintances who simply did not reply to letters, who were never where they had said they would be, and whose telephones, when they had them, broke down the moment that they were subject to common usage, that it did not strike him as the least astonishing that Edmund should fail to effect any concrete business. "That is how it goes. *How* it goes! One spends three-quarters of the life in uncertainty, and the last quarter in despair. So—one must remain unmoved. Life will most certainly continue—excuse, please, while I make this call, and we will then have some kind of good dinner when we have located where are my friends who so much want to meet you if only they can be found. You will see. All simply cannot turn out for the worst." But Edmund was simply anxious for anything to turn out at all. If he found a suitable site for building, he could not find or deal with the owners; if he found a villa, it always seemed uncertain whether the people who were reputed to own it actually did, or whether they were making, or had made, other arrangements. Once he was shown a whole island: no water on it, but a small and very beautiful place. This might be bought for hardly any money at all, Mr. Andros said, but he did not know for how much, and whoever owned it seemed unattainable. In the end, Edmund abandoned himself to making lists of places, houses, islands, beaches, and people. He also found that the life in Greece was extraordinarily enjoyable: amusing, restful, zestful, and easy. When he thought of returning home, it was to a—by now—distant decision, which lost none of its horror by its distance: and his natural disinclination to make decisions was encouraged more in this country than any he had ever been to. One night he got very drunk with Mr. Andros and told him that he had two women in his life. Mr. Andros politely concealed his lack of astonishment at this, and said that this was the lot of all men. In his opinion, he said, some three hours later of his opinions, the only way to deal with this was to marry as well as possible for the children and family life, and to have the right kind of girl on the side for one's amusement and pleasure. This, he said, was not at all difficult: most women here were glad of respectability and children, and, for the rest, if Edmund did not mind his saying so, there were plenty of attractive foreigners whose attitude was entirely different. Edmund found that he less and less minded Mr. Andros's saying such things. He concealed from him the fact that he had no children, since they seemed to rank diplomatically high in Mr. Andros's estimation. But he enjoyed the partial confidence, and the fact that Mr. Andros clearly thought the more of him for his infidelity. "It is natural. For us, it is a part: for women it must be all, or they are bad women, with whom one would not wish a permanent alliance." The family came first, although the day-to-day order would seem to be sporadic. Edmund, very drunk, agreed with him. Mr. Andros took him tenderly back to his hotel and put him in charge of the excellent night porter. Next day, Edmund, with a hangover, sent two more cables: to his office and his home. UNABLE RETURN. DEALS NOT YET COMPLETED. And DESPERATELY SORRY. BUSINESS HERE FAR MORE COMPLEX THAN

ORIGINALLY ENVISAGED. This latter cable arrived indecipherably mangled at Mulberry Lodge.

"Beeznis more *what?*" Anne and Arabella hung over the telegram together and laughed, and tried again and gave it up.

One of the best things, Anne thought, about their relationship, was the way in which Arabella, at least, never seemed to load it with anything. By "anything" she meant the extraordinary and wonderful nights that sometimes they spent. The days were so good that Anne did not mind the sometimes part of the nights at all. If it happened, it happened, and whether it did or not, their days were filled with the most active intimacy. She taught Arabella something about cooking, and also about novels: Arabella showed her her favourite music and imparted to each day a holiday air. Sometimes Anne's illness overcame her, and she had simply to lie in bed, throat and glands aching, a fever and a headache. Then the sweetness of Arabella came into its own. She looked after Anne; she looked after the house; she betrayed none of the irritable impatience that all men—even Edmund, Anne reflected—would have betrayed to her. Between them, they decided to write a letter to the solicitors who sent Arabella her money when she asked her mother for it. They wrote it for hours, until it came out in the shortest, most businesslike manner. Arabella wished simply to know whether her father had left her anything absolutely, either in the form of investments or actual capital.

The weather continued to be fine: they began eating artichokes. They went for a picnic on the river, in the punt that Edmund had bought when they moved there but hardly ever used. They went about midday and returned late. By now, they had become completely easy with each other. Nobody had ever made Anne proud of her breasts, and when she realized that Arabella actually envied them, she said (that day, in the punt), "But yours have got much larger: I've noticed."

"Have you?" asked Arabella. She looked almost frightened.

"What shall we do when Edmund does come back?" Anne had asked that evening.

"Wait and see *how* he comes back. There is nothing to worry about: we don't have to lie to one another."

Anne began to say, "But what else could we do?" when Arabella started to make love to her, and she couldn't and didn't want to say anything.

Arabella did most, if not all, the driving into Henley or Maidenhead for supplies. "There is no reason why you should ever leave," Anne said one evening. Arabella had not replied to this. She had had an answer from the solicitors to the effect that their only instructions from the Princess Radamacz were to pay her five hundred a year. They had not handled her family's estate, and therefore could not give her any further information. Five hundred! But she had paid that man with his rubber gloves a hundred and fifty and thought nothing of it. She started to think about being independent—possibly with a dependent. Nothing added up at all. Everything, she imagined, might be changed by what Edmund felt about the whole situation.

A letter came from Clara telling her that she absolutely must join the yacht by the end of the month, as there had, in fact, been delays in refitting her, and so everybody had been stuck in a villa at Cannes. She also sent her a cheque for five hundred pounds— "and for goodness sake buy yourself some reasonable cruising clothes"—and a note authorizing Arabella to take the jewels left by Clara with Cartier on her last visit to London and bring them to Cannes. Her first-class air ticket—open, not dated—was also enclosed. These communications set up a miserable conflict in Arabella. Anne quickly realized this, and it was not long before she was shown the letter and ticket. The note for Cartier Arabella kept to herself. She did not quite know why she did this, and she determined not to try and find out. When Anne had helped her to stop feeling too awful about Clara, she managed to write a short note back. *Edmund is still away*, it went; *Anne had glandular fever (which I may very well have caught from her), so I cannot possibly come out to you until it is known I am not infectious.* This, she knew, would get Clara, who was terrified of any infection, even common colds, and glandular fever would fill her with alarm and abhorrence. In fact, a cable arrived within two days: ON NO ACCOUNT LEAVE COUNTRY UNTIL CLEAR OF INFECTION it ran. So that was that.

"Now you can stop worrying, darling Arabella," Anne said gaily.

They were in the greenhouse, and she was potting up the tomato seedlings—now a good three inches high. Arabella was helping by cracking up bits of broken pots to put in the bottom of unbroken ones—for drainage, as Anne had explained to her. Together, they had mixed up the potting mixture—Anne made her own brand—in a wheelbarrow. The greenhouse, whose top windows and door were open, smelled, nonetheless, of bruised tomato leaves, damp earth, and a sweet, fruity aroma that came, perhaps, from the early-ripening nectarines on its main wall. Mr. Leaf had painted the top windows with greeny-white paint: he had done it very badly, like a child painting in a rage, so that the corners of panes were bare and the middles streaky. Bees came in and out like sightseers—nothing much here, let's move on; funny, it smelled all right from a distance. The light was either aqueous or shot with the brilliant streaks of sun that shone in the bright blue sky.

"Shall I half-fill some pots now?" Arabella asked.

"You can do the whole thing, if you like."

"Oh, no! I'd be afraid to. I might kill the poor things."

"You've got to learn. Supposing I take a turn for the worse half-way through this, what would happen to the seedlings?"

"All right."

Arabella watched carefully while Anne showed her how to prise out a seedling with a knife—so gently that it came out with all its roots intact—put it into a half-filled pot, and then sprinkle and press more earth round it.

When she had done one, she said, "I used to be perfectly happy doing this entirely by myself: now I can't really imagine feeling perfectly happy doing anything without you."

Arabella looked pleased and at the same time nervous. Anne, who was, by now, acutely sensitive to almost anything connected with Arabella, put down her flowerpot and knelt beside her on the greenhouse floor.

"What is it? You're worrying about something. Is it this wretched business of feeling you have to go on the yacht? Is it Clara you're worrying about? Because, even if I can't, I'm sure that Edmund can cope with her—if he really tries."

"Supposing he doesn't *want* to try?"

"Why shouldn't he?"

Arabella turned away. "If you can't see that, I can't explain to you."

Anne *could* see, but she very much didn't want to. The implications of Edmund's return were, literally, beyond her. What she tried—and generally succeeded in—feeling was that she and Edmund loved each other, she and Arabella loved each other, so surely, unless Edmund took a positive dislike to Arabella (which he had shown no signs of doing before he went away), *surely* things must work out somehow?

As though Arabella could read her thoughts, she now said, "It depends what he—what Edmund—asks. And then what he feels."

Anne thought, He'd never *think* of asking that: because he'd *never* think of that possibility. Then she thought again, and said, rather timidly, for she was a creature without natural vanity, "You don't mean that you might feel, you might find that you would be—"

"Jealous? No, that's not what I meant. I think it would be much better if we all loved one another without any secrecy or bad feelings."

"Well—I don't think I'd like—in fact, I'm sure I *wouldn't* like to spend the night in bed with both of you." This seemed to her an absurd idea; it had not occurred to her that Arabella's instincts and feelings might be as varied as her own. As usual, when this topic occurred, which it did as little as possible, they stopped it by mutual consent before it ran either of them into some (possibly different) cul-de-sac. For the rest of the afternoon, they potted tomatoes: Anne did fifty and Arabella ten. Then they lay under the cedar and drank iced and well-minted Pimm's and listened to the birds, changing from blackbirds to owls as the sun went down, a creamy mist rose from the river at the end of the garden, and the stocks began to fill the air with their scent.

"Have you any money?" Arabella asked, much later in bed.

"How do you mean? Oh. None of my own. Edmund gives me everything I need."

"Oh. I see," she added, with careful lightness.

The beginning of the fourth week of Edmund's absence, Anne's illness seemed very much on the wane. Her literary agent friend rang up and asked if she could come down for dinner and the night, and Anne, although she did not at all want her, was too honest to lie about Edmund's absence or her illness, and therefore was left with no decent excuse.

"Len is coming for one night. Just dinner and one night," she told Arabella.

"Who is he?"

"She's a she. She's really called Leonora, but she hates that, so everybody calls her Len. She's one of my oldest friends," she added, not saying that, in fact, she was her *only* old friend. Except for Mrs. Gregory and Dr. Travers—who in their different ways hardly counted as company—Anne and Arabella had not spent any time at all with a third person, since, of course, Edmund. The first question was where Len, or Leonora, was to sleep. Ordinarily, she could have had Arabella's room—which she now used simply to keep her numerous possessions in and which was otherwise dominated by increasingly active and rather wicked kittens, whose characters, Arabella said, were going to the dogs, as their mother seemed to have got tired of them. They were lapping up bowls of milk, Farex, and minced-up fish by now, and stamped and swore at each other throughout their numerous meals. Ariadne still cleaned them up and played a few half-hearted games of ambush with them—letting them win—but on the whole she preferred to leave them to their intense and monotonous devices. These consisted of fighting/playing with each other almost all the time that they were not asleep, being washed, or eating. It was decided that Len should be put in the other spare room, and that Arabella, who had, in any case, been rumpling up her bed each morning for Mrs. Gregory's sake, should spend a night of unknown frightfulness with Ariadne's brood. "Although, really, I think it is time they were shoved out. Why don't we do that anyway? They can jolly well sleep in the scullery."

"I think I'd like *one* night with them. Let's do it the next day."

So Mrs. Gregory prepared the spare room, and Anne and Arabella went shopping for food. Their usual ways of eating—delicious snacks whenever they felt like it—would have to be forgone. "Len thinks I'm a frightfully good cook," Anne explained, almost apologetically.

"Well—you are."

They planned on iced borsch, a haddock mousse and a green salad, and some cheese—whatever could be had.

"There are always raspberries," Anne said. "We may be a bit tired of them, but *she* won't be."

"And I suppose we can't watch 'The Avengers' if she's here."

"We could, if we brought the set downstairs."

"Not worth it. Anyway, she'd probably think it rude. What shall we be talking about?" she enquired later, as she drove—barefoot, as usual—into Henley. With Anne, she drove very slowly and carefully, much in the way she had driven on the first occasion by herself.

"It's funny: I always think of you as a very dashing driver."

"Not with people. I don't mind being driven fast—in fact, I like it—but I never do it myself, because I don't want to be the killer or killing person."

"Do you mean, you wouldn't mind if someone else killed you?"

"Yes."

"Oh, darling! I would!"

"Oh, darling, I won't let them, then."

They bought the food, and then Arabella wanted a Mars bar and the shop that sold them also sold ice-cream, so they each had one of those. Anne refused more than a bite of a Mars bar because she said she would get too fat. Arabella said there was nothing more annoying than somebody wanting one bite of anything that the other person was meaning to have all of. Anne then bought six Mars bars for Arabella, which were put into a weak paper bag.

Len arrived about seven. Arabella, who was changing out of raspberry-stained jeans into something tidier, heard her arrival, looked out of a window, and saw a gentle-looking middle-aged woman with her hair in a white bun get slowly out of a red drophead MG. She carried one small, expensive-looking brief case and was wearing a green linen suit. Arabella, still watching, saw Anne come out of the house, greet and embrace her in a manner both familiar and perfunctory. They had obviously treated each other in this way for years. Then they disappeared through the front door of the house and she heard it shut. She picked a jasmine flower from outside her window and idly sucked its nectar. Then she wondered what she ought to wear, as she felt anxious about making a good impression with Anne's friend. In the end, she settled for a pale-pink sleeveless silk jersey that had a gold chain belt to go with it. She had some pink sandals some-where, if only she could find them. As she brushed her hair, she suddenly felt rather sick, and then so sick that she knew she would have to go and be it. By the time this was over, she had washed her face, and was again brushing her hair, Anne was calling to her: "Come down and meet Len."

Len and Anne were sitting at the entrance to the french win-dows in the sitting-room. Len was drinking a pink gin and soda, and Anne said that she had opened some champagne. Arabella said she would rather have a brandy and soda. Anne looked faintly surprised, but said nothing, and, having introduced the two women, went to get Arabella her drink.

"I hear you've been looking after Anne while she's been ill and Edmund is abroad."

Len smoked small cigars, and offered one now to Arabella, who shook her head.

"It hasn't been very difficult. In fact, I've enjoyed it."

"And Anne is looking as though she is far better, and Edmund is due back any day now?"

As these seemed to be statements, rather than questions, Arabella simply nodded. Then, she asked, "What is being a literary agent like?" She felt it might be useful to know, in case she hadn't enough money and it turned out that she could be one.

"Well—*I* like it, or I wouldn't have stuck it for the last fifteen years. But it is rather like dealing with a host of egomaniacs on one side and a lot of artists *manqués* or businessmen *manqués* on the other."

"How do you mean?" Anne had come back into the room with Arabella's drink, which she took gratefully, refusing a cigarette at the same time.

"Well—nearly all authors are in need of endless comfort. *They* call it encouragement, but what it really is is flattery. They can't help it, poor things, it's the solitary confinements they are so constantly prey to. Writing," she added to make her point clear. "And then, most publishers either think they have a genius for picking a good writer without anyone else's help, or, and often, they think they are public servants, scraping along with the minimum of backing, and therefore fearfully astute to be there at all. This makes them tend to be stolid and mean. I'm in between. I have to negotiate the proper price for material that the solitary genius feels is priceless and the publishers often feel it is rather kind of them to publish at all. It is frightfully funny a lot of the time. They're both wrong, you see, nearly always, but it is hopeless to say so."

"If you think that, why aren't you a publisher? Or a writer?"

"I'm not a writer because I'm not a writer, and I'm not a publisher because nobody has every asked me to be one. Also, I enjoy the freedom of being this kind of middleman. I *like* flattering authors because I've sincerely learned how awful it must be to be one, and I *like* dealing with publishers because a lot of them care about their product, as it were. Not all, of course, but some. I'm in it for the people, really," she finished. Then, looking at Anne, she said, "A far cry from our Pitman's Intensive Course. I've never seen you looking so well. Glandular fever must have its points."

"I feel fine now."

"The other good thing is that every now and then, out of the blue, one finds a really good writer. That makes a lot of the rest of it worth while. I've always told Anne that she would make a marvellous manuscript reader. She's omnivorous, you see. And if you stay like that long enough, you acquire a taste. Are you a great reader?"

"I'm hardly a reader at all. Anne has been introducing me, as it were. It isn't one of my resources—if indeed, I have any."

"You have music. Arabella is devoted to music, and she knows a hell of a lot about it." Anne said this to Len, and, in a way, this set the tone for the evening. Anne was constantly extolling one to the other, and having these encouragements either ignored or given the minimum of attention. Len wanted to talk about the past with Anne, and the present in her work. Arabella wanted to talk about the present with Anne, and not very much at all with Len, whom she did not dislike so much as feel afraid of. She had some odd idea that a person who read constantly—and chiefly fiction, at that—might know some difficult things about human nature that she did not want to have explained to her.

They had dinner in the kitchen. Arabella ate very little, which worried Anne, who tried to conceal this and succeeded with Len and not at all with Arabella. "I ate some Mars bars: they've filled me up," she explained to Len. Len ate a great deal, talked considerably—and not boringly, Arabella decided—and the small forays that were made into Anne and Len's past were obviously now too routine to them both to require much audience or indeed time. After raspberries—only Len had them—they decided to have coffee in the sitting-room.

While Anne was making this, Len and Arabella were left on their own.

"What are you going to do when you leave here?" Len asked.

"I haven't the slightest idea." Arabella said this stiffly, because she was so frightened by the prospect that she could not imagine anyone's asking her from either idle or amiable curiosity.

"I'd like to get some sort of job, I suppose."

"What kind?"

"Well—you see, I don't know. I'm not in the least qualified for anything."

"Can you type?"

"No. Honestly, I can't do anything," she said, having tried a Gauloise and found that she still didn't want to smoke.

"*Get* qualified, my dear. That's the only thing to do, unless you fall in love or don't care whom you marry."

Anne arrived with the coffee at this point. Arabella felt then so unhappy, so hopelessly out of what must be presumed to be her depths, that she felt she should go to bed. However, she did not want to worry Anne, so she drank some coffee and a little green Chartreuse that Len turned out to have brought with her as a present.

"Do you remember? *Don't* overtype, Miss Hayling. That awful woman in a spotted muslin dress and spots everywhere else, who prowled about and changed the gramophone records."

"And you always managed to get away with murder. They simply gave me up when it came to shorthand."

"Nonsense! *You* gave it up. You met Edmund. People like Edmund are thin on the ground," she added, turning to include Arabella in this part of the conversation.

"I met Edmund *long* after that—" Anne began, and then couldn't be bothered to finish the argument. She suggested that Arabella put on some music, and so she did. This did not pre-cisely bring all conversation to an end, but it provided, as Ara-bella had previously noticed that it often did, a let-out in the way of serious attention. Divide the attention: that was the thing.

But the time came when Anne said that she was going to do one or two things in the kitchen, and would Arabella look after Len. She said this so firmly that neither of the other two thought of arguing with her. When she had gone, shutting the door behind her, Arabella got to her feet to take off the record, and said, "Would you like some more of your own drink to drink?"

"What I would really like would be a whisky and soda, if that's possible."

"Oh, yes, I think so." Glad of the employment, she opened the drinks cupboard and found the whisky and a glass. "It's really Edmund's evening drink, that's why it's put away."

"Have you known Edmund and Anne for long?"

"Only a few weeks. And Edmund had to go away after I'd been here about a week." She decided to give herself a stiff brandy and soda, and to have one more shot at a cigarette. She sensed danger —not hostility, but danger, which was somehow far worse. The cigarette seemed all right: she took a deep draw on it and said, "Edmund and I are sort of related. My mother was once married to his father."

"And are you and Anne sort of related too?"

"What do you mean?"

"You know what I mean."

Arabella turned to face her steadily. "Right. Well, yes, we are —since you ask."

"I didn't really have to ask: I knew."

"Why did you, then? To get me to admit?"

"No. To get you to see." She lit another small cigar and leaned forward. "Look: I'm not a bitch or full of prurient curiosity. But if in one evening—in a few hours—I can tell what the situation is, what do you think will happen when Edmund gets back?"

"Men don't notice the same things as women," Arabella said weakly.

"No: not always, but it does depend on the thing. I think Edmund is very devoted to Anne, and I know she has been very happy with him, so I don't see much future in subterfuge there, do you?"

"I have never been in favour of subterfuge," Arabella said coldly.

"Oh. Just in favour of messing up other people's lives."

"*No!* I *don't* want to do anything to hurt Anne—or him. I just want a peaceful happy life with . . . people who want that too—with me in it."

There was a short, painful silence, while the hopelessness of Arabella's desires sank deeply into her, leaving a gap between her conscience and her heart.

This white-haired woman, who looked much older than she can have been, knew far too much too easily and soon, and the implications of this were obvious. *Anyone*—or almost anyone—would know. A wild vision of taking Anne away with her to some little croft in Scotland where they could live on the practically nothing that five hundred a year seemed now to her to be, with Ariadne, perhaps, there would be fish in the sea and she would not be expensive to feed . . . The whole vision went out too soon, like a damp firework, leaving the desert dark.

"I'm afraid I haven't thought properly about it. Although I know I've got to," she said at last, unaware that her voice was shaking.

"Look, Arabella—if I may call you that—if you're stuck, you could always come and stay with me. I've got a flat in London with a spare room of sorts. I won't complicate your life, but it might come in useful."

"It is very kind of you, but I am quite all right. My mother, who has a lot of money, has rented a yacht and wants me to go on a Mediterranean cruise with her. So, you see, I don't need anyone's help. Thank you," she added. Tears were burning in her eyes, and she longed more than anything to get away from this kind, perceptive stranger. "I'm just waiting," she went on almost inaudibly, but not realizing it; "I'm just waiting until I'm out of danger from Anne's fever—that's all." She turned her back on Len, as she leaned against the fireplace and drank all the rest of her drink as quickly as possible.

Before Len could reply—if, indeed, she was going to do that

) 229 (

—Anne returned. Almost at once, Arabella said, "I'm off to bed. Good night, everybody." She gave a general, unseeing nod to the others and left.

She undressed in what all the time had been supposed to be her room, went to the bathroom, got enough kittens off the bed and into an open suitcase with a cardigan in it, and got into bed. All this time, she did not put on any light in her room. She had shut the door, and the moment that she lay down, she wept. She dimly heard the others come upstairs, their exchange of good nights, and could tell by the crack under her door that landing lights were put out. Still, she cried. From sheer practice, she had learned to cry silently: it was too long since the bitterness of being unhappy had ever been assuaged by the presence of anyone else. I am a crier, she told herself. I cry about anything: it's a kind of reflex—doesn't even count. All the times when matrons at schools had assumed her to be homesick (homesick!) or sickening for something, or people whom she had thought she might come to know and who had turned out to be total strangers when it came to the frightening point, or her mother had told her to pull herself together, or her mother's men had lied, first to her and then to her mother—infatuation—very young—been spoiled (how?)—oh, yes, far too much money too young—a change of scene would make all the difference, and, by god, it had, but not of the kind they had in mind: all these times had taught her secrecy and silence that broke down only when her mother assailed her in front of other people. Then she could not contain herself. But it was all frivolity; it must be: nobody went through life with such an anonymous undercurrent of unhappiness unless there was something missing in *them*. So the bitterest tears were private ones: music was the only thing that made her cry *and* feel joy—as though her heart was growing and the tears were a release. It was not being different from other people that frightened her, it was being worse. Churches that she had so often gone into alone at different times of the day in different countries, they had all made her weep from feeling this. Even Christ had had friends—even though they temporarily let Him down, nonetheless He had them. She did not seem worthy of a friend.

She must have wept for the best part of an hour, until her eyes were nearly closed from the burning flow and the rest of her body cold with the effort of trying to bear it or stop, before the door opened and Anne came in. She shut the door at once, got straight into bed, and, feeling the soaking pillow and wet hair, took Arabella in her arms. For a long time, she didn't say anything, simply comforted; she didn't ask questions or assume that she knew why Arabella was unhappy, and these two omissions made everything much better. It was as though Anne was talking to her through her gentle hands: saying that she loved her, and that everything was all right, that there was nothing wrong about any kind of true love. The only thing she said in the end was, "I *do* love you, and if you love me, it must be all right." They kissed then, and touching Arabella's salty, soft mouth, Anne felt a tenderness, a sense of exaltation that she must, at all costs, protect. "I love you also," was all that Arabella managed to say. They slept in each other's arms in the same position for the rest of the night.

The next morning, Anne, kissing Arabella once more, slipped out of bed and left to make breakfast and behave as though nothing had happened. She had wondered, the previous evening with Len, whether Len had had anything to do with Arabella's state, but had concluded that she couldn't have. Len had spoken of her with merely objective, intelligent kindness. Anne had known Len during the one great affair of her life, but the man had died of throat cancer, and Len, having seen him through that with all her heart, had nothing left that she felt like giving to anybody else. She had therefore concentrated upon her career: she was extremely good at it, and consequently reached a position that most women with careers cannot reach, since too much of their emotional energy is siphoned off by whatever man they are involved with. To women writers she was a mother or very good schoolmistress, to men a mother and a very good agent. It worked, and she was not unhappy now. Nothing she said to Anne could give the latter any idea that she had tried to or had inadvertently upset Arabella. All the same, Anne was relieved when, after coffee and orange juice, Len climbed into her little red car and made off for London and her office.

By the middle of the fifth week in Greece, it became clear to Edmund that there was really going to be nothing more that he could possibly do after the following week-end. The week-end was, or had become, that admixture of business and pleasure in which Mr. Andros so much excelled. They were to go out in a caïque, with a suitable accompaniment of pretty girls, to places that Edmund could not possibly see without the caïque. Edmund, by now, looked forward to it with simple pleasure. His life, he felt, had either been corrupted or enlarged by Mr. Andros, and whichever this might turn out to be was at the time so enjoyable that he did not much care. He had had one letter from Anne, in which she had said that she had glandular fever and that Arabella was dealing with it admirably, and the whole thing seemed distant, and immediately distasteful. He loved his sense of not being responsible. He loved the late hours, the fact that he need only look at and enjoy things without having to make decisions about them, and he reflected, with a touch of self-pitying defiance, that it was high time something—of this sort—happened to him. The last night of all, Mr. Andros took him to Turkoleimon, where the clam merchants with their suitcases and the children with their gardenias and jasmine gave him a feeling of well-being and excitement that was by now familiar. This was the life: this was the country for the life. He ate clams and lobster (Mr. Andros kept explaining that if only he stayed a few more weeks there would be quail) and drank a great deal of retsina, ate a very good salad and delicious grapes. The evening blood heat of the air, the violence of the lights installed by the new mayor, the stench from the water that the mayor had not somehow begun to work upon, all made him feel at home. Another dark-haired girl with whom he had spent one—not entirely satisfactory—night seemed on this evening to promise better things. He was due to fly at midday on Sunday. Make the most of it. He bought a sponge for Anne and a Greek bag for Arabella, and a bottle of Citro from Naxos for himself. He decided that, in future, he would ask Sir William to send him anywhere. This was far more interesting than catching the commuters' train to and from Waterloo. And he felt, by now, that he could view both Anne and even Arabella in their proper perspectives. The girl came back with him to his hotel, and they spent an enquiring night with some good moments.

Mr. Andros insisted on seeing him off. His pale, rather greasy face was contorted with dismay at Edmund's departure. They embraced awkwardly. "Bring back your wife. Or anyone at all," was Mr. Andros's open and warm invitation. But, after this time there, Edmund could not imagine being in Greece with one's *wife*. Arabella, perhaps, but she had had none of the—almost indigenous—desire to please that Edmund had encountered with the girls Mr. Andros had provided. He got into his aeroplane, feeling heroically injured by he didn't know whom.

When he reached Heathrow, he rang Anne, who answered almost at once. She sounded nearly aggrieved that he hadn't given her more warning. "I'll be back in about an hour, I expect," he had concluded. Actually, it would be far more than that. The sun seemed muted after Greece, the sky far more compromising, and he felt almost cold until he put on his macintosh. He had to go to London to fetch his car, which he now saw he had stupidly left there. The alternative was to take a taxi from the airport home; somehow, this did not appeal to him. He decided that he needed the time the bus and fetching the car would take to adjust himself to whatever he was going to find that he felt on returning to Mulberry Lodge. How dull and ugly England looked, he thought, as he gazed out of the airport-bus window. As it was a fine Sunday, there was a good deal of traffic into London. He wondered what Marina would be doing now.: stretched on her bed with the shutters drawn, or sitting in her office—a tourist bureau—answering telephones and foreigners, switching from her rapid, husky Greek to her enchantingly halting English, or, indeed, probably several other languages for that matter. He remembered giving her the gardenia he had bought for her, and how she had cupped it in her hands—not olive, nobody's skin was the colour of any olive, more like parchment with a faintly green tinge to it. She had taken the flower, enjoyed its smell, smiled and thanked him in Greek because she knew that he understood that word, and then with a single, most graceful movement, fastened the flower in her hair. English women would have been hopeless at that, fussing away with pins, etc. and getting it in the wrong place and having it fall out, but Marina seemed always to make only the necessary, successful movements—like a cat. He wondered whether she was missing him at all, even giving him another thought as he was now giving her; then he stopped thinking about her. She was somehow not the kind of girl one saw again: next time he went to Athens he would find that she was engaged, or married even, and mournfully at home with children while her husband went out with girls such as she had been. On the whole, everything had turned out for the best: if he had to confess anything to Anne, he had now a suitably distant, passing, and unreturnable-to infidelity to confess. *Much* easier than the other one: the nearer he got to that, the less he wanted to think about it.

The bus was rushing down Cromwell Road at last: stopped at the Earls Court lights, but nearly there. Passengers began fidgeting with their hand luggage on racks, putting on coats and hats, telling each other that they were nearly there, wondering whether Marion or Ernest or Paul would meet them, and, if they were obviously foreign, staring ahead with that compound of apathy and panic that the end of any hiatus in a strange country usually induces. They were safe in the bus, need do nothing about it: in a few minutes they would be called upon to struggle with the language, find their luggage, get taxis and tell them where to go. For the first time, Edmund felt glad that he was returning home, rather than departing from it.

Edmund's announcement of his return—unheralded by any cable—had affected both Anne and Arabella, although in different ways. In Anne it induced a kind of nervous bustle, in Arabella a kind of clumsy aloofness. She was never to be found; did anything she was asked very slowly, dropped things, even broke a pudding basin. Just about the time that Edmund was due (they thought) to arrive, she said she thought she would have a bath. Anne, who was putting aspic onto eggs with a leaf of tarragon, looked up, surprised.

"Couldn't you have it later? I mean, after he gets here: there's an awful lot to do."

"Not things that I'm much good at."

"Well, you could do the flowers: you're marvellous with them, and you know what not to pick. I've got the fish salad *and* the bloody old raspberries to pick."

"I'll pick the raspberries, then," Arabella said, almost sulkily.

"Let's do it all together: *please.* Darling—I know you're worried that everything won't be all right, but I *know* it will be. If only we—"

"We what?"

"Behave naturally, I suppose."

"Behaving naturally would be me kissing you when I felt like it, and you don't mean that, do you?"

Anne looked at her nervously. She seems to want to *quarrel* with me! she thought incredulously. "No, of course I don't mean that. But Edmund *is* very fond of you, and he *is* coming home, and he always makes a sort of celebration of that. He'll think I don't care, if he feels I haven't taken any trouble, even if he didn't give us much notice."

"And you do care, don't you?"

Anne went to her where she was stooped upon the kitchen floor sweeping the broken pieces of pudding basin very slowly into the dustpan. She put her hands on Arabella's shoulders and pulled her up. When standing, Arabella was far taller than she, and now her arms were stretched above her round Arabella's neck. "I don't know *what* I feel. All I know is that we've got to try and make everything normal and unsurprising. *You* know what I mean."

After Len's visit, Arabella certainly did. She bent to kiss Anne, and, for a second, each wanted the other very badly, but because this feeling was mutual, it was possible for them to feel like that and stop feeling like it.

Arabella said, "You're perfectly right, of course. We *will* do it all together."

At this moment, Ariadne trotted into the kitchen with a shrew in her mouth. "A really rotten contribution," Arabella said, expertly prising open Ariadne's jaws and taking the shrew from her. "They simply make you sick or thin. A bad example to your children," she scolded, putting the shrew into the rubbish bin, while Ariadne watched with burning resentment.

So they picked the raspberries, made the fish salad, put the *oeufs en gelée* into the fridge, and made a large, rambling-rose arrangement for the sitting-room. At the end of this, there was still no sign of Edmund.

"Perhaps we'd better have baths and change. Wear that lovely white trouser suit you bought in London" (Mrs. Gregory had carefully washed and stretched it and ironed it until it was almost as good as new).

"Oh, no. I'm sick of it. I'll find something."

"I love you in it."

"I'll find something."

But Anne had bathed and had changed far faster than Arabella, and, as Edmund had still not arrived, she turned up in Arabella's bedroom to persist so much about the trouser suit that Arabella thought, What the hell, and agreed to wear it. He probably won't remember it even, she thought: in her experience, few men actually remembered clothes.

She had been sick again while having her bath, and when Anne suggested that she make her martini with cucumber juice, etc., Arabella said that she would, but that what *she* wanted was some brandy. Anne, wearing a navy-blue voile dress with an enormous white collar, looked far more as she had when Arabella first saw her. But, then, they had spent the past five weeks in shorts, in jeans, in bathing dresses, and in nothing at all.

One reason why she decided upon the trouser suit was that it was very comfortable, and she felt the need of that. She had washed her hair because being sick made her feel so dirty, and now she thought that some make-up would be a good thing. Make-up, for Arabella, was rather a taking-up-action-stations affair. It buoyed her up: made her feel that she could not cry because her mascara would smudge and she would look silly when she felt least like it. She also used a great deal of scent. She lined her eyes with pale grey, brushed her eyelashes with several layers of black, plucked her eyebrows, which she kept rather thin and arched, and put on a dark, clear, rather greasy lipstick. She drank the brandy that Anne brought up to her while she was doing this, and, as Anne stayed to watch her make up, she said, "You see, I *am* trying: dressing up for the returning traveller."

They both heard his car at the same moment, before it had turned into the drive. They looked at each other with some mute, passionate appeal for support, and then Anne went downstairs to greet her husband.

Arabella heard distant apologies for his lateness—something about having to fetch the car in London—and Anne's laughing disclaimer that it didn't matter in the least. She heard something about Anne's saying Sunday traffic was awful, and they moved out of earshot—to get drinks, Arabella thought. Better get on with it, she said to herself, and, finishing her brandy, went down with the glass in her hand.

When she entered the sitting-room, Edmund and Anne were raising their glasses to each other, and both turned to her as she stood in the doorway.

Anne felt nothing but tremendous relief at the sight of her: she had discovered that she was truly glad to see darling Edmund again; she also realized, seeing her, that she also loved Arabella. She had the two people she loved most in the world present. She finished her drink and felt wonderful.

The moment that he saw Arabella, Edmund realized that the last few weeks with their adventures—sexual and otherwise— made not one whit of difference. She is wearing that suit on purpose, he thought, with mounting excitement: it must mean

) 237 (

that she, too, feels as I do, that parting made no difference at all, has simply accentuated what had not time to be resolved before.

"My dear Arabella," he said, with what he felt to be admirable aplomb: "how wonderful you look. Have a drink quickly and catch us up."

"I've had one already so it is not a question of catching, but, yes, I would like another."

As she moved towards him, expecting a cousinly kiss from Edmund, she noticed his knuckles white round his glass and moved aside.

"Arabella, for reasons best known to herself, is drinking brandy," Anne said.

"Wicked Arbell." It came out without out his meaning it to or thinking about it.

"Ar*bell?*"

"I told Edmund once that sometimes I am called that." Arabella took the cigarette she did not want from Edmund and moved away from him.

"You never told *me.*"

"Dear Anne, you never asked me. I think I did, though. There's no secret about it—no secret at all."

She went through the motions of explaining this arrangement of her name while Edmund got himself and Anne martinis and Arabella her brandy.

"Tell me about Greece," Anne said.

"Greece was extraordinary—and, now I am home, seems quite unreal." Edmund looked so frantically round the room when he said this that Anne asked; "Nothing has been changed here: is that nice—or nasty?"

"Oh—nice, of course. What coming home should be," he said mechanically, and trying not to remember Arabella by the lake. She wouldn't be *wearing* that suit if she didn't care, he thought. We must both be very careful: the evening must go with its usual swing—if that is the word for it.

They ate in the kitchen: Edmund duly admired and deplored the kittens. "I hope they haven't been allowed to monopolize your room?" he asked Arabella, who answered, "Oh, no, we managed quite well. But now they are sleeping in the scullery."

At dinner, Edmund talked disjointedly, and rather boringly, about Greece. About every twenty minutes, he recollected himself and asked what sort of time they had been having. The answers to this, mostly given by Anne, were dull and satisfactory. She had been ill. She was getting better. Arabella had looked after her like an angel (she said this not looking at Arabella). Dr. Travers had now pronounced her fit for general society. Len had been down for a night.

"Oh?" Edmund said. Then turning to Arabella: "What did you think of her. *I'm* quite sure she's a Lesbian. Not that I mind that in the least," he added generously. "I simply think Anne is too blind, or too partisan or whatever, to realize it."

"Edmund," Anne said, as she had always said when this topic arose, "what on earth makes you think that? I told you about Gordon. It was terrible for her. She never got over it. I do think it is frightfully unfair if women are faithful to one love in their lives, and he dies, they should be branded Lesbian just because they get on with their work alone."

"I've told you, I'm not against Lesbians: I think they're probably rather exciting. All I've ever said is that I think Len is one. What do you think?"

Arabella, with no hesitation, answered, "I think you're wrong. I don't think she is one. But I don't think it is a very easy category to put people into or out of."

Here was a silence. Edmund spooned up the rest of his raspberries; he felt that at all costs he could not embark upon a serious argument with Arabella. He felt too violently about her, and was too confounded at discovering this to do more than exchange practicalities or platitudes.

It is always easy to lower the level of any conversation, and as, on this occasion, nobody had the nerve or desire to elevate it, it transpired that, by the time they got to coffee, nobody had anything at all to say.

Music, as so often, was the way out. Edmund suggested it. He was wondering how on earth he was going to manage a credible night in bed with Anne, and he decided that a great deal of drink and loud enough music would let him out. For tonight. The next day—or indeed any days to follow—he simply could not bear to contemplate. So they listened to sixteen Scarlatti sonatas. During this time, they all drank a good deal, Edmund more than both women put together and far more than he usually drank. Anne noticed this in the end, with a small, half-protesting, half-indulgent smile. It was the indulgence that he didn't like, Edmund thought—supposing that before he had never really noticed it; forgetting that it had been one of Anne's attributes he had basked in. It made him feel as though he was a child, hardly old enough to make up his own mind, or with nothing serious to make up his mind about. By God, that was wrong.

"Darling, as you're still convalescent, oughtn't you to go to bed?" He realized that he had to be careful how he said "convalescent."

"Well—fairly soon. I'll just put the kittens to bed—or, rather, shut them up in the scullery for the night."

Arabella said at once, "I'll do that."

"No, darling, you stay and talk to Edmund. I've got to leave some supper for Ariadne as well." And she moved with her small, light steps out of the room.

Anne, thank God, always shut doors behind her: it was a lifelong habit and had nothing to do with privacy or the time of year. Edmund looked at Arabella. She was sitting on the arm of the big arm-chair, one foot swinging, a single lock of hair hiding part of her face.

"Arabella!" he began—but she interrupted him in a resolutely childish voice.

"One of the kittens—the stripy one—hasn't the slightest idea of what size it is. It thinks it is a tiger and we should all be in a state of terror."

"If you knew how much I've wanted you," for he was confused enough one way and another to feel that if he wanted her so desperately *now*, he *must* have been wanting her all the time in

Greece without realizing it. It was one of the many things of this kind that people say to each other that are neither true nor untrue.

Arabella looked as though it was untrue. "*Wanted* me?" she asked, conveying at the same time astonishment and complete incredulity.

"Oh, more than that—I—" he had an inspiration. "I'm going to find some dance music on the radio, so that I can hold you in my arms and we'll be dancing if Anne comes back."

Before she could say anything, he had turned the knob, and—just like a play—actually found some dance music at once. He turned to her: she had risen defensively and was looking at him rather as though she was at bay. I mustn't frighten her, he thought, as he remembered more exactly how she had made him feel. She is very, very young, compared with me: must keep remembering that. "It is you who have caught me," he said, holding out his hand to her. "Not I you."

She put her—very cold—hand into his, and he drew her to him and began to dance, hardly moving on the carpet. He bent to kiss her neck; she smelled of the scent he had forgotten and now remembered—it obscured her own smell that he knew he had loved and could not now remember. Her dancing with him, her total passivity, her not speaking or kissing him back or even looking at him made everything seem like a dream. He touched the little square end of her chin with his hand and tilted it up to him, so that for a second their eyes did meet: her eyes seemed enormous and they looked at him as though she was blind. "Darling Arbell. Don't be so frightened; there is nothing to be afraid of. I will look after you. You must love me a little too, or you wouldn't be wearing what you are wearing. I won't rush you. I want you too much to risk anything."

The music changed from the blues to a quickstep: far more difficult to dance upon a carpet and not suited at all to his mood. But he could not bear to let her go. He was an old-fashioned dancer, but in spite of this, she followed him perfectly—her body melting, but like ice, in his arms. If she was happy—or more sure of herself—she would be humming this tune, or at least the catch phrase of it: "That's why the lady is a tramp," but she made no sound, and seemed almost to be shrinking—or to be becoming more insubstantial with each movement they made.

Anne came into the room towards the end of the piece. "That's why the lady is a tramp," she sang. "You *do* look good at it: a pair of pros."

Instantly, Edmund felt a fool. Better than being caught out, as it were—but, in his state, only just.

Anne went on, "Isn't it a pity they don't seem to invent dances for three people."

Arabella slipped from Edmund's arms. "You dance with him: it's your turn."

But the quickstep came to an end as Anne advanced into the room towards Edmund, to be followed by something much newer.

"You dance this without touching people," Arabella said, and began dancing not with Edmund but rather at him. Edmund tried to respond, but he neither knew nor wanted to know how to—and Anne, who had reached him by now, put herself firmly into his grasp. Together, they danced, but the music was not right for either of them, and they soon abandoned the mutually self-conscious efforts they had both made. At once, Arabella stopped, and they all three stood, with the music going on, as though they had all become frozen in some ludicrous TV advertisement.

"Dancing's a marvellous idea!" Anne said. "The radio's far too unpredictable: find the old records, Edmund, the ones we always used to dance to."

"It's too late," Edmund said, "and I'm too drunk. I got used to drinking up to all hours in Greece, and this, I'm afraid, is what you get for it."

"Where is Ariadne?" asked Arabella.

"I let her out. She can always get in again through her door, but she likes to hunt at night."

"I think I'm going to bed."

"We must all go to bed," Edmund said, a shade too heartily.

The radio and lights were turned off, and they trooped upstairs.

"Good night, Arabella, sleep well," Anne said, and then, as though it was an afterthought, stretched up and kissed Arabella's face. Edmund looked as though he would do likewise, but Arabella held out her hand—in so royal and commanding a manner that he could do nothing but bend, with the courtliness of one half drunk, and kiss it. They parted.

Arabella, who had badly wanted Ariadne for company, opened her windows wide: Ariadne had been known to climb up and down the wisteria when so inclined. She took off her clothes as quickly as possible and sat for a long time in a patch of moonlight on the floor: frozen with fear and the expectation of despair. It was like approaching rapids with two people who thought that a rowing boat would do all three of them quite nicely.

Anne and Edmund entered their bedroom with the same, mixed feelings. Neither wanted the other, but neither wanted not to be wanted. Usually, if Edmund had ever been away (and he had certainly never been away for so long before), their reunion was something that the whole evening built up towards: their mutual hunger and knowledge of each other had always made something particularly good, and not always in the same way. Sometimes, Edmund wanted her so badly that she had not had time for herself; sometimes he had been able to prolong everything for both of them until Anne could be satisfied as much as he. This was the first time in their lives that things were not the same, and neither was able or willing to say why not. So their lies to each other—she had been ill and must not be overtired, he had been travelling all day and was clearly drunk—were eagerly accepted by each of them. Behind the acceptance lay a small, anxious seed of doubt that germinated in the dark, as each pretended to fall instantly asleep. If he was simply drunk, Anne thought, then he would have taken me clumsily and too fast, but it would have happened. If she was really feeling too tired because she has been ill, she would have put her arms round me and explained all that, Edmund thought, and then thought that those times had often ended in his having her in spite, or because, of the explanations. The morning, each of them thought, and decided that they would rather sleep than think of it. The morning was sure to be different.

The morning was naturally not the same as the evening before, but the ways in which it was different eluded all three of them. Edmund woke with a terrible hangover: in Greece he had seemed able to drink an unlimited amount of what he liked or was available; in England martinis, wine, whisky, and brandy were taking their toll. The thought of getting up and making breakfast for himself and Anne actually nauseated him, and he was greatly relieved when she said that she would make him some coffee and then go back to bed, as she had been doing, she explained, throughout her recent illness. So he cut himself shaving because his hands shook and he felt too awful to try, and drank a lot of coffee after a long, hot shower, and dressed, and felt sorry for himself about the impending day—lunch with Sir William an absolute certainty, and no time or privacy to resolve anything that really mattered. Anne's making him coffee and being about the house meant that he had no chance at all to see Arabella, as he had hoped and planned to do. If she would only come to London for one day, they could have a proper talk and sort things out. (Whenever this possibility diminished, he felt it to be the only solution; had it loomed, he would have been panic-stricken at the prospect.) But he did not see Arabella and got wearily into his car, having snapped at Anne and stumbled over a blasted kitten, which hurt him, he was sure, far more than it hurt the little beast.

The moment that she was sure he was really gone, Anne flew to Arabella's room. Arabella was fast asleep. Anne, who had brought her grapefruit juice and tea, woke her up.

"He's gone. It's me," she said.

"Did you tell him?"

"Of course not. Anyway, he didn't ask," she added, knowing this fitted with Arabella's moral code. "I don't tell lies," she lied, because the kind she had told were not the kind that one could explain to anyone else. And some pride in her also wanted not to tell Arabella that the asexual night she had just spent had been by mutual agreement. In a way, she wanted Arabella to think that Edmund had wanted her and that she had—very kindly and intelligently—got out of it. This state of affairs could not continue, she knew, with Edmund, but it would be better if Arabella was eased into it. She wanted it to be all right for both of them, with both of them wanting her. Because I love them, she thought.

Arabella drank her fruit juice and tea quickly, and then said, "Could I borrow the car?"

"Darling, you know you can always drive the car. I thought we might do a shop together: we're going to need it."

"In that case, I'll take a taxi. I've got to go to London."

"*London?*"

"Yes—London. Just for the day."

"What on earth for? I mean, why today—particularly?"

"I'll explain when I get back, if you don't mind. Can I call a taxi?"

Anne, deeply hurt and disappointed at not having Arabella to discuss Edmund with—nor to *be* with all day, said stiffly, "I'll drive you to the station. And if you call me when you are coming back, I'll meet you."

Which was what she did. Arabella put on her yellow suit and all its accessories, and Anne drove her—silently—to the station. When they got there, she said, "I wish you'd trust me. I wish you'd tell me why you want to go to London today."

"You'll have to trust me," was all she got in reply.

"We'll have a celebration *lunch*," Sir William shouted, so loudly and so near to Edmund's ear that he nearly jumped.

"Good," he said weakly.

"Food? Of course we'll have food. And drink. That's what lunches are for. I expect you're fed up with all that foreign messed-about stuff they give you. I've been eating cold game pie for a week," he continued at full-volume wistfulness.

"Why for a week?" Edmund yelled—or so it seemed to him: it certainly made his head ache.

"Had a touch of indigestion last Tuesday from it. Won't be beaten by trifles like that. Eaten it every day since: if you give in to your digestion at my age, you're done for. Might have a day off with you, though. See you at a quarter to one." He stumped out of Edmund's office. Edmund sent Miss Hathaway out for some Alka-Seltzer and put on his dark glasses.

"There is only one problem that I can see, my darling one."

"My dear Vani, problems have never been your *métier*. I'm surprised that you can rise to *one*."

"The English sarcasm is completely and utterly wasted on me."

They were sitting on the terrace of the large hotel that looked out onto the sea, confronted by a line of middle-aged and wind-weary palms, the smell of petrol fumes, and two champagne cocktails that had been made with very indifferent champagne. They had officially left the villa, and were due to board the yacht that evening. So they were lunching and spending the afternoon in the hotel that Clara usually frequented at such times. Clara had had her hair done that morning, her legs waxed, and her nails on hands and feet painted.

The Prince had read some of the *New York Times*, been shaved, and bored. He was now—with no gambling in sight—spoiling for some intrigue, however small and removed from his real interest.

"The problem," he reverted portentously, for him, "—and this, my dear one, is a secret in some ways, although naturally, like most secrets, far from complete—is that poor Ludwig— I fear that Ludwig is not— He is many years older than might appear— it has never been satisfactory for him—"

"For God's sake, Vani, don't beat about the bush. You mean

he's sterile, or impotent or something. There's nothing new about that."

"You have hit upon it. But that is not the major factor. It would not be of the least interest to speak of his bed life, excepting that he needs an heir. An heir," he repeated dreamily: the last thing he would ever want to be saddled with. He considered it extremely open-minded of him to contemplate such differences between one man and another.

"If he begets not an heir, his truly unspeakable cousin inherits all. This he would shoot himself to avoid. He has said so many times. He has only the one way. He must marry, and his wife must have a child. *Now* you are comprehending me."

"You mean, Arabella must get married to him and then find someone who'll get her pregnant. Well, really—I don't see much difficulty in that. We all know that she is capable of pregnancy, and I should think anyone married to Ludwig would welcome a change. Or anything," she added.

"You do not regard this as an insuperable problem, then?"

"Why should I?"

"I think Ludwig would—reasonably enough—wish to have some sayso in who it might be. He would hardly care for it to be his head gardener, or some unstable, displaced person."

"I am tired—really absolutely *sick*—of trying to plan that girl's future. If she marries Ludwig, I shall be delighted: she will be off my hands; she will then have enough money for me to stop worrying about her ever."

"But she has the money surely, yes?"

"Unmarried, she has five hundred a year, and anything I feel like giving her. Married, she gets everything her father left, which is in a trust for her. It is his will—nothing to do with me, but naturally I shall not tell her this unless she agrees to marry Ludwig. Then she will have quite enough to restore his castle and pay anyone to go to bed with her."

"I do not think she would have to spend money on that."

"Don't you? That is really rather ungallant of you, Vani. A

mistake." She finished her cocktail. "She does not know about the money. If you tell her, it will be the end of you and me."

It was going to be the end, anyway, but she wanted as many excuses as possible.

The Prince tried to smile. "I would never on my life tell her," he said.

Henry had certainly gone to Oswestry, and had done, in fact, four days' filming. But he had not returned. Janet had, by now, finished her post-office savings money. She did not know where Henry was: their telephone had been cut off because the bill was simply unpayable, and she was down to her watch and her wedding ring. Lack of proper food or anybody sensible to talk to, and the children's ceaseless needs—most of which it was becoming impossible to fulfil—had so sapped her energy and intelligence that she now behaved like any starving, unloved, despairing person might behave. She had lived for nearly ten days now from her hand to the children's mouths. She felt dizzy, stupid, omnipotent, and sick, by turns. She made one effort to find and see some sort of welfare person, but she chose the worst time of day, when nearly everybody (who wasn't on holiday) was out to lunch. She couldn't face going any distance with both children, and she couldn't leave them for long. She knew how to make a public call box work without money and used it to try and trace Henry's agent, but he, too, was on holiday. Back at home, she faced the milk bill—unpaid for too many weeks for the milkman to put up with it any longer—the half loaf of stale bread, the greasing margarine, the fish paste that she thought might have gone off and dared not give to them. She no longer cared what happened to her: it was what she should do about the children. Leave them on the doorstep of some hospital? Or police station? Leave the poor little buggers to a fate of institutions and fostering? Finish *them* off too? She no longer knew what she felt about them: they had become such a chronic, enormous, and insuperable problem in her life that she thought of them almost as she thought of the telephone bill or the milkman. I could just leave them here and go to the town hall and ask them, she thought, but the idea of the long, uphill climb of walking in the heat to that place seemed too much of an effort. Almost any effort made her sweat and feel cold, as though she was going to faint. But people were supposed to be kind to each other. Supposing she called the police and said what her difficulties were. But if a telephone didn't work, it didn't work. I could go to a call box, she thought: 999 calls did not cost a thing. "My husband seems to have left me, and now I have have no money and can't buy food for the children, and I don't know what to do." Even if I knew, could I bear to do it? She had a dim, spasmodic feeling that possibly her mind was failing her. Surely this was an idiotic situation to have got into? All around her were houses and flats, and they were full of people; couldn't she just ring a bell and tell someone and they would help her? But she had begun to be afraid that nobody would believe her, and she did not feel that she could take not being believed. Also, she was afraid of utterly breaking down while she told them, and she had been taught that breaking down —about anything—was a very bad thing to do. They might simply think she was mad.

Every now and then, in a spasm of energy, she would search her worn handbag, with its broken handles, in case she had overlooked some money. Or pockets of clothes. Or pockets of the few clothes that Henry possessed. Once, a week ago, this search had yielded a shilling, and so she kept on feeling that some more cash might turn up. But it hadn't and didn't. She didn't feel in the least hungry any more, but she would have given anything for a smoke—or someone who *knew* her to talk to so that she wouldn't have to explain everything. Every day, she wondered whether Henry would come back, because if he did that, he would *have* to do something. His returns always coincided with pubs' shutting, so she had two periods in each twenty-four hours when it was worth hoping. But after three weeks—no, three weeks and four days—there didn't seem much point in that. When he hadn't come back by four in the afternoon, she'd had enough. She wrote two letters, which she put in one envelope.

She had to use Samantha's drawing pad to write them, which meant writing over her faint scribbles. Samantha was nearly three and spent most of her time talking crossly and bossily to a rabbit that she had had since she was a baby. Luke sat on the floor sucking his left thumb and pulling his left ear with his right hand. He did this for hours, so that his thumb was swollen and his left ear lobe a different shape, but any attempt to stop him made him howl. The people immediately above her were away on holiday, but the old woman on the top floor, whose husband had a bad rheumatic condition that had affected his heart, was at daggers drawn with Janet about the noise that her children made. Samantha kept asking her what she was doing, and Janet had to tell her dozens of times that she was writing a letter, be quiet because I've got to think, I'm writing a letter. She wrote one to her family in Australia and one to the police with the address for the Australia letter to be sent to. She found it difficult to write either letter, and both were full of apologies. *I'm sorry to be such a nuisance,* she found she had written three times. It took her hours—until long after the pubs were open again for the evening. She put the letters, folded, into the envelope, which she then put out of Samantha's reach. Then she went to look at the fish paste. It smelled all right: if she scraped the top off, she could fry some of the bread (the electricity bill hadn't come in again yet) in the marge and put the paste on it for the children's supper. She didn't want to give them food poisoning, poor little sods, but there really wasn't anything else. She washed them and put them into their night things. Luke still wore a kind of spaceman's suit to sleep in, but he had grown out of it, so that she had to cut off the feet. She cleaned their teeth with their toothbrush and cold water. Luke had eaten the remains of the toothpaste yesterday. She made their suppers, frying the bread very carefully, as there wasn't really enough marge, and spreading the paste thinly on each fried and hot slice. Samantha loved it, but Luke turned his head away and said no, one of his few and much-used words. In the end, Samantha ate both slices. Then she gave them each a glass of water, into which she had put a Disprin—saved for the occasion. She wanted them to sleep well. They had bunk beds, one above the other, Samantha on top, Luke below. He climbed into his, while she lifted Samantha, clutching her rabbit, into the top bunk. She tucked them up, as usual, and read them one of the much-read and tattered books. *Peter Rabbit* was Samantha's choice, and, as Luke didn't have any literary preferences, she was always allowed to choose. When she had finished, she kissed them. Samantha hugged her and gave her a very loud and rather wet kiss. "*I* love you, but *he* doesn't like you at all." This was the rabbit.

"Never mind," Janet said. "Perhaps when he's had a good night's sleep, he'll wake up in a better temper."

"He won't. He can't. He hates good tempers."

"Well, it's very kind of you to look after him."

Luke lay on his back, and simply endured, or perhaps accepted, her kiss. His skin was so soft and felt so thin stretched on his forehead that she kissed him very gently. "Me too," called Samantha from the top. She was jealous of Luke. Luke began his thumb sucking and ear pulling while she gave Samantha a final hug.

"That's that," she thought, with no emotion at all. It was now nearly nine o'clock: there was still time to put in. The rules she had set herself were now rigidly superstitious: she must wait until he *couldn't* come home from the pubs before she posted the letter. She spent the next hour and a half trying to read: a paperback of a novel about prisoners trying to escape. At half past ten, the children were quiet, and she let herself out of the house and went the block up the hill to the letter box. She hadn't got a stamp, but she had put THE POLICE on the envelope in capital letters and was fairly sure that this would mean delivery. She had included her address, and a Yale key to the flat, which Henry must have left. She walked very slowly down the hill back to the flat. It was hot, and there was a smell of cooking, dust, petrol, and dogs' shit.

"I wish I had something to drink," she thought. "Dutch courage, or cowardice, or whatever." But she hadn't. The plane trees were dry, and their leaves crackled slightly in any faint breeze. Their zebra bark, a piecemeal way of tidying themselves up, looked simply unsuccessful and alien. She let herself into the flat very slowly, looking round once more at the long road lined by these trees that had cars streaming up and down it with people who were doubtless going through all sorts of things. When she shut herself into the flat, the silence struck her. She went straight to the kitchen, where she had put the bottle of carefully saved Carbitrol—given her by a doctor after the birth of Samantha. She filled the largest glass she could find with cold water—running the tap until it really was cold so that the taste of chlorine wouldn't be so bad. She went to the lavatory, brushed her hair, kicked off her shoes, and took the pills with systematic care. Not too fast, or she might choke or retch; not too slowly, in case she should change her mind. The glass of water just about did for the pills. She lay down on hers and Henry's bed to wait. She had one fleeting thought that he might have effected some reconciliation with that rich bitch, but this passed, and, in the end, she simply lay, looking at the damp patches on the ceiling and waiting to die. I hope I haven't been too wicked, was the last thing that she thought before she could no longer think anything and she was past fear or anxiety or responsibility or life.

"But you have no appointment made."

"I know. I said I'll wait."

"The doctor is extremely busy."

"I only want to ask him one thing: it won't take a moment."

The woman went away, and Arabella tried to read a very old copy of *Country Life*. Any room in which one waited for anything was always, somehow, depressing. This one contained an ugly stained-wood table, on which out-of-date periodicals and magazines were stacked. It also had four ugly, uncomfortable high-back oak chairs with plastic seats. After she had waited for what seemed like ages, the door opened and the foreign bitch ushered a nervous-looking woman into the room.

"Vill you chust vait here," she said. She did not look at Arabella, or, rather, she looked firmly through her—once—to make her point, whatever the hell that might be.

The newcomer sat down: she was neither young nor old, neither pretty nor plain. She met Arabella's eye once, and then looked down at the table with the papers on it. She did not attempt to read one. She behaved not exactly as though Arabella was not there but in the classic way that patients in waiting-rooms do behave, as though the other person, or people, were there, but would be there anyway, like the table and the chairs. Arabella had noticed this before, at all kinds of doctors' and dentists'. A feeling of anonymous tension simply grew. Eventually, the foreign bitch returned, and said, with evident sulkiness, "The doctor will see you for a minute, Miss *Smith*."

On the table once more, she said, "I thought you could probably tell whether I am, whether I've—"

"If you are pregnant again? I have told you, my dear, that you should be particularly careful after what you have a few weeks ago had. You are much more open to conception at those times."

"Well—could you tell me, please?"

"It is possible—not certain, but possible. But I warn you, my dear, that I will do nothing about it at this stage. I do not agree with the English doctors on this point. I will do nothing until three months, you understand."

Arabella lay back so that she need not see his face while he prodded about with his rubber gloves. He took some time, feeling deeply inside her, which was unpleasant. "Relax more," he said once, and it was not so bad. When he had finished, he shook a rubber finger at her and said, with what seemed to her horrible jocularity, "Indeed, I am afraid you have done it again. What a girl! What a life, eh? You may have a urine test if you wish, but there is little point: I am very seldom wrong in these matters."

Arabella sat up, to finish things off, but he pushed her gently back saying, "You go to many lengths for so small a pleasure. Do you know if I touch you—here—and in the right way, you can have an orgasm?"

Arabella swung her legs over the side of the high table. "I don't want one, thank you."

He shrugged—perfectly amiable. "You must come back and see me in two weeks. Make an appointment next time, you naughty girl."

"Thank you." It was difficult to maintain her dignity, putting on her knickers.

He watched her, but he was also washing his gloved hands in Dettol and water. The smell rose strongly in the room.

"What do I owe you?"

"Nothing now. You will pay what you paid before next time you come." He smiled quite kindly and patted her shoulder. "Do not upset yourself: you will be quite safe with me. I am a very good doctor for women. But you must be more careful next time. Next time, I will arrange matters for you so that you will not need to get into this condition." He was still smiling in the middle of his moustache, his dark eyes fixed on her face with an expression both cynical and understanding. "Men are devils," he said. "I hope at least you make him pay for it."

"Good-bye, and thank you for seeing me."

"Good-bye for the present. No funny business, you understand? Or I will not touch you. In my hands you are safe: go to no others." He nodded and turned away again to wash the hand that had patted her shoulder. He is at least conscientious, she thought, as she walked, rather slowly, out of the room. Outside, the foreign woman sat at a desk with an appointment book.

"You wish to make a further appointment?"

"I'll ring about it, if I may."

"It is better if you make it now."

"I'll ring you."

Outside, she walked slowly down the street feeling very strange. There was an extraordinary gap between suspecting something and having it more or less confirmed by someone else. For she had no doubt that he knew his job. She felt suddenly very

) 254 (

hungry, and went into a very small Italian-run coffee-and-sand-wich place. Even if one of them accepted the idea, would the other? Reason rejected this ideal as absurd: but her feelings were stronger at the moment than any thinking she could do about it. She ordered a salami sandwich and a cup of coffee. If she called her mother at the villa and told her *this*, she would be let off the yacht: might even be let off any more ghastly-getting-through-the-days-in-different-climes nonsense. It was much simpler for Ariadne, she thought sadly, when she had finished her sandwich and asked for another. As she paid and walked out, she thought that all she could do was ask them: she would not lie about it, but she could, at least, ask them.

Anne was rung by Clara at about three-thirty. Where was Arabella? In London: oh, well, would she kindly call the follow-ing number the moment she got back? The number was given. Was Arabella, by the way, out of quarantine, or whatever it was? When Anne said yes, Clara said that she hoped that *she* (she could not remember Anne's name) was better as well. Anne said that she was. Then Clara said that she had had an awful time trying to get Edmund at his office, but he appeared to be out having what seemed like an interminable lunch. She had tried at half past twelve, and again now, and still he was out, that was why she had troubled Anne. She would be most grateful if Anne (only she still said "you") would exercise her influence on Arabella to come to Nice by Thursday. The air ticket had been sent; it was quite simple. She rang off after that.

Anne, whose feelings about Arabella's going to London with-out telling her why had not yet subsided, was put back entirely onto Arabella's side by this conversation. Even from a distance, Clara sounded awful, a totally unsuitable person for poor Ara-bella to have to deal with. She is not capable of machination, Anne thought tenderly; her mother could easily manoeuvre her into an impossible position about having to marry someone. She thought that she must have a really serious talk with Edmund about Arabella's future. It would bring her and Edmund together: make everything much sounder and more complete. She decided to make an especially good dinner for both of them when they returned. This prospect galvanized her: she loved the idea of their sitting—Edmund on her right, Arabella opposite—praising and enjoying what she had made for them. Arabella would not go to London every day. She started planning and collecting ingredients.

They had all three sat through the candlelit dinner that Anne had taken so much trouble over. Edmund had eaten very little: he had explained and complained to everyone about his lengthy lunch with Sir William. Arabella's condition, as she, by now, very well knew, precluded her eating very much in the evenings, but she had picked at everything with loyal intent, although, as Anne had observed, to little purpose. All three turned out to have so little to say to one another at dinner that Anne's intention of having a good, private talk to Edmund about Clara and her machinations had by now evaporated. Arabella had arrived much earlier than Edmund, but she had not called Anne from the station, had taken a taxi and arrived saying that she didn't want to be a bother.

"This is your home: you're never a bother," Anne had said, and for a moment, Arabella had clung to her. Then she had detached herself and said that she wanted to have a bath and a rest, if Anne didn't mind, and Anne, who did, couldn't.

Now they all sat, not eating the *fromage à la crème* and black cherries that Anne had provided for the end of the meal. Interrupting Edmund's desultory, and clearly forced, narration about Greece and Sir William's reaction to it, Arabella had suddenly said, "I think we have all got to talk."

Both Edmund and Anne looked frightened by the prospect. Arabella went on: "I think we'd better make a lot of coffee and have it in the sitting-room."

So Anne obediently made coffee, while Arabella and Edmund variously cleared the table. Anne, who hoped that the talk would turn out to be about Clara and how they were going to deal with that situation, tried to believe or pretend that she was looking forward to it. She had told them that Clara had rung, and Edmund turned out to have known that Clara had twice rung and failed to get him at his office. But Edmund did not look as though he was looking forward to a talk—of any kind.

Eventually, in the sitting-room, with everybody provided with coffee and brandy and ensconced in their customary places, there was no putting this off. Anne had turned on only one light, so that it was a kind of electric twilight in the room, towards the centre of which moths collided and stunned or hypnotized themselves. There was a complete silence.

Arabella said, "I am having a baby. That's what I went to London about. It isn't absolutely certain, but pretty nearly. And *I* am sure."

There was another—more charged—silence.

Then Anne said uncertainly, "How *can* you be? I mean, you said that you had an abortion just before you came to stay."

"That was perfectly true. I wouldn't have said it otherwise." She took a cigarette and lit it, hoping that she would be able to smoke it. "I had to tell you, because you've been so very kind to me."

Anne thought back to the day that Arabella had gone to London with Edmund. So did Edmund.

"You mean that day when you went to London and there was that awful storm?"

"Yes."

"My poor darling—we'll help you, won't we Edmund?"

Edmund said nothing. His heart was pounding, and he thought that everyone must hear it, but he couldn't speak.

Arabella said, "How?"

"Well, you don't want to have it, do you?"

"That depends upon you."

"Upon *me?*" Anne put down her coffee cup. She was beginning to be afraid now of what Arabella might be going to say about them.

"Upon both of you."

) 257 (

Anne said faintly, "How do you mean?"

"It is Edmund's child. That's what I mean."

The silence now was horrible.

Arabella looked desperately at Edmund, who still seemed speechless. *He* was not going to have an atom of courage: he was going to leave it all to her. She looked at him steadily for a moment, and Edmund felt more awful than he had ever felt in his life.

Then, Arabella said, "I have not been to bed with any other man. So it must be his."

Anne looked at Edmund: his silence, and his face, and indeed everything about him proclaimed this confounding truth.

Anne, looking at Arabella as though she had only just seen her, said, "Do you mean to say— Can you honestly admit, that you —that you went to bed with Edmund in order to have his child?"

"I didn't do it for that. But that is what has happened." She tried again with the cigarette and, knowing that she would be feeling sick anyway, decided to go on with it.

Anne, looking from one to the other for denial, reassurance, for anything she could see that might help her *not* to understand, fell back upon saying, "But Edmund loves me!"

"I know. *I* love you, too."

"You can't love two people!"

"Can't you? How do you feel? Don't you love Edmund and me? Or have you decided whom you love? Don't *you* want it both ways?"

Edmund said now, at last, and barely audibly, "How do you mean, both ways?"

Arabella looked at Anne, but she was speechless now. She was not going to help: she was going to leave it all to her. She answered, "While you were away, Anne and I—we discovered that we also loved each other." She looked at Anne steadily for a moment; there was still time for her to have the courage, but as Edmund also stared at Anne, she looked away. Anne had started to blush, slowly, deeply, as the confusion of jealousy and guilt collided. Edmund looked from Anne back to Arabella, he seemed

) 258 (

literally unable to understand either of them.

"What do you mean, you discovered that you 'loved each other?' "

"Just that. We went to bed with each other."

Anne, in a voice that neither of them had ever heard before said, "You've really torn it now, haven't you?"

Edmund asked, but in tones of near credulity now, "You've been to bed with *my wife?*"

"Yes. Because I loved her."

"But you went to bed with *me!* You're not that kind—"

Anne interrupted venomously, "Behind my back! You did it behind my back!"

Edmund turned upon her furiously. "Well, you are hardly in a position to complain about that, are you? After—what is it—five weeks of behaving in this—this disgusting, unnatural manner?"

"It is Arabella who has deceived everybody!"

Arabella, her voice shaking, said, "I have deceived nobody. And it was *not* disgusting, don't please say or think that. I have not told either of you lies, if that is what you mean."

"Oh, yes, but *your* conception of morality is that you don't have to tell anyone anything unless they ask. As far as I can see, that counts for precisely nothing."

"*Anne*—we've been talking about love, not morality!"

Before Anne could answer, Edmund said, "And in your view, all love is equally immoral—or perhaps 'amoral' would be a better word for it."

Arabella shook her head: she was finding it more and more difficult to say anything.

Anne, back to the point where her pride had stumbled over her humiliation, said bitterly, "How can you imagine that it would ever have occurred to me to ask you, simply because you went to London for the day with Edmund, whether or not you had been to bed with him?"

Edmund, with equal bitterness said, "Perhaps you've noticed that, even when you tell me *several times,* I don't find it very easy to understand that you and Anne— How can you ever have thought that it would have occurred to me to ask you about that?"

Anne burst into tears. Both looked at her: neither knew what to do about it. Edmund thought viciously that this was how all women behaved as a way out of anything; Arabella, clenching her hands together, thought that whatever happened she *must not* cry.

In this she succeeded: as a result of which Anne thought her brazen and Edmund, even more unfairly, thought her callous.

Arabella got shakily to her feet and took some more brandy. Nobody said anything. Anne searched for and found a handkerchief, which she held to her eyes as she rocked slowly back and forth in her chair. This rather operatic picture of unhappiness touched neither of the other two. Arabella thought it was irrelevant and Edmund irritating.

Finally, making her last effort that she felt she could ever make, Arabella said, "The reasons that I told you this were because it is true about the child and, secondly, I thought that perhaps—" her voice began to fail her here—"perhaps if we *really did* love one another, you would be glad about it: it would just be another good thing in our lives."

She sat down again with her brandy, finding herself unable to stand.

Edmund, not for the first time, imagined himself married to her, living with her and their child. He looked expectantly at Anne: perhaps she would provide a way out.

Anne, recovering from the shock of what she recognized to be a single interlude with Edmund, as opposed to her weeks with Arabella, started imagining Edmund permanently in Greece, out of the way, and she and Arabella bringing up this child. But it was *Edmund's*: this was what she couldn't stand. If it had been some anonymous conception, how kind, how protective and gentle she could have been! But it was not. If anybody was to have Edmund's child, it must be she.

Arabella imagined nothing: she was simply wondering—for

the hundredth time in her life—what anyone meant when they said that they loved anyone. No answer.

"Anyway," she said, being very careful about her choice of words and how she said them, "it's no go. I can see that. I'll be off, then."

"You can't go at this time of night! There won't be any trains."

The confirming blow of what she had always dreaded.

"Well—I can go first thing in the morning. I'd better go up now and pack."

Anne, recovering herself, after Edmund's—to her—conciliating remark, said, "But what are you going to *do?*"

"I think you have both made it very clear that that is my business." She got up, stood for a moment till she felt she would be able to walk, and looked at them: at Edmund, who seemed to her to have no courage of any conviction at all, and at Anne, who had determined to have, on her own terms, both things both ways and never mind the lies. And she managed to think, Perhaps *it is* all my fault. Perhaps it is I who can't love anyone, am just a kind of limpet, sticking to whatever seems to be suitable scenery. That's awful: I must not do that.

"Good night, both of you," she said, "and thank you for having me to stay."

Upstairs, she packed mindlessly for hours: everything she possessed had to go into all the cases. Looking round this room, in which, in fact, she had spent so little time, she had still the violent sense of loss and fear. She had to start again, somewhere, somehow. It was like being cast into the middle of a wood, or a desert, or a sea, entirely alone, knowing only that those who had cast her would be glad that she had gone. When the packing was done, she lay, dressed, upon the bed, and tried to think without feeling. The knowledge that absolutely nobody in the world really cared a damn about her when it came to any kind of point had to be accepted and dealt with. I have no choice about people, she thought, and then, she thought, that, yes, she had one choice. That should be enough for anyone. She could have the child.

Nobody on earth could stop that. Discovering this, at last, made her able to weep for everything else she had lost. As usual, she made no sound.

Edmund and Anne, left in the sitting-room, spent some time just being there, their minds charged with separate, unspoken thoughts. Anne, hating it, thought, He can't make a decision: it has to be somebody else—usually me.

Edmund thought, with that dichotomy between excitement and revulsion, There she is: my wife. She's had an affair with a woman, but really she wants to stay with me. *I* am supposed to protect her from the world.

Both felt that they were there to protect the other: neither wanted the results of the protection. Each thought of what he had to do to sustain life for the other; each considered his efforts and translated them into nobility and unselfish determination. Neither of them was prepared to consider aloud what his feelings for Arabella had been, or were. Both of them—in different ways—wanted to regard the situation as an extraordinary and, because of the other person's behaviour, nightmarish aberration.

Anne looked round the familiar room that she had decorated and collected and made things for: the ten years that had slipped by, bringing with them the imperceptible growth of comfort and stability and routine. The roses she had first planted had grown high up the walls round the windows; sofa covers had worn out and been replaced; they had gradually collected the pictures painted on glass depicting the death of Nelson; had more bookshelves built. She had tried and failed to make the lamp shades, had covered the chairs and stools with petit point instead. Generations of kittens who had galloped and scrambled over the arms of chairs that now all bore the marks of their wicked pioneering (the Cornhills are *mad* about cats). The seasons; the log fires and drawn curtains with supper on a trolley; the cold, blue twilight of the early springs with their own snowdrops or daffodils or forsythia that she arranged so well; the arguments about where they should go for their holidays and when: looking at maps spread out in front of the fire; the recurrent discussions about whether they should keep a donkey, a parrot, a goat, or a mynah bird (but *never*, not once a child); Christmas and their birthdays: small sieges of pleasure, and always, in between, the telegraph poles of week-ends that propped up the five week-days and prevented any sagging into loneliness. It had been a routine, with small, controllable variations: exactly, in fact, what she had thought she had always wanted. But if everything about it had been so right for them, how could it be so easily disrupted? If Edmund decided to leave her . . . she would be free to make the other plan. Without looking at him, she got stiffly out of her chair and poured some more brandy. The coffee was cold, and she did not feel like reheating it. Then she did look at Edmund, sitting with his head in his hands, and thought that they had been ten good years, and that all that had probably happened was that she had discovered that she loved him, but *in a different way*—which, of course, he must never know, or find out. At least, she thought, we both understand each other well enough to realize that this is no time for talking, that we both need silence and time to—to understand—get over the shock. She remained silent.

Edmund felt, in some confused way, that everybody had let one another down: that some reparation, some explanation—but not, of course, in hot blood—was necessary. It seemed to him that he had been shown up as narrow-minded, blind, and indecisive; and none of these aspects had ever impinged upon his view of himself until now. His old life was gone, as far as he could see: he could not imagine that his feeling about Anne could ever return to its original state, but he could not envisage what could be put in its place. He still wanted Arabella, but felt that he ought not to like her; he supposed that he still liked Anne, but he certainly did not want her. He wondered whether she would leave him . . . free to make some other plan. But would he actually want to marry Arabella and have their child, if it came to the point? He had a feeling that she was somebody to encounter, rather than someone to live with. She seemed not only to have bad luck, she seemed to have managed to disseminate it. What he really hated was that she seemed to have *shown them all up*. Nobody was the better for what she had done or been responsible for—he suddenly remembered Clara on the telephone saying, "Don't let her exploit you," and wondered whether that was what Clara had meant. He and Anne should surely now be *talking* about it, not sitting in this tense and dreary silence, which, it seemed to him, simply underlined the dismal fact that when they had something really serious to discuss, they had nothing to say. For surely it was up to her to begin? What he had done was what any man might have done: fallen for the provoking attractions of a young, and certainly not innocent, but beautiful girl. Once. Only once it had happened (no thought of that never having been his choice now entered his head). But what Anne had done seemed to him—well—odd, extraordinary; most people's wives didn't dash into bed with other women the moment their husband's backs were turned. (What did they *do*, anyway?) It was up to her to do some explaining. If he had to give up Arabella—he had swivelled back to this being a sacrifice—then he deserved some kind of . . . help. The idea that possibly Anne didn't want to stay married to him recurred. If she didn't—well, then, then he might do anything. He would have to sort out his feelings afresh, and, in a way, that was what he would most like to do. A picture of himself and Arabella sunbathing on the deckhouse of Clara's yacht flashed.

At this moment, Anne said, "I think we'd better go to bed."

He looked at her. She was wearing an extraordinarily uncharacteristic dress, or housecoat or whatever. Her hair was longer and, now that her tears had subsided, she was very pale. She was at one and the same time the person he had thought he knew best in his life and somebody whom he wondered if he'd ever known at all.

"I don't mean the same bed," she said, and began moving towards the door.

"Don't you think we ought to talk?"

"No. Because I can't think of anything to say. I don't like myself much, and I imagine you must feel the same."

Instantly, he did: he disliked her for this piece of perception, but the echo of some respect for her stirred.

Together, they put out the lights, shut the door, and went upstairs.

In their separate beds, a different, but in both cases quite selfish, longing for the girl who was crying silently in hers possessed them.

Arabella, who had slept in the end, woke early. This was because she knew that she was going to have to travel, that she did not know where she would be spending the next night, and that all her feelings about this place, and her illusions—or delusions?—about its owners had to be dragged up by the roots. Her business was to collect all the luggage, find a taxi, and go to the station, to London. She went down at eight to the kitchen to make herself a cup of Nescafé. Ariadne was there: for a moment Arabella's determination and control broke down; she hugged this silky, black, fairly indifferent, but acceptable cat, and then put her down because she could not afford to care.

Both Edmund and Anne came into the kitchen while she was drinking her coffee. Arabella said that she had ordered a taxi (which she had) and would be leaving very soon. Her attitude was both apologetic and proud. Edmund, not looking at Anne, said, "If you are having an abortion, I want to pay for it."

Arabella said, "Thank you, but that really is not necessary. As you know, my mother has a great deal of money."

Anne said, in tones both guarded and light, "Are you going to join her in France?"

"I don't know. I haven't decided."

There was a silence. Anne was making proper coffee, and Edmund was collecting bread for toast and so forth. Both were wearing dressing-gowns and both looked much older to Arabella than either had done before.

The front doorbell rang. Everybody knew that it was the taxi, but when they all three went into the hall, Edmund realized that she had, touchingly, or misguidedly, carried all her pieces of luggage down for herself. The taximan loaded his cab, and they all stood, frozen, waiting for this departure. Then, while the man was putting something on the rack of his cab, Arabella said, "I'm truly sorry if I've made either of you feel unhappy. I didn't mean to: I really never meant that."

They did not know how to say good-bye to her, but she made it easy for them—by running suddenly out of the hall into the cab. "Good-bye," she called, as though the cabman would expect that.

"Good-bye," they said, galvanized by this end and the lack of pressure. Edmund went outside.

"Please look after yourself," he said.

"You must know by now that that is what I am worst at. Still, it is a good thought."

Anne came out, and Edmund turned away to allow her her chance. But Anne said, "If only you'd told me, it would have been all right."

"You know that that is not true. You look after Edmund: he will look after you."

Then she went, and they watched the taxi out of sight, with no clear idea of how its occupant might be feeling.

Arabella knew that she had so much to go through that it would be sensible to get out the other side of some of her feelings on the way to the station. So, all the way there, she thought about Mulberry Lodge and the haven it had seemed to be, and she made the two people she had known there . . . agreeable puppets. It was all her fault. She had wanted to belong, to join them; they had not. Perfectly reasonable. It's lucky I don't feel sick in the mornings, she thought. She could not think about *them* very much, because she could not bear to think ill of them.

At the station, she tipped the driver to help her onto the train with all her stuff. Now I am going to London, she thought. I shall never, in my life, go back there.

In London, she went to Cartier. She presented the man who attended her there with her mother's letter and, after due time, he produced the emeralds. They were in a beautiful and expensive-looking case. She signed a receipt for them, and then wrapped them in brown paper and put them in a plastic carrier bag. "I don't want to be shot," she said to the man, who seemed to understand this. The commissionaire at Cartier got her a cab to take to Chelsea and Neville's flat.

Standing outside Neville's flat made her remember Henry, and, for the first time, she wondered *what* lies—there were bound to have been some—he had told her about his wife—what was her name?—Marjorie or Janet? Henry had said that she was very stupid, dull, had not even been a good actress, but with her long, blond hair and rather widely spaced but anaemic features, she had been given a chance at an acting school, which was where they had met. No, no children, he had almost snapped; but she had trapped him into marrying her by saying that she was pregnant. No, he had never found out whether this was an actual lie or whether she had miscarried. All he knew was that she stuck to him like some parasitic creeper, preventing his growth as an artist. "For Christ's sake, don't let's talk about this any more," and they hadn't, and Arabella had not given Janet, she was sure now that it had been Janet, another thought. Now, she wondered. But she had not any means of getting hold of Henry since she had left him. She asked the driver to wait, until she found out whether Neville or anybody else was at home. Her luck was in. Neville answered the door in a most gorgeous dressing-gown; his look of dismay was most fleeting, before he got his welcoming smile into action.

"My dear girl!" he said.

"I haven't come to stay," Arabella said quickly, "but I would be grateful if I could dump my stuff here and ask you something."

"Of course. I'm afraid Rodney is out, so do you think this frightfully kind man would help with the cases? I'm not supposed to carry anything."

The driver, whose feelings were divided between natural amiability and the intuition that Arabella would prove to be a good tipper, agreed, and so he and she made the necessary journeys.

She took the plastic carrier bag first, and dumped it in the kitchen behind the door before going back for some of the other things. She gave the driver ten shillings for his trouble, and he drove off feeling that it took all sorts to make a world and that he and Arabella were two of the better sort.

"Now, dear," Neville said, when the door was finally shut and the small passage crammed with Arabella's suitcases. "Something tells me that all is not well. Let's have some coffee and settle down and be comfy and you can tell me anything you wish."

He bustled about in the kitchen getting a tray, in the middle of which, he called out, "What an extraordinary carrier bag! One of those psychedelic affairs. Rodney can't bear them, I must warn Mrs. Hotchkiss—"

"It's all right, it's mine." Arabella came into the kitchen and took it.

"Whatever have you got in that, dear? Not your style at all, if I may say so."

"Emeralds," Arabella answered, without thinking.

Neville burst out laughing. "That serves me right for asking awkward questions, I must say." He brought the wobbly pottery cups full of delicious coffee on a papier-mâché tray into the sitting-room. "Here we are. You don't take sugar, do you? Or cream?"

"No, thank you. Black's fine."

Then, as they both sipped their coffee, Neville put his down and said, "Your mother rang me yesterday: about twelve, I suppose. She seemed to be trying very hard to find out where you were." His bright-blue eyes were fixed upon her face.

"What did she say?"

"Well, between you and me, dear, rather a lot, but I don't want to be indiscreet." His tone implied, "unless you are, too," "You're looking very pale, darling. Has the country air not agreed with you?"

Arabella put her cup down and sought in her bag for a cigarette. She felt suddenly so awful, so much wanting to fling herself into his kind, avuncular arms (if only he *was* her uncle) and tell him everything, but she had to concentrate very hard on finding and lighting the cigarette not to. He was no relation of hers, rather a friend of her mother's—one of the very few whom she liked and who had been kind to her.

"Come on, dear, just treat me like an old Dutch uncle. Lots of people do."

"Could you tell me first what my mother said to you?"

He looked at her with his head upon one side: he reminded her of some kind of exotic bird, his silvery hair ruffled like a crest and smoothed now by one of his beautifully shaped hands, this characteristic movement effected without his taking his eyes from her face.

"Let me see. Of course, she is *most anxious* that you should join her on the yacht in Nice. A number of people seem to be going: we were asked, but Rodney insists on going to that stupendous exhibition in Paris, and that doesn't leave us enough time. But from what I gathered—" he paused, as though choosing his words, but he wasn't, she knew: he was a great diplomat, but with a passion for gossip. "What I *gathered* was that there is some Italian painter in whom she is interested, and in order to have him there *en famille* (hers, not his, you understand), she has asked one of Vani's old friends—dearest friends," he hastily amended: the idea of age in anyone horrified him.

"Somebody she thinks I might as well marry."

"So you *have* talked to her, then! I must say, it is a teeny bit sly of you, darling, not to tell me first. I might have said all sorts of things."

"I haven't talked to her; it's just that she's done it before."

"Done what, dear?"

"Tried to palm me off on some awful drip to placate whoever she's got tired of."

"Dear girl, that *is* plain speaking, and no mistake. Well, between you and me, he doesn't sound exactly right for you. Although I believe he has a most interesting estate. And frankly, I think there may be something of a *rumpus* on the yacht, as I told Rodney, so that although one adores cruising—"

"*I'm* not going," Arabella said.

"Ah. And what does that mean, pray?"

"It means I'm getting out—for good."

"Has Mr. Right appeared at last? Or S*ir* Right? Darling—I'm so glad for you."

"No." She put out the cigarette and lit another one immediately.

"Tell Neville. I'm the soul of discretion, because I so adore being told things."

So she told him what she wanted. *She* did, indeed, choose her words with care, because she was in no position to trust anybody for the moment. She wanted to hock the emeralds and the air ticket. She was a bit short of money, and she wanted to start a sensible life on her own—*not* dependent upon her mother's innumerable whims. The thing was that she didn't at all know how to set about hocking the emeralds, without its being done by someone.

Neville listened to all this in sparkling silence. She could not tell what side he was on, but she kept telling herself that, really, she had no choice: if he would not help her, she did not know who could, or would, and she knew that she would make a mess of it by herself.

"One cannot help wondering where you got the emeralds from," he said at last. She knew that he knew that her mother was particularly fond of emeralds.

"Oh, from Cartier," she said carelessly. "You know how Clara loves them. Well, I went to get some from there. I knew they would be good, you see."

"But why did you get them, if all you want to do is sell them?"

Arabella gathered herself together for a really intricate and convincing lie. "*I* didn't exactly get them. They were—sort of—given to me. But I've finished with him, so now I want the money. I don't want to go back to Cartier with them, it would embarrass Mummy."

"I *see.*"

She wondered anxiously how much he did.

At that moment, both heard a key in the front door, its slamming, and somebody coming upstairs. It was Rodney. Luckily, Arabella had met him before, which meant that he knew who she was, which in turn meant that he did not have to worry about her.

"Ara*bella!*" he cried. "What a marvellous, gorgeous surprise. No sooner is my back turned," he added to Neville, "than you collect the most attractive girl in London and indulge in wild orgies of coffee, I see."

"Rodney will help you," said Neville fondly. "He is simply marvelous at selling things for more than one has paid for them."

"What things?"

"Arabella has some dear little emeralds in that disgusting bag. She wants thousands of pounds as quickly as possible."

And it all worked out. They went to lunch in some bistro, for which Neville insisted on paying, and Arabella, with her new-found—perhaps comparative—poverty, did not struggle. Rodney, once he had seen the emeralds, was wild about them. "All that platinum *thrown in,*" he kept saying. "*So* ugly, and *so* valuable. I shall feel of real use to you if I can rid of you of such horrendous luxury."

He bought an evening paper after lunch to look at the racing. On the back page there were four lines that said an actor's wife had committed suicide in North London, leaving two children. None of them saw or read this. After lunch, Arabella agreed, at Neville's instigation, to write a letter to her mother. They did not want—and, indeed, did not have room for—her to stay, so it was easy for her to depart. She did not want them to know where she would be, and they were, really, glad to see the end of her. She arranged that the money from the emeralds and the air ticket be sent to her bank in London. She trusted them, she said, and meant this: she did. She had—as delicately as possible—offered Rodney a commission for his work, but before he could reply, Neville seized one of her hands and cried, "My dear, don't be so utterly absurd! Rodney would do anything for you—and so would I—you must know that!"

"Thank you very much. Will you—will you manage to do it fairly soon? I am a bit short of money, you see."

"Rodney will *shoot* out first thing tomorrow morning. We have a nice friend who will be able to value them, so Rodney will be sure to get the right price. So tiresome having to worry about money. Are you sure you're all right, dear?"

"Fine, and thank you for my lovely lunch."

She acquired another taxi, and Rodney this time helped her downstairs with all her luggage. She kissed them both, got into the taxi, thanked them again, and was off.

"Well, well, well," said Neville, as he climbed the narrow stairs again with his friend. "She's in some sort of trouble, poor dear; but whatever it is, we must be on her side about it." Clara had once made an absent-minded pass at Rodney, and Neville, who was fully aware of Rodney's penchant for high life, had been made quite upset. Rodney fervently agreed. He divided his time between doing this and sulking, and he knew that if he did his best about the emeralds, Neville would make it up to him in Paris. "I've brought you your paper," he said. "Have a little rest now; you know the doctor said it was sensible." He tucked Neville up on the sofa, putting a rug over him and an ash tray and cigarettes within reach. Then he went to the other room and started telephoning the friend who would be so good at valuing the jewels.

Rodney could be an angel when he liked, Neville reflected comfortably: and that was more than could be said of most people. We all have our little ups and downs, he thought, as he began to drop off for his afternoon nap, which every day it was pretended was an exception, but was, in fact, the rule.

"Where to?" the driver asked, the moment they were on the move. Panic struck Arabella. She had not the slightest idea. What she wanted was a cheap hotel, where she could unpack a bit, be sick if she had to be, and be alone, which she certainly had to be.

"Do you know a good, quiet hotel?"

The driver scratched his head and drove slower. "How quiet?" he asked at length.

"Cheap quiet."

He had thought that that was what she meant. "It's not easy, just like that, you know."

"I know: that's why I'm asking you. It is only for about two nights, I think."

"O.K. But don't blame me if we don't hit it off first go."

They didn't. It took four tries before a very depressing place in Pimlico turned out to have a room. Arabella still had some pounds left from the ones she had cashed before she started being careful with them. She paid the driver, and felt almost sad at parting with him, since he was now the only link between being with people and being entirely alone. The room was small, dark, and noisy with traffic and trains. It was ugly as well, but she had not expected anything from it. There was no bedside lamp, she noticed, and this made her guess that the single ceiling light would be so dim that reading at night would be nearly impossible. A man who looked as though he never slept got her to fill in a form saying who she was and what her last address had been. She wrote her name, but when she got to Mulberry Lodge, she made up where it was. The man gave her a key that looked identical to the other keys on the board but had attached to it a wooden label saying 7. He did not like the look of her luggage, and she had to carry most of it up herself. It filled the room, so that she could hardly walk. She shut the door, sat on the bed, and tried to think. Her plan was that, as soon as the money for the emeralds came through, she would take a train to Inverness and find somewhere very small and quiet to live and have her child. She had not thought beyond this, and was unable to imagine what it would be like. She wanted her mother not to be able to find her, and this seemed as good a way as any, but the prospect, now that it was one move away, terrified her. She remembered her fleeting thought at Mulberry Lodge that first morning with Anne when she had imagined a cottage and a cat. Well, it was going to be more than fleeting. I could have a cat as well as a baby, she thought, as her eyes began to burn with tears that she did not want to start upon.

Then, she remembered telling Edmund about Nan (how *could* she have done that?) and her mourning, which seemed always to be lying in wait, never to be further away from her except in time; seemed of itself only to increase her need for this one person who had once known her; resolved itself, as it always did, in painful grief that had never been softened by anyone in the world hearing it and understanding. She lay on the bed, as she had lain on the beds in Switzerland and America and God knew how many since, and cried bitterly for the only person who had cared for her and then died—therefore, unwittingly leaving her to feel that love, in any shape or form, was all over the place.

There was a thunderstorm that evening that began as Edmund got into his train and continued for nearly the whole journey. By the time he reached his home station (having changed), it had nearly stopped: the sky was streaked with livid yellow and harsh greys. Drops fell heavily from the trees, and, as he got into his car, he unwound the windows to smell the fresh, moisture-laden air. He had taken a later train to London in order not to travel with *her*, in order not to upset Anne any more. But he had come home by the usual one, so that she should not feel anxious about his being late. Resolutions had formed themselves and dissolved again all day: he knew only how to do the next thing; he was not capable of any policy. But now, he could not help wondering what he was going back to.

The only thing that Anne had not known what to do with was the ring that she had been given. Selling, giving, throwing it away seemed variously inappropriate. In the end, she opened the wooden lid of the well head and dropped it down. The ring was too light and the well too deep for her to hear it reach the bottom.

Anne met him in almost artificially the same way that she had always done. She wore her usual blue linen trouser suit, her hair seemed back to its normal length and shape, she had put on a little scent, and had made the drinks. She was busy in the kitchen when he entered the house, and at once called out, "I'm in the kitchen," before he could begin to wonder or worry where she might be.

"I've done dinner," she said. "Let's drink next door."

The rose arrangement from yesterday had gone, and she had made a bowl of mixed white flowers. The gramophone records that Arabella had always left strewn about the room had all been tidied away. He sat down with a heavy, to-be-heard sigh of relief.

"Did you have a storm here?"

"Yes: like anything. Still, it has freshened everything up, washed things away, and done a lot of good to the garden, really."

They sipped their drinks, covertly not looking at each other. Then Anne said, "Edmund, I've been thinking of going away."

He was startled. "Where could you possibly want to go?"

"Not me: us. I think we could both do with a change of scene. If you know what I mean."

He felt at once relieved and depressed. A piece of him wanted it to be *his* tact, *his* understanding that effected whatever kind of reconciliation they were going to try to have.

"I was thinking the same thing," he said rather coldly.

He refilled their glasses and stood up with his.

"Well, we could talk about it at dinner. I'll just go and see to the oven."

She always said that when she felt that he wanted a chance to change, to wash, or relax, or potter round the house after work.

Upstairs, he noiselessly opened the door to Arabella's room. The bed was made: the room empty, tidy, organized, waiting for its next guest. There was no trace of her: he could not even picture her clearly in bed, because the disorder that had been removed seemed to have anaesthetized his imagination. A window was slightly open, and he could hear a blackbird. There was nothing on the dressing table, and the wastepaper basket was freshly lined with white paper. He shut the door and went to his —or their—room. When he had washed and put on a comfortable evening jacket, he went down to the kitchen. Anne at once got the jug of martinis out of the fridge. "Where's your glass?" He didn't know. "Never mind, darling. Here's another one."

As he finished his third, and last (they never had more than three, and these got successively weaker because of the ice), he had an idea. It might not work, but on the other hand it might: it was certainly worth trying. What they needed was something serious to talk about that *wasn't* Arabella, and this, he realized, he could provide.

So, at dinner, he told her all about Marina. He told it humbly, as an escapade that he was now ashamed of, but at the time had been too weak to resist. It wasn't that he cared for her, he said more than once, it was simply that he had felt lonely and she had been *there*. He did hope Anne understood this: he had to tell her in any case, because, they, of all people, must not have lies between them. As he finished, he pushed back his chair and said, once more, "I do hope and pray you understand—and don't mind —too much."

"Of *course* I understand, my darling. And of course, I don't really mind too badly." She looked as though a load had been taken from her, as though she had, like some trapped fish or bird, been put back into her element. "I'm sure that if *I* had to spend weeks by myself in some strange place where I didn't know anyone, *I* would have done the same."

Edmund looked at her for a long time without answering. She had done it for him: made him feel that something which might have been hard for her to take was not only easy, but exactly what she would have done. His feeling for her began to return to its familiar, erotic devotion.

He looks as though a load has been taken from him, Anne thought. I have always known how to do that. That is why he loves me. Her feeling of protective, almost maternal, care for him was exactly what it had always been. In fact, his confession, she thought, like the thunderstorm, had simply cleared the air.